Tony Park was born in 1964 and grew up [...]
of Sydney. He has worked as a newspape[...]
tary, a PR consultant and a freelance writer. He also served 34 years
in the Australian Army Reserve, including six months as a public
affairs officer in Afghanistan in 2002. He and his wife, Nicola, di-
vide their time equally between Australia and southern Africa. He
is the author of eighteen other African novels.

www.tonypark.net

Also by Tony Park

Far Horizon
Zambezi
African Sky
Safari
Silent Predator
Ivory
The Delta
African Dawn
Dark Heart
The Prey
The Hunter
An Empty Coast
Red Earth
The Cull
Captive
Scent of Fear
Ghosts of the Past
Last Survivor

Part of the Pride, *with Kevin Richardson*
War Dogs, *with Shane Bryant*
The Grey Man, *with John Curtis*
Courage Under Fire, *with Daniel Keighran VC*

Blood Trail

Tony Park

For Nicola

Author's note

Much of this story deals with African traditional beliefs and medicines. I have researched and consulted as widely as I can on this subject in the hope of ensuring accuracy and sensitivity.

For consistency, I have used the following spellings: *umuthi* or 'the/their *muthi*' (plural: *imithi*), a term which encompasses a range of traditional medicines, and *sangoma* (plural: *izangoma*) for a traditional healer.

The settlement of Killarney is fictitious, as are Lion Plains and Leopard Springs game reserves and the Hippo Rock Private Nature Reserve. The Sabi Sand Game Reserve and adjoining Kruger National Park are real, safe and beautiful places. I urge you to visit them as soon as you can.

Chapter 1

South Africa, in the time of COVID-19

A lion roared outside. The deep, longing call came from the pit of its belly, and made the glass pane of her bedroom window vibrate. Normally, she loved that sound, and, being that close, she might once have found it a bit scary.

Now, Captain Sannie van Rensburg felt nothing, just empty.

As she did up the buttons of her blue uniform shirt, she felt detached, as if she was dressing one of her three children, not that she'd done that for many years. Her youngest, Tommy, her *laat lammetjie*, was turning thirteen in a month and it wouldn't be too many years before her late lamb didn't need her at all. Normally she would wear plain clothes to work, but her washing basket was overflowing.

Sannie started to cry and didn't bother even trying to wipe away the tears as she buckled her belt and adjusted the holster holding her Z88 pistol on her hip.

She went through to the kitchen. The house was still chilly in the morning, although this winter, which had seemed like it would never end, was slowly, begrudgingly, giving way to the warmer weather, which would bring rain and fresh growth. She put the empty bottle of Nederburg sauvignon blanc from the night before in the bin and rinsed her glass; she did not need more rolled eyeballs from her two sons.

1

The lion called again, searching for his brother or warning others to stay away. Increasingly, lions were crossing the Sabie River from the Kruger National Park into the adjoining Hippo Rock Private Nature Reserve, a housing development in the bush, where Sannie lived. Many of the houses in Hippo Rock were holiday homes and with their occupants stuck in Gauteng or the Cape or, for the foreign owners, overseas, because of travel bans, the estate had been far quieter than normal during the pandemic. The animals were, literally, taking over.

There was never a good time for a pandemic, Sannie mused as she made herself a cup of rooibos tea and a single slice of toast, hoping it would settle her stomach. The wine had been flowing last night, when she'd been at the home of her friend, Samantha Karandis. Even though sales and transport of alcohol had been banned during South Africa's draconian lockdown, Samantha had not been miserly and the three of them – Samantha, Sannie and their friend Elizabeth Oosthuizen – had come close to finishing six bottles between them, including the half bottle Sannie had taken home and finished herself, alone.

'I've got a well-stocked cellar, darling,' Samantha had said, more than once, but Sannie, an experienced police detective, had also noticed the briefest look that passed between the two other women. If Samantha had a secret source of booze then she was surely not the only one in South Africa. Sannie had bigger crimes to worry about.

'Mom?' Tommy said behind her, breaking into her thoughts.

She didn't look over her shoulder. 'Yes, my boy?'

'At least turn the light on.'

'It's not even six am, go back to bed.' He might talk to her like a surly teenager, but she still thought of him as her little boy.

'Lion woke me.' He went past her to the fridge, took out the milk and swigged it from the bottle.

Normally she would have told him not to be so rude, but there was no normal any more. He was getting taller by the day, looking more and more like his father, and the resemblance would only grow as he filled out. Nature was conspiring to prolong her grief forever. She looked out the window, not wanting him to see her tears, but not caring if he did.

'Christo will help with your homeschooling today. Do as he says, hey?'

A couple of sullen seconds' silence. 'All right, Mom.'

Her middle child, six years older than Tommy, happened to be at home with them. Christo was studying zoology and botany at Wits University and had been doing a practical with the Kruger Park's veterinarians when the government announced the country was shutting down because of the virus. As the veterinarians' work was an essential service, Christo was able to stay in the park, or move to and from their house in Hippo Rock at will. He had slept at home last night.

Sannie's eldest, Ilana, was studying medicine at Stellenbosch University and had decided to stay in the Cape for the lockdown. Inter-provincial travel had recently reopened, throwing a slender thread rather than a lifeline to the tourism operators, but Ilana was prepping for exams.

They'd had a fight last night, Sannie and Tommy, over him spending too much time on the computer. She'd never said so to his face, nor to her husband, Tom senior, but she thought the boy was too English, spoiled by his British father who'd had no other children of his own before meeting Sannie. Ilana and Christo were by her first husband, an Afrikaans detective, like her. She felt guilty, now, that she had ever questioned Tom's loving parenting, even silently.

'Are you crying?'

She looked at the kitchen window and saw now that he had been watching her reflection. She wiped her eyes for the first time.

He put a hand on her shoulder. 'I miss him too, Mom.'

Sannie covered Tommy's hand and gave it a squeeze. 'I know you do, my boy.'

He forced a smile. 'I just saw on Facebook that there's a leopard with a kill at the golf club.'

'Animals are taking over the place,' she said.

'Please will you try to get a picture for me on your way to work, Mom?'

'Sure.'

Sannie's latest posting in the South African Police Service was as the head of the Stock Theft and Endangered Species unit, which was based at the MAJOC – the Mission Area Joint Operation Centre – the headquarters for anti-poaching in Kruger, alongside Skukuza Airport. Sannie and her small force of STES detectives were responsible for crime scene investigation and prosecutions arising from rhino and other poaching incidents. From Hippo Rock it was a fifteen-kilometre drive to the MAJOC, through the Paul Kruger entry gate across the river. She liked to get an early start on the day, especially as work was one of the few places where she could busy herself enough to not think too much about Tom. Her daily short cut through the Skukuza staff village took her past the golf club, so she could easily divert there to look quickly for Tommy's leopard.

The Skukuza golf course, which was open to big game all the time, was being overrun by elephants and other herbivores feasting on the greens now that no one was playing. The predators, too, were arriving in numbers.

Despite a lull in rhino poaching at the start of the lockdowns, crime had been returning with the progressive reopening of the country. Poverty was a perennial problem in the communities that bordered Kruger, but with the collapse of the tourism industry due to worldwide shutdowns, many more people than usual were unemployed, adding to the police's problems.

Sannie kissed Tommy. 'Say goodbye to your brother for me and tell him I love him.'

'Will do, Mom.'

Tommy opened the laptop sitting on the kitchen counter.

She held up a finger to him. 'And do your schoolwork today. No computer games.'

He turned the laptop around to show her the screen, tapping the volume key as he did so. 'No games, Mom. The Stayhome Safari morning drive's just started.'

A young white woman with short, dark hair swivelled in the seat of her open-topped Land Rover game viewer and smiled at the camera while an older African man sat on the tracker's seat attached to the front left-hand fender, watching the bush and the reddening sky. '*Good morning from sunny, cool South Africa, and welcome to Stayhome Safari, wherever you're logging on from in the world. I'm*

4

your ranger and field guide, Mia Greenaway, coming to you from Lion Plains Private Game Reserve, inside the world-famous Sabi Sand Game Reserve, and behind me is my very talented and knowledgeable tracker, Bongani Ngobeni. Behind the camera today is our Jill-of-all-trades Sara Skjold, all the way from Norway, though stuck here in South Africa these days. Now, let's go find some lions!'

Sannie shook her head and manufactured a smile for Tommy. 'Shame, you live in a nature reserve with lions calling and you have to go online to watch them.'

He grinned, and he looked so much like his father that she had to wipe her eyes again.

'Mom?'

She picked up her car keys out of the carved wooden bowl on the bench top. 'Yes?'

'It's OK to cry.'

She drew a breath and ruffled his hair. It wasn't like she was the only one who had experienced loss during the pandemic. People had died; Samantha's husband John had committed suicide because his tourism business had collapsed due to coronavirus, and Elizabeth's husband Piet had left her for his secretary and escaped with the woman to Dubai, unable to face the prospect of not seeing his mistress during lockdown. 'I know.'

As soon as she opened the front door the chill hit her hard. The lion was quiet now, but she knew he – and probably the rest of his pride – was close. She didn't care. She went to her Toyota Fortuner, clicked the alarm remote, got in and started the engine.

As she drove off, she realised she hadn't even bothered to check for the lion. Ordinarily, she would have had her powerful torch, scouring the surrounds for danger first.

Sannie didn't care any more.

*

Mia had parked her Land Rover by Crocodile Pan, but the big reptile of the same name who normally resided here seemed to have taken a leave of absence. It was 6.30 am and while the early bird had the best chance of catching Africa's big cats on the move, it had been a quiet game drive so far. The online audience, Mia had learned during lockdown, could be as demanding as the rudest rich real-time guest when it came to the Big Five.

Mia took out her binoculars and began scanning. 'We'll just sit here a few moments and see who might come down to drink,' she told her worldwide audience of several thousand armchair safari experts. 'Look at that beautiful sunrise.'

While Sara – the statuesque volunteer who did indeed seem to be able to turn her hand to anything around the game reserve – panned the camera and focused on the dawn, Mia checked the Stayhome Safari Twitter feed for questions.

@Atlanta_Alice where are lions?

@UKJim how about a leopard?

@Jozi_Babe maybe one of the hot guy safari guides would be able to find some animals? Just sayin'.

Mia smacked the phone down on the front passenger seat. Bongani languidly lifted a hand and pointed to a tamboti tree. Mia had already spotted the tiny riot of colour.

'Sara ...'

But Sara's eyes, too, were accustomed to the telltale signs of movement and she was already swinging the camera around to track the tiny bird.

'Oh my,' Mia said, not needing to manufacture any excitement for the online crowd, 'that's one of the most beautiful birds in the bush, and one of my favourites, the pygmy kingfisher.'

Mia took a couple of seconds to focus her binoculars and marvel at how such a staggering palette could be present in a bird that would have fitted nicely into the palm of her hand. 'Although this is a kingfisher, the pygmy actually doesn't feed on fish. They eat insects and small reptiles, such as lizards.'

Mia flipped over her phone and looked at the feed.

@Bwana_joe it's just a bird.

@Big_Frikkie it's a malachite kingfisher. She needs to check her bird book.

Mia closed her eyes, then picked up her binoculars again and started to focus on the bird once more. *Why am I doubting myself over some jerk sitting at home big-noting himself online?*

Mia knew the answer to her own question and it rankled her.

'Mia?'

She turned and saw Sara running her finger across her neck. 'They've cut the feed. They've found some lions in the Timbavati.'

Mia put down her binoculars. Stayhome Safari was also webcast from an additional three reserves around South Africa. The production director, mindful of the attention span of many of their viewers, would always choose a big cat over a bird.

Bongani looked up from his phone, which he had taken out of his pocket. 'The bird *was* a pygmy kingfisher. You were correct. Why did you just check with your binoculars?'

She felt her cheeks burn with a mix of embarrassment and anger. Her best friend in the world knew her too well. Bongani was right; she had doubted herself. It was like a cancer, eating away at her.

Mia spoke into her radio to the Stayhome Safari producer, Janine, who was based at a lodge in the Timbavati Game Reserve, about a hundred and twenty kilometres north of where Mia was. 'Lion Plains closing down for a break, over.'

'Roger, you may as well,' Janine said.

'That guy on Twitter's a jerk,' Sara said.

'Whatever,' Mia said. 'Frikkie' was, given his name, most likely a South African, like her. She and every other safari guide in the country knew that locals were often the hardest to deal with on game drives. Many of them had experience in the bush and knew their birds and animals, and all of them thought they did.

Sara took a Thermos flask out of her Fjällräven daypack. 'Want some?'

'Sure,' Mia said.

'Bongani?' Sara asked.

'Not for me, thank you.' He yawned and stretched, face turned up to the morning sun, eyes closed.

Mia checked her Instagram, making the most of the phone signal, which came and went in this part of the reserve. There were large tracts of Lion Plains where there was no coverage, particularly in the areas closest to the perimeter fence. This corner of the Sabi Sand butted up against the community of Killarney and her boss, Lion Plains' wealthy owner, the British business tycoon Julianne Clyde-Smith, had deliberately avoided paying to have mobile phone coverage extended across her property – rhino poachers used their phones to tip one another off about targets and anti-poaching patrols.

Sara leaned over from the back of the Land Rover, around her camera, and passed Mia a steaming cup. 'Nothing tastes better than coffee out in the field. I remember one time in Afghanistan –'

'Are you going to tell us another war story?' Bongani interrupted.

Sara laughed.

Their banter was good-natured, and it went some way to lifting Mia's spirits. A few other trolls were baiting her on the Twitter feed now, about not spotting any lions this morning, and Mia regretted opening the morning's drive with a promise to her audience that she would try to find them. That was not her, and not the way she would normally conduct a drive for in-the-flesh guests. She was out of sorts.

Sara gave her a big smile. The tall blonde was wearing her old Norwegian Army desert-pattern camouflage shirt which she had worn in Afghanistan, where she had served prior to leaving the forces and embarking on her bid to see as much of the world as she could. Her adventure had started and ended in South Africa, where she had become trapped due to COVID-19.

Sara sipped her coffee. 'When will you get to make another attempt at the master tracker's qualification?'

Mia had been trying to focus on some of the positive comments on Twitter and Instagram and just like that, with an innocent, kindly meant question, Sara had brought her back to the one thing she didn't want to think about.

'Not sure,' she said, trying to sound light. 'COVID's affecting everything, including assessments. I'm not sure I'm ready, anyway.'

'You have been ready for that assessment for at least two years,' Bongani said, without bothering to open his eyes.

'Easy for you to say,' Mia shot back. 'You didn't fail your exam.'

Bongani said nothing. Mia picked up her phone again and opened Twitter.

@rajiv_mumbai that bird was beautiful, like you, Mia.

'Fuck.' Mia threw her phone down on the passenger seat. When she looked up and, as she habitually did, around her, she spotted the twitch of an oversized grey ear.

'What are you upset –' Sara began, but Mia held up her hand to silence her and pointed at the slow-moving bulk of a white rhinoceros coming into sight. Sara shifted to get a better view, and in the process she knocked over her flask, which fell onto the metal floor of the Land Rover with a loud clang.

The rhino, which had seemed so ponderous, spun around ninety degrees to confront the noise.

The sound of a gunshot split the morning's peace.

Chapter 2

Once inside the Kruger Park, Sannie took the turn-off to Lake Panic and the Skukuza golf course. The greens were deserted when she arrived, a low mist hanging over the dam which served as the water hazard. In normal times a couple of golf buggies would have already been on the move, now that it was light enough to keep a lookout for predators and other dangerous animals, such as hippopotamus and buffalo.

A hippo honked somewhere nearby. She, too, had seen the leopard on Facebook, awake a couple of hours before Tommy, staring at her phone, scrolling through photos of her husband until they ended, abruptly.

She had not wanted to get out of bed. It was an effort most days and sometimes she just wanted to hide. On her days off the boys either forced her to get up – perhaps they could see what was going on – or, more often than not, she had to be up first to get *them* organised and moving.

Sannie stopped by the clubhouse and identified the tree where the leopard had hoisted its kill the previous afternoon. Sannie remembered lunches and brunches here with friends; birthday parties. It was a Kruger Park staff hangout. Tom had played golf, occasionally, with John and Piet, while Sannie drank wine in the sun with Samantha and Elizabeth. Her friends Hudson Brand and Sonja Kurtz had come sometimes, on the rare occasion when Sonja wasn't off somewhere in the world killing people or bodyguarding.

'Close personal protection,' Tom would have corrected her. Sannie had done the same job, when they had met, though she never fought the public perception that they were bodyguards.

Close personal protection.

Tom had protected all sorts of people – politicians, bureaucrats, heads of state, rock stars. Everyone. Except himself.

Sannie had buried the man she loved, Tom Furey, former UK police protection officer and loving father, just three weeks earlier, and every day since, when she woke, she had cried when she remembered she was alone.

Of course, she wasn't alone – she had her children, and her memories of Tom. Try as she might, however, the reminiscences that rolled over and over in her mind like a continuous video loop were of the fights they'd had and her guilt at letting Tom go back to Iraq. At the end of the day it always came back to one thing.

Money.

Stupid, God-cursed money was the reason Tom was dead. Like so many other people in South Africa they had struggled to make ends meet. Sannie had gone back to fulltime work in the South African Police Service after Tommy had started school, and while Tom senior had fancied himself as a farmer, they had been unable to make a profit from her family's banana farm near Hazyview. They had lost the farm, in any case, to a land claim, and Tom had taken work overseas, as a protection officer for VIPs in Iraq.

An ISIS rocket, fired at one of the coalition's last toehold bases in that terrible country, had indiscriminately robbed her of her second husband, as well as taking the lives of three soldiers, including a woman in her twenties.

Sannie reached to her side and closed her fingers around the grip of her Z88. She drew it out, aware of the whisper of steel against leather. She sat the handgun in her lap and glanced down at it.

She had only ever loved two men, and now they were both gone.

Sannie glanced in the rear-view mirror, saw the dyed blonde hair, the crow's feet at the corners of her eyes. She was too tired and it was too early for makeup. And who would she be trying to impress anyway?

Ilana was a young woman now, pretty and brilliant, strident in her views and independence. She would be fine. Christo was strong-jawed and handsome, fair like his father, in looks and temperament. Tommy was smart, dark, brooding, perhaps a writer-cum-safari guide. A thinker. They were all good kids. The older two had never thought of Tommy as anything other than their blood, and all of them had been exposed to their share of trauma and tears.

'Tom ...' she croaked. 'Why?'

She knew exactly why. Because of her.

Deep inside her she knew that Tom had not just gone to Iraq because of the money, but because he was unhappy. She had been part of his problem, because she'd returned to duty in the police force. Tom was a good guy, but he was a man, with an ego, and she had sensed for some time, despite his words to the contrary, that it irked him that she was back in the police service, working, earning money.

He'd gone back to Iraq because of her. She could have tried harder to stop him, to help him find different work, but the truth, as much as she hated to admit it, was that she was relieved when he went. It was what he wanted, and the fights had stopped. But now, in addition to her grief and depression, she felt a crushing guilt.

Sannie looked at the weapon. It was old, but loved and well cared for. It had never let her down.

It was a cliché, she thought, wasn't it? The cop who put the gun in their mouth and pulled the trigger. Men did that, like the gambler she had seen in the public toilet stall in Riverside Mall. He'd lost too big at the Emnotweni Casino, and then calmly wandered next door to the shopping mall where the poor cleaners and some super-market worker on his break had had to deal with the aftermath.

Women used pills. Was that about vanity? It was not about certainty.

No, she would use a pistol, if her time ever came, like John Karandis had. And because she was the only cop Samantha knew, her friend had called her first. She hadn't been part of the investigation, but it was clear John had set out to do the job properly.

Sannie's heart felt like it would never mend. She did not want to go through the pain of losing someone again, and anyway she couldn't imagine ever meeting anyone new. The thought was almost too much to bear.

Sannie looked at her pistol.

Samantha had a son from a previous marriage, but he lived overseas somewhere, like many of her friends' older children. Elizabeth was Piet's second wife and they had never had children. Samantha seemed to have come through her grief – Sannie envied her – and Elizabeth told them both that she was well rid of Piet.

'A handsome *younger* helicopter pilot is a good remedy for a broken heart,' Samantha had said last night, looking pointedly at Elizabeth, but when Sannie had gently pressed for more information, Liz had said she could neither confirm nor deny such rumours – just now, at least.

Thinking about Tommy, Sannie told herself that kids were resilient. Tommy's hurt would heal with time.

Her phone rang, jolting her out of her dark thoughts, even more so when she saw it was Tommy.

'Hello, my angel.' She coughed to clear her voice as she holstered her pistol. 'Are you all right?'

'Mom, Mom, someone's shooting.'

'Where? At the house? I'm coming –'

'No, Mom, on Stayhome Safari, now, check. Have a look at your phone, Mom, Mia's chasing a rhino poacher right now. It's hectic!'

'Mia?'

'One of the guides. Hurry. Sheesh, you might even be able to catch the poacher, or help them. Someone fired a gun at them, Mom!'

'OK, I'll call you back.'

Sannie wiped her eyes. This was a first, she thought, even for South Africa – a live-streaming poaching incident. She went to Facebook and found the Stayhome Safari page. Fortunately, the signal was good at the golf course and in a few seconds the live stream loaded. She saw a shaky view of a Land Rover bonnet crashing through the bush.

'*We can see him, one adult male, over,*' the young woman driving was saying into her radio as she spun the steering wheel, one-handed, then quickly used the same hand to change gears.

Sannie caught a glimpse of a figure darting through the trees as the camera operator managed to focus.

Sannie's phone rang, just then. She tore her eyes away from the feed.

'Van Rensburg.'

'Howzit, Sannie? Henk here.'

STES fell under the South African Police Service's Organised Crime Division and Captain Henk de Beer was the organised crime liaison officer at the provincial capital, Mbombela, still referred to by many by its old name, Nelspruit. 'Fine, Henk. Are you watching this stuff on Facebook, the live safari thing?'

'What? No. What are you talking about?'

'Lion Plains lodge in the Sabi Sand do a live-to-air game drive twice a day. My son's addicted to it. One of the guides is chasing a poacher right now, live.'

'Serious? That'll be good for their ratings.'

'I'll call Sabi Sand security, get an update,' she said.

'Sure. I was just calling to tell you the boss has asked if you can go to Killarney for us this morning.'

'What's happening there?'

'Missing girl.'

'What's that got to do with STES?' Sannie asked.

'It's become political. The local community is threatening to protest, like in America. They're saying poor people's lives don't matter. The grandmother of the missing girl says she'll only talk to a senior female officer. The boss thinks you're the closest and best person for this one, Sannie, and this time I happen to think she's right.'

'How old is the missing girl?' Sannie asked. The crime was serious and would make a change from viewing yet another dead rhino carcass.

'Thirteen. The boss asks if you can please go there now, try to talk to the girl's family, maybe defuse things before the people gather this morning?'

Thirteen. Same age as Tommy. 'OK, I'm heading there now.'

'And keep me up to date on this rhino poacher thing if you hear anything more. I'll call Sabi Sand security – you drive.'

'Will do; Killarney's close to the gate so I can head into the Sabi Sand afterwards.' She started the engine. Sannie knew that with the police stretched so thin during the pandemic there was no way she or any other police could get to Lion Plains quicker than the reserve's private anti-poaching operators. She set her phone on the dashboard so she could keep an eye on the online hunt to find the rhino poacher while she did a U-turn in order to head back out of the park to Killarney.

'Jissus,' she said out loud as she drove, 'only in Africa.'

*

The Land Rover bucked like a bronco as Mia drove over a fallen tree trunk. Bongani lurched to one side and for a second looked in danger of falling off. Sara clung to her camera mount.

'*Mia, Mia, this is Sean Bourke, over.*'

Mia keyed the handset. 'Go, Sean.'

'*Mia, we're looking for a breach in the perimeter fence now, over.*'

'Stand by, Sean.' Mia glanced over her shoulder. 'Kill the audio.'

'No, no, no!' the producer Janine shrieked in her earpiece. 'This is going viral. We're getting thousands of people tuning in, Mia!'

'The bloody poachers will be watching as well and we're not going to give them any information they don't have,' Mia told the producer. 'Go to channel four, Sean.'

'*Roger, Mia.*'

They both switched to the other channel, which was reserved for private talks.

'*My dog team is following up,*' Sean continued, '*I've been told Captain Sannie van Rensburg, a senior cop from Kruger, is on her way to Killarney now. Looks like that's the direction where the poacher has come from.*'

Mia's phone vibrated on silent in her pocket. 'Wait one, please, Sean. I've got Vulture messaging me.'

On the screen was a WhatsApp message from Graham Foster, one of Sean's anti-poaching rangers, who was sitting in an unmarked air-conditioned portacabin hidden away in a small clearing in the bush and surrounded by its own electric fence a hundred metres from Lion Plains' luxury lodge, Kaya Nghala, which meant 'home of the lion'. The Vulture system, named for the bird's incredible eyesight, was an array of sophisticated long-range cameras – which used infrared and laser designators to see at night – trail cameras, radar, and motion-sensitive alarms and cameras positioned along Lion Plains' section of the Sabi Sand Game Reserve perimeter fence. This impressive and expensive collection of monitoring devices was controlled via a bank of computers and four large screens in the cabin where Graham had been sitting since he crawled out of Mia's bed at midnight, doing his best not to wake her, when he went on shift.

'*I'm getting the messages as well,*' Sean said.

Mia put down the radio handset and dialled Graham on WhatsApp as she continued to drive, using Bongani's hand signals to navigate by.

'Mia, hi,' Graham said as soon as he answered. There was no time for small talk. 'We've got movement. I'm trying to raise Sean on the radio, but he's not copying.'

'He's in the north of the reserve checking for breaches in the fence. Sean's getting your WhatsApps and I've got radio comms with him, so I can relay. Is our target on the move?'

'I think so, yes.'

'You think?'

'I just spotted him, moving two hundred metres northwest of your position – I can see you both on the radar and camera, towards the perimeter fence, but it looks like he doesn't have his rifle any more.'

Mia stopped the Land Rover and turned off the engine. Bongani looked over his shoulder and gave her a questioning look. To her tracker partner she said: 'He's on his way to the fence, not far from us.'

Mia put the phone back to her ear. 'Maybe he cached the rifle, doesn't want to get caught with it.' That way, Mia thought, the man would claim he was simply setting or checking snares and get off with a small fine and a slap on the wrist.

'We should follow him on foot,' Bongani said. 'The bush is so thick here we'll be faster than in the Land Rover, and he won't hear us coming and hide. If he is unarmed, he is not a problem.'

Mia glanced back at Sara, sitting behind them but leaning forward, straining to hear what was being said on the radio.

'She will be fine. I will look after her,' Bongani said.

Mia raised her eyebrows. 'You?'

He smiled. 'You will be tracking. I'll watch over you, and Sara will be behind me, safe and sound. It will be good practice for your assessment.'

Mia wasn't sure. 'Graham's got a visual on him. We can relay the message to Sean and he can send some guys, or call the police, to intercept this guy wherever he tries to get over or under the fence.'

Bongani held his tongue, but Mia could see the hunter in him was itching to go after this man. Bongani had grown up in the bush when there was still enough wild space and game for him and his siblings to track and catch small animals and birds to supplement the family diet, the way his people had always lived. If his circumstances had been different, he might very well have been a poacher, but as someone whose living depended on wildlife in a different way, he was more than ready to track down this intruder.

'Stand by, Graham,' she said into her phone.

'OK, babes.'

She frowned at Bongani's grin and called Sean on the radio.

'*Go, Mia,*' Sean said.

'Graham picked up the poacher on the Vulture system. He gave me a rough direction in which the guy is heading.'

'*I'll send a patrol down the fence line. We'll catch him on his way out.*'

'Roger, Sean.' She took a deep breath. 'We're going to track him on foot.'

There was a pause. Sean eventually keyed his microphone. '*This isn't your responsibility, Mia.*'

'Graham says the guy's ditched his rifle. We'll follow him, keep him in sight, but we won't engage.'

'*Copy,*' Sean said. '*Just be careful.*'

'Come,' Bongani said, impatient. 'Let's see if we can pick up some tracks.'

Mia was undecided. This was not a good idea, particularly with a volunteer in tow, but a poacher was on the move and Mia hated the idea that a rhino might die because she did nothing, or was afraid to go after an armed man. She lifted her rifle from its cradle on the dashboard, unzipped the green canvas padded carry case and drew it out.

'Yes!' Sara said.

As Sara took off her headset Mia could hear their Stayhome Safari producer, Janine, yelling into the earpiece, demanding an update.

'Switch off the camera and leave it,' Mia said. Sara nodded and complied.

Bongani slid off his tracker seat, stowed his poncho, and then took a panga, a wickedly sharp machete, from where he kept it wedged behind the vehicle's plastic radiator grille. The blade was in case they came across low-hanging thorny branches when tracking big game off-road or small trees that had been pushed across roads by elephants.

'I wish I had a rifle,' Sara said.

'I wouldn't let you bring it if you did,' Mia said. 'You're a volunteer, not an anti-poaching ranger. If you shot someone you'd end up in prison.'

Sara looked miffed, but she was raring to go.

Mia worked the bolt on the .375-calibre hunting rifle, took five rounds from the hand-tooled cartridge belt around her waist and loaded the weapon. She rammed the bolt home, then passed the weapon to Bongani. He gave her the panga.

As they set off, she wondered what had happened to the poacher's rifle.

Chapter 3

Jeff Beaton sat opposite the two men in camouflage fatigues in the room that served as the kitchen and meal room for the anti-poaching rangers at Lion Plains Game Reserve.

The place had the feel of a military camp, the vibe enhanced by the webbing gear and LM5 semi-automatic assault rifles waiting expectantly beside the dining table and the radio in the corner that occasionally hissed to life with updates about a poacher being pursued.

Jeff guessed the younger of the two men he was interviewing, Graham Foster, was close to his own age, twenty-six. Foster checked his chunky watch.

'I won't take too much of your time, I promise,' Jeff said as he opened his laptop. 'I imagine you're keen to join in the pursuit of the poacher.'

'We're on standby,' Foster said, 'so, like, sorry, bru, if we have to split. You're American?'

'Canadian. A common mistake.'

'Sorry, no offence.' Foster held up his hands.

'None taken. Happens all the time.'

Jeff typed Graham Foster's name into the survey form on his screen. 'And Oscar ...'

'Mdluli,' the older man said. He looked to be in his early thirties.

Jeff entered the details. 'Thanks for your time, guys. As you've probably been briefed, my studies focus on the use of imithi – you know, traditional medicine – by poachers, and –'

19

'Primitive bullshit.' Foster took a toothpick from the container on the table, leaned back in his chair and started picking his teeth.

Oscar folded his arms. Jeff looked at him and raised his eyebrows. 'Oscar?'

'Yes?'

'What do you think?'

'About what?' He glanced sideways at his younger white partner, who looked up at the ceiling.

Jeff consulted the survey form he had prepared. 'In the course of your duties, when you have apprehended or otherwise encountered a poacher, how often, if ever, have you encountered evidence of the poacher using umuthi?'

'Otherwise encountered?' Oscar asked.

'Slotted,' Foster weighed in.

'Slotted?' Jeff asked.

'Killed, right? That's what you mean by "otherwise encountered", as in the ones that get shot, as opposed to the ones we catch.'

Jeff shrugged. 'It's open to interpretation.'

'Like your *study*. Look, man, no offence, again, but this stuff is nonsense, hocus-pocus. Izangoma, the traditional healers, sell the poachers magic charms to make them invisible, to turn our bullets to water, to make the magistrates and the judges in the courts fall asleep, or the prosecutors lose their evidence. These people are preying on the poachers' ignorance and stupidity.'

Jeff looked to Oscar again, who shrugged.

'Oscar, how often have you encountered –'

'All the time,' Oscar said.

'Umuthi?' Jeff asked, starting to make notes.

Oscar spoke evenly, quietly: 'This is our culture, our beliefs, the way we are, that we are talking about,' he looked to his partner briefly, 'not people selling something to gullible people.'

'*Kak*, man.' Foster looked to Jeff. 'Translation: bullshit.'

Oscar turned to Graham. 'You go to church every Sunday that you are not on duty, and you have a Bible, yes?'

'Of course, man. I'm a Christian, like you say you are.'

'I *am* a Christian. You came to my son's baptism.'

Foster nodded. 'I did. So, don't tell me you believe in this rubbish.'

Oscar looked to Jeff again. 'Faith is invisible, yes?'

'Absolutely,' Jeff said.

'We believe certain things, in religion, to be absolute,' Oscar went on, 'even if we cannot scientifically prove them.'

Foster rolled his eyes. 'Here we go again.'

Oscar continued, ignoring his partner. 'The poachers believe in the ... the talismans they are given, the spells. That is the important thing. It gives them confidence. A confident enemy is an effective soldier.'

'What about your beliefs?' Jeff asked.

Oscar looked down at the table, across to Foster, then back at Jeff. 'They are my business.'

Jeff nodded. 'For sure, I understand and respect that,' he made eye contact with Foster, 'and I'm not here to judge anyone.'

'Nor am I, bru.' Foster reached over and grabbed Oscar's shoulder and squeezed it. Then he threw back his head and laughed.

Oscar exhaled. 'There are some things that cannot be explained.'

Jeff typed into his laptop. 'Such as?'

'We were tracking a man, a couple of weeks ago, and –'

'*Sjoe*, not that one again, bru.'

'Please,' Jeff said to Foster, 'I'm interested in what Oscar has to say.'

Foster held his hands up in surrender again, then leaned back in his chair and went back to picking his teeth.

'We followed a man to a mostly dry spruit, the Manzini, near where there is a waterhole. I was tracking him, his footsteps quite clear, and then we came to a place where there was water, a little bit ... and he disappeared.'

'You lost the spoor,' Foster said under his breath, toothpick resting on his lower lip.

Oscar glared at his partner. 'I did not lose anything.'

Foster shrugged. 'So the guy backtracked.'

'He was not backtracking,' Oscar said.

'How do you know?' Jeff asked.

'Even the best, most skilled poacher who backtracks will eventually put a foot wrong, he will step so that his foot is not exactly in the first track he made. I checked. He was not walking backwards.'

'Right,' Foster gave an exaggerated nod, 'he ascended to heaven, or was beamed up by aliens.'

Jeff thought about the two men's testimony. 'Could he have gone upward? Was there a low-hanging branch of a tree or something like that?'

'No,' the other two said in unison.

At least they agreed on something.

'You said there was water there, in the dry "*sprite*", is that how you say it?'

'Close enough. Creek, to you,' Foster said. 'Where there is water, poachers will walk along a stream and then exit somewhere downstream or upstream to try to confuse a tracker or throw a dog off the scent. We then cast up and down the far side until we find his spoor – his tracks, as you would say.'

Jeff nodded. 'I see. And what did you find?'

They looked at each other. 'Nothing,' Oscar said.

Foster spread his hands wide. 'What can we say? Sometimes we win, sometimes we lose. The *oke* could have taken off his shoes, swept the sand, used a pole and pole-vaulted for all we know. It's never easy to track in sand. Maybe we just didn't try hard enough.'

Jeff looked to Oscar, whose mouth was crinkled into a frown. 'What do you think, Oscar?'

Oscar looked up from the tabletop and into his eyes. 'That man, he disappeared.'

'You think he had help? Some medicine – some muthi?'

'Sheesh, Oscar,' Foster interrupted. 'It's bad enough these simple poachers believe this stuff, but *you*?'

Jeff made a mental note to interview the anti-poaching rangers individually from now on. Foster's scepticism was intimidating Oscar, or so he thought.

'I was confused that day, when I saw those tracks disappear,' Oscar said.

'*Babelaas*, more like it,' his partner scoffed.

'I was *not* hungover.'

'Sorry, man,' Foster said, then chuckled.

'Izangoma, they give the poachers imithi not just to protect them, but also to affect us, to make us not see clearly, to confuse us.'

Jeff nodded. 'So I've heard. Was there any indication you picked up, while you were following him, that he might have been using umuthi?'

Foster reached in his breast pocket and pulled out a packet of cigarettes. 'If you don't need me any more, I'm going outside for a smoke.'

'Fine with me,' Jeff said, 'thanks for your time.' Thanks for nothing, he meant, though to be fair, Foster was entitled to his beliefs and he was not alone in them. Many people saw the whole business of umuthi as a rip-off, a con played by izangoma against scared men who were risking their lives to hunt rhinos.

'Do you think you were affected by the poacher's umuthi, Oscar?'

Oscar looked to the door, perhaps to make sure Foster was out of earshot, then back at Jeff. 'I do not know. I can track a man, but I am telling you, this man, he disappeared. We cast along the water, both sides, upstream and downstream, and there was nothing. I felt sick that night.'

'Sick? You were ill?'

'Yes.' Oscar patted his stomach. 'I was not right inside, you know? But that morning I was fine. I wondered if it was umuthi. You asked about evidence?'

'Yes.'

'I did see a sign, near the last track of the man we were following.'

'What was it?'

'Some string, like a small rope, made from bark that had been stripped from a tree and braided. It had been laid across the track.'

'What did that mean?'

Again, Oscar looked to the door. He ran a tongue over his lips. 'Danger.'

Jeff was confused. 'Do you mean it was a threat?'

Oscar shrugged. 'It was a spell.' He straightened, sitting taller in his chair. 'I was not afraid of this man or his magic.'

'Of course.' Jeff made some more notes. 'What happened, after you lost the man?'

Foster walked back into the room, his cigarette finished, and he was carrying a green canvas satchel bag. 'What happened was that we found a dead rhino, covered with branches. The poachers do that so the carcass can't be seen from the air, by helicopters or by vultures.'

'Vultures?' Jeff said.

Foster nodded. 'Often that's the first notice we get of a rhino being killed – the vultures will spot the dead animal and lead us to it. Poachers hate vultures; sometimes they even poison them deliberately just to take them out of the game.'

'The man you were tracking killed the rhino?' Jeff asked Oscar.

Oscar nodded, a grave look on his face. 'Yes, we picked up his tracks by the carcass. It was the same man.'

'And he vanished.' Foster snapped his fingers. 'Poof, into thin air. Magic.'

Oscar looked up at him.

Foster again put his hand on Oscar's shoulder. 'It's not your fault, bru. We've all been outsmarted by these bastards one time or another, but we'll catch that one and we'll drill him, hey?'

Oscar gave a small nod.

'Do you know,' Foster locked eyes with Jeff, 'that there are now more gunfights per year in the greater Kruger Park – including here – than there were at the height of the old South African Defence Force's war in Namibia?'

'I did not know that,' Jeff said. 'Do you ever get scared, Graham? Do you pray for protection?'

'God is on our side,' Foster said, his eyes not wavering from Jeff's. 'Of that I have no doubt. You can write that in your laptop.'

Jeff nodded. 'I will. Belief systems play a role in many conflicts. In some, like the fighting in the Middle East, and in extremist terrorism, they're the root cause.'

'You know they tried to get izangoma on side, in the Kruger Park?' Foster said.

Jeff knew what Foster was referring to, but he wanted to hear his take on it. 'Really?'

'*Ja*. They called all these witch doctors together for an *indaba*, a big meeting, and urged them not to supply umuthi to poachers. It was all a PR stunt.'

'You don't think it did any good?' Jeff asked.

Foster shook his head and rubbed his thumb against his fore-finger and middle finger together. 'It's all about money. Those guys will say one thing and then charge some dumb poacher a fortune for a spell or some potion or whatever to keep him safe.'

'I have seen pictures, videos, on Facebook,' Oscar interjected, 'of American soldiers in Afghanistan and Iraq taking communion before they go into battle. Isn't that the same thing?'

'No.' Foster slapped the table. 'Those men are praying that if they get killed, they will go to heaven.'

'Not for protection?' Jeff asked.

Foster shrugged. 'Well, maybe.'

'Then it's the same thing,' Oscar said to his partner.

'But,' Foster said, 'they're not paying for it. This is about izangoma conning people who don't know any better.'

Oscar said nothing, but he looked to Jeff like he was seething. Jeff decided he had *definitely* better keep these interviews to one on one in the future. He needed to change the subject. 'You said you had some samples to show me, of stuff you'd confiscated from poachers?'

'Sure,' Foster said. He went to a storeroom adjoining the mess area and came back with a cardboard filing box. He set it down on the table, took off the lid and rummaged inside. Oscar pushed his chair back from the table.

Jeff craned forward to see what was inside.

Foster started taking out some of the objects, laid them on the table and gestured to them with a sweep of his hand. 'Check.'

Jeff could see thin brown roots, a bundle of leaves and a snuff container. There was also a small pouch, decorated with what looked like hyena hairs on the top; it was partly open with dark powder inside. There was also a length of string or wool, dyed red and knotted in places.

'This was gathered as evidence, but the cops don't need it any more,' Foster said.

'We should put this away,' Oscar said.

Curious, Jeff picked up the length of string. He looked to Oscar. 'Do you mind?'

Oscar shrugged. 'It's fine.'

'This is a *xitsungulu*, right? Hunting band?'

Oscar raised his shirt to show he wore a similar thing above his hips. 'Not just for hunting, for protection.'

Graham stared at the ceiling and exhaled.

'Cool,' Jeff said. 'The Catholic church has a similar tradition, with people wearing a scapular.'

Oscar lowered his shirt. 'We take this stuff seriously.'

'I respect your feelings, Oscar,' Jeff said, next examining the pouch. 'I'd like to find out what this is made from and what its significance is.'

'Its significance,' Foster said, taking up a clump of dried roots, then grinding them up between his hands, 'is *kak*.'

'No!' Oscar reached for Foster, who brushed the fragments from his hands, stood and ground them into the cement floor with the heel of his boot.

Jeff looked down at his laptop screen.

'Don't do that, man,' Oscar said to Foster.

Graham stared at him, mouth half open, and started blinking.

'*Aaagh ...*'

Jeff looked up.

Foster was clutching his chest near his heart with two hands. His legs began shaking and he dropped to his knees, head slumped forward.

Oscar sprang to his feet, as did Jeff.

'Is there a medic or someone here?' Jeff asked.

Foster was rolling on the floor, groaning.

Oscar dropped to one knee beside his partner and put a hand on his chest. 'Tell me what's wrong!'

Jeff went to the door of the dining room. 'Help, help!'

Foster shuddered once more, and was then still.

Jeff darted around the dining table to get to the young man, who looked to be unconscious. 'Heart attack?'

Then Foster thrust an arm up and grabbed Oscar by the shirt-front and started laughing.

Oscar fell back, out of reach, gasping. 'You scared me to death.'

Foster sat up. 'Got you!'

Jeff sat on the floor of the dining room, waiting for his heart rate to settle.

Oscar, to his surprise, joined in, laughing heartily as he helped Foster to his feet and embraced him.

Jeff shook his head. These anti-poaching guys were crazy.

The radio on the table hissed. '*Kaya Nghala, this is Sean, over.*'

Graham wiped the tears of laughter from his eyes and took up the handset. 'Sean, this is Kaya Nghala, go.'

'*Graham, I'm trying to raise your new helicopter pilot, Mike someone, over.*'

Graham pressed the send button. '*Ja,* Mike de Vries. Sorry, Sean, he tells me the bird's gone to the mechanics in Nelspruit again. Bloody thing seems to be on the ground more than it's in the air these days.'

'*Copy, thanks, Graham.*'

Jeff wondered if the helicopter was needed to chase the poacher on the loose in the reserve. Graham told Sean he would send the pilot a WhatsApp message and then he and Oscar began going through a check of their gear, readying for battle. Jeff took his cue to leave them to it.

*

Mike de Vries had his phone in a car mount in front of him, on the control panel of Julianne Clyde-Smith's Robinson R44 helicopter. He saw the message flash onto the screen but ignored it, concentrating instead on safely landing on the neatly manicured lawn in front of a sprawling faux-Tuscan manor.

The house was set in the rolling hills on the Sabie Road between the quaint historic town of the same name and Hazyview, the rather chaotic tourist town that serviced the Sabi Sand Game Reserve, the Kruger Park and the surrounding villages and farming areas.

Even before Mike had settled into the grass he saw Elizabeth stride from the house to meet him. Mike settled the chopper and let the engine run, blades still turning above him, to cool down. That didn't stop Elizabeth Oosthuizen.

Bent at the waist, she jogged to the R44. The doors had been removed from the helicopter to improve visibility and to allow

Mike's passengers to fire rifles at poachers or dart guns at the animals he was often called on to help capture or immobilise for other reasons.

Elizabeth stood and leaned into the cockpit as Mike undid his safety harness and lowered his mouth to meet hers. Already her hand was in his lap, feeling for him. Any thought of responding to the phone message disappeared from his brain.

As he swung towards her she grabbed the lapels of his shirt and half dragged him out as he slid down. She wore black lycra activewear – yoga pants and a singlet top punctuated with those wonderful nipples.

Mike was able to shut down the engine, but she still had to raise her voice over the dying whine. 'Howzit, my lovely? I must be quick, I've got to get to Killarney to keep up the pretence of being the good Christian lady.'

'You?' He laughed.

She slapped his face, not hard, but with enough force to send him over the edge. He pulled her to him and kissed her hard.

'Here,' she said. 'Now.'

'What?'

'Like I said, I must go. Come.'

'Yes, ma'am.'

The grass was wet and she nodded to the open rear of the helicopter. He grinned. She backed away from him and shimmied her bottom onto the floor of the cargo area, boosting herself up with her tiptoes on the chopper's skid. Once in, she kicked off her expensive Nike shoes.

Mike unzipped his shorts as he came to her and grabbed the elasticated waist of her pants. In one motion he pulled them and her G-string off.

'I've been thinking about this since I woke up, even while doing pilates,' she said, waiting for him to put on some protection.

He moved between her legs, which she then hooked over his hips, drawing him in. It was effortless. 'I can tell.'

She clung to him as he stood on the skid, their bodies interlaced as he arched his hips, bringing them together.

'Quickly,' she whispered, 'Samantha's due here any minute.'

'Maybe she can join us ...'

She grabbed his bottom and pinched it. 'Dirty.'

'OW!'

Elizabeth giggled, but Mike took her breath away as he entered her again. Over her shoulder he glanced at his watch. He was also conscious of the time. Elizabeth met his every thrust, clinging to him, eager to finish. Soon – too soon – they were done.

'I want to spend a day doing this,' he said.

'Me too.' She jumped lithely down from the open door of the helicopter, with the help of his hands on her waist. They both pulled their pants up just as they heard a vehicle coming up the long driveway behind them. Samantha's white Amarok pickup came into view.

'The wine?'

He grinned. 'All part of the service.'

Samantha drove up to the chopper, stopped, leaving the engine running, and got out. 'I see I'm just in time for the express delivery.'

Mike reached into the back of the helicopter and took out a box of six bottles of sauvignon blanc.

'Howzit, Mike,' Samantha said. 'You can put them both in my vehicle.'

Samantha kissed Elizabeth on the cheek, and Mike couldn't help but think of the suggestion he'd made to Elizabeth. Both women were quite a bit older than he, but Elizabeth was crazier than any girl he'd been with. He was, however, on a tight schedule. He unloaded the second box and put them both in the back of the truck, which was already full of bulging plastic shopping bags. Samantha reached in and camouflaged the contraband wine under bags of food.

'You're a darl, Mike,' Samantha said.

'My pleasure.'

Elizabeth reached into the phone pocket of her yoga pants and took out a wad of hundred-rand notes, which she handed to Mike. 'For services duly rendered.'

He touched his forelock. 'My pleasure. Sorry ladies, I have to go.'

Mike climbed up into the pilot's seat and began a quick check.

'Are you all right, Liz?' Samantha asked as the two of them backed away towards the *bakkie*. 'Your rosy cheeks make you look like you've just done a hard cardio workout.'

Mike was still grinning as the engine spun up and he lifted off from the farm. There were some things happening under COVID that troubled him greatly, but it wasn't all bad.

Chapter 4

Captain Sannie van Rensburg held the sobbing woman to her chest and let the grandmother's tears soak her uniform shirt. It took all the strength she had left in her not to join the woman and let her own grief spill out.

Sannie wore her face mask and should not have been holding the woman, but her innate sense of compassion won out over regulations.

Around them, in the unpaved road that ran through the middle of the village, a mix of women, children and a few men crowded her, the arrival of the police causing a commotion and a distraction from day-to-day life. A few wore masks, but social distancing was almost impossible to enforce in tight-knit communities such as Killarney. Even a hobbled cow looked up from the banana peel it had been sniffing on the roadside. Sannie was acutely aware how quickly such crowds could go from curious to angry.

Sannie sighed into her face covering. Her job was the only thing, other than her children, that was keeping her functioning. 'We are here to help,' she said into the woman's hair.

Nomvula took a deep breath and nodded. She broke from Sannie and brushed her hands down the front of her dress. She set off away from the crowd, which was losing interest as fast as it had gathered, and Sannie followed. Parents sat on plastic chairs outside their homes, fanning themselves as they contemplated the goings-on. The village was a mix of the new and traditional; single-storey brick homes with tin roofs and circular thatched huts with brown walls made of mud brick. Interspersed were half-finished builds, owned by local people who had been forced to go to Johannesburg or further afield to find work and who then constructed their family home one room, one window frame, at a time as they made their money. Too many of these absentee residents were now out of work and there was no building going on right now. Children darted through the backyards of houses, not-so-secretly following their progress. Nomvula yelled at the small ones in Xitsonga, telling them to go to their homes. The children obviously respected, perhaps feared, the old *gogo*.

Nomvula took Sannie off the main dirt road down a pathway lined with upended green Castle Lite beer bottles, an example of putting litter to better use. What had once been a hectare or so of vacant land on the edge of the settlement, cleared of most of its trees and used as a dumping ground, was now a fledgling community project, indicated by a sign that said 'Sustain – Non-Profit Organisation'. It was hot already, the sun beating down on red dirt and young trees, newly planted but struggling to grow. The village children were supposed to be watering them, part of their environmental studies, and despite the kids' best efforts some of the leaves were wilting and dried; in Killarney, the water supply was intermittent – watering plants was a luxury when there wasn't enough for humans. Hope had been nurtured here, but now it was struggling.

'I'm so sorry,' Sannie said, trying to build rapport. 'I can only imagine how you must feel.'

'What do you know of my pain?' Nomvula Ndlovu said as they walked, just a few curious youngsters in tow now.

It wasn't said in anger, more in frustration at the perceived lack of a speedy response by the police, and the woman could not know how Sannie had suffered, but the words stung her nonetheless.

She wanted to scream, *The man I love has been taken from me, killed! And if you want to know if I understand your pain, the answer is yes, because this was the second time it happened to me.*

Nomvula stopped and looked up into Sannie's eyes. 'You *do* know.'

Sannie blinked, still fighting back her own tears. 'About loss?'

Nomvula nodded.

'Yes,' Sannie said quietly. 'Everyone in this country knows about that. I am here to help you.'

Nomvula wiped her eyes. 'My granddaughter, she is gone.'

Sannie took off her mask and put it in her pocket. 'Yes. Tell me everything, please. Let's sit under that tree. Start from the beginning: what she was doing, and where you last saw her. Come.'

They were still within sight of the road and Sannie saw that the earlier crowd had reconvened, its attention now drawn to the arrival of a white Volkswagen Amarok *bakkie*, which pulled up about fifty metres from Sannie and Nomvula. The people who had been clustered around Nomvula, vociferously sharing her outrage and grief, now had other priorities; they formed themselves into a more or less orderly queue that ended at the tailgate of the big pickup truck.

Sannie thought she recognised the vehicle and her suspicion was confirmed as her two friends, Elizabeth and Samantha, got out. Both were dressed in activewear, having just done their morning on-line pilates class with their instructor, Taryn, which Sannie did not catch often enough. Both were toned and, despite their misfortunes, still had enough income or savings to keep themselves well-groomed like the rich men's wives they'd both been until recently. So much of life in South Africa, Sannie mused, was about keeping up appearances. Elizabeth, blonde and blue-eyed like Sannie, spotted her and waved.

'You know them?' Nomvula said. Samantha, unlike her Afrikaner friend, was of Greek descent, with smooth olive skin and lustrous black hair. She had already opened the tailgate and begun handing out shopping bags to the waiting people, who filed past. Samantha was the more organised of the two and it was she, Sannie knew, who had arranged the food relief program.

'Yes.'

'They bring food to us, every few days,' Nomvula said. 'They are good people.'

Sannie saw the look in Nomvula's red eyes. As consumed as she was with the need to find her granddaughter, Nomvula also needed to eat. Unemployment had been rife in Killarney even before the

33

pandemic hit, and just trying to make ends meet was a fulltime occupation. Even those with jobs barely scraped by.

'Come,' Sannie said. 'We'll get your share, then you can show me where Lilly disappeared.'

They walked to the truck. 'Howzit, Sannie,' Elizabeth said as she, too, began handing out bags that Sannie could now see were filled with maize meal, vegetables, cooking oil, sugar and long-life milk. 'I hope you feel better than I do after last night.'

In truth, she still felt a little queasy. 'Fine, Elizabeth. Can we maybe sort Nomvula out with a bag? She and I have business.'

'Hundred per cent.' Elizabeth selected a bag and passed it over.

'Shame, Sannie,' Samantha said, not breaking her rhythm of dispensing the COVID aid parcels. 'Is this the lady whose little girl has gone missing?'

'I am,' Nomvula said, taking the bag from Elizabeth, 'it's my granddaughter, and thank you.'

Samantha stopped her work to come around the *bakkie*, ignoring the scowl of the man who was next in line, and put a hand on Nomvula's arm. 'We're all praying for you, and for the girl.'

'You heard about this already?' Sannie asked.

Elizabeth nodded as she handed the man a bag. '*Ja*. We've been here in Killarney quite often, so we pick up the local gossip; we had permission to travel all through lockdown.'

'It's good of you to be doing this,' Sannie said. Samantha had run a thriving business before the virus, but from what Sannie knew of Elizabeth, her idea of hard work was Parkrun on Saturday mornings. Sannie had got to know the other women through a book club at Hippo Rock. Samantha lived on the estate, but Elizabeth and her husband had previously had enough money to keep a house there for weekends and holidays, even though they had lived only forty kilometres away. Sannie wasn't sure how Elizabeth was doing, financially, as a result of Piet leaving her.

Samantha shrugged. 'Yes, well, we both feel some responsibility. Many of the people in Killarney had been hoping for jobs at the hotel, and Piet and Elizabeth's company had been employing a few locals during construction. Those jobs all went as well.'

Nomvula nodded her head slowly, confirming what they all knew. Samantha was the head of the Hazyview Tourism Association and she and her husband John had been devastated by the coronavirus lockdown and suspension of international and domestic tourism. Sannie knew they had overextended with the bank to finance construction of a new boutique hotel on an old citrus farm very near to where they now stood.

The development was going to be a boon for Killarney, and not just through the promise of jobs. As part of gaining approval for a lease on the land from the local chief and community, John had started building a new and expanded school and major infrastructure works to prepare for a second stage of development, an upmarket housing estate in a future wildlife estate, much like Hippo Rock, with animals roaming between the houses. The long-term plan was that the old citrus farm would be incorporated into the Sabi Sand Game Reserve and adjoining greater Kruger National Park. Now Piet, Elizabeth's husband, had shut down the construction and infrastructure development work, mothballing everything and then running away.

'It is hard for all of us,' Nomvula said to Samantha.

Samantha swallowed and blinked a couple of times before turning back to her work.

As usual, Elizabeth was putting on a brave face. 'Might need a *loop dop* later, hey, Sannie?' Elizabeth whispered.

Sannie gave a small shake of her head. The thought of another drink, 'one for the road' as Elizabeth had suggested, turned her stomach even more, and she had serious work to do. They said their goodbyes and Sannie and Nomvula left the women to their charitable work.

Nomvula led Sannie to a mahogany tree. They each sat on old kitchen chairs on the raked dirt.

'When she didn't come home, I called the police, but they did nothing.' The woman took a handkerchief out of her bra and mopped her face.

'I understand,' Sannie said, taking a notebook from the side pocket of her cargo pants. 'I have come to say sorry for that, and to listen to you. Now, tell me, from the start, what happened.'

Nomvula sighed. 'I have a job in Hazyview, where I work at the Pick n Pay. I am lucky that the supermarkets are considered essential – so many people here have lost their jobs. On Thursday I left early, as I always do, at six in the morning. My granddaughter Lilly left at the same time to go to visit one of her friends. With the schools closed because of the virus, Lilly and her friend help each other with their homeschooling. Lilly spent the day with her friend and the girl's *gogo*.'

'Is it mostly the grandmothers who care for the children here?'

Nomvula nodded. 'Often, yes. Most of the mothers are away working. My daughter, Sibongile, Lilly's mother, died three years ago. She was very sick with tuberculosis.'

'I am sorry for your loss.' Sannie wondered if Sibongile had been HIV positive as well. Often it was TB that caused death for people whose immune systems were low.

'Does Lilly ever miss school?'

Nomvula shook her head, emphatically. 'No, she is a good girl. Some of the children, *ai*, they grow up with not enough supervision and they get into trouble, but not my Lilly. She even has an award from the teacher for her attendance. I can go to my house and find it for you, show it to you so you can see and ...'

Sannie reached out and put a hand on Nomvula's shoulder as her body heaved beneath her touch, the fear threatening to overwhelm her. Sannie could not imagine how she would feel if one of her children went missing, but Nomvula seemed to be fearing the worst already. 'How about Lilly's father?'

Nomvula gave a flick of her head. 'He works in a mine in North West province. I have left a message for him on his cell phone, but that one, he is no good. He has not seen Lilly for nearly eight years now.'

Which meant, Sannie calculated, that he'd left when Lilly was just five years old. This did not sound like a case of a parent kidnapping his own child.

'There was another girl taken, you know?' Nomvula added.

'No. When?'

'Two weeks ago, but the police were not interested in her, either.'

Two girls, Sannie wrote in her notebook. 'I will need her name. Tell me, why do you think the police were not interested in these disappearances?'

36

Nomvula looked over her shoulder, as if there might be someone eavesdropping. 'The other girl was Thandi Mnisi. She was different from Lilly. Thandi was only Lilly's age, maybe a little older, fourteen perhaps, but she was wise beyond her years. She had been in some trouble, with drugs, alcohol, boys.'

'Do you think both girls might have been abducted?'

Nomvula nodded. 'Yes, I think so – now.'

'Now?'

Nomvula glanced at the crowd, some of whom were drifting away now that the initial excitement was over. 'At the time Thandi went missing, well, many of us dismissed the reports, you know? We thought, "Ah, Thandi, she has just run off with some boy, or maybe gone to Joburg, or, God forbid, to one of the shebeens to work".'

Sannie shuddered. The thought of a girl just turned thirteen or fourteen going to work as a prostitute in a bar was as repugnant as it was illegal, yet in the poverty-stricken communities of South Africa it was not inconceivable.

'Who reported Thandi missing. Her mother?'

'No, Thandi's mother has passed and her father is somewhere else. Her friend, Sonto, made the report. I feel bad now. Maybe I, too, was too quick to judge Thandi and Sonto. They are alike.'

'This Sonto, is she still here?'

'Somewhere, yes. I can't see her now, but she is not far. I saw her before you arrived. Perhaps ...'

'Perhaps what?'

'Perhaps she is afraid or does not trust the police. She has been in trouble with the law in the past.'

'I see.' Sannie made some more quick notes then looked up. 'What did Sonto tell you?'

'She was upset. She said that Thandi had disappeared. At first,' Nomvula looked up into the branches and leaves of the tree, as if searching her memory, 'at first I asked Sonto if Thandi had run away. She said, "No, Mama, it is not possible – she would have told me, would have asked me to come, if she was going to run away."'

'Go on,' Sannie said.

'Sonto said they had both been out in the evening – she said they were going to a Bible study group, but I know that was a lie. They took my Lilly with them at first, though she came home early. The way the other two were dressed, the usual smell of liquor on their breath – well, I am sure you know how some young women behave.'

Sannie forced a smile.

'Sonto said they were walking through the bush and her friend Thandi was walking slowly and Sonto lost Thandi.'

'Lost her?' Sannie made a note.

'Yes, well, as you can imagine, Captain, I thought the girl would probably show up, with a *babelaas*, somewhere, you know?'

Sannie nodded. She knew the feeling of being hungover all too well these days, but did not want to be reminded of her own problems. 'Yes, I know.'

'I told Lilly she could not go out with these girls again after dark. Thandi did not show up. Sonto went to the local police, but they dismissed her, telling her Thandi would surely be back sometime soon.'

Sannie shook her head. The local officers should have at least opened a docket. 'I will find out what happened.'

'Yes, well, even when Thandi did not show up again, no one was too worried until, that is, now, when my Lilly did not arrive at the library.'

'Tell me where Lilly was last seen and what she was doing, please.'

'Lilly was last seen in the same place where Thandi disappeared. Lilly was on her way to the library, to do some of her own study, but she never made it there.'

'Where is this place where she was last seen?' Sannie asked. 'Can you show me?'

Nomvula glanced around her, as if she was checking for someone listening in, then cast her eyes down at the ground. 'I went, but I cannot go back there.'

'Why not? We have to find your granddaughter, and this could be the scene of ... well, this is a place we definitely have to investigate.'

Nomvula looked up and swallowed. 'This is a bad area, a place of ... evil.'

Sannie bit her tongue. Part of her was tempted to tell this woman to stop talking in riddles and to worry less about evil spirits and get on with the important information about what might have happened to her granddaughter, but she knew enough about the local Shangaan people to know that their belief system was as ingrained and deep as it was complex.

'Tell me.'

Nomvula licked her lips. 'There were signs where the girls disappeared.'

Sannie said nothing, an old interrogators' trick designed to make a suspect, or, in this case, interviewee, fill the void.

'Umuthi.'

Sannie made a note.

'There were some small packets of herbs or other medicine, some string made of plaited vines.'

'Warnings?' Sannie said.

'More like actual spells.' Nomvula copied her body language, more at ease, perhaps, knowing the white policewoman was not going to ridicule her beliefs.

'There is a sangoma here who thinks those girls have been taken by the spirits, that they have been corrupted.'

Sannie desperately wanted to interject, but held her tongue. She made a note to find and talk to this sangoma as a matter of priority.

'But I don't believe that.'

Sannie looked up. 'You don't? Why not?'

'I might be an old woman, Captain, but I was young, once. I know men. The one thing these girls have in common – two, in fact – was that they were young and beautiful.'

'You think they were abducted by men – the same man or men? Do you have any idea who, around here, might be interested in young girls?'

Nomvula stared at her for a few seconds as if she should know the answer to the question. She sighed. 'Captain, I don't have to tell you that the lockdown has been hard on all of us. Too many of the men who would normally be away at work are here now. They are restless, angry. Although alcohol has been banned there are still some who make a plan. Also, there were many workmen who came here to work on the new hotel and the school and so forth. Not all of them went back to their homes. Some stayed here, hoping for work. They are poor, hungry, like so many of us. Things were bad enough for women and girls before all of this.'

Sannie nodded. Not all men were abusers, and nor was this 'evil' restricted to any race or tribe, but as a police officer she knew all too well the seriousness and scale of this problem in her beloved country.

Nomvula went on. 'There are bad men in our community, criminals.'

This, as well, was not news to Sannie.

'Very bad men,' Nomvula said.

Sannie looked up from her notebook, into Nomvula's eyes. The older woman frowned. She was mulling over something, Sannie thought, deciding whether or not to tell her. Nothing Sannie could say, she knew, would force Nomvula to speak. It had to be her idea.

Nomvula glanced around again and lowered her voice. 'There are rhino poachers here.'

It was all Sannie could do to keep her composure. One of the greatest problems she had faced during her time in charge of the anti-poaching unit was getting assistance from the local communities. For certain, some of the poachers walked across the border from Mozambique, but there were others who came from within South Africa, from communities like this one, which bordered the Sabi Sand Game Reserve and the adjoining Kruger National Park, and it was very rare for anyone within these tight-knit clans to expose one of their own as a criminal. Sannie waited.

'None of my family,' Nomvula said quickly, 'but I hear things. We all do, but no one speaks up. We are afraid of these men.'

Sannie gave a tiny nod, nothing more, and made a point of putting her pen back in her pocket, to further encourage Nomvula to keep talking. She would write up her notes later, but for now she knew Nomvula would be more forthcoming if she assumed that what she said was off the record.

'You people ...' Nomvula began.

Sannie smiled, inwardly. Two simple words, 'you people', that in any other part of the world would not count for much, were laden with the evils of prejudice and hatred in South Africa, most commonly a precursor to criticism of another tribe or race.

'You people, your police, army, national parks rangers, are too good at catching poachers, now.'

Sannie had not expected the compliment and her words slipped out. 'Thank you.'

Nomvula shook her head, as much, Sannie thought, to tell her to keep her silence as to disagree with her. 'No, you misunderstand. I am not congratulating you. This is part of the problem.'

Now Sannie was confused, but she went back to being quiet.

'The poachers came, many of them from outside of the area. Some were violent men who turned to crime in Johannesburg and Durban, using guns to hijack cars and rob the cash in transit vans. Then they came here to kill rhinos, because, a few years ago, this was easy money for them, with very little risk. However, as your people started killing more and more of them, and their export markets dried up because of border closures,' Nomvula checked her surroundings again, 'they started looking for new business.'

Sannie knew of the successes, although it sometimes felt like the incoming tide of poachers would never end. For every criminal who was caught or killed while illegally hunting in the Kruger Park or the neighbouring private game reserves it seemed like there were ten new recruits to take his place. Not even the dreaded COVID-19 had slowed the poachers, who knew that fewer tourists and game drive vehicles from the luxury lodges meant fewer eyes on the ground. They had used the period of peace and tranquillity for the animals to ramp up their efforts.

Nomvula looked like she might be regretting opening her mouth; she continued to look around her. It was time for Sannie to prompt her. 'What type of business?'

'Drugs – they are a problem, but worse is the taking of children.'

Sannie drew a breath, fearing the answer to her next question. 'Why do you think the girls were taken?'

Nomvula looked at her as if she was as reluctant to answer the question as Sannie had been to ask it. 'Men. These girls may be taken for immoral purposes, maybe for worse things.'

It was hard to imagine anything worse than the rape and abuse of a child, but Sannie could. 'Umuthi?'

Nomvula gave a small, tight nod. 'There is evil here. Some izangoma, the bad minority ... I am sure you know, they will charge very much money for pieces of a human body, especially pieces from a child. There is a belief, also, among some men that to lie with a child will cure them of the illnesses they have caught.'

Sannie shuddered. She had heard it all before, seen children with terrible injuries, and even little bodies, but the horror never ceased to have an impact on her. The day she felt nothing, she thought, she would be dead, in spirit if not in the flesh.

'Nomvula, listen to me, please, and tell me the truth. Has anyone contacted you asking you for money?'

The older woman shook her head. 'No. I would tell you if they had.'

A thought crossed Sannie's mind. 'With all the police and army patrols at the moment, because of COVID, how are the criminals moving about?'

'Their magic is strong,' Nomvula said without hesitation.

Sannie exhaled. 'You think they make themselves invisible.'

'Either that or their muthi makes your police officers, or the soldiers, confused, or they go somewhere else, when these men move at night.'

Sannie checked her notebook again. 'You say the area where the girls went missing, this bad place, is near the border of the Sabi Sand reserve?'

Nomvula nodded. 'Yes, it is close.'

'We've had extra patrols along the perimeter fence, private antipoaching patrols on the reserve's side and police on this side.'

'See? Like I said, even with all your extra people patrolling, the *tsotsis* are able to get past them.'

That was true, Sannie admitted to herself. Even Julianne Clyde-Smith's intensively patrolled and monitored property, Lion Plains, had lost several animals lately. She expected the internet coverage of the female guide chasing the poacher this morning would go viral, putting renewed pressure on the government to do more, and that a wave of shit was heading her way.

'And their muthi is strong,' Nomvula added.

As respectful as Sannie was of people's beliefs, she did not believe there was any potion or spell that could make a human being

42

invisible or a police officer blind. However, she was well aware of how people could allow their faith to convince them that something scientifically impossible had actually happened. In her faith people called those occurrences 'miracles'.

Trying to enforce the lockdown had been a nightmare and despite the still-high numbers of infections, Sannie was glad the restrictions were gradually being lifted. How did one convince people who lived hand to mouth, day to day, to stay indoors for weeks on end, with no work, no income and no food? South Africa's president had been commended, not just at home but internationally, for taking the country straight into a tough lockdown, but the reality was that people had resorted to breaking the rules of self-confinement and there were not enough police officers or soldiers on the streets to stop them.

Sannie's view was that the government had known all along how tough it would be to enforce a full lockdown. While other, more law-abiding countries, had introduced a phased approach, in the knowledge that by and large people would do the right thing when it came to staying at home and social distancing, the South African president had introduced draconian measures in the knowledge that a percentage of the population would ignore them. It probably had the same net result, Sannie thought – or, rather, hoped.

'I need to look at the place where Lilly was last seen,' Sannie said. She had come here to be the face of the police service, to appease the local community and listen to Nomvula, but she decided, on the spot, that she would take the case and open the docket herself. It was not that she did not trust the local police, but she knew, instinctively, that this case was what she needed, to take her mind off Tom, and because she felt Nomvula's loss, almost personally.

Nomvula started wringing her hands. 'I want to help you …'

'Then take me there,' Sannie reached out and touched Nomvula's arm softly, 'please. I know it will be difficult for you, and you may fear going to the place where Lilly disappeared, but think of the greater evil, if we can't find her. You know umuthi doesn't affect us white people, as we don't believe in it. You won't need to touch anything and you'll be safe with me. Please. Every minute is crucial.'

Nomvula eventually nodded, and led Sannie further through the sustainability project, a collection of ambitious initiatives that were sadly showing the signs of hibernation and neglect because of the on-again, off-again lockdowns. There was a curio shop whose corrugated iron sheeting shutters were closed, and no children were using the second-hand play equipment outside the creche.

'You said Lilly was on her way to the library when she went missing?' Sannie asked.

'Yes. Like I said, she is a good girl, Captain,' Nomvula continued. 'It was after school, early evening. She knows that the ability to speak and read English very well will be important for her when she does her Matric, but her teachers in junior school, they struggled with English themselves so these after-school classes are important, especially for the young ones. My Lilly was a tutor before coronavirus, helping the small children with their English after school and at the same time improving her own knowledge.'

'Your English is very good,' Sannie said.

'Thank you. I practise every day with the English-speaking customers through my job at the supermarket, and I helped my Lilly. Although the library has been closed because of the virus, Lilly was going there to do her own study, in peace. She was trusted enough to have been given her own key.'

Sannie was touched, both by the plight of these kids, and a thirteen-year-old's dedication and devotion to others and her own learning during the pandemic. There was no excuse for breaking the lockdown, but at least Lilly had not been disobeying the rules to drink or take drugs and party. At least not according to her grandmother. Sannie resolved to keep a clear mind.

A road, once sealed, but now more potholes than tar, marked the boundary of the settlement of Killarney and the old citrus estate of the same name. Nomvula led her across and onto the former farm. There were gnarled stumps where trees once heavy with fruit had been cut down, and they walked along and over furrows that now resembled ancient earthworks. Nature was returning, with buffalo thorn trees recolonising what man had taken and long grass – no doubt a fire hazard – bending in the soft breeze. Through the regrowth Sannie glimpsed an old farmhouse or packing shed, a whitewashed brick shed with skeletal charred rafters.

Sannie knew this old farm well; it had once been a major thoroughfare for poachers coming to and from the Kruger Park, but Lion Plains, under Julianne's iron fist, had upgraded its share of the Sabi Sand's fence, and seeded it with electronic sensors and alarms.

They came to a new road, graded smooth enough to be out of place in the otherwise neglected-looking landscape. 'Where does this lead – to the new hotel?'

Nomvula pointed up the road. 'Yes, work was nearly finished on the boutique hotel, as they call it, and the swimming pool, as well as the new school, which still has no desks or other equipment.'

COVID-19 had put an end to that, Sannie knew.

'That is the new library; close to the new school and to the hotel, so rich foreigners can visit and make their donations, to feel good about themselves,' Nomvula said, gesturing to a large, circular mudbrick building. The grass thatch on the roof was still bright yellow, indicating it had only recently been constructed. The grass would turn almost black with age.

'The volunteers from Europe only finished it two weeks before the virus came,' Nomvula added, confirming Sannie's observation. 'And now with no volunteers or tourists we have no more money, nothing with which to continue our programs.'

Nomvula led her to the edge of the former agricultural land, up a small rise which looked out over a band of bushland with a perimeter fence a hundred or so metres beyond, running left to right in front of them. A cow mooed somewhere. This, Sannie knew, was a buffer zone between the old estate and the Sabi Sand Game Reserve, with its wild and dangerous animals hemmed in by the fence.

On the crest where they stood, looking over the wilderness which stretched away to the Kruger Park, was a cluster of boulders with another excellent view of the lands beyond. One big flat rock looked like an ideal place to sit and take in the vista. Nomvula climbed onto the rock, slowly, her old joints taking the strain.

Sannie followed and below the rock she saw the remains of a fire and a pile of empty and smashed beer and spirits bottles. There were cigarette butts and a woman's shoe, and an old, partly scorched mattress. This was a place on the fringe, perhaps where teenagers came to party, perhaps something more sinister. She would need to organise a forensic team to search the area.

'This place,' Nomvula sniffed, 'this was where my Lilly was last seen, by Sonto; they parted company here.'

'I must talk to Sonto.'

'I will find her for you, Captain, as soon as we get back.'

Sannie's phone rang and she excused herself, climbed off the rock and walked a short distance from Nomvula to take the call. It was Sean Bourke, the head of anti-poaching for the Sabi Sand Game Reserve. She had known him for a few years, since he first started working in the reserve as a tracker dog handler. He quickly filled her in on the action on the Lion Plains property that morning.

'We're tracking the poacher now. We suspect he's making a run for the perimeter fence near Killarney, probably via a new hole in the area around the old citrus farm,' Sean said, completing his report.

'All right. Thanks, Sean. I'm actually near there now. I'll take a turn by the fence as well.'

She ended the call, came back to Nomvula and put her phone away and her hands on her hips. Sannie looked around her.

'Can you feel it, Captain?'

'Feel what?'

'This place.'

Sannie knew, from what she had been told, that something had happened here, but she was not given to believing in the spirit world. All the same, this semi-abandoned construction site was a place where no one might hear a young girl scream. 'I will find out what happened to your granddaughter.'

Nomvula hugged herself and looked into Sannie's eyes. 'You did not answer my question, but you can feel the chill. I can see it in you.'

It was, Sannie knew, most likely the power of suggestion, but she shivered nonetheless.

Chapter 5

Mia studied the ground in front of her. This was no exercise and she was not as keen and excited as she would have been if she was tracking, say, a lion.

She had picked up a clear footprint, a running shoe, near the edge of the road and it had been relatively easy to hold on to the trail until now. They were close to the Manzini Spruit, where the man had been spotted on the Vulture system.

Bongani came up beside her. 'What do you see?'

She pointed to the flattened clump of grass, and then ahead of them. 'He is moving, but not in the direction where he was first seen.'

'There are two of them, maybe?'

'I'm not sure,' she said. 'These tracks are fresh-fresh and we would have seen another man here, easily. I think he has moved while we were driving.'

Bongani nodded slowly. 'A good deduction. But remember, we must not try to make the tracks fit what we believe – it must be the other way around. The tracks will tell a story, perhaps in another language, and it is up to us to translate that story, to understand it.'

He'd said the same thing to her before, and he was right. A novice tracker would find some evidence and then try to make it fit what he or she believed was a pattern, their assumption of where the quarry had gone and what it would do next. With animals it was, in fact, easy to do this and be right, but with humans, it was dangerous. A man would set out to deceive.

Mia saw a scuff mark on a rock, where the poacher had climbed over a granite boulder in his way. Perhaps he thought that by rock-hopping he could throw her off his scent.

'Good work,' Bongani said, noticing what she was looking at. They followed the trail over some boulders. 'He knows we are after him. He is trying to put us off.'

Mia tried to think what she would do next.

'Is that the dry creek bed, up ahead?' Sara asked, catching up to them.

Mia looked up. 'Yes. That tall leadwood tree is a giveaway.'

Sara smiled. 'I thought so. I'm getting to know this place.'

'Slowly, now,' Mia said. She put a finger to her lips and Sara nodded. Bongani seemed to grip the rifle more tightly, judging by his knuckles. There was something about his eyes, as well. It was as though he was nervous, and Mia could not recall ever seeing him afraid of anything. Mia led the way.

She picked up the trail again, and it led to the edge of the dry stream. She could see where the poacher had half slid, half run down the bank to the sandy bed. Mia knelt and took a closer look as Bongani and Sara closed up on her.

'He went down here, but look,' she pointed to another set of scuff marks in parallel, but going back up the bank, 'he's exited here again at the same place. Sloppy work.'

'Those tracks look fresh,' Sara said.

'Yes.' Mia stood and scanned the bush. 'We can catch him. Graham thought he must have cached his rifle somewhere.'

Heavy-calibre hunting rifles were hard to come by, Mia knew, and poachers sometimes resorted to violent raids on farms to get hold of them – reasoning that an isolated farmer would be more likely to have a rifle than anyone else. If they caught this man they could always come back with a dog trained to sniff out ammunition and firearms and look for the weapon.

'All right,' said Mia, as it seemed she was the one calling the shots, 'we follow him, but once we have him in sight we tail him, without him knowing, and we call in Sean and his guys. Agreed?'

Both Bongani and Sara nodded.

'That sounds like fun,' Sara said.

Mia frowned, quietly fuming. 'Tracking a man is not "fun". It's dangerous work and he still may be armed.'

'Sorry,' Sara said.

'OK.' Mia checked the ground again then looked up. Surprised, she had to stop herself from crying out in alarm. She could see a man, much closer than she expected, and he was carrying something cradled in his arms. 'Shit.'

*

Mia's phone vibrated in her pocket. It was a message from the Vulture control room, from Audrey Uren, Julianne Clyde-Smith's personal assistant, who, like many of the lodge's support staff, had been trained to operate the monitoring system. Audrey and Alison Byrne, the British-born lodge manager, had relieved Graham and Oscar.

Lost sight of target. We think he has gone into the drainage line of the spruit. Radar and cameras having trouble picking him up.

That made sense, Mia thought. She wondered if someone at the lodge had been leaking details about the system. It seemed this poacher knew how to evade the electronic gadgetry. It was proof that poachers were clever and that technology, while useful, had its limitations.

Mia tapped out a message: *Copy. We have visual on him now.*

Roger, Audrey replied. Mia smiled to herself – she knew Audrey loved working on the system as it gave her a break from her more mundane day-to-day work and made her feel like she was playing a role in the war on poaching.

Mia knew that there were other sensors and hidden cameras in and around the reserve and along its perimeter fence that would, hopefully, pick up the man on his way home, if they lost him. For now, she was locked onto his trail. He was making no attempts to cover his tracks, and every now and then they caught sight of him. He was wearing a pair of running shoes, quite new judging by the crisp tread pattern and logo and brand name she could occasionally pick up in the dust.

He was moving carelessly, and did not seem to be looking behind him at all. Each time Mia glimpsed him she went to ground, but their target trudged on. He was not swinging his arms because of whatever it was that he was carrying, and she could see no sign of the rifle that Graham had spotted earlier.

Mia thought more about the rifle. She knew that poachers sometimes used take-down rifles – weapons that could be disassembled into two pieces, but this man was not wearing a backpack or satchel in which to hide a rifle.

She'd read about poachers in Zimbabwe who cached AK-47s in game reserves, for good reason. In that country if a person was seen carrying a weapon in a national park or game reserve they could be shot dead on sight. In South Africa there was no such law and anti-poaching rangers, police and military operators could technically only fire in self-defence. It was, she thought, a technicality that was very much open to interpretation, but to the best of her knowledge Sean Bourke was a strictly law-abiding commander who instructed his rangers to treat any poacher firmly, but fairly. She did not think he was the shoot-on-sight type.

The man stopped.

Mia waved her hand, signalling the others to stop. She looked over her shoulder, and once she saw they were settled she showed them an open palm, telling them to stay where they were. She crept forward, keeping a stout jackalberry tree between her and her quarry.

The man appeared to be checking his directions, standing still in the open, the bundle still in his arms. The sun had climbed high now and she got her first good look at him. He was, she saw, a young man, not much more than a boy, long legs and thin arms and a body not fully filled out. When he looked her way, not at her but in the general direction, she took a sharp breath.

Sipho, she said to herself. She was surprised.

Mia knew the boy – she had gone to school with his older sister, who now worked in Johannesburg as a hairdresser. Sipho was a promising student, who had been raised by his grandparents until they passed away. The old man had been a hunter in his day – or, depending on the lens he was viewed through, a poacher – but he had seemed honest to Mia other than that. Sipho now lived alone, except for a large collection of snakes and other reptiles that had given birth to his nickname, 'the Snake Boy of Killarney'.

She brought her radio up to her mouth. 'Sean, Mia, over?'

After a few moments he replied. '*Go, Mia.*'

'I've got our man in sight. He's a kid. No weapon, over.'

'*We still need to arrest him, over.*'

Who, me? she wanted to reply. 'I'll keep him in sight until you can send someone, or intercept him at the fence, over.'

'*Affirmative, thanks Mia,*' Sean replied.

Sean had his hands full this morning, but he seemed calm. Mia knew Sean had served in Afghanistan, and had an impressive record in catching poachers and running the reserve's security – until recently.

Sipho turned around and Mia could see, for the first time, what he was carrying. A pangolin.

'Shit,' she whispered. She had been toying with the idea of turning a blind eye to the boy and letting him go. The last thing he needed was a criminal record – growing up where and when he had, he was already at a disadvantage – but she could not let him get away with a pangolin.

She was about to tell the others when they all heard a bang, from behind them.

'That was a gunshot,' Sara said, cocking her head.

Bongani nodded. 'Heavy calibre.'

'Sean, Sean, this is Mia,' she said into her walkie-talkie. 'We've got gunfire ...' There was another loud crack. 'Two shots, southwest of our position.'

'*Roger,*' Sean said.

'I'm heading there now,' Mia said. 'We're going back to our vehicle.'

'*What about your suspect, over?*' Sean asked.

The others had both turned and started jogging to the Land Rover. 'He's ... a kid, though he's got a pangolin,' Mia panted. 'I think I can ID him. I'll ... follow up with him later.'

'*OK,*' Sean said. '*He may have been a decoy all along for the real shooter.*'

'Affirmative,' Mia said. The same thought had just crossed her mind, yet the Vulture system had only been able to pick up one person earlier. Something funny was going on this morning. Mia paused to call Audrey, but the signal was disappearing.

'Mia … can you hear me?' Audrey said into the phone. 'I got a glimpse of a second man, and this one has a rifle! I've lost him, but I last saw him heading back towards the dry riverbed, where we first saw him go to ground.'

'Just one man; I mean, he's moving by himself?' Mia asked.

'Yes, one man, but you're breaking up. Also we can see a baby rhino running around by itself and …'

Mia swore to herself again and resumed running. 'Send me the coordinates off the computer screen.'

'Losing you,' Audrey said. 'Can't hear you.'

They reached the Land Rover and Mia and Sara climbed aboard. Bongani sat in the tracker's seat again, but this time he kept the rifle cradled across his knees. They would never have driven like this with guests on board, but there was at least one armed man out there somewhere.

Mia felt a shift within her. She had been raised, in no small part, by the same community that Sipho and Bongani were from. It was quite possible that she knew the shooter they were now chasing. She had begun the morning not wanting to do the anti-poaching rangers' job, of tracking down a human being, but the blood lust was coursing through her body now. She felt as much of a kinship with the animals of this reserve as she did with the people in the surrounding communities.

Mia was about to use the Land Rover's radio to call Audrey again when Bongani signalled for her to stop and pointed to the ground. Mia rose in her seat and, peering over the front of the vehicle, picked up the tracks of the rhino cow and her calf.

She turned to Sara, sitting behind her. 'Hold on.'

Mia swung the steering wheel and the Land Rover bounced on its coil springs as they left the graded surface. Thorny branches whipped the side of the truck and there was a loud crack as Mia drove over and split a dead branch. She turned fast and confidently to navigate around a termite mound.

Bongani's tracking skill was as good as any GPS and Mia barely needed to check that they were still on course. He held up his hand and closed it into a fist. Mia pulled to a stop and switched off the engine.

They heard a high-pitched whining, bleating noise and it pierced Mia's heart as surely and as keenly as a blade.

'What the hell is that?' Sara asked.

Mia opened her door and got out of the Land Rover. 'Baby rhino, calling for its mother.'

Bongani climbed down from his seat and led them through the bush. Sara raced to keep up with them. The noise became louder.

Mia pushed through the branches and leaves that scratched her bare forearms and hooked her green shirt, ignoring the blood. She came to a clearing. It had been done quickly, the poacher not even bothering to cover the carcass. The poacher knew they were out here, looking for him and his suspected accomplice, Sipho.

She knelt by the dead female rhino and touched her fingers to the wound. 'Clean shot, to the heart. At least she didn't suffer.'

'But the horn's still attached,' Sara said. She stood over the dead animal, put her hand over her mouth and started to cry.

Bongani cast around the scene, walking in a circle, looking for spoor. The baby rhino emerged from the bush, took a look at them, bleated some more, then retreated away from them. Mia knew it would not go far from the body of its mother.

'We have disturbed the poacher. He will be close. We must find him,' Bongani said, his voice dispassionate, businesslike, 'now.'

Mia looked up at him. Once more she found herself in the same quandary. She wanted to get the bastard who had done this, but he was armed and they had a volunteer with them.

'Let's go,' Sara said.

Mia stood, wiping the blood from her fingers on her shorts. 'We know this one is armed.'

'So are we,' Sara said.

'The tracks lead back to the road,' Bongani said.

Mia nodded. 'We'll drive there. Sara, you can stay with the Land Rover. The vets will need to come and dart the baby, to rescue it and take it to one of the rhino orphanages. You can help them, lead them to the carcass.'

Sara put her hands on her hips and shook her head. 'No.'

'It's important and will be a great experience for you,' Mia said, trying to sound kindly. This was what these volunteers wanted, to save wildlife, to take home memories they could show off to their friends like souvenirs, before they drifted into their corporate jobs and safe, first-world lives.

Sara pointed at the dead rhino. 'I want to catch the bastard who did this.'

'That's not our job, Sara.'

'I *know* it isn't, but don't tell me you're not angry about this.'

Mia sighed. 'Of course I'm angry, but that's not a good mood to be in if you're tracking a man with a gun.'

'You're good at your job, Mia. You need to get off the fence, get some skin in the game, as the Americans always say. You can follow this guy.' Sara looked to Bongani. 'What do you think?'

Bongani shrugged. 'I work with Mia, she is my partner, not you. These men who poach, they are dangerous, and this one is lone, like a dagga boy, an old buffalo bull. That either means he is tough and clever – to come out here and track by himself, without a protection man with an AK-47 – or crazy. In either case, we do not want to corner him.'

Sara continued to stare at him. 'You people are scared.'

Mia glanced at Bongani, whose face was impassive for a few seconds, and then he spat on the ground. The insult meant little to Mia. Sara didn't understand the dangers involved, and like too many people from western countries, she was impatient.

Mia looked to Bongani. 'What do you think?' she asked in Xitsonga.

'Ignore this woman,' he said to her in their shared language. 'Think what is best for the reserve, and for this rhino. It is dead. This man has bested us.'

Mia gave a small nod. Julianne was fiercely protective of her rhinos and both Bongani and Mia felt the loss as keenly as Sara, even if they didn't show it. And Bongani was right, this poacher had got the better of them and that did not sit well with either of them.

Mia was shorter than Sara, but she squared up to the other woman and jutted her chin forward. 'You stay behind us, and you do not say a word. If there is trouble your job is to run – and I mean run – back to the Land Rover as soon as it goes down. Understood?'

Sara looked like she might answer back, but Mia held her stare and Sara backed down, giving a small nod. 'I understand.'

'We find him and we fix him,' Mia said to both of them, 'and we wait for the cavalry. No stupid heroics.'

Bongani worked the bolt on the rifle and chambered a round. 'Come. Time is wasting. He will be moving fast.'

They climbed back into the Land Rover and Mia reversed and turned, retracing their tracks through the bush and driving as fast as she dared. When she came to the gravel road she turned left. Bongani leaned forward in his tracker's seat on the bonnet and Mia craned her head over the driver's side, checking the ground as they drove.

After scanning ahead for a while, Bongani held up a hand. Mia stopped. He pointed to the right and Mia swung off the road. He stopped her again.

'It's too thick to drive through here and follow the tracks,' he said. 'We will go on foot from here.'

'Sara –'

'I told you, I'm coming with you,' Sara interjected.

Mia held up a hand. 'Hear me out. I want you to take the Land Rover, keep driving in this direction. If he's going to head for the perimeter fence, which is logical, he'll have to cross this road again some time. Also, the poacher will be able to hear us now; if we turn off the engine he'll know we're after him on foot, but if you're driving he won't know we're tailing him. You can act as a cut-off, or whatever it is you call it in the army.'

Sara bit her lip, perhaps debating whether or not to continue the argument. 'All right.'

'As an ex-soldier you don't need me to ask if you know how to use a radio, right?'

Sara half grinned. 'You do not need to – what is the expression? – butter me up any more.'

Mia smiled. 'Thank you.'

She and Bongani set off into the bush, Mia tracking, Bongani keeping watch over her with the rifle at the ready.

*

Sara drove along the road, imitating Mia, looking over the driver's side door, searching for tracks, but it was hard for her to make out anything. The higher the sun rose, the less distinct the shape of tracks became.

She slowed down, scanning the bush instead, hoping to catch a glimpse of movement.

Sara stopped to remove her fleece. She was warming up. While the sun was out, there were dark clouds building on the horizon. The weather, she already knew, was about to change.

Once she had shrugged the garment over her head, she froze in her seat. From her left she heard movement over the noise of the idling engine. Even though Mia had told her to keep driving, Sara decided to switch it off, to better hear.

Not daring to move, she cocked her head. There it was again, the swish of something moving through the bushes. Sara looked around the vehicle. There was nothing she could use as a weapon. She felt her heart pounding and reached, slowly, for the ignition key again. If she saw the bastard poacher she would restart the engine and run him down.

If he was making that much noise, Sara reasoned, he would not be aware she was there. *Swish, swish, swish.* The man was crashing through the foliage now. With her other hand she reached for the radio and brought the handset up to her mouth. Glancing down, she noticed that the light on the screen was off. It had obviously needed power from the engine to function. Sara placed the handset down on the passenger seat and pushed a button on the radio.

It came to life with a musical chime that sounded as loud as a church bell.

The sound of movement from the bush stopped.

Sara realised the man had heard the radio coming on. He had a gun. She was unarmed. She tried to think back on her training. The smart thing to do in a situation like this would be to pull out, get reinforcements and come back. She started the Land Rover, but as she put the vehicle in gear a dark shape exploded from the bush beside her.

Sara screamed. When she looked around, however, at the blur of movement that ran behind the game viewer, she saw the angry pug-face of a honey badger staring up at her. The creature, small but fierce, snarled at her. Sara exhaled.

'My God, you scared me.'

'And you me.'

She jumped and looked back to where the honey badger had erupted from the bush and saw a man in black clothes and a ski mask moving around to the front bumper of the vehicle. He was pointing a Czech Brno hunting rifle at her. His bare hand, and the finger inside the trigger guard, told her he was African.

Neither of them said a word. The man licked his lips, but kept the rifle up in his shoulder and stared down the open sights at her.

'Turn the engine off,' he said to her, at last.

'Don't shoot me. You don't want to add murder to your list of crimes. Why don't you just go? I won't tell anyone I saw you.'

'Where are you from? Your accent is not Afrikaans.'

'I am from Norway. I've heard it said that if a South African commits a crime against a foreigner then the police come down on you harder.'

He nodded. 'That is true. Now turn the engine off and throw me the keys.'

She made a show of looking around the steering wheel. 'I am sorry, I am not normally the driver.' As she pretended to scrabble for the key she picked up the handset of the radio and keyed the send button, keeping the handset low, out of his line of sight.

'I *said*, turn off the engine, now, and get out of the vehicle.'

'Are you going to kill me?'

'Not if you do as I say. Quickly now. The key. Switch it off.'

She pretended to fumble again. 'I'm trying!'

He started to move sideways. Sara knew she had only one chance. She put the gear lever in first and depressed the clutch.

She pressed her foot down on the accelerator, revving the engine.

The man pulled the trigger.

Chapter 6

Mia had stopped Bongani when she heard Sara's voice on the radio. She started at the sound of the gunshot.

'Vulture, Vulture, this is Mia, over,' she said into the handset. 'For God's sake, answer!'

'*Go Mia,*' said Audrey, at last, replying via the radio.

'Give me a location on our game viewer, please, Audrey. Sara's in it and I think she's just been shot. Then call Sean, get him to send a team there ASAP. We may need a helicopter casualty evacuation.'

'*Roger, Mia ... stand by.*'

Mia turned and led Bongani the way they had come, towards the road. The poacher had obviously doubled back on them.

'*Mia, I've got the Land Rover on the computer screen now. I'm zooming in on it with the camera.*'

Mia was breathing heavily as she ran through the bush. 'Any sign of movement?'

'*Um ... negative. Wait ... I can see Sara. My God, she's lying on the ground, over. She's west of Little Serengeti. There's a tree partially blocking the road, if that's any help.*'

Mia knew the place. The tree had come down in a windstorm last week. 'Send the GPS coordinates to Sean. Where the hell's our chopper been today?' Mia said a silent prayer they were not too late, but it didn't sound good. Dark clouds covered the sun, and thunder rumbled.

'*The helicopter had some maintenance issues,*' Audrey said. '*Julianne already had me check on that, over.*'

Mia fumed, although she knew it wasn't Audrey's fault. 'OK. Sorry. But please tell Sean he needs to find a chopper from somewhere.' She looked up at the sky. A storm wouldn't help when it came to air support. As much as everyone loved the first rains, this was *not* a good time for the dry season to break early.

Bongani, still holding the rifle, ran ahead of Mia as she slowed to talk. He burst out onto the road before her and looked both ways, and at the ground.

'Come, this way.'

He led her at a jog and as they rounded a bend Mia saw the tree partially blocking the road and the Land Rover beyond. Bongani charged ahead and dropped to one knee as Mia, panting, joined him. She put two fingers to Sara's neck.

'She's got a pulse.' Mia ran her hands over Sara's body. 'Help me roll her over.'

Her right hand came away sticky. 'She's been hit in the shoulder,' Bongani said.

'Put your hand on the wound. I'll get the first-aid kit.'

Mia got into the truck and fetched the pack with the red cross on it from behind the driver's seat. She unzipped it and ripped open a wound dressing.

Bongani moved his hand, which was drenched with blood, and Mia applied the pad. With Bongani's help they tied the dressing. It started to rain, fat drops spattering them, but they continued to work.

Sara came to and started screaming. Mia held her hand. 'We're here, we're with you, Sara. Help is on the way.' Mia looked to Bongani, who grimaced.

The radio squawked and Bongani picked it up as Mia cradled Sara in her arms. Bongani got up and walked a few paces away.

'I'm … I'm sorry,' Sara said. Tears mixed with raindrops streamed down her cheeks. 'I'm sorry I disobeyed you. I tried to run him down.'

'It's OK,' Mia said.

'No.' Sara shook her head. 'He was wearing a ski mask, so I couldn't see his face. He was about one-eighty tall, solid build, deep voice. He was African.'

'You did well to get those details.' Mia held her tight, keeping her hand on the wound.

'I ... I saw his hands,' Sara said. 'They looked old – thin, you know?'

Mia nodded. 'Good work.'

Bongani returned to them. 'Good news. National Parks is sending one of their choppers from Kruger, and their doctor. They'll get you to Nelspruit in no time, Sara.'

Bongani was staring into the bush, shifting his weight from one foot to the other, the rifle held tight in his hands. Mia read his mind. 'No, Bongani, it's too dangerous.'

'What?' Sara croaked.

'I will go find him,' Bongani said.

Mia shook her head, 'No.'

Sara grabbed her arm, and her grip was weak. 'Yes. Go. Get him. He killed that mother rhino. Don't let him get away on my account. There is nothing Bongani can do for me.' She shuddered as the pain racked her body.

Mia smoothed the other woman's golden hair, now wet from the rain and tinged red with the blood from Mia's hands.

Bongani stood and Mia saw how his eyes instinctively cast about on the road for tracks. His stare locked on to something.

'He'll be running for his life,' Mia said.

'Get him, catch him, Bongani,' Sara said.

He looked down at her and nodded. 'I will, you can count on me.'

Bongani left and Mia was worried for him. Nothing was right about this situation – the older man disappearing, Sipho appearing out of nowhere, Sara being shot. There was, of course, always a danger of non-combatants being injured in the war that was being waged against poaching in South Africa, but to date it hadn't happened. The security forces – national parks rangers, the police, military and private anti-poaching companies, such as Sean's – ran rings around the poachers, tactically. That didn't stop them coming.

Mia checked Sara's dressing. It was almost soaked through. She held the other woman to her breast and picked up her handheld radio again. 'Audrey, this is Mia.'

'*Go Mia.*'

'Do you see anything? Bongani's gone after the guy with the gun.'

'*How's Sara, over?*'

Mia looked at Sara's face. Her skin was pale, her breathing shallow. 'Could be better,' was the best she could manage. 'Now tell me, what do you see?'

There was a pause as Audrey rechecked the Vulture computer screens. '*Nothing, I'm afraid, Mia. Rain's not helping either. The unarmed guy, the one we think was the decoy, is out of our area of operations now; literally off the screen, over.*'

Mia nodded to herself. The cameras and other sensors covered a finite area, and while it was a broad arc of coverage, they could only be turned and readjusted so far. 'Roger. And the other guy?'

'*Lost visual. It's weird, though. I'm tracking Bongani, plain as day, but the guy with the gun has literally disappeared from my screens, over.*'

Mia felt a chill.

'*Mia, do you copy, over?*'

'Um, affirmative, yes, I'm still here. Just thinking, over.'

'*Thinking what?*' Audrey said. '*I could use any guidance you can think of. Is there maybe some tracking trick this guy is using? Unless he's lying flat under a bush, I don't know where he's gone. None of the cameras or sensors are picking up movement, over.*'

'Keep looking,' was all Mia could think of.

'*Helicopter's inbound,*' Audrey said over the radio a couple of minutes later.

Mia heard the chop of rotor blades cleaving the air. 'Hang in there, Sara. Can you hear the chopper?'

Sara blinked and nodded weakly. Mia laid her gently on the ground, got up and went to the Land Rover and switched on the headlights. The pilot came through on her radio and Mia talked him down into a clearing next to the roadway about fifty metres away. As the pilot descended, Mia went back to Sara and crouched over her, using her body to shield the wounded woman from the cloud of dust and twigs and leaves that washed over them.

A ranger in a green uniform, carrying a folded stretcher, and the Skukuza doctor, a woman dressed in jeans and a khaki blouse, carrying a medical pack, jumped out. With Mia, they all shifted Sara onto the litter and carried her to the waiting helicopter.

'Do you want to come with?' the ranger yelled in her ear as the doctor inspected Sara and inserted a cannula into her arm.

Mia shook her head. 'I've got a man in the bush looking for the shooter.'

'Be careful!'

Mia gave the man a thumbs up and she watched as the helicopter started to lift off. She could see the doctor had already connected Sara to an IV line. As soon as the chopper was out of sight she set off into the bush after Bongani.

She was easily able to follow his trail, but still kept an eye out for dangerous game.

After a few minutes she came to the banks of the mostly dry Manzini Spruit. Here and there the sandy stream bed still held puddles, and there was a pumped waterhole, which they often checked during their game drives as the clean water was a magnet for game. Bongani was standing by the waterhole, scratching his head.

'What is it?' she said softly.

He turned and shrugged. 'I don't know.'

'What?'

'I mean,' he said, 'I've lost him.'

'Don't tell me he made himself invisible or turned himself into an impala.'

He frowned at her flippancy. 'Do you see any impala here?'

Mia cast about, walking in a circle. She picked up tracks – hers and Bongani's, and a third set, that came to the waterhole, where she had found Bongani. 'Where did he go from here?'

'That's what I want to know.'

They heard a vehicle from the direction in which they'd left their Land Rover and decided to retrace their tracks back to the vehicle. A curious black Belgian Malinois, Askari, met them as they approached the road.

Askari's handler, Phillip, along with Graham, Oscar and Sean Bourke joined them. They all exchanged greetings and Mia filled Sean in.

Sean nodded. 'We need to secure the rhino carcass as a crime scene, for the police and forensics, and I've called Doc Baird, the vet, to come dart the calf.'

It felt to her like he was verbalising his to-do list as a means of trying to assert some sort of control over what had been a terrible morning for all of them.

Graham came to her and gently took her elbow, leading her away from the others. 'Howzit, babe?'

She shrugged. 'Could have been a better morning.'

'*Ja*, affirmative.' He leaned forward and kissed her cheek.

Sean glanced away and Mia felt self-conscious. There was important work to do, but it was nice that Graham was thinking of her. Despite his bluster and extroverted nature, which could border on arrogant sometimes, inside he was a softy. He was also ridiculously good-looking, and brave. His partner, Oscar, nodded to her in greeting. Mia forced a smile for him.

Sean called them back over. 'Right. Mia, if you and Bongani are up to it, can you help us track the armed guy?'

Mia was shattered, but there was no question of her going home to her room at Kaya Nghala just yet. 'Sure. Can do – we've just been looking for his spoor, but we seem to have lost him.'

'Graham, Oscar?'

'*Yebo*,' Graham said.

'Mia says the rhino still had its horn when they last saw it. You guys go secure the carcass and keep eyes on the calf until the vet gets here. There's a chance this *skelm* will double back to try to claim his prize.'

'Roger,' Oscar said.

Graham nodded to Mia and he and Oscar jogged away.

Bongani came to Mia. 'You take the lead. Perhaps I was tired, maybe I missed something.'

It was a measure of Bongani, she thought, that he could admit he may have made a mistake in trying to track the man, or that Mia might do a better job.

Mia led off, with Phillip the dog handler and his Belgian Malinois on her heels, followed by Bongani and Sean.

There was spoor everywhere. Mia realised that she was seeing Bongani's footprints, those of the older poacher, and also those of the boy, Sipho, with his distinctive running shoes. If he was going to have a career as a criminal, she mused, he would need more nondescript footwear. Bongani's tracks went both ways, to and from the road, as did the older poacher's and her own. It would have been confusing if she didn't already have some oversight of what had happened during this crazy morning.

She stuck to what she believed were the freshest tracks. The first light shower of rain, which had helped her distinguish the freshest and crispest tracks, turned into her enemy as the skies opened up.

'This is not going to help,' she heard Sean say behind her.

He was right. The fresh imprints began to fill with water, but Mia, undeterred, carried on. The dog sniffed impatiently behind her as he picked up the scent of the poacher. The anti-poaching dogs were trained to ignore the scent of people who worked at the lodge, a time-consuming process that involved using items of clothing worn by each of them, which the dog would come to recognise and then ignore while tracking.

Sean caught up with her, overtaking the canine handler. 'We can let the dog go on ahead if you like.'

Mia shook her head. 'No, I want to see where Bongani got to before the rest of us mess up the spoor. I'm only going to get one good look at this before the rain washes it away completely.'

'OK,' Sean said. 'But only because it's you and I know how close you are to your master tracker's qualification.'

'Thanks,' Mia said. She was the first to recognise and appreciate the tracker dogs' phenomenal abilities, but following scent, just like her looking for tracks, meant taking in only one piece of this puzzle. A dog could not think like a human, and nor was it as devious – or as cruel.

Mia followed the spoor down into the stream bed. A trickle of water was now flowing in the deepest part of the sandy watercourse. She came to an area of flattened sand.

'This is where he sat, resting or hiding; he even lay down for a while,' Mia said, wiping rainwater from her face.

She carried on, the others content to leave her in silence, not commenting or venturing opinions. Mia felt the pressure start to build, just as it had during her last assessment for her master tracker's qualification when the two men who had carried out the assessment scrutinised her every move and muttered quietly to themselves as she, and they, inevitably came to the conclusion that she would not pass.

She had failed. She had been tracking a lion – a lioness in fact, moving about on its own. It was a difficult and potentially dangerous animal to track. A pride of lions, anywhere between four and twenty-four animals, was easier to follow because of the sheer amount of spoor, but it was easy to lose the trail of a single animal. Lions were generally sociable animals, so Mia knew that if this female was on her own then it was either because she had been injured and become separated from the pride, or she had left of her own volition, most likely because she was heavily pregnant and about to give birth to cubs, or she had just done so and was hunting or returning to wherever she had stashed her young.

Every theory about why this animal might have been alone spelled danger. An injured animal would be under pressure, hungry and extremely defensive; however, by reading the spoor Mia had seen no evidence of blood trails or limping, which would have been indicated by the damaged leg leaving a fainter paw print. Also, judging by the distance between the tracks the animal had been making good speed, with a healthy, natural gait. She was a big girl, as well, Mia had noticed from the size of the pug marks, meaning she was in her prime, and this tended to discount the theory that she might be an injured loner.

If she had not yet given birth the lioness would be acutely aware of her vulnerability, and quick to defend herself. If she had given birth her protective instincts would be in overdrive. Lionesses left the pride to give birth and to tend to their newborns because the tiny cubs were at risk of being trampled or otherwise injured by the boisterous, downright violent day-to-day life of lions; it was only once the cubs had their little eyes open and were mobile enough to keep pace with the pride that their mother would return to the fold with them.

Several times Mia had lost sight of the big cat's tracks, but that in itself was not unusual. Rocky ground, water and other variables made it hard to spot spoor, but tracking was also about knowing an animal's patterns of movement, behaviour and individual habits. Mia had known there was a waterhole nearby and that given the time of day the lioness, assuming she had cubs and needed to ensure she was lactating sufficiently, would need water.

Mia had headed towards the waterhole, sure she would pick up some clear tracks at some point, but it didn't happen. She had begun to doubt herself. Backtracking, she had returned to the last identifiable pug mark, but then the self-doubt had overcome her.

'Mia?' Sean said.

She realised she had been standing in the rain, staring down at the last clear footprint the poacher had left on his return to the stream. She had followed his spoor out of the snaking sandy bed, and then back into his lying-up position, and now there was no sign of him.

Mia ignored Sean for another few seconds. In front of her were half a dozen granite boulders, sticking up from the sand, worn smooth by generations of seasonal rain.

She looked back at Sean. 'He might have used these rocks, like giant stepping stones, to confuse us – me.'

'The dog?' Sean said.

Mia wavered, doubting herself once more. She needed time to put herself in the poacher's mind, but time was something they did not have. She felt a hand on her shoulder and turned to see Bongani standing beside her.

'You can do this,' he said.

She shrugged off his touch. She was the head ranger on the Lion Plains reserve and she knew that several of the other male guides, most of whom had been sent home because of COVID, resented the fact that a woman had been promoted above them and still had a job. She often felt she had to be twice as good as the male guides just to be treated as an equal. Now, she had many people watching and the added pressure of tracking a man who had just tried to kill one of their own. 'In this rain, with so many tracks? Bongani, I ...'

'He is a man, so he does not think like an animal. He is smarter, though perhaps also arrogant. He will have made a mistake somewhere around here, and if he has not today, then he will next time.' Bongani surveyed the sand. 'There is the boy's spoor.'

Mia followed Bongani's finger, pointing the way the boy Sipho had passed through the gully and left.

Mia sighed and looked back at Sean. 'Get the dog.'

Phillip came up and Askari bustled past her, straining at his lead and sniffing the ground, sucking up scent like a vacuum cleaner. The dog went past one, then a second boulder and then dropped down on his haunches, to his belly.

'He's indicating,' Sean said.

Phillip moved forward, then waved to them to approach.

On the ground was a green canvas satchel bag.

Mia stopped and let Sean go past her, but instinctively she looked for spoor around the bag. It didn't make sense. There was no sign the poacher had lain or rested there, or knelt to check or retrieve something from the bag, which he had subsequently abandoned. There was no tree which could have snagged the carry strap and the bag was too big to have slipped from his shoulder unnoticed.

'Sean ...'

'I'm on it,' Sean said. 'It could be booby-trapped. Stand down,' he said to Phillip, who motioned for Askari to stand, then gave the Malinois his rubber toy to chew on, as a reward for finding the bag.

Sean picked up a stick and dropped to his knees in front of the bag. He used the tool to carefully peel back the front flap of the satchel.

'Shit. Get back,' Sean said. 'Grenade.'

Mia and Bongani backed away as Sean dropped to his belly in the wet sand, in order to peer inside the bag without further opening or disturbing it.

'Bongani and I are going to cast further down the spruit, to see if we can pick up his spoor again,' Mia said.

'OK.' Sean continued looking in the satchel, presumably for tripwires or other detonation devices. 'Just keep your distance.'

Mia and Bongani skirted the boulders and moved along the stream bed, both of them searching the ground intently.

Bongani shook his head. 'Nothing.'

Mia straightened her back and brushed away the wet hair plastered to her face. 'He can't have just bloody disappeared.'

Bongani was silent, but he was looking at her. 'No,' he said eventually.

Mia held up a hand. 'Don't give me that look.'

'What look?'

Bongani glanced past her, to Sean, who was still preoccupied. Nevertheless he lowered his voice. 'You know there is something going on here, Mia.'

She sighed.

It was Bongani's turn to hold up a palm. 'Remember, I told you about my cousin, the ranger.'

Mia put her hands on her hips. 'Yes, Alfred. You told me he was part of a reaction team chasing a poacher north of here and the man disappeared.'

Bongani nodded. 'The poacher turned himself to water, Alfred said.'

Mia closed her eyes against the rain and the thoughts, the ghosts, the demons that were creeping their way up her spine, chilled already by the rainwater running under her collar, and lingering at the corners of her subconscious vision.

There *were* things she believed. When she passed an *umkhanyak-ude*, the beautiful, almost iridescent fever tree, she would rub her hand over the lime-green bark, and the fine golden pollen would stick to her palm. This she would smear on her forehead for good luck, to help her in whatever endeavour she was undertaking. Sometimes, she thought, it helped her find a leopard for a demanding guest. She had anointed herself on the morning before she met Graham.

And yet, she had performed the same ritual on the morning of her last assessment, when the lioness had evaded her.

Bongani pointed to her wrist. 'Why do you wear that *isiphandla*? To impress people by pretending to be the white Shangaan woman, to remind them you were brought up by my people?'

She did not like his mocking tone, nor the challenge he was laying down to her. Mia fingered the knotted bracelet of goatskin and hair on her right wrist. 'You know I respect your culture – our culture. I wear this in honour of your mother, may she rest in peace. I was honoured to be given it at the cleansing ceremony for her; you know that.'

'You say you are one of us ...'

It was the same with any faith, she told herself. One could be a good Christian without believing everything in the Bible. Surely it could be the same with the customs of Bongani's people – her people – that beliefs could be a guidebook to living a good life, full of parables and old wives' tales meant to teach people by example, and nothing more.

'Your mother's religion taught you that a man rose from the dead,' Bongani continued. 'I, too, am a Christian, and I believe that is true.'

'We're not talking about miracles here, Bongani.'

'Agreed. This man has vanished. We are talking about the opposite of a miracle here.'

'What?' He was speaking in riddles.

'Evil.'

Chapter 7

Sannie accompanied Nomvula back through the stumps and furrows of the former orchards into the main street of Killarney. People watched them, from front doors and windows, or from old chairs on their *stoep*s as they walked down the dusty street.

They had taken a walk around the new library, but had found no tracks or any other sign of Lilly around the building, which was locked. Peering in through the windows they could clearly see there was no one inside the sparsely furnished two rooms.

A stray dog darted away from them. Nomvula pointed out the home of Sonto, the last girl who had seen Lilly.

'I must go see to my other grandchildren, Captain.'

'Sure,' Sannie said. 'Go to them. I will call you if I have further questions.'

As Sannie came abreast of a side street she saw a man in dirty two-piece overalls stop and stare at her. The man paused, as if he didn't know which way to go, then ran off, down the street. Another man emerged from behind the house and when he saw Sannie he, too, ran.

These two *skelms* were running like they had done something wrong.

Sannie set off after them. At least she was dressed for a pursuit, in sensible, sturdy boots and her blue trousers and short-sleeved uniform shirt.

She had thrown herself into her fitness in the last few weeks, hitting the treadmill that she and Tom had bought for the kids – though they rarely used it. Running was not advisable around Hippo Rock, because of the potential for dangerous game such as leopard and hyena, even the occasional lion, to join in the chase for joggers.

The nearest of the men had a fifty-metre head start on her, but Sannie was fast. The second man was clearly not a good runner.

'Stop, police!'

Here and there neighbours emerged or popped their heads out of windows to see what the fuss was about. A couple of young men whistled, either derogatorily at Sannie or in encouragement of the fleeing men.

'Stop!' Sannie turned down a side alley. She drew her Z88 pistol as the men led her past the rear of a line of houses, backtracking in the direction she had come from.

The first man charged on, but the second, struggling, turned his head to check on her as he ran. Distracted, he tripped and sprawled in the dirt.

Sannie closed the distance between them and got to him as he was getting to his feet. He pulled a small knife from a sheath on his belt.

Sannie levelled her pistol at him. 'Drop that, *now!*'

The man seemed to realise she was serious and dropped the knife.

'On your knees, hands behind your back.'

The man complied, albeit slowly. Sannie went to him, holstered her pistol and cuffed him. She lifted him to his feet and spun him around. 'What the *fok* were you playing at, man? I could have shot you. Why did you run?'

He glared at her.

'Captain?'

Sannie turned and saw Nomvula emerging from the rusty rear gate of a modest green-painted house.

'I heard your voice,' Nomvula said, then looked to Sannie's captive. 'Solly?'

The man glanced at her, but said nothing.

'Oh, Captain,' Nomvula said, 'I think there's been a mistake.'

Sannie nodded to the man, Solly. 'He ran when he saw me.'

'Poor Solly,' Nomvula spread her hands wide, 'he is like a child, you know, not fully developed. He cannot speak.'

Sannie frowned. 'Can he hear?'

'Yes.'

Sannie looked to the man. He nodded, but now looked fearful and she wondered if he was more worried about Nomvula's stern look than being chased by the police.

'He works at the charity project,' Nomvula said. 'He is one of our gardeners.'

'Why did you run?' Sannie asked him.

Solly looked to Nomvula and then back to Sannie with a flick of his head, as if asking Nomvula to speak on his behalf.

Nomvula sighed. 'Solly has been in trouble with the police a few times, nothing serious, but minor theft from the local stores. He is a bit of an outsider. We have taken him in on the project, partly to keep him safe.'

Sannie looked him up and down. By the state of his clothes and face it looked like he had been working hard, and his body smelled of sweat. 'Turn around.'

Solly presented his back to her and Sannie undid his handcuffs. Solly rubbed his wrists and backed away from her.

'What about the other one?' Sannie asked Nomvula.

Nomvula drew a breath and nodded. '*Ai, ai, ai*, Richard. Something of a troublemaker, but so many of our young men have been in trouble. It is the unemployment, Captain, the lack of opportunity for them. The new South Africa has not been kind to everyone.'

That was an understatement, Sannie thought. 'Go home,' she said as sternly as she could to Solly, who turned and walked away from her.

'Tell the other one, Richard, that I want to talk to him, if you see him. He may have seen something suspicious around where Lilly disappeared.'

Nomvula put a hand to her mouth, as if the mention of her granddaughter had brought her fears back to the surface, which it probably had. 'Of course, Captain, I will.'

Sannie touched the peak of her cap, put away her handcuffs and walked back to the main street, towards the house where Sonto lived.

She found the dwelling Nomvula had indicated and knocked on the door. She heard a child crying inside and the door was opened by a woman with a baby in her arms – the child was the source of the noise.

The woman eyed her suspiciously. 'Hello, how are you?'

'Fine, and you?'

The woman nodded and bounced her baby a little, cooing in its ear.

Sannie introduced herself and held up her identification card. 'I am looking for a girl named Sonto, does she live here?'

The woman's eyes narrowed. 'Why?'

'I need to ask her some questions about the disappearances of Lilly and Thandi.'

'My Sonto had nothing to do with that.'

From further inside the small house, perhaps the next room, Sannie heard the tinny sound of rap music playing on a phone.

'It's important,' Sannie said.

The woman frowned. 'What is important is that I have no job any more. This stupid situation means we have no money, no food. Why aren't you doing something about that?'

'Don't you think the disappearance of two children is important?'

The mother pressed her lips together and then looked over her shoulder. 'Sonto!'

The girl appeared in the doorway, tall and pretty, her hair elaborately braided. She froze when she saw Sannie's uniform.

'Come here, girl,' the woman said. 'This police lady wants to talk to you.'

Sonto looked around, as if for a means of escape. Sannie saw the back door, which probably led to the privy out the back, and stepped in. 'You've done nothing wrong, Sonto, and I've done enough running for the day.'

The mother scoffed. 'I saw you chasing that boy, Solly. Why are you harassing us poor people?'

Sannie ignored her. 'Sonto, where can we speak in private?'

'Mama,' Sonto said beseechingly.

'You are not taking my child to prison.'

Sannie sighed. 'No one is going to prison. Sonto, don't you want a walk in the fresh air?'

'Prison might be more fun than being locked up here,' Sonto said. 'At least there might be some dagga.' Her mother gave her an admonishing look, but Sonto just poked her tongue out at her. 'Just let me get my shoes on.'

Sannie craned her head past the mother to make sure Sonto was not running away, but the teenager was clearly glad of any excuse to escape the house. She returned with a pair of sneakers on her feet.

'We won't be long,' Sannie said to the mother, who eyed her warily as Sannie led Sonto outside.

'I got nothing to say to you,' the girl said, but all the same, she fell into step beside Sannie.

'You don't know what I'm going to ask you.'

The girl glanced over at her, but said nothing more.

'What do you think happened to Thandi and Lilly?'

The girl shrugged.

Sannie stopped. They were past the last house on the road, next to an abandoned car that had been stripped down to a metal carcass. Sannie took out her notebook and pen. 'We can do this at the police station if you like.'

Sonto looked around. 'At least it would be a change of scenery.'

'Don't push me.'

'You can't arrest me.'

'I have no desire to do so.' Sannie said nothing more, just waited.

'I'm not sure about Lilly, but ...'

Sannie stayed silent and did not take any notes.

'Um, people were not too worried about Thandi, at first, when she went missing,' Sonto said, carrying on. 'It was like they didn't care about her.'

Sannie paused, but when Sonto didn't continue she prompted her. 'What did you think about Thandi going missing?'

Sonto shrugged. 'Thandi would sometimes disappear, like, even when we went out together. There was a boy she liked ...'

Sannie raised her eyebrows.

'Sipho. Her mother didn't approve of him.'

Sannie made a note. 'Surname?'

'Nyarhi.'

'Why didn't Thandi's mother like Sipho?'

'He had been in trouble with you people, the police.'

'What for?' Sannie asked, underlining the boy's name.

'He likes snakes. The cops came one time and said he had to have a permit. He was fined.'

'Was he around the night she went missing?' Sannie asked.

Sonto shrugged. 'Maybe. Thandi and me, we were drinking … like, cool drinks, not alcohol, and I had to go … you know, behind a bush, and when I got back she was gone.'

'What time was this?'

'After dark. Maybe twenty-thirty.'

'Had you been drinking a lot of *cool drink*, by then?'

Sonto shook her head. 'No.'

'You didn't go looking for her?'

'Sure,' Sonto said. 'I called her name, like, many times. And I walked around looking for her. I figured that maybe Sipho had been following us. He did that once before, scared us in the dark, and he and Thandi talked, and then she left me … went off with him.'

'Why would he do that, creep up on you, in the shadows?'

Sonto seemed to think about the question for a few seconds. 'I don't know. He was like that, secretive, sneaking around, you know? And the whole snake thing was creepy. He lives alone – his parents are dead – and his house is full of slimy reptiles; snakes and stuff.'

'Did all of you, or Thandi and Sipho, meet at that place with the big flat rock, near where the construction work has been going on?'

'Maybe.' Sonto couldn't meet her eye. 'That's not a place many people go.'

'Why not?'

Sonto looked around her. 'It's, I don't know the word … scary? No … more like, spooky.'

'Spooky?'

The girl nodded.

'Why?'

She shrugged. 'It's a place most people stay away from. There's a sangoma who has a hut in the bush near there, on the edge of the old farm.'

'Why would people stay away from a sangoma?' Sannie asked, as much to herself, out loud, as to Sonto.

Sonto lowered her eyes and shrugged.

'Sonto? Look at me. Who is this sangoma? Why do people stay away?'

Sonto looked up and around again, and Sannie thought she saw fear in her eyes. The girl lowered her voice. 'We're all told to stay away from that one.'

'Why?' Sannie persisted.

Sonto fidgeted with her hands. 'Sipho said that bad men go to that sangoma. He showed me and Thandi the sangoma's hut; hidden in the bush, but then he told us we must never go there. It was like Sipho wanted to show off, or scare us with his inside knowledge.'

Sannie made some more notes. When Sonto didn't fill the void she looked up. 'How did Sipho know about this sangoma?'

'He said he went to the sangoma once, for some medicine, umuthi, you know?'

Sannie nodded. 'What did he need umuthi for?'

'To protect himself.'

'From what, from whom?' Sannie asked.

Sonto said nothing, and looked away.

'This could be important. You know that, right? It's why you told me, isn't it, Sonto? If you're scared, you don't need to be. My job is not to hurt you or put you in danger, it's the opposite.'

Sonto looked her in the eye now and stuck her chin out. 'You say that, but then you people come around here with your uniforms and your guns, and you beat us for not obeying the lockdowns. You say you care for us but you bring the army and you hurt us, shoot us. I've seen it, on social media – the police were killing more people than the virus at the beginning of the lockdown. You don't care about us.'

'I've got three children.'

'So?'

'So, I take the disappearance of young girls seriously.'

Sonto pursed her lips but did not say anything more.

'What did Sipho need umuthi for, and where did he get the money to go to a sangoma? Does he work?'

Sonto shook her head.

'Where did he get money?'

'A man gave him some.'

'Why?' Sannie sighed inwardly, but knew that patience would be her best weapon with this teenager. She sensed from the girl's body language and continual vigilance that she was more scared than defiant. 'I'm waiting.'

Sonto shrugged. 'He wanted him to do something for him, but Sipho isn't bad like that.'

'Like what?'

'Like bad or stupid enough to get himself killed.'

Sannie sat back on the log, giving the girl a little distance. She had heard of this kind of thing, all too often. 'Did this man give Sipho money to become a poacher?'

'I did *not* say that,' Sonto said, urgently.

'I didn't say you said anything. I know how the system works. Rhinos are getting harder to kill and the work is becoming more dangerous for poachers. It's not unusual for the poaching syndicates to go to a young man, to offer him money and a rifle and to send him into the game reserve to try his luck.'

Sonto looked up at her again and blinked. 'He never had a gun.'

Sannie went back to her notebook and wrote in it, deliberately saying nothing more.

'You have to believe me; he never had a gun, he was not going to shoot any rhino or anything like that.'

Sannie looked her in the eye. 'So why did he receive money from a poacher? Why did he need umuthi to protect himself?'

Sonto bit her lower lip. She probably realised she had been lured into revealing as much as she had, and was now trying to think of a way out, to backtrack from what she had already said. 'I want to talk to my mother.'

Sannie closed her notebook. 'Fine, we will all go to the police station together, with your mother present.'

'No, no, no!'

Sannie sighed. 'Then what more do you have to tell me?'

'Sipho *was* told to go into the game reserve, but he did not have a gun and he was not going there to kill a rhino.'

Sannie opened her notebook again. 'For what, then?'

'To check snares. You know?'

Sannie grimaced. 'Yes. Bushmeat.'

'He is not a killer, not even of animals, even though we are all hungry. Someone else sets the snares, he just paid Sipho to check them. Sipho came home with nothing.'

Sannie shook her head. 'He still broke the law. I need to talk to him.'

'You will arrest him.'

'Listen to me, Sonto. My priority right now is finding your two missing friends and it should be *your* only concern right now, as well. If this boy has information about what might have happened to them, then I need to find him and talk to him. I'm less concerned about him jumping the fence in the game reserve than I am about the girls. Will you help me?'

Sonto's lower lip started to tremble. 'I will try.'

'When and where did you last see Lilly?'

'She was on her way to the library. I was ... I was busy with someone else. I saw her walking through the bush, towards the library, and then ...' Sonto wiped her eyes. 'I never saw her again.'

'Tell me, what do you think happened to Thandi and Lilly?'

The first tear rolled down Sonto's cheek. 'I don't know, but I am scared.'

Chapter 8

The rain beat a tattoo on the corrugated tin roof of the staff quarters at the rear of Kaya Nghala Lodge, where Mia lived and Graham was an increasingly frequent visitor.

Mia lay on her bed, naked under a sheet, her wet clothes piled in the corner of the simple, one-room suite she called home. Graham stood in the open doorway, still in his camouflage trousers but bare-chested, exhaling cigarette smoke outside. Mia checked her watch. It was half past eleven in the morning – she had slept for half an hour. The constant surges of adrenaline, the highs of pursuit and the lows of failure, had exhausted her. So much had gone on during the handful of hours since dawn, but she still needed to collect guests from the airport. That, in itself, should have been the highlight of her day given the lack of tourists during the pandemic. Now, it was a chore she almost did not want to think about.

'No one disappears into thin air, Mia,' Graham said, as if continuing a conversation he'd been having in his mind, or maybe he had been talking to her, not realising she was asleep.

Mia crooked an arm behind her head as she leaned against the wall. All of them, even Askari the dog, had failed to pick up the second poacher's trail beyond the stream bed. Graham and Oscar had searched the area around where the female rhino had been shot, also to no avail. The one piece of good news was that Dr Baird, the veterinarian, had been able to dart the baby rhino and had taken it to the rhino bomas at Skukuza. Graham was still wired from the fruitless chase.

'I know,' she said, 'but –'

'But what? *Jislaaik*, you can't believe this black magic mumbo jumbo.'

She frowned. 'Don't use language like that, please. These are people's beliefs you're talking about.'

'*Ja*, but which "people"? You? Look, I know you love the Shangaan and maybe think you're one of them.'

She was silent for a moment. 'My Shangaan nanny all but adopted me.'

Graham finished his cigarette and ground out the *stompie* on the concrete *stoep*. '*Ja*, I know you had a rough upbringing, but you can't really believe all this superstition.'

Mia quietly fumed. When and where did any religion start or stop being a superstition? Her rational mind, the one that had been moulded at university through a scholarship for gifted girls, told her there was no basis to Bongani's conclusion that the older poacher with the gun had disappeared, or turned himself invisible; but the other part of her, the side of her that had turned her back on a qualification that could have seen her practising environmental law and made her return to the only home she had ever loved, the bush, told her there were some things in life that could not be explained.

Mia's greatest source of frustration was that both she and Bongani had lost the tracks of the man they were following.

'Maybe he backtracked?' Graham said, in a more conciliatory tone. 'Maybe he's just really good at it.'

'Maybe,' Mia said. She had considered the possibility and both she and Bongani had taken some time to inspect the various tracks at the scene. 'That would have been easy for him to do in the soft sand, in the dry riverbed, as the tracks there were never going to be crisp or well defined, but then it started raining. You try walking backwards in those conditions and see if you can get your boot to fit in *exactly* the same position as the first track you made, in every single footprint.'

Graham leaned against the doorframe, staring outside. He didn't look at her as he spoke. 'Of course, if the guy didn't use umuthi to turn himself into water, or make himself invisible or just vanish into thin air, then the only other explanation is that you and Bongani lost his trail.'

There it was, the accusation. Graham was saying that she and Bongani had blamed magic instead of admitting their failing.

'The dog didn't do much better,' Mia said after telling herself to stay calm.

'Sure,' Graham agreed. 'He had plenty to occupy him – scent from the two poachers, plus the hand grenade in that satchel. Might have just been, like, sensory overload.'

'Bongani's cousin –'

Graham ran a hand through his wet hair as he closed the door and walked back inside. 'Alfred, I know. I heard the story. That *oke* claims he saw a poacher disappear. You have to be careful with this shit, Mia. If people like you and me start believing it, or giving it credence, then it takes hold. Next thing my anti-poaching guys will be too scared to go out looking for the bad guys and they'll be blowing even more of their pay than they already do on their own imithi.'

Mia said nothing. Graham was right, she told herself. She was being irrational. It was one thing to accept that izangoma knew about herbs and other bush remedies that actually worked in the treatment of a variety of ailments, and another to believe that a sangoma could give a poacher a potion or a talisman that would make him vanish into thin air or assume the form of an impala.

'There has to be a rational explanation,' she said.

He crossed the screed concrete floor to the bed and sat beside her, reaching out to brush a strand of hair from her eyes. She was tired, and a little annoyed at him, but his physical presence was invading her space and her senses. She felt her body start to respond, a kind of magic all of its own that she was unable to control.

'What are you smiling at?' he asked her.

'Nothing.'

'I'm sorry, I didn't mean to criticise you,' Graham said.

'It's OK. I'm annoyed at myself for losing that guy's tracks.'

'Blame the rain. He just got lucky. We'll catch him next time.'

'I hope so,' Mia said.

Graham leaned closer and kissed her. Again, she was acutely aware of her body responding to his. She just wished he could be a little more tolerant of her other friends and their beliefs.

'Are you all right?'

'Hm-mm.' She kissed him back, forcing her mind back to the job at hand. She felt down and she knew that being held, caressed and loved now was what she needed.

Graham's lips tracked down her neck to her chest and, as he lowered the sheet, her pulse started to race. She closed her eyes and tried to concentrate on his touch and her pleasure.

Unbidden, and unwanted, the face of Sipho, the teenage poacher, came back into her vision. He was holding the pangolin, his eyes wide as she spied him. He would be in so much trouble.

Graham had stopped kissing her and had rolled back to the edge of the bed so he could take off his boots and loosen his belt. Normally Mia was as voracious as he was, and enjoyed touching him, seeing his arousal, but now she stared at the ceiling.

'What's wrong?'

Graham was standing, wearing just his boxer shorts, looking down at her. Mia blinked up at him.

'Is it us?'

She shook her head, quickly. 'No. I was thinking about that boy.'

'What bloody boy?'

'The one we tracked first, the decoy or whatever he was. I know him.'

'You do? Why didn't you say, Mia? We can arrest him, interrogate him.'

'You're not going to torture anyone. I told Sean I think I know who he is.'

'No one said anything about torture, and you just said that you *do* know who he is. You have to tell me, Mia. The cops need to know.'

She shook her head. 'I'll talk to him. I'm sure Bongani will, in any case. He's respected in the community.'

Graham sat down on the bed beside her. 'Mia, I know you're close to these people.'

'*These* people are *my* people, Graham.'

'That's my point, Mia, you *are* part of the local community and that's mostly a good thing and really one of your strengths as a person. You're not like most of us in this bloody country. You don't have a race or a tribe, you just do what most of us tell ourselves we do: see people as people. But now you're acting like too many people in this community do; you're turning a blind eye to crime, covering up for someone.'

She glared at him. 'That boy made a mistake. He shouldn't go to prison for it and he might just be able to help us find the guy who's killing the rhinos.'

'Julianne wants blood,' Graham said.

'No. She wants her rhinos protected, and so do I. We're all on the same side, Graham.'

He stared at her, saying nothing.

To hell with Graham, Mia thought, if he thought she was on the opposing side to him just because she didn't want to see a slightly odd schoolboy arrested and put in prison.

'OK.' He ran a hand down his face then stood and went to the chair where he had dropped his muddied camouflage trousers. He pulled them on and zipped them up, then reached for his shirt.

'OK, what?' she said, ready for a fight. She had grown up tough, fighting off racial slurs from white kids who thought she was too friendly with black kids, and black kids who felt no need to be friends with the child of a white soldier.

Graham pulled on his cap and opened the door. 'Bye, Mia.'

He closed the door and she sank back into the bed. She felt bad – he had wanted to make love to her and part of her still craved the release of sex, the need for touch after the traumatic events of the long morning.

Mia punched her pillow. This afternoon the lodge was welcoming its first guests since the last lockdown had begun. She should have been excited and raring to go, but instead she had lost two poachers, seen another rhino shot, and had failed, yet again, at the one thing in life she had thought she was good at. On top of all that her boyfriend, if that's what he was, had just walked out on her.

*

Jeff Beaton stopped his Toyota HiLux outside the neat row of staff accommodation units, got out and avoided as many puddles as he could. He found unit eight and knocked on the door.

He checked his watch, confirming he had the right time, but there was no answer. He knocked again and waited.

'Who is it?' called a woman from inside.

'Jeff Beaton. Mia Greenaway? We've got an appointment.'

'Oh.' It sounded more like a groan. 'Hang on. I'm coming now-now.'

He waited on the porch, nodding to a tall African man in khaki who walked past.

The door was opened by an attractive woman, short with dark hair, sleepy, but with a fast-recovering sense of perpetual energy about her. She wore only a long, stretched T-shirt; her bare legs were muscled and tanned.

'Is now not a good time?'

She checked her watch. 'Good as any. I needed to get up. I've got sixty minutes, less shower time.'

'That should be plenty,' he said. 'I did make an appointment.'

'Yes, yes, I remember the email now. You're the Canadian?'

He smiled. 'Most people say American.'

She motioned for him to take a seat at the small writing desk in the corner of her unit and went to a washbasin and squeezed toothpaste onto a brush. 'I deal with people from around the world every day – at least, I did before the virus. I know the perils of addressing a Canadian as a Yank, and vice versa.'

'So,' he said, as she wiped her mouth, 'I'm here to interview people about –'

'Traditional beliefs, umuthi, that sort of thing.'

'Yes.'

'I remember now, though to tell you the truth I forgot you were coming today. We had quite an eventful morning.'

'So I heard. I was with Graham and Oscar – I believe you know them – when they were called out, after finishing their shift on the Vulture system.'

Mia dried her hands. 'I really need a shower.'

'I'll wait outside,' he said.

She shook her head. 'No, it's OK. You don't look like the serial killer kind. I'll just go next door. You can ask your questions if you like. Safari guides are used to multitasking and when you usually start work at four in the morning you learn to shower and dress and eat quickly.'

'OK.'

She opened a door to a small en-suite bathroom, went in and closed it. Jeff stood and indulged in a quick snoop around the room, the woman's home. It was not much bigger than a small suite in a hotel, and Mia was the head guide. How long had she been living this life? he wondered.

There was a wardrobe made of canvas and wood and he saw a small collection of clothes: khaki shorts, shirts and trousers on one side, and on the other a pair of jeans, some blouses in earthy tones and a token sundress with flowers on it. The shoes beneath were two pairs of boots, a pair of sneakers and a couple of pairs of sandals.

On the bedside table of cheap unfinished pine was a faded colour portrait of a woman with long straight hair wearing a cro-cheted top, maybe from the seventies. In a similar plastic frame was another shot, this one of a man in military uniform sitting atop an armoured vehicle, a rifle across his lap. He had a drooping mous-tache and cold dark eyes fixed on some distant horizon.

The books piled beside Mia's bed were field guides, mostly, to birds, reptiles, mammals, trees and even grasses. There were a cou-ple of novels set in Africa he thought he recognised.

'Are you still there?' she called from the bathroom over the noise of a shower.

'Yes.'

'Then stop snooping and start asking questions. You're on the clock!'

He smiled to himself. 'You've heard about my research?'

'Sure have.'

'OK.' He took out his laptop, thinking that this was the oddest interview he had conducted in his time as an academic. There was also something mildly arousing about knowing his subject was naked on the other side of the door.

'So, you interviewed Graham and Oscar last?'

'Yes. The odd couple.'

She laughed. 'Let me guess, Graham ridiculed everything about traditional beliefs and medicine and Oscar was quietly reasoned.'

'Exactly.'

'Those two are not what they seem,' she said. Her voice was clearer now that she had finished her shower and turned off the water.

'So,' Jeff said, 'I'll just launch into it. Do you support the premise that traditional beliefs in Shangaan culture influence not only poachers but the rangers and other indigenous members of the security forces arrayed against them?'

'Yes,' she said without hesitation.

'Can you explain how, and why, you think this is so?'

'Because it affects me.'

Jeff pushed his glasses up the bridge of his nose. That surprised him. 'How so?'

'I was brought up to believe many of the – superstitions is the wrong word – traditions of African people. For example, if you look at my bed, you'll see something weird about it.'

He glanced down and noticed, for the first time, that the legs of the bed stood on old tin cans. 'What's that for, to protect the wood from insects?'

She laughed on the other side of the door. 'No, to protect me from tokoloshes.'

'Spirit men. Little guys?'

'Yes.' Mia opened the door. She had put on a khaki button-up shirt with a Lion Plains logo above her left breast pocket, and a pair of green shorts. She towel-dried her hair as she took a seat on the bed. She patted the duvet. 'The tins raise the bed up so that I can see under it, and therefore the tokoloshe can't hide underneath it. Silly, right?'

He smiled. 'I'm certainly not here to judge. The opposite – I'm here to learn.'

'Graham thinks it's crazy. It's not even a Shangaan belief – my nanny had lived in Johannesburg and she picked up her fear of the tokoloshe from some Xhosa women she knew, and it stuck with her.

She figured I needed to be safe from everything. That's how I grew up, learning about tokoloshes instead of bogeymen, or whatever it is kids in Canada call that thing that scares them.'

'Clowns.'

She laughed and put the towel down.

He carried on: 'Tell me about your childhood.'

She looked at him, her smile dropping. 'I'm pretty sure that's not one of the questions on your list.'

He scrolled down his fresh document and turned the screen towards her.

'*Tell me how, if at all, your formative years have influenced your belief or otherwise in traditional cultural beliefs or medication,*' Mia recited. 'I'm impressed.'

He nodded. 'So?'

'Have you got a week?'

He checked his watch, theatrically. 'Couple of days. I've been looking forward to interviewing you.'

'Why?'

'Because more than one person told me that you are probably the most culturally aware white person they know, when it comes to the local people. I've been told you speak Shangaan –'

'Xitsonga, there's a difference.'

'My bad, Xitsonga – as well as or even better than most local native speakers.'

She gave a small shrug. 'That could be true, especially of the local kids. They grow up in households where some of their family speak the local language, but at school they're also expected to learn English. Their teachers sometimes struggle with both languages, so kids end up graduating – or not – with a lack of fluency in both their mother tongue and English.'

'I hear you're doing something about that,' Jeff said.

'I volunteer at an after-school English language program when my shifts allow, if that's what you mean.'

'It is.' He was impressed by her already. 'I think that's great.'

'I'm no Mother Teresa. Ask anyone who knows me.'

She was being modest. 'I also hear you're one of the best – if not *the* best – trackers in the Sabi Sand, and that you'll soon be awarded the master tracker qualification – and be the first female to ever reach that position.'

Mia frowned. 'If you saw my last assessment you wouldn't be so sure.'

'Well, I wish you luck,' he said.

Mia fetched a pair of hiking boots, retrieved a sock stuffed in one of the boots and put it on.

'So, my formative years?'

He nodded and prepared to type.

'The short version is that my mom died and my dad was away for much of my childhood. My white aunts weren't interested in me so I was more or less raised by my nanny. Lots of white kids say they have a close connection to the domestic person or staff in their house, but for me it's actually true. My nanny, Prudence, was the closest thing I had to a mother.'

'So you would say you share the cultural beliefs of the Shangaan people and their attitudes to traditional healing.'

'I don't share them, they're mine, simple as that.'

'May I ask, and you don't have to answer this,' he looked up from his screen, 'are you a Christian or do you follow any other religion?'

Mia smiled. 'Like most of my Shangaan friends I am a Christian and I go to church every Sunday at the all-denominations service at Skukuza unless I'm working.'

He made a note. 'Have you ever visited a traditional healer for medical and/or other issues?'

'I have.' She laced one boot and put on her other sock.

'Do you believe in the efficacy of traditional healers?'

'I'd be silly to go to them if I didn't. Many are women, wise and experienced. If I can get the makings of a tea made from local plants to fix an upset stomach or relieve the symptoms of a cold for the fraction of the price of western medicine from the Hazyview pharmacy, then I'd be mad not to, wouldn't I?'

He smiled and entered the answer. 'I've been to that pharmacy.'

She nodded as she did up her other lace. 'Then I guess you've seen all the love potions and spells and whatnot.'

'I have. It was quite an eye opener.'

'That's just people making money, and, from the point of view of the patients, wishful thinking, but there's nothing wrong with that.'

'No?'

Mia got up, picked up a brush from her bedside table and ran it through her hair. 'If someone wants another person to fall in love with them and they buy a harmless potion that does nothing, then at least they maybe feel better about themselves and come across more confident and relaxed.'

'So, a placebo, you mean?'

She nodded. 'Exactly.'

'And you don't have a problem with people making money out of that?'

'People waste money on stuff they don't need every day. What's wrong with buying a little confidence?'

He smiled. She was kind and genuine and it seemed like she wouldn't find fault with anyone in the world. 'How do you feel about the traditional healers who charge poachers for umuthi to make them bulletproof?'

Mia placed her hands in her lap and gave him a beatific look. 'I want to kill them.'

Jeff swallowed. 'OK. Why?'

'Talk about using your powers for evil. The whole point, I believe, of a lot of traditional healing, even practices better known in the western world, like reiki, is that you capitalise on – or in this case, prey on – people's belief systems. These men, the poachers, they trust their traditional healers to care for them, to look after them when they're physically and mentally unwell. They believe in their powers, and here we have izangoma exploiting that trust to tell these men that because of what they've paid for, they will turn to water, literally, when a bullet is fired at them, and the round will pass straight through them.'

'And to be perfectly clear,' Jeff looked up from his frantic typing, 'you don't actually believe that a sangoma can help a man disappear, or turn to water?'

'I believe that some people fervently believe that, and that's what's important.'

'Why is it important?'

'Because that belief is not just confined to the poachers who pay for umuthi, it's shared by many of our own anti-poaching rangers, and most likely our soldiers and police involved in the war on poaching. That's a problem for us, because every time we catch a poacher and he's carrying umuthi with him, our guys are thinking that someone is maybe casting a spell against them, and that freaks them out.'

'But, to play devil's advocate, if your guys catch or kill a poacher, then that means, doesn't it, that the sangoma's medicine was weak, that it didn't work and the poacher was exposed. Doesn't it undermine the whole thing?'

'Yes and no. Even the ones who get captured believe that when they go to court the magistrate will be confused or the police will lose their evidence – they pay for that as well. The courts are so overburdened here that prosecutions don't always proceed smoothly or quickly, so there's a good chance the poachers will think they're getting value for money. If a guy is killed then the belief is that, well, he didn't believe enough, or pay enough, or take his medicine correctly. Enough poachers get through for the rest to believe that umuthi will help them.'

Jeff typed some more notes, then looked her in the eye again. 'With respect, Mia, you didn't answer my question. For the record, do you believe umuthi can make a man disappear?'

She held his gaze.

'I don't mean to push you,' he said.

Mia closed her eyes and shook her head.

He could see she was troubled by something.

'What is it?' he asked.

'It's just that … we lost a poacher, two in fact, this morning, and a young woman was shot, as was another rhino.'

'How's the volunteer doing?' Jeff said.

'She'll be OK, according to the doctors. She's as tough as a honey badger.'

'That must have been terrible for you.'

'Yes,' Mia said, 'and worst of all, we couldn't catch the guy who did it. In fact, we lost his trail completely.'

He raised his eyebrows. 'Does that happen often?'

She shrugged. 'The weather was bad, as you know. That doesn't make tracking easy, but ...'

'But?'

'It was weird that neither Bongani nor I, not even the dog, could catch the guy. We lost his trail – all of us.'

Jeff looked over the top of his laptop screen at her. 'So, what? He really disappeared?'

Mia stood and walked to the door and opened it. 'I have to go to work now, to collect some real-life clients, my first in months.'

He closed his laptop and stood. 'You didn't answer my question.'

She gave him a weary smile. 'I know.'

Chapter 9

Mia walked briskly towards her Land Rover in the parking area, nodding greetings to several of the lodge staff on her way. For a change they were dressed in freshly pressed uniforms instead of their casual clothes, which had become dress of the day during the lockdown.

One of the maids, Adella, stopped her. 'I want a selfie with you, now that you're properly famous.' Mia forced a smile as Adella snapped a picture of both of them. 'Stayhome Safari is going crazy with comments!'

Mia excused herself. There had been something of a buzz about Kaya Nghala the last couple of days, in anticipation of the return of guests. Hospitality staff had been cleaning and making up a guest room and the chef, Pretty, seemed to have been cooking nonstop for twenty-four hours. Mia smelled fresh bread that made her stomach growl, as she passed by the kitchen.

Pretty spied her, picked up two paper bags and came out. 'For you and Bongani. A little snack to prepare you for your first guests in some time.'

Mia smiled. 'Thank you.'

Bongani was waiting for her, leaning against the green open-top Defender. 'You look worried.' Mia handed him his food packet.

She opened the door and got into the driver's seat. Bongani climbed up onto the tracker's seat on the fender.

'Don't you want to sit next to me until we get to the airport?' Mia started the engine then opened her bag. She found a smoked salmon bagel and took a big bite out of it.

He shook his head as he started on his snack. 'No. I want to look for tracks, of humans.'

'You think the second poacher's still on the reserve somewhere?'

'He must be. Don't you think? He went to ground somewhere, I'm sure of it.'

Mia drove out of the staff area, past the workshops and onto one of the game-viewing roads. Julianne's property, Lion Plains, was in the Sabi Sand Game Reserve. In addition to the luxurious Kaya Nghala Lodge, where Mia and Bongani worked and lived, there were two other camps on Lion Plains: the Manor House, a small lodge with four bungalows set around an old but renovated farmhouse, suitable for a single group; and Leopard Lodge, which consisted of twelve double rooms pitched at a level more affordable than Kaya Nghala. Both the other camps had been mothballed due to COVID, with only Kaya Nghala remaining open to house a care-taker contingent, the anti-poaching rangers and canine unit, and Mia and a couple of other guides and trackers who provided the daily Stayhome Safari webcast game drives.

Mia slowed and turned right, leaving the Lion Plains concession and joining one of the main roads through the reserve that, eventu-ally, led to the adjoining Kruger National Park. Guests arriving at Lion Plains, like several other lodges in the south of the Sabi Sand reserve, often flew into Skukuza Airport, inside the national park.

'It's possible.' The thought had crossed her mind. 'Maybe he hid somewhere from us, waited for the rain to stop, and then set off. But which way did he go?'

Bongani glanced back at her. 'I'm thinking that this guy might be Mozambican and that maybe he's travelling east, back to the bor-der of where he came from.'

Mia nodded to herself. That could also be correct. The Shangaan people had historically straddled both modern-day South Africa and Mozambique, and Mia knew it was not unusual for people in one coun-try to have family in the other. There was a good deal of cross-border movement, legal and illegal, between members of the local community.

'The quickest and easiest thing for him to do would have been to make for the western perimeter,' Mia called over the engine noise. It was turning into a pleasant afternoon, the clouds having cleared, and the rain had left the air fresh and clean.

'I think this is a man who does not do the quick or the easy thing,' Bongani said.

Mia thought about the boy, Sipho. It was possible that if he truly was a decoy, and not just some hapless unarmed lone poacher checking his snares, he could have been working with the older guy and deliberately set off in the opposite direction to the senior man, blazing a clear trail for them to follow.

As if reading her mind, Bongani said, 'We need to go find that boy and talk to him.'

Mia voiced her agreement, but for now they had work to do. They drove on in silence, each mulling over their own thoughts on the recent events. At the airport there were half a dozen other game-viewing vehicles parked, which meant an encouraging number of lodges had guests to collect. Bongani waved to another tracker he knew well and sauntered over to him and bumped elbows.

Mia left them to chat and headed to the terminal. Skukuza Airport was unlike any other that Mia had been to, although to be fair she had not travelled widely outside of Africa. The airport was small and tasteful, and walking past the life-size statue of a white rhinoceros into the thatch-roofed arrivals and check-in area was more like entering the reception of a well-designed luxury safari lodge than a terminal.

The other rangers and trackers from the Land Cruisers and Land Rovers outside were already there, all waiting with sign boards for the guests to be disgorged from the first South African Airlink flight from Johannesburg in months.

'I never thought I'd be so excited to see a bunch of tourists.'

Mia turned and saw the speaker was Jake, one of the rangers from a neighbouring game lodge.

'Howzit, superstar.'

'Fine,' she lied, 'and you?' Jake was older than her by about fifteen years, but it could have been fifty given the patronising way he treated women. She'd been told by a friend that he had boasted that a woman would never be appointed head guide at any lodge he worked at, if he had anything to do with it.

'Fine. Hey, I heard on the radio what happened this morning. Sorry,' Jake said. 'How's the blonde?'

'Sara. She's in hospital, but Julianne called just now and the word is she's fine.'

'What about you? I'm surprised to see you here ready to pick up guests.'

Why, because I'm a woman? 'I'm fine, like I said.'

'*Ja*, but you couldn't find the poachers, right? I thought maybe you'd still be out there looking for them. Or doing a re-enactment for your internet fans.' He snorted. 'You can be a proper *influencer* now – our very own Kim Kardashian in khaki.'

His barb about not finding the poachers hurt even more than this ridiculous comparison. 'Sean and his guys will keep up the search.' Mia busied herself in the folder she had brought from the vehicle, checking the names of the guests she was to collect. The family name was Barker, mother Sue, and a thirteen-year-old daughter, Laura.

'Well, after losing those poachers you better brush up on your tracking skills before you sit your master tracker's assessment again, my girl.' Jake walked off to talk to one of the other male guides, but paused to look back over his shoulder. 'Let me know if you want a little one-on-one tuition.'

Bongani came into the terminal and walked towards her. Mia tried to ignore the laughter of the other guides Jake had just joined. Seeing her face, Bongani said, 'Pay no attention to that fool of a "great white male".'

'I'm not, or at least I'm trying not to.' She managed a smile for Bongani, who had just parroted one of her favourite sayings back at her.

Mia heard the whine of a jet engine as the Airlink Embraer touched down. She and the other guides readied themselves, Mia turning her folder inside out so the surname, Barker, was clearly visible.

It wasn't long before the passengers, almost all dressed in uniform green and khaki designer safari wear, were walking across the tarmac from the small aircraft and into the terminal. A woman with a blonde bob and a girl with long fair hair waved to them. Mia went to them and introduced herself and Bongani.

'We will go and collect the luggage now,' Bongani said to the girl, Laura.

'What does "Bongani" mean?' Laura asked as they walked.

'Laura,' her mother said from behind them, 'don't be so forward.'

Bongani smiled. 'It is no problem. My name means to be grateful, or thankful.'

'And are you?' Laura asked. Her mother mouthed 'sorry' to Mia.

'I am.' Bongani laughed. 'I live in a beautiful country, I have a wonderful family and I have the best job in the world.'

'Will we see rhinos?' Laura asked Bongani as she pointed out their luggage from the collection two porters were bringing out from the terminal onto a small deck for identification.

'I hope so, and if that is what you would like to see I will make it my business to find one for you.'

'Find one, how?'

Bongani lifted a second wheelie bag down and Mia walked past him, leading them to the Land Rover.

'By finding and following its tracks,' Bongani said. 'Do you have a phone, Laura?'

'I do.'

'Then it is very important, if we do see a rhino and you take its picture, that you do not tag the location with any information that might show where it is, and share it on social media. The poachers are clever and they monitor various Facebook pages where people post their sightings of animals.'

Laura nodded emphatically. 'Understood.'

Mia helped Bongani load the bags as Sue and Laura climbed up onto the Land Rover and selected the row of seats behind the driver's position.

'I don't want us to be too far from you, Bongani,' Sue said.

'In case a lion jumps in the truck?' Laura said in mock horror.

Mia opened the driver's side door.

'Oh, will you be driving us to the lodge?' Sue asked.

Mia looked back and smiled. 'I'm your ranger, I'll be driving you on all your game drives, and taking you for a walk, if you wish.'

'Sorry,' Sue said, 'I thought Bongani ...'

Having secured the bags in the back, Bongani came around to the front of the vehicle. 'Mia is a very good guide, Sue,' Bongani glanced at Mia, 'for a woman.'

Sue's cheeks had coloured and it took her a fraction of a second to get the joke, but then she burst out laughing. Mia hoped the mirth and relief were genuine. It wasn't unusual for her to be mistaken for one of the hospitality staff or lodge management.

Mia climbed aboard and sat on the steering wheel, facing Sue and Laura. 'It's just a short drive to the lodge, but we'll be going through the reserve, and we will start seeing animals, so I need to give you a quick briefing. Most importantly, please stay seated while we're driving, and at sightings.' Sue and Laura both nodded. Mia gave them a thumbs up and carried on.

'The animals in the reserve are used to the sight and presence of our vehicles, but, importantly, they're used to seeing us all sitting down. If one of you stands up when we're looking, say, at some lions, you'll break the familiar silhouette of the Land Rover with people sitting on board and the lions will most likely get up and run away.'

When they were ready, Bongani climbed up onto his tracker seat and Mia took her seat and started the engine. They drove off, through the airport security gate that marked the border with the Kruger Park, and into the Sabi Sand Game Reserve.

'Bongani will watch the road ahead, for tracks,' Mia explained over the rumble of the Land Rover's engine, 'and if we see something he might go and investigate on foot.'

'With a gun?' Sue asked.

Mia shook her head. 'No, he's so experienced that he doesn't need one when he's by himself, especially if he's not tracking a lion or leopard. We might all go for a walk at some point, and if we do I'll be carrying a rifle.'

'That makes me feel slightly more at ease,' Sue said, 'ever so slightly.'

Mia smiled to herself. Within a day or so their nerves would be gone and they would be complaining about not getting close enough to lions for better photos.

Bongani held up a hand and Mia slowed to a stop. He flicked his head to his left and Mia saw the giraffe in the distance.

'What is it?' Sue asked.

'Off to the left,' Mia said.

'Giraffe!'

'You've got good eyes, Laura,' Mia said.

'How on earth did any of you spot that?' Sue said.

Laura and her mother scrambled for their phone and a camera respectively. Mia took out her binoculars and handed them to Sue. 'It's a female.'

'How can you tell, at this distance?' Sue asked, working to focus the binoculars.

'Look at the two horns on her head, which are actually bony protrusions. You can see tufts of black hair at their tops. The females have hair up there, but the male is bald, with the white caps of bone showing.'

'Amazing.'

'They're so beautiful,' Laura said.

Mia reeled off her standard spiel about giraffes – including the fact that they only have seven vertebrae, the same as a human, and that their young are nearly two metres tall at birth. As if on cue, a baby giraffe emerged from a thicket to nurse from the mother, to the delight of the two guests.

Ordinarily Mia would have relaxed into and enjoyed the sighting, but there was too much on her mind. She felt guilty about Sara being injured and desperately wanted to visit her in hospital. Mia knew full well that she should not have caved in to Sara's demands to join them in tracking the poacher, even if the Norwegian woman had military experience. Mia was expecting to be disciplined over that lapse in judgement, and as Jake had made painfully but accurately clear, her inability to track the man with the gun had not gone unnoticed either.

Not only that, things had gone badly with Graham when he had visited her. He had probably only wanted to comfort her, and she should have let him, instead of rebuking him. Added to all that, Jeff, the researcher, had unsettled her by forcing her to examine her own beliefs.

She didn't really believe someone could make themselves vanish by taking umuthi, but the poacher had, for all intents and purposes, clearly done that, somehow.

Mia looked at her guests and was able to judge, by the way they glanced to her and relaxed into their seats, that they were ready to go on. She took the main road through the reserve back to the lodge. Although it was longer, distance-wise, than the short cut they could have taken, Mia could stick to the fifty kilometre per hour speed limit and make just as good time. The shorter route was very bumpy and while the bucking and bouncing of the Land Rover was something she and Bongani were accustomed to, she didn't think this mother and daughter were quite ready for a rocky ride. Besides, they had more chance of encountering interesting game on a slow drive through the bush than on the slightly busier main road and Mia did not want them ticking off the Big Five – lion, elephant, buffalo, leopard and rhino – on their first road transfer. The Barkers would be with her for three days and she wanted to do a slow reveal of Africa's wildlife, managing their expectations along the way.

A little further on they came to the place where Sara had been shot. It seemed the police, thankfully, had been and gone. There were tyre tracks and footprints everywhere, but neither she nor Bongani drew this to the Barkers' attention.

A few hundred metres on, however, Bongani raised his hand and Mia stopped.

'What is it?' Sue whispered behind her.

'*Wanuna*,' Bongani answered.

'*Rin'we?*'

Bongani nodded. He was looking at the tracks of a man.

'Is it an animal?' Sue asked.

'Yes,' Mia lied, 'a hyena, he thinks.'

Bongani slid down from his tracker's seat and bent at the waist, inspecting the tracks.

'*Nkari muni?*' Mia asked.

He rocked his hand from side to side. '*Tiawara timbhiri.*'

Shit, Mia thought. She had asked Bongani how long ago the tracks had been made and he had answered: two hours. 'Is it him?' she let slip in English.

Bongani nodded.

Mia felt a mix of dread and excitement. They needed to report this, but she did not want to alarm her guests, or, as she had with Sara, lead them on some wild goose chase after a poacher.

'I am going to follow him,' Bongani said, sticking to their shared language.

'No!' Mia opened the driver's side door, got out and joined him.

'Keep your voice down or you will alarm our guests.'

'Don't talk to me like a child, old man.'

'Call me "old man" and I will treat you like a child, Mia.'

'Get back in the vehicle.'

He returned to the Land Rover, but instead of getting back on his seat he reached into the front of the vehicle and retrieved one of the two handheld radios they took with them, in case one or both of them left the vehicle tracking an animal or escorting guests on a walk.

'I'll radio Sean. He'll have someone here in twenty minutes,' Mia said.

Bongani looked at the track again. 'This poacher is practising counter-tracking, using a branch to sweep behind him, and he missed this one. He will be moving slowly. I'll stay on his trail until I work out exactly where he is headed and how long since he passed through here.'

'No,' she tried again, though with less conviction. Mia glanced back at the guests.

'What is it?' Sue called.

'Just checking some tracks,' Mia said. She lowered her voice and reverted to Xitsonga. 'This is crazy – you are crazy.'

'We lost him, Mia.'

That stung her, but she now realised Bongani had been just as hurt as she had by their inability to do the one thing in the world that both of them prided themselves on most.

She sighed. In Xitsonga she said, 'I will take the clients to the lodge and come back for you.'

He nodded. '*Hi ta vonana* at Impala Road.'

'All right.' Mia got back behind the wheel and started the engine. Bongani was only going to traverse one block of bushland and he would see her at Impala Road, which ran parallel to the route they were following. The network of roads on the reserve, laid out in a grid pattern like city blocks, made the tracking of animals relatively easy. If the spoor of, say, a leopard, was picked up crossing a road, then by driving the roads around the grid square in the direction the cat was headed the ranger and guide could, theoretically, work out if their quarry was still in the block by the presence or otherwise of exit tracks on the roads, where prints were easier to detect. 'I'll drive the square as soon as I get back.'

'What about Bongani?' Laura asked in alarm as Mia drove off and the tracker disappeared into the bush with a casual wave.

'He's just following up on some hyena spoor,' Mia lied.

'Oh, OK. He'll be safe, though, right?' Sue asked.

'Bongani's been walking in the bush alone since he was a little boy,' Mia reassured her, and was tempted to add *and so have I.* 'He'll be fine.'

The mother and daughter's interest was soon diverted by a small herd of zebra and Mia stopped to let them quickly take some pictures. Much of the Sabi Sand, and Lion Plains in particular, was covered in thick bush along the banks of the Sabie River, so plains game, such as zebra and wildebeest, were less common than in other, more open, parts of the reserve and the adjoining Kruger Park.

Mia didn't dally, however, and radioed the lodge to let them know she was two minutes out. 'Lunch is waiting, I'm afraid,' she said to Sue and Laura.

As soon as she had handed her guests over to the manager, Alison, Mia got back in the Land Rover and drove as fast as she dared back to the block where she had left Bongani.

She slowed the vehicle as she circled the spot where Bongani had last been seen, and tried him on the radio.

'Bongani, Bongani, this is Mia,' she said. After a few seconds, she tried again. There was no reply.

He might, she reasoned, be in a dip crossing a dry creek bed, or he might have turned down the volume on his handheld, if there was dangerous game nearby.

'Bongani, Bongani, Bongani?'

Mia leaned over the top of her door, scanning the road for tracks.

She tried Bongani again, but once more, there was just silence. Mia completed a circuit of the block into which Bongani had walked but there was no sign of his tracks exiting the area. The ground was still soft from the morning's rain and there had been no vehicles on the roads since she had taken Sue and Laura to camp. Even a first-time tourist would have been able to follow Bongani if he had crossed any of the gravel roads; that meant he was still in the block. Mia felt a chill run down her spine.

Mia circled back to where she had left Bongani. When she arrived she drove the Land Rover just off the road and parked it with the nose pointed into the bush in the direction in which she was headed – if something happened to her then any experienced guide who passed would at least know which way she had gone.

From the cradle racks on the dashboard she took the rifle bag, unzipped it, and drew out her .375.

Bongani's footprints almost leapt off the ground at her. Less distinct, and older, were the poacher's tracks. She studied them and concluded, as Bongani had, that it was the same man they had failed to find that morning.

How on earth, she wondered, had he eluded them? Whatever the case, Bongani had done well to pick up the poacher's spoor. Given the condition of the ground, it was easy for her to follow Bongani's path from the road into the bush. Even amid the thick undergrowth and leaf litter, to her trained eye his trail was as clear as if he had marked it for her.

Mia engaged all her senses. She paused and listened, wondering if she might pick up the low growl of a leopard or lion, or, even worse, the sound of bones being crunched. She sniffed the air; some animals such as elephants were, ironically given their huge size, most easily detected by their musty smell rather than the noise they made. When she came to a flattened pat of buffalo dung she dropped to one knee and touched it – the scat was cold, which was good. Of all the animals that might pose a threat to Bongani on foot, even with his decades of knowledge and experience, a lone male buffalo was the most dangerous.

She carried on, her rifle up and at the ready, but had to stop for a moment as she experienced a painful cramp in her stomach. She drew a deep breath after the spasm passed.

This was dangerous country in which to walk alone and she cursed herself for agreeing to let Bongani set off by himself. What was clouding her judgement? she wondered. She had foolishly agreed to let Sara accompany them when tracking the poacher and now she had abandoned her friend. Had something or someone been distracting her?

Mia felt light-headed.

She stopped, took another deep breath and her vision started to swim.

'Bongani! Bon ...'

Mia felt hot bile burning the back of her throat. She doubled over at the waist, planted the butt of her rifle on the ground to steady herself and threw up. She dropped to one knee, coughing and retching.

She had no idea what was wrong with her. Mia wiped her mouth and used the weapon to help her get to her feet. She staggered forward at a jog, feeling her stomach flip with every movement. Her eyes were teary from the effort of being sick, but she forced herself to look for spoor.

Mia heard a groan.

'Bon ...' She could barely form the name.

'Here,' a voice croaked from in front of her. 'Stay back.'

Mia dry-retched, but summoned enough strength to raise her rifle. 'Where are you?'

'Go back!'

She shook her head, trying to clear her thoughts, and staggered forward.

Bongani lay on the ground, one arm forward, clawing at the dirt, his whole body heaving. The smell of his vomit was harsh and strong in the air and Mia held a hand to her mouth and nose to stop herself from throwing up again. She gagged.

Bongani half rolled and half pointed up at something.

Mia followed his line of sight and saw something white in a young tree.

She went forward, the rifle still up, though she realised there was no dangerous animal here. Something else had laid Bongani – and her – low.

'What …' she spat, 'what is it?'

'Do not … do not go close to it.'

Mia half walked, half stumbled to him. Bongani was on his hands and knees now, coughing, but at least he was alive.

Mia went closer to the tree, shaking off Bongani's hand that grabbed weakly at her ankle, trying to stop her.

Wedged in a fork of branches was a skull.

Chapter 10

Mia and Bongani sat on the ground next to each other, slumped against the same tree.

Mia spat bile into the grass and wiped her mouth. 'What was that all about? And don't say evil spirits.'

Bongani coughed. 'I was going to say the smoked salmon bagels Pretty packed us.'

Mia's stomach churned. She leaned to one side and heaved, but, mercifully, nothing came out. 'I think you're right.'

'We'll have to tell Alison,' Bongani said.

'Agreed.' Mia rolled over onto her knees and used the tree trunk for support as she stood. She picked up her rifle and looked at the skull. 'What does this mean?'

Bongani, also slowly standing, shrugged. 'A warning? To stay away?'

'From what?'

'He's carrying this muthi with him, leaving it, to discourage us,' Bongani said, looking briefly at the skull, which they could both see, on closer inspection, belonged to a baboon. Bongani took two steps back from it.

'You're not scared of this?'

'Of a baboon skull? No. But it is a little unnerving, it's not something a poacher would normally carry around the bush. It's too big.'

Mia shook her head. 'This is bullshit. Theatrical, almost.' She was talking braver than she felt. She had initially panicked when she'd started throwing up, not even considering the possibility that it was food that had caused her illness. 'What did you think, when you were sick?'

He blinked. 'That someone had poisoned me.'

'Deliberately? Pretty?'

He smiled. 'No, not Pretty. As I was being sick I saw the skull. I thought it was related to that. Not the skull itself, but that a spell had been left for me, to throw me off the trail.'

'Well, that worked, for both of us, even if the salmon was the cause. Has anyone ever been sick from Pretty's food in the past?'

Bongani didn't pause. 'Never. She is scrupulous in that kitchen. Her staff sometimes complain about how strict she is. She supervises the cleaning herself, every day.'

Mia checked her watch. 'Either way, whether Pretty's food made us sick or we were subjected to some magic spell, we've been thrown off the track.'

Bongani cast about, though every couple of steps he put a hand to his stomach. Mia felt like she was through the worst of the attack, though she had only eaten half her bagel and had a recollection of Bongani wolfing his down on the way to the airport.

'I have lost him, again.'

Mia came up behind Bongani and looked where he had been searching. She, too, found no obvious spoor that she could follow and, besides, they needed to be back at the lodge soon.

'Let me check the road,' Bongani said.

He went on ahead of her. Mia examined the skull up close, and looked around the base of the tree. There was no obvious sign of recent disturbance. Mia looked up, but there was no poacher clinging to an upper branch.

The sickness had brought on a headache and she realised that the vomiting had probably left her dehydrated. They were both in need of water, to drink and to rinse their mouths out. They could hardly undertake the afternoon game drive smelling of spew.

'Bongani?' she called.

'*Yebo?*'

'I'm going back for the Landy.'

'All right. Drive around the block. I'll wait for you on the road.'

'Affirmative.'

Mia retraced her steps, checking the ground for spoor. She saw Bongani's footprints, here and there, and traces where he had passed – flattened grass, a broken twig – but there was no sign of the poacher he had been looking for.

Mia heard a rustling noise off to her right. She stopped and listened. Slowly, she turned her head. She saw nothing, but heard the crunch of dry leaves.

Animals were quiet.

It was not scientific, but it seemed to her that there was an inverse relationship between the size of an animal and the amount of noise it made when passing through the bush. The biggest, the elephant, was one of the quietest, literally tiptoeing on spongey, cushioned feet. At the other end of the spectrum the first indication she'd had of the presence of animals close to the ground – honey badgers, porcupines and even a cape clawless otter – was the sound of them stomping through the vegetation. Small birds such as robins tossed leaf litter about, searching for insects, and made more noise than a buffalo.

And then there were humans.

Mia brought her rifle up, painstakingly slowly, aware that movement was one of the big giveaways for man and beast in the bush. She saw it, now, a glimpse of brown moving through some thick vegetation, roughly where she thought she had heard the sounds coming from. Mia held her breath. She brought the butt of the rifle into her shoulder.

She looked down the open sights of her Brno, her finger sliding through the trigger guard. A bush moved, as if someone or something was brushing it aside, or holding it down. The twig bounced back up into place. All of Mia's attention was focused on the spot where she had just seen the bush disturbed.

A ray of afternoon sunlight pierced the trees as an errant cloud was blown to one side, and it glinted, for just a fraction of a second, on burnished metal. Mia made out the barrel of a rifle, poking through the leaves, maybe thirty metres from her.

'Contact!' a man yelled, and three shots rang out.

Bullets whizzed past Mia and one thudded into a tree next to her. She dropped to her belly. 'Don't shoot! Cease fire!'

Footsteps pounded towards her and Mia struggled to bring the rifle up from her position on the ground. When she looked up she saw it was Graham running towards her.

'Mia? Hell, I nearly killed you!'

'I know that, you idiot!'

She stood and brushed herself down. Graham and Oscar came to her.

'Don't call me an idiot. What are you doing out in the bush at this time of day?'

'Looking for the poacher who disappeared. Bongani picked up some spoor, then lost it again. What are you doing here now?'

He set his rifle down, butt first, on the ground, wiped sweat from his brow and took a breath – to try to compose himself, she thought. 'Same thing. Sean's as pissed off as you two that we all lost the poachers, so he sent us out again. Did you find some new spoor?' Graham asked.

Mia shook her head. 'No. I was looking for his tracks, the ones Bongani had seen, just before you tried to kill me.'

Graham frowned. 'Sorry.'

'It's OK.'

Graham looked at his boots. 'And for before.'

'What?'

'For walking out on you. I love you, babe,' he said.

Oscar looked away, giving them a moment.

Her heart softened, a little. She found it weird telling him she loved him, especially in public, though she was sure, deep down, that she did have strong feelings for him. There was just so much going on in her life right now. 'Thanks.'

'So what do we do now?' Graham said, not seeming to notice or care that she had not responded in kind.

'Let's go find Bongani, see if he's had any luck.'

They walked through the bush, still mindful of the presence of dangerous game, to Mia's vehicle. Bongani, having heard the shots, called her on her radio and Mia explained what had happened.

'Any luck?' she asked him.

'*Aikona*,' he replied, which meant he'd found nothing.

Mia gave Oscar and Graham a lift to their vehicle and they drove in convoy to where Bongani was waiting on the side of the road.

'You look like hell, man,' Graham said to Bongani.

Mia leaned over and opened the passenger-side door for Bongani, but he shook his head and, instead, climbed slowly up onto the tracker's seat on the fender. 'I will keep searching.'

*

Back at the camp, Alison Byrne, the manager, was waiting for them, hands on hips. 'What happened to you two?'

'Ask Pretty,' Mia said. 'Food poisoning. We both ate the fish.'

'I'll take it up with the kitchen, if you're sure that's what it was?'

'That's all we ate in common,' Mia said.

'I must go to the bathroom,' Bongani said, and excused himself.

'Your guests are at lunch,' Alison said. 'Quite a handful, if you ask me.'

Mia nodded. 'They should count themselves lucky they're out here in the bush before all the international hordes return.'

'I hear you,' Alison said, 'but try telling that to the mum. She's high maintenance.'

Graham, who had been lagging behind Mia to stay out of the dust wake of her vehicle, pulled up under the impressive thatched portico in front of Kaya Nghala.

Alison took a step closer to Mia and lowered her voice. 'The boss lady is here. She wants to see you.'

As if on cue, Julianne Clyde-Smith walked out of Alison's office behind the curio shop.

'Mia.'

'Ma'am.'

'I've told you, Julianne is fine.'

Mia gave a small nod. Julianne was dressed in her characteristically casual style – jeans, open-necked white blouse with wooden beads, and an elephant-hair bracelet, although Mia guessed the billionaire's sandals were worth more than what she earned in six months as a ranger. Julianne's hair was natural grey; she was attractive, and affected the same air of laidback confidence as Richard Branson, to whom she had often been compared, but Mia knew her boss could be as hard-nosed and demanding as any man in a three-piece suit.

'I hear you were looking for this morning's poachers,' Julianne said.

'Yes ... Julianne.'

'And?'

'Nothing, I'm afraid.'

'I'm always being told what a good tracker you are, Mia. It's one of the reasons the company paid the expenses for your attempt at gaining your master tracker's qualification.'

The emphasis on 'attempt' was ever so slight, but nonetheless unmistakable. Mia felt miserable, and not just because of the salmon bagel.

'If we are to survive this current crisis, if the jobs of everyone here are to be protected, then Lion Plains needs to be in pole position when the world starts travelling en masse again. We need to uphold our reputation as the safest game reserve in Africa, for guests and for rhinos and other endangered game.'

'I understand,' Mia said. What did the woman think, that she was an idiot, or didn't care about rhino poaching?

'I've spent a fortune on the Vulture system and we've invested time and money on your education, and that of all the trackers and rangers and anti-poaching patrol members. And yet, I am told that once again a man has vanished into thin air on my reserve.'

'Yes, ma'am.'

Julianne didn't bother correcting her again. She took a deep breath. 'Sorry, I'm not blaming you personally for the rise in rhino poaching, or for the fact that Facebook is awash with armchair experts telling each other it's not safe to go on safari even if COVID disappears.' She exhaled. 'I know that's not your fault and I'm just pleased that neither you nor Bongani were hurt and that Sara is OK. Tell me what's going on, Mia. Is there something more at play here?'

'The weather didn't help,' Mia said, knowing the words sounded lame as soon as she uttered them.

'A little unseasonal rain should help you find tracks, shouldn't it?'

'Yes, for a time, but then it washes them away, as it did this morning.'

'Yes, and the poacher *disappeared*. I'm not an idiot, Mia.'

Mia looked her in the eyes. She was not going to be cowed by this woman. 'I don't think anyone thinks that.'

'Good. So, tell me, what else is going on here?'

'He's good.'

'The poacher? An old guy, yes?'

Mia nodded. 'We think so, yes, and we think it's the same man who has given us the slip several times now.'

'So, we know he's experienced. As are you.'

Mia drew a breath. 'Today, just now, if we had more time, Bongani and I might have been able to pick up his trail and work out how he's been avoiding us.'

'What else?' Julianne asked again.

'What do you mean?'

Julianne lowered her voice. 'Could this be an inside job? Is someone on our staff tipping off the poachers, or maybe turning a blind eye to tracks, or even covering them up?'

It took a split second for Mia to comprehend what Julianne was asking, and a moment longer for her to stop herself from exploding. 'Bongani is not a criminal. He's the closest thing I have to family.'

Julianne brushed a hair out of her eye. 'Yes, well, one hears of experienced rangers in the Kruger Park being corrupted, and Lord knows, the money ...'

Mia stared at her. 'Not Bongani.'

'Very well. I gather you were both ill.'

The woman was on top of everything. 'Yes.'

'Did that impede your ability to track?'

That and my boyfriend nearly killing me, Mia thought, but she said nothing as she had no wish to get Graham in trouble. 'Yes.'

'A coincidence?'

Mia thought for a moment. 'You think Pretty might have poisoned us so we wouldn't find the poacher?'

'Unlikely,' Julianne said. She frowned, as if she, too, was now out of ideas.

'Look,' Mia spread her hands, 'I've seen counter-tracking measures used by poachers in the past and I've learned about the practice from expert trackers, one of whom was a poacher, and this guy is good. He must know every trick in the book, but the thing with counter-tracking is you can only employ it for so long, whether it's walking backwards in your own tracks, sticking to rocky ground, wading through streams or using a leafy branch like a broom to cover your tracks – everyone makes a mistake eventually. We've just had a combination of factors working against us, from rain to dodgy salmon, and poor Sara getting shot. Those have stopped us catching this guy out. We'll get him.'

'You and Bongani?' Julianne looked slightly dubious.

'Yes.'

'But you're not my anti-poaching team.'

'I know, but they haven't caught him either. That's why you and I are having this conversation.'

'Yes,' Julianne admitted. 'I've been on enough game drives and walks with you, and others throughout Africa, to know that combined, you and Bongani are probably one of the best tracking teams on the continent.'

'Thank you.'

Julianne pursed her lips. 'I'm not complimenting you, Mia, I am telling you to go out there and do what you do best.'

Mia nodded. 'I understand. I think. What do you want me to do about our new guests?'

'They're important to me as well. Keep taking them on drives, but I also want you on standby, ready to follow up any electronic or physical reports of poachers on this reserve. Bongani as well. Understood?'

'Yes.'

Julianne sighed. 'I like you, Mia. You're not afraid. I remember the time we were on a walk and you stared down a charging lion, held your ground. I nearly wet myself, but you didn't flinch. I need you, now.'

In truth, Mia remembered, she'd nearly had the same reaction, but she knew the number one rule when it came to predators was not to run away from them. That applied to bosses as well as poachers, but at the moment she felt like going to her room, crawling under the duvet and hiding. 'I understand.'

'Good. Find this clever bastard for me, Mia. If I have to I'll recruit extra anti-poaching rangers or more canine teams – whatever it takes – but right now you and Bongani are probably my best bet. The chopper's yours if you want it, ditto the Vulture system. We can turn it on, day and night.'

'All right,' Mia said. The Vulture system was normally only manned at night-time, but she was not going to thank Julianne again. As for her helicopter, from what Mia had heard – and experienced this morning – the damn thing seemed to be on the ground or off for maintenance every time they'd needed it during the recent contacts with poachers.

'Are you fit to go out on a drive this afternoon?'

Mia swallowed. She was desperate to brush her teeth. 'I am.'

'Good. I'll come with you. These two tourists are important to me and not just because they're our first post-lockdown guests. The woman's husband is a potential future investment partner. We need to make sure his wife and daughter enjoy themselves while they're here.'

'I'll give them a safari they won't forget.'

'For all the right reasons, please. And we've got two more women for the game drive, Samantha Karandis and Elizabeth Oosthuizen.'

Mia vaguely recognised the names. 'Samantha's head of the local tourism association, right?'

'Yes,' Julianne said. 'It'll be a long time before hordes of foreign tourists start coming back to South Africa so we're going to need all the help we can get attracting domestic visitors. Samantha will help with that – and Lord knows she needs to, as I hear the bank's about to repossess that empty hotel she and her late husband built near Killarney.'

'Shame,' Mia said. 'I heard about the husband. Who's the other woman?'

'Elizabeth. Her husband's big in construction; did a bit of infrastructure work here in the reserve, waterholes and roads and such. Basically, she'll be another pretty face for today's Instagram posts, and in the right post-COVID demographic – wealthy local South Africans. Take plenty of pictures for the social media people.'

'Got it.' Sensing the pep talk was over and she was dismissed, Mia excused herself to go to her room.

Kaya Nghala was built into and around a granite koppie, a boulder-studded hill that overlooked a grassy area of open savannah, punctuated in the middle by a waterhole fed from an underground bore. In the distance the grassland gave way to thicker bushveld.

Mia detoured up the stairs from reception to the dining area. As well as a more formal indoor setting, with a big square table around which most guests and their rangers sat each night, there was a timbered deck overlooking the place where animals came to drink.

Sue and Laura Barker were finishing lunch, watching a lone bull elephant slurping up trunkfuls of water and alternately drinking and showering himself.

Mia greeted them, but young Laura seemed more interested in the elephant. 'Look, he's showering. Is he washing himself?'

'No, not really,' Mia said. 'He's squirting that water on his back to wet down his skin. Next, he'll suck up some dust and spray that over his skin so that it sticks to him. The layer of dried mud on his back helps cool him and protect him from parasites, such as ticks.'

As if on cue, the elephant moved a few paces away from the water, kicked the ground with one big front foot to loosen some soil, and inhaled the dirt. He reached back and coated himself with dust.

'Wow,' Laura said, looking back at Mia, 'you're amazing.'

Mia smiled. 'Not really. It's just that part of this job involves learning a lot about animal behaviour, so I know what they're going to do next.'

'Still, very impressive,' Sue said. 'What's the plan for the rest of the day?'

'When you finish your lunch you're free to head to your room, perhaps for a siesta, or you can hang out here or by the main pool. Your room has a private plunge pool as well.'

'Brilliant,' Laura said. 'I'm going to sunbathe.'

'Well, if you don't put on sunscreen,' her mother said, 'I'll smother you in mud, like an elephant.'

'We'll meet back here at 3.30 pm for afternoon tea,' Mia said, 'and then we'll go out on a game drive. Julianne Clyde-Smith is coming with, and two other guests.'

'That's fine,' Sue said, as though she had final approval over who was coming on the game drive. The sense of entitlement of some guests, especially the very wealthy, never ceased to amaze Mia.

'OK, great. Bye for now.' Mia retraced her steps, then took a side path to the staff quarters. Bongani was sitting on the small *stoep* of his room, cleaning his boots.

'Did the boss lady give you a dressing down?' he asked.

'You heard?'

'I hear all, like an elephant.'

'Nice of you to stick around and back me up, partner.' He gave a small laugh. 'We're under pressure, friend,' she added.

'Aren't we always?' He inspected the toe of his boot, gave it a buff and looked up at her. '"Find me a leopard, find me a lion, find me a rhino, find me a poacher." It's all the same.'

She looked at him, wondering, for just a moment. 'Are you all right?'

He shrugged. 'I miss my wife and my children.'

'But this is nothing unusual for you. You're normally away from them this long, or longer.'

'Yes, but it is the uncertainty, in these times. We take things, people, for granted when we know they are always going to be there, even if we don't fully appreciate them. I think, now, what if one of my kids, or Thandeka, gets the virus, and has to go to hospital? We have no money, and only I have medical aid.'

This was a man whom Mia had seen stare down big cats and elephants. Bongani had even survived being charged and tossed on the horns of an angry buffalo bull. She had always thought of him as fearless, indestructible, and now she was reminded he was simply human.

'I am sure they will be fine. And at least you've been able to keep your job thanks to the Stayhome Safaris.'

'Yes ...'

'Yes, but what? Is something wrong?'

Bongani looked away from her, clearly uncomfortable. It wasn't like him, she thought, to be evasive. They had long since shed the racial, cultural, age and gender barriers that would have stopped them being close friends – at least, she thought they had. 'Is it money? We're all doing it tough – we certainly all relied on our tips before the virus, of that there's no doubt.'

He drew a breath and exhaled. 'It's ... it's not just my family who I have to provide for with my wages.'

Why hadn't she thought of that? Mia cursed her insensitivity. 'Of course, you've probably been supporting your extended family and half of Killarney.'

He gave a small shrug. 'Not quite half ...'

Mia shook her head. She should have known – did know already – that a person of importance and comparative wealth, as Bongani was now in these tough times, would be expected to share his fortune with those less well-off.

'I'm so sorry, my friend. Can I help?'

'We both know how much you make – minus tips,' he said.

She sighed. 'You're right. But let me know if there is anything I can do.'

'Of course.' He slapped a hand down on his thigh. 'In the meantime, we must find this poacher.'

'You do hear everything; I'm sure you were eavesdropping on me and Julianne.'

He smiled up at her. 'Yes, so you don't need to brief me on our extra pax. But apparently you and I do not see so well any more. We cannot let this man get the better of us, Mia.'

'He already has.'

'Yes, but not for long. I think we need help.'

'What kind of help? Julianne said she'll bring in more anti-poaching rangers and dogs, but that will take time.'

Bongani shook his head. 'As good as they are, we cannot use the dogs for what I have in mind. How do you track an animal, Mia?'

She put her hands on her hips. 'Is this a trick question? I'm too tired for jokes, Bongani.'

He shook his head. 'No. Answer my question, please.'

She sighed. He could be like this sometimes; she called it his Yoda mode. 'Find us some spoor, we do.'

'Very funny. Go on,' he said.

'Physical evidence, like flattened grass, scat, broken branches, blood.'

'And ...'

'And our knowledge of the animal's behaviour.'

Bongani spat on the toe of his other boot and rubbed it with his cloth. 'You're getting warmer.'

'Get into the mind of the animal we're tracking. But that's anthropomorphism, pretending we know what an animal's thinking, or giving it human-like emotions.'

'True.' Bongani set down the boot he was working on. 'And we want to avoid that, when it's an animal, but this is a human we are tracking so we *do* and we *can* and we *should* get into his mind.'

Mia sat on the concrete *stoep*, literally at Bongani's feet. He was the teacher once more, as he had been when she had first come to the reserve, fresh from university. It was almost comforting, being the student again, not having to call the shots or make the decisions, as she so often did these days when on a game drive. 'Tell me.'

'No, you think. You're doing well. What is in his mind?'

'Greed.'

'You're thinking like a white person now, or some politician, thinking, how can I better myself, how can I make more money, get more possessions? That may be part of this man's motivation – in fact it most definitely is – but there is more to him.'

Mia nodded slowly, taking in Bongani's words. 'He is not a young man, so he is not foolish – well, not too foolish.'

Bongani smiled. 'Go on.'

'This is not a game he is playing, but he knows he is besting us.'

'Yes. Why?'

'Because his life depends on him outwitting us.'

'Now we are getting there,' Bongani said. 'He is using his brain, and he is using every tool and skill at his disposal.'

Mia thought of the skull in the tree. 'Like umuthi, you mean?'

'Yes, perhaps. But why? Does he believe in umuthi?'

Mia chewed the inside of her lip. The temptation was to say 'yes', that this man they were tracking was putting his faith in medicine, potions or spells, in the belief that they would make him invisible.

That, of course, was not possible. If the man believed some powder or a tea made from a root or being anointed with something would make him vanish then he would be careless when being followed, putting his faith in the magic rather than his skills. Plenty of younger, less experienced poachers had been shot dead carrying umuthi.

She closed her eyes for a few seconds, then opened them. She looked at Bongani. 'He believes that we – or some of our anti-poaching operators – believe in umuthi.'

'He knows,' Bongani went on, 'that if things like that skull, or other evidence of his traditional medicine are left behind, then our men will know he has been using umuthi. Some may believe in it, just as the young poachers do, but, importantly, if our guys cannot track him, cannot find him, they may think that his magic is strong – stronger than whatever they believe.'

'It's a cop-out, you mean? Like, some of our guys won't try so hard, but rather blame umuthi?'

Bongani shrugged. 'Something like that.'

Mia thought a little more. 'It's like psychological operations that some armies use, preying on their enemy's perceived weaknesses.'

'Yes,' he said.

'It gives him an edge.'

Bongani nodded. 'My cousin Alfred was a good soldier, when he was in the army. He is no coward. He is not as good a tracker as me – or you – but when he lost his poacher, it was easier for him to say that the man had used umuthi to make himself disappear than to admit defeat, or his own lack of skill.'

The same thought had crossed Mia's mind, though she had not wanted to offend Bongani by suggesting such a thing about his relative. It was OK, though, if it came from him.

'So what else is motivating our man?' Bongani pressed.

'Like I said, his life depends on how good he is. That's what is motivating him.'

Bongani raised his eyebrows. 'Saving his own life? If he was worried about that he would stay home and farm or drink beer and listen to the radio.'

She shook her head. 'No, he wants to be the best, better than you and me.'

Bongani nodded slowly. 'Now we are getting closer. This is important to him, eluding us, perhaps even more than killing rhinos and making money, to be known as the best tracker – or, in this case, counter-tracker – in the land.'

Mia thought about that. 'So what was he, a hunter?'

'No doubt,' Bongani said, 'when he was younger, but in this day and age it is hard to practise such skills on a daily basis. For one, until this current surge in demand for rhino horn, there was no need – people had access to food by other means; at least most people are not starving in this country. This man has spent a life perfecting his craft.'

'Like us,' Mia said.

'He is not just like us,' Bongani said.

Mia nodded again, understanding now. 'He is one of us.'

Chapter 11

Mia parked the Land Rover under the portico out the front of Kaya Nghala Lodge. Bongani stayed with the vehicle and Mia went through to the dining area where afternoon tea was being served.

'How are we all doing?' she asked Sue and Laura.

'Fine thanks.' Sue set down her cup of tea. 'We have high hopes for this afternoon's drive.'

'We want to see a leopard,' Laura said.

'Do you now?' Mia had mixed feelings when guests demanded what animals they wanted or expected to see. Mostly it was good-natured, but some guests would complain, behind her back, if she did not serve up every animal they had imagined they would see. It was fine if she knew that a particular guest or group had their heart set on something, and she would do her best to deliver, but she much preferred those clients who were happy to be out in the bush and accepted that, in the spirit of the animals being wild, it was never a hundred per cent guaranteed they would see lions, leopards, buffalos, elephants or rhinos. Also, if the reserve was operating as it had pre-COVID, there would have been half a dozen or more other guides, trackers and vehicles full of guests out roaming the bush from Lion Plains' three lodges, and they would be sharing their sightings with each other, thus making finding a particular animal much easier. Today, even with a Land Rover full of the first guests in months, they would be on their own.

One of the waiters came to Mia. 'Can I get you something, Mia?'

'I'll just help myself to water, thanks.' Mia saw two other women standing to one side, sipping coffee. She recognised Samantha Karandis from photos she had seen in the *Hazyview Herald*. 'Mrs Karandis?'

'Samantha, please.' The woman raised an elbow theatrically in the COVID-era version of a handshake, and nodded to the other woman. 'And this is Elizabeth.'

'Howzit,' said the blonde woman, who was well-groomed, beautiful.

'I'm Mia. I'll be your ranger, and our tracker is Bongani. He's –'

At the table behind them, Sue held up her wristwatch. 'I hate to interrupt, but, well, time is getting on.'

Mia groaned inwardly. Sue was clearly a woman used to setting the agenda and getting what she wanted.

Elizabeth looked to Mia. '*Sjoe*, but I just need to finish my iced coffee.'

Mia gave a polite smile, grateful that Elizabeth had stood her ground. 'No problem. We're good for time and we're waiting for one more.'

Julianne Clyde-Smith walked into the dining room, a green canvas and brown leather satchel bag over one shoulder. 'I'm just in time, I see. Hi, everyone. Sorry I'm late. Sue, have you met Liz and Sam?'

'We did, earlier,' Sue said. 'Laura and I are all set and ready.'

Mia forewent her glass of water. She knew from past drives with Julianne that the boss lady never drank anything before she went out. Perhaps, Mia thought, she did not want any of the staff to see her doing something as human as sneaking behind a tree to go to the toilet. Elizabeth finished her drink, slowly. Mia liked her style.

Mia and her guests walked out to the portico and the women and Laura sorted out who was sitting where. Mia reflected that she had probably been unfairly harsh on Julianne. The woman did everything for a reason and was a fair employer. The pay at Kaya Nghala was above the industry average – Julianne prided herself on delivering the best service in the Sabi Sand Game Reserve, so she wanted to attract experienced workers.

Mia was sure Samantha and Elizabeth, as locals, had been on game drives before, but quickly reminded them all of the basics, especially about not standing up in the vehicle.

'Under*stood*.' Sue looked at her watch again.

Mia was finding herself disliking the woman more and more, but Julianne struck up a conversation with Sue as they drove off, so Mia could concentrate on finding some animals for them.

The other two women joined in, telling Sue a little about themselves.

Bongani scanned the road ahead as Mia drove, searching for tracks. She wondered if he was still suffering from the bout of mild food poisoning they had both gone through. She was feeling better now that she was outdoors, with the breeze on her face and the afternoon sun warming her back as she drove through the reserve.

'Are you in the tourism business as well, Sue?' Samantha asked.

'My husband's an investment banker,' Sue said.

'And no talking work on game drives, Sam.' Julianne laughed, but Mia had the distinct impression that if anyone was going to be discussing business with the banker's wife it was going to be Julianne. If her employer, the richest woman Mia had ever encountered, was worried about her investments, it was no wonder economies around the world were on their knees.

'Shame, Mia,' Elizabeth said, 'I saw on Facebook you had quite the morning. Are you all right?'

Mia glanced back at the blonde woman. 'Fine. Yes, it was quite hectic, but thanks for asking.'

'What happened?' Sue asked.

Bongani held up a hand and Mia spotted the elephant he was looking at. Mia was grateful she didn't have to explain to the prickly woman and her daughter about what had gone on that morning. She guessed Julianne was grateful for the distraction as well.

Mia stopped and switched off the engine. All talk behind her ceased. 'Over there, on the left.'

'What are we looking at?' Sue asked.

Mia swivelled in her seat. Laura was also staring at the bush; Julianne was making the most of the last vestige of mobile phone reception before they got too far from the lodge's booster tower to check her emails or messages.

'Elephant,' Mia said.

'Where? No way.' Sue sounded incredulous.

'You need to look *through* the bush, not at it. The elephant's grey skin is actually perfect for camouflage and it's hard to imagine the biggest land mammal in the world can be so hard to spot in –'

'I see it!' Laura was jubilant and she scrambled to find her phone.

Elizabeth and Samantha held up their hands to shield their eyes from the afternoon sun and watched the elephant.

'It's like the giraffe earlier,' Sue said, now sounding impressed as she raised her camera and started clicking away. 'I still don't know how you do it.'

'Part of it's just practice – it's my job – but there's more to it, of course,' Mia said. 'You'll find that in a day or two you'll be seeing more, Sue. When you live in a city, like you do, your horizons are limited, literally. You can't and don't need to see past the next block, but here your eyes are taking in a lot more, at greater distances. A few things give away an animal – its size, its shape, its colouring and, especially, movement.'

'Thank you, Mia, and well spotted, Bongani,' Julianne said.

'We all good?' Mia asked her guests. 'That's a lone bull – we'll probably see more elephants on our drives, and if we come across a breeding herd I'll get in closer.'

They all nodded and Mia started the engine and drove off. They saw a bachelor herd of impala and Mia reeled off her standard spiel about the pretty but numerous antelopes as she drove slowly past. Bongani studied the road for tracks and, as part of a never-ceasing routine, swivelled his eyes right through left, looking for movement and other signs of game.

Bongani held up a hand and pointed to the road ahead. '*Yingwe. I famba.*'

Mia slowed, inspecting the tracks for herself as she came alongside them.

'What is it?' Sue asked.

Julianne no doubt knew that the Xitsonga word for leopard was *yingwe – ingwe* in Zulu – but she kept quiet, adding to the suspense.

'We're just checking something,' Mia said, letting the excitement build.

The tracks veered off the road into longish grass at the side and for a moment Mia thought that was it, but Bongani had spotted something further ahead. He swept his hand from left to right. Mia looked where he was indicating and saw the drag mark.

'Fresh,' she said.

It was not a question, but Bongani nodded his agreement.

Mia put the Land Rover in gear and, engine still running, crept forward. When she reached the scuff marks that crossed the road, she turned off to the right into the grass on the other side. Bongani held up a hand for her to stop again, drew his machete, then slid down to the ground.

'Where's he going?' Laura whispered. 'Will he be safe?'

'Bongani knows what he's doing,' Mia assured her. Mia leaned out of the vehicle – she had crossed the leopard's path and now the trail of flattened grass was on her right. She saw the specks of fresh blood.

Mia switched off the engine and Bongani stood a moment, cocking his ear. He sniffed the breeze which, to further help them, was coming towards them. The cat would not catch their scent before they reached it.

'Are you all right?' Mia asked Bongani softly.

He nodded. His eyes still looked a little sleepy to her, but she knew that his body, like hers, would now be infused with a shot of adrenaline. The hunt was on.

Bongani moved away from the vehicle into the bush, following the sign of where the leopard had dragged its kill. Mia noticed some tufts of grey hair, which led her to believe the leopard had just killed a common duiker, a small antelope. She looked to her guests.

'We'll just sit here quietly for a bit. Bongani's following up on something.'

Bongani reached into his pocket, took out a pinch of something and put it in his mouth and started chewing.

Mia knew it was a concoction of herbs that his regular sangoma had given him, to protect him from dangerous game and to heighten his senses. He chewed as he walked out of sight and Mia knew that every few metres he would be spitting out a little saliva mixed with the potion, to keep the leopard from attacking him.

In her western-educated mind she knew that what was keeping Bongani safe on foot were his senses of sight, smell and hearing, and even his sense of touch as he no doubt reached out for a stem of grass and judged the time since the leopard passed from the wetness of the duiker's blood. But in his mind umuthi gave him the extra edge he needed to stay safe and be successful in his quest.

Mia's great-grandfather had been a South African Air Force Spitfire pilot, flying for the RAF during the Battle of Britain. She remembered him from when she was a little girl, showing her the lion's tooth he wore around his neck.

'This kept me safe through the war,' he had told her. 'I never flew without it.'

Talismans and superstitions were part of any culture. And who knew, perhaps there was a pinch of something in Bongani's concoction of roots and leaves that gave him a physical kick of some sort. Mia had met plenty of creative types and office workers who had claimed, before it became unfashionable, that nicotine made the synapses in their brain fire better.

Mia's radio hissed. She knew that the single click, breaking static, was Bongani signalling to her.

'Go, Bongani,' she said softly into her handset. For all she knew he was face to face with a leopard.

'*Come,*' was all he said.

Mia started the engine and drove off-road, into the bush, navigating her way around larger trees and driving over the top of saplings.

'Isn't this bad for the environment?' Sue asked.

'Good question,' Mia said as she concentrated on a tight turn and ducked to dodge a low-hanging bough of a buffalo thorn tree. 'Don't touch that branch; it's covered in tiny thorns. We only go off-road in pursuit of important sightings, like the one we're looking for now, and we do spend a lot of time out of hours on the reserve doing bush regeneration work. You have to remember that during our wet season, which lasts from October through to around March, there is massive regrowth as well.'

'*I hear you,*' Bongani said into his radio. '*Come left.*'

Mia wondered why Bongani had strayed off the trail the leopard had left, which she had been following.

She glimpsed him through the trees and drove up to him. Bongani climbed up onto his seat and smiled broadly at the guests. He used his machete to point in the direction in which Mia had been heading. Softly, he said: 'The *yingwe* is in a big tamboti, about a hundred metres further on. He's feeding and didn't notice me.'

Mia raised her eyebrows, wondering why he had moved to where he was.

Bongani read her enquiring look. 'I will tell you soon, when we get a chance,' he murmured.

They were, Mia thought, almost like an old married couple who could tell what one another was thinking.

Mia navigated back to the leopard's path and manoeuvred the Land Rover close to the tamboti tree. Samantha was the first, other than Mia and Bongani, to spot the leopard.

'There, second branch from the bottom,' she said.

Mia imagined that Samantha had logged plenty of time on game drives. She had good eyes.

'Where ... what ... wow!' Sue said. 'That's incredible.' The mother and daughter frantically started taking pictures.

Elizabeth gave Samantha a high-five. 'Well spotted, hey, Sam.'

Before beginning her talk about leopard behaviour to her guests, Mia said to Bongani in Xitsonga, 'Tell me.' She glanced back to see if either Samantha or Elizabeth were suddenly paying attention, but they were both gazing at the leopard, with Elizabeth trying to get a picture of her friend with the big cat in the background.

Bongani hooked an arm over the back of his seat as he turned to face her, and replied in the local language. 'He is close by.'

The poacher? Mia mouthed.

Bongani nodded. 'I was on his spoor when you found me. I picked it up by accident, as I was tracking the leopard. He crossed the *yingwe*'s path.'

'How long ago?'

He shrugged. 'One hour, no more.'

'Shit, I have to radio it in. Which way was he heading?'

Bongani pointed northwest.

'That would take him to the Manzini Spruit, where we lost him last time.'

'He could be there already. Gone.'

'Is it just the one man?' Mia asked as she reached for the handset of her radio.

Bongani nodded.

'Eagle, this is Mia, over,' she said, calling Julianne's anti-poaching unit.

'*Howzit, babe,*' Graham replied a few seconds later.

'Um, Eagle, I have guests, remember? Over.'

'*Oh. Roger. Go, Mia.*'

'Fetch Oscar, please.'

'*Affirmative,*' Graham said.

Mia glanced around and saw that Julianne was staring at her. Their guests were still alternating between photographing and staring at the leopard, which was still feeding on the carcass of the duiker.

'*Mia, this is Oscar, over.*'

Graham only spoke a few phrases of Xitsonga, but with Oscar Mia could switch to her second language and not alarm her passengers. Quickly, she filled Oscar in on the location where Bongani had picked up the poacher's tracks.

'*Is it the old man, over?*' Oscar asked.

'We think so, yes,' she said.

'*Roger, wait.*' Mia checked the leopard – it was still feeding, so it was relaxed. Oscar came back on the air. '*I've told Sean. We're bringing the canine team now.*'

'Roger. We'll pull out of the sighting and meet you near here on the road.'

'What was that all about?' Julianne whispered from behind her when she'd replaced the radio handset. But before Mia could reply, Sue called to her from the rear of the vehicle.

'I'll explain in a bit,' Mia murmured to Julianne, then she turned to Sue. 'Yes, Sue?'

'I'm really sorry, but Laura has just told me she needs to go to the bathroom.'

'Mum!' Laura whined. 'I said it's not urgent.'

Mia smiled. 'Not a problem at all.' Laura's need gave her the excuse she needed to pull out of the leopard sighting much sooner than she ordinarily would have. She needed to get these guests and her VIP employer out of this area if there was an armed poacher on the loose, and let the anti-poaching rangers do their work.

Mia started the engine and reversed. 'We can come back to this leopard later, maybe.'

'I'm sorry to ruin everyone's fun,' Laura said.

Samantha leaned over from her seat and patted Laura on the arm. 'I have to go as well. No harm.'

Mia executed a tight turn and took a shorter, more direct route to the road. Once there she drove in the opposite direction to that indicated by the poacher's tracks.

Mia pulled over into a cleared, grassy area where she sometimes stopped for sundowners or morning coffee and rusks on game drives. There was a termite mound about two metres high near the edge of the clearing.

Mia turned off the engine, got out and walked over to the big grey mound, around it, and back to the Land Rover. 'OK, everyone, let's have a leg stretch.' She took a small cylindrical green canvas pouch containing toilet paper out of the front of the vehicle and passed it to Laura. 'You can go over there behind the termite mound.'

'You're sure it's safe?' Sue asked her.

'She'll be fine,' Mia said. 'Laura, just sing out if you have a problem.'

'OK.' The girl took the pouch and walked off.

'I'm off to find a tree of my own,' Samantha said.

'Not too far, please,' Mia called to her.

Samantha gave a wave without looking back as she headed in the same general direction as Laura, but on a slight tangent.

'We might as well have a drink here now we've stopped,' Julianne said to Mia. Sue and Elizabeth got off on the other side of the Land Rover, chatting about the leopard as they climbed down.

Julianne took Mia aside and lowered her voice. 'Are we actually safe here?'

'Yes, it's fine. Graham, Oscar and the dog team will be deploying on the other side of where the leopard was.'

'All right,' Julianne said. 'In that case I'll have a G and T, but let's make it a quick drinks stop, then clear out.'

Bongani went to the rear of the truck, opened the tailgate and dragged out a green cooler box which he brought to the nose of the game viewer. Mia lifted up and secured a hinged folding table made of welded steel mesh which formed part of the bumper bar, in front of the radiator. She had another box with snacks, glasses and a starched white linen tablecloth, which she set up on the impromptu bar. Bongani set about fixing their employer her drink.

'Sue?' Mia asked.

'Dry white wine?'

'Elizabeth?' Bongani asked.

'White wine as well, please, and Sam will have the same. With ice, please.'

'Coming right up.' Mia fished a bottle from the cold slurry of ice, unscrewed it and poured. She took out a Coke Lite for herself and a can of soda water for Bongani, knowing his preference off by heart.

'I feel like brandy,' he said softly to her as he took his drink.

'Me too.' For one thing, it might settle her stomach, she thought.

Bongani walked a little way from the rest of them and, out of habit, scanned the road for tracks. Sue and Elizabeth walked over to him and Sue asked Bongani what he was looking at. Julianne seized the opportunity to beckon Mia to walk with her, a little way in the opposite direction.

'Do you think this poacher has been somewhere on my reserve all day?'

'I don't know,' Mia said. 'The guys on the Vulture system should have picked him up if he'd left or come back onto the reserve. These old poachers are skilled at living in the bush. He could survive out here for a long time and the Vulture's technology might not pick him up, especially if all the gadgets are facing the wrong way. Our camera traps and alarms on the fences are all primarily focused on picking up people coming or going. If we're looking for one man living out here in the bush it's literally like looking for a needle in a haystack. The dog team will help, though.'

'Good. I'm sure Sean and his team will pick him up.'

'Let's hope so,' Mia said.

'Bongani thinks he's found another drag mark,' Sue called to them. 'There's even a blood trail!'

'Well, no shortage of leopards, at least,' Julianne said. She lowered her voice for Mia's sake: 'I don't like this.'

Neither did Mia. She did not like being bested by the poacher, nor having to rely on dumb luck, but at least Bongani had been doing a good job, not becoming so focused on tracking the leopard that he did not see anything else. They walked over to the other two guests.

Sue showed her new-found tracking skills to Julianne, pointing out the scrape in the dirt where the leopard had dragged its prey, and the pug marks either side.

'Same leopard?' Mia asked, although she knew that the possibility that the same leopard had made two kills in a short period of time, or that there might be another close by which had also happened to kill in the same time period, were both statistically unlikely.

Bongani took her arm and led her away. 'No leopard,' he whispered.

'What?'

Bongani put a finger to his lips. 'There was an impala carcass dragged or carried across the road – there is blood and hair from the antelope – but I picked up a partial boot print. They dragged the impala across the road to cover their footprints.'

'They? What makes you think it was more than one person?' Panic started to rise inside Mia's chest, like heartburn.

'The leopard's pug marks are fake, made by two humans using their fingers. One did a good job – he fooled me – the other was not so good, and he left a fingerprint in the sand nearby.'

'Holy shit,' Mia whispered.

'Laura!'

They looked around. Sue was standing with Julianne, Elizabeth and Samantha, who had rejoined the group. Sue shaded her eyes against the setting sun as she looked towards the termite mound. The girl had been taking her time, Mia realised, checking her watch.

'Laura, are you all right? Come take a look at these tracks when you finish,' Mia called.

Julianne, sensing something was up, excused herself from the other women and came to them. Bongani quietly filled her in on his discovery as Mia went to the Land Rover, took her rifle from the dashboard and extracted it from its carry case.

'Laura?' Mia called again as she loaded the .375. To Bongani she whispered: 'I didn't see any drag marks or tracks around the termite mound.'

'They could have gone into the bush, by the mound, when they heard us coming,' Bongani whispered.

'Shit,' Julianne said.

'What's going on?' Sue started heading to the mound, with Elizabeth and Samantha striding to keep up with her.

'Get in the truck, everyone, please,' Mia ordered the women. Elizabeth and Samantha paused, then turned and headed back to the Land Rover. 'Laura!'

Bongani peeled off, instinctively knowing what needed to be done. He intercepted Sue. 'Please, just give Mia a moment to check.'

Sue shrugged off his gentle touch on her arm. 'Get out of my way!'

Mia brought the rifle up into her shoulder as she came abreast of the termite mound. She drew a breath, her finger curled through the trigger guard.

'No!' Sue shrieked.

Chapter 12

Sannie made it into the Sabi Sand Game Reserve and onto the Lion Plains property, where Kaya Nghala Lodge was situated, in less than half an hour. She had driven as fast as she dared, navigating towards the WhatsApp pin that she had been sent.

The lodge and the place where the crime scene had been set up were, as the crow flew, less than two kilometres from where she had just been, in Killarney village, looking for a sangoma who was not home. Annoyingly, however, the road to the gate followed the boundary of the reserve for a much longer distance north, then through the gate, and then back down the fence line and into the wilds of the reserve.

Julianne Clyde-Smith, the owner of Lion Plains, was with the girl's mother, whom she introduced to Sannie. Surprisingly, Sannie's two friends, Elizabeth and Samantha, were standing nearby, leaning against a Lion Plains open Land Rover. Sannie remembered now her friends telling her over drinks the night before that they were going on a game drive this afternoon, but she had not recalled them saying which lodge they were visiting. They both gave her a little wave and she nodded to them, keeping it professional.

'Thank you for coming so quickly, Captain,' Julianne said.

'Quick?' Sue Barker, the Englishwoman, glared at Sannie. 'My daughter has been missing for ages and no one is doing anything.'

Julianne put her arm around the woman. 'My two best trackers are on the trail and our dog team is coming in from the east.

They were called out earlier after a suspected poacher's tracks were seen.'

Sue pulled away from Julianne. 'What? You knew there were criminals here on the reserve and you let my daughter and me continue on a bloody game drive?'

'It's not like that –' Julianne began.

Sue grabbed two handfuls of her own hair. 'What do you bloody mean it's not like that?'

'Mrs Barker,' Sannie said, taking out her notebook, 'we're mobilising more police as we speak.'

'My helicopter is on its way,' Julianne said. 'It had to go for maintenance this morning, but I've passed on a message for the pilot to hurry back.'

Sannie nodded. 'Good. What have we got here?'

Julianne led Sannie to a termite mound, Sue Barker following them, wiping her eyes, and the other two women trailing along at a distance.

'I've tried to keep everything as undisturbed as possible.'

A green fleece hoody, a small woman's size by the look of it, lay on the ground, along with a cylindrical green canvas pouch of a type which Sannie recognised. She had one herself, for carrying toilet paper when she and her family had gone camping. It was unopened.

'That's ... that's my daughter's jacket,' Sue said, and started crying.

Sannie moved forward slowly. She needed a crime scene investigation team here, now, but they were still a couple of hours' drive away and there was no time to waste.

'We can use the radio in the Land Rover to get an update from my people,' Julianne said, 'but right now I think they're better off concentrating on finding the girl, don't you think, Captain?'

Sannie agreed, but this was her investigation, not the wealthy lodge owner's, no matter how many anti-poaching rangers she employed. Only in the time of COVID-19 would she be the only officer at such a scene. She looked at the ground. 'Signs of a struggle?'

Julianne stepped forward, but Sannie held out a hand to stop her walking over the tracks. 'Yes, my people say there are the tracks of two men, barefoot, leaving the scene.'

'Why,' Sue Barker sniffed, 'why would they not have shoes?'

Sannie looked up after inspecting the footprints. 'Poachers take their shoes off sometimes. They know that we can match the tread of their shoes and use that as evidence. A foot is not like a hand, which leaves a distinctive fingerprint, especially not in the dirt.'

'My trackers said the men were moving as though carrying someone,' Julianne said.

Sannie nodded and moved in the direction of the tracks, skirting them so as not to contaminate them. Even she could see how the one footprint rolled out to the side and was firmly pressed into the dirt, as if carrying an awkward, perhaps struggling weight. 'You heard nothing?'

'No,' Julianne said.

Sannie looked back to her friends, who both shook their heads.

'I was in the bush as well,' Samantha volunteered. 'Answering the call of nature, like poor Laura. I heard nothing. Whoever it was moved like ghosts.'

Sannie cast her eyes around the base of the termite mound. There was no obvious evidence that the girl had actually relieved herself.

Sue gasped and started crying again. 'Do something!'

Sannie checked her watch. It was nearly six. It would be dark soon. 'You say your chopper is coming?'

Julianne nodded. 'Yes, and I have a wide area surveillance system.'

Sannie was writing in her notebook, but something caught her eye. She glanced up to see Samantha staring, point blank, at Elizabeth, whose cheeks turned red when Sannie looked to her. Odd, Sannie thought. She directed her mind back to the facts, as she was trying to establish them.

'Yes, I've heard of it. The Vulture system,' Sannie said to Julianne.

'We'll pick them up as they try to leave the reserve, if my teams don't catch them first.' Julianne put an arm around Sue's shoulders.

Sannie went back to the girl's jacket, found a stick on the ground and used it to lift the garment without getting too close to the obvious scuff marks in the bare sandy patch of earth where the girl, Laura, had been. She lifted the jacket and checked it. There was no sign of blood on it.

'How long was Laura alone?' Sannie asked.

'She was *not* alone.' Sue wiped her eyes. 'We were all here, just on the road.'

Sannie looked back. 'About thirty metres away. What were you doing there?'

'What are you insinuating, Captain?' Sue said.

'Please, Mrs Barker, I just need to establish the facts.'

'We were looking at tracks,' Julianne said, 'and Laura was relieving herself, as was Samantha.'

Sannie made a note. 'Tracks of what?'

'Leopard,' Julianne said. 'At least, Bongani thought it was another leopard. We had just seen one up a tree with a kill – it had dragged its prey across the road. Even I thought that was weird, two leopards in such close proximity, but stranger things have happened. Bongani thought there was something suspicious about –'

'Wait.' Sue stepped between the two women and confronted Julianne. 'You knew there was a problem and you didn't call for Laura then and get us all back on the truck?'

'It all happened so fast, Sue,' Julianne said.

Sannie saw that Sue's hands were balled into fists by her sides. 'Ladies, please.'

Sannie manoeuvred herself so she was between the two women. Elizabeth and Samantha hung back, not wanting to take sides, Sannie guessed. 'The most important thing now is that we find Laura. More police are on the way. I think we should check in with your teams.'

Sannie shepherded them all to the Land Rover.

'Julianne, this is Sean, over,' came a voice through the radio.

'Sean Bourke, head of anti-poaching,' Julianne said as she opened the front door and reached across Mia's seat to get to the handset.

Sannie nodded. 'I know him. Good man.'

Julianne pressed the transmit button. 'Go for Julianne, Sean.'

'Julianne.' Sean was panting. *'We're closing on them ... heading west, towards the perimeter fence. One of my guys ... says he just caught a glimpse of them.'*

'Roger, Sean, give me a reference and I'll send the chopper to you as soon as he's overhead.'

Sannie had her phone out.

'They'll hit the fence about four kilometres north of the R536, over.'

'Copy,' Julianne said.

Sannie sent an SMS to the police tactical unit and the crime scene investigators, both of whom would be in the area soon, if they weren't already. Julianne looked to her. Sannie nodded. 'Got it.'

'Roger, Sean,' Julianne said into the handset. 'The police are here and they're directing their people to go to the fence to assist.'

Then Sannie looked up from the screen of her phone when she heard, quite clearly, a gunshot over the radio.

*

Mia and Bongani dived to the ground, searching for cover, as two more shots were fired, this time at them.

'The dog,' Bongani said, his hand on his chest as he lay there, gasping for breath. Mia kept fit by using the gym at Kaya Nghala, but with each passing year Bongani was getting bigger and slower. 'I think they shot it.'

'Bastards,' Mia said.

The dog handler, Phillip, had let Askari off the lead to chase down the men as soon as they had been sighted. Phillip had run after Askari, bringing his R1 rifle up to bear and readying for a shot when one of the poachers had opened fire.

'Askari!' Phillip yelled, then fired his weapon.

Mia put her head up. There was no sign of the dog. Phillip got to his feet and then the gunman fired again, this time on full automatic.

'AK-47,' Mia yelled, realising their enemy had an assault rifle.

Phillip, either heedless of his own safety or worried for his four-legged friend, fired twice and ran forward.

The poacher opened up again and Phillip fell.

'Phillip!' Mia rolled over and handed her hunting rifle to Bongani. 'Cover me.'

'No, Mia.' Bongani shook his head. 'Wait for Sean.'

'There's no time,' Mia said. 'The guy will show himself as soon as I start running, but he'll have to be a good shot to hit a running target. He'll be focusing on me, so as soon as you see him, you plug him, OK?'

Bongani shook his head again. 'You're crazy.'

She put a hand on his arm. 'Do this, now, or these guys will get away with Laura.'

Bongani took a deep breath and worked the bolt of the rifle back a little to confirm it was loaded and ready.

'On three,' Mia said.

He nodded.

'Wait.'

'What is it?' Bongani asked.

'That muthi you chew, the herbs or powder, or whatever it is the sangoma gives you to keep away danger. Give me some.'

'You sure?'

'Yes. There are no non-believers in foxholes.'

'What?' He dug into the pocket of his fatigue trousers.

'Old white people's saying.'

He passed her a pinch of his potion. Mia took it and put the stuff in her mouth. She started chewing. It was tangy, bitter.

'Spit as you run,' Bongani said. He handed her a folded paper packet containing the remaining muthi.

Mia put it in her pocket. 'OK. Ready?'

Bongani adjusted himself so the rifle was pointing around the trunk of the tree, towards where the gunfire had last come from.

'Three!' Mia stood and ran.

With her legs pumping she expected to hear shots from the poacher at any second. As much as she dreaded the thud of the bullet into her body – her father had told her once, drunk, that it didn't hurt, at first – she knew that if she was not fired upon then the poachers had already left, and that meant Laura would be further out of reach.

The man with the AK-47 fired a burst of three rounds. Mia heard the *crack-thump* of a bullet as it cleaved the air close to her face. The gunman must have been firing wild, as another skidded across the ground near her foot. Her heart felt like it was ready to explode. She saw Phillip on the ground in front of her; he rolled over, to face her, and raised his rifle.

'It's me!'

Mia barely registered the louder bang of her own rifle going off as Bongani, at last, fired. No more rounds came her way from the AK-47 as she dived like a Springbok winger sliding in for a try, ploughing her way along the rough, dry earth and brittle grass.

'Sheesh, you're crazy,' Phillip said.

She looked up and wiped dirt from her face. Phillip was pale, and despite his forced smile he was wincing. 'Where are you hit, Phillip?'

'*Ag*, in the lower right leg, only, but I can't stand.'

Mia leopard-crawled closer to him, staying low, and worked her hands down his leg. He flinched as she pulled up his trouser leg. 'I'm no soldier, but I can see an entry wound and an exit wound, so I think you'll live. Have you got a bandage or something?'

'A field dressing, in my pack.'

Mia helped Phillip shrug the daypack off his back, unzipped it and found the dressing.

'Can you do it yourself?' she asked him.

He blinked at her. 'You're not ...'

'I have to go, Phillip. I can't let them get away with that girl. They've stopped firing at us, which I think means they're moving.'

Phillip shook his head. 'They're desperate men, Mia, they've already shot me, and poor Askari. They're looking at serious prison time after taking that tourist kid. They'll kill you, sure as nuts.'

Mia handed Phillip the wound dressing and when he started to unwrap it, a job that took both hands, she snatched his rifle up from the grass.

'Hey, give that back!'

'Tell Sean I'll radio through any updates. I'll get Bongani to come to you.'

'Mia, wait ...'

She ignored him, stood, and ran forward, before her fears could paralyse her. Finding some cover, Mia slowed, took her radio from her belt and told Bongani to go to Phillip. She heard whining and, ahead of her, saw Askari the dog.

'Bongani, the dog's alive as well. Please see to him if you can, over.' She stooped quickly to ruffle his fur. 'Good boy.'

Like his handler, Askari looked as though he had also taken one in the leg.

Mia steeled herself and moved off.

She picked up the tracks of the men and came to a patch of flattened grass. There were spent copper casings from an AK-47 lying where the man had opened fire on them. Mia quickly cast about and found blood on the grass. It was not, however, where the shooter had been lying. She found two other indentations on the ground, but only the one in the middle – presumably Laura – had been bleeding. Dread, mixed with adrenaline, both terrified and fuelled her from within. She prayed none of them had accidentally shot Laura in the exchange of gunfire.

She grabbed the cocking handle on the left of Phillip's R1 and, as Bongani had with her rifle, made sure there was a round chambered, ready for action.

Mia saw where the men had picked up the girl again and set off. It seemed as though one man now had her over his shoulder as his tracks were deeper than those of his partner in crime.

There were no more bullet casings so Mia presumed only the one man was armed. That made things slightly fairer.

Mia tried to put herself into the mind of her quarry.

These men would be desperate and their movement would be slowed by the burden of the girl. They were heading west towards the perimeter fence.

'Julianne, this is Mia, over,' she said into her radio as she jogged, keeping her eyes down and, as always, scanning the bush ahead – the last thing she needed now was to bump into a pride of lions or a cantankerous old buffalo bull.

'Go, Mia.'

'Julianne, tell our people, or the cops, or whoever you can, to stop any vehicle traffic on the road along the fence line outside the reserve. These guys might have a vehicle waiting for them.'

'*Roger, Mia, will do. The police are here now, with more reinforcements on their way and heading to the fence as a blocking force.*'

'*Mia, Mia, this is Sean. Copy?*'

Mia could hear the urgency in the normally unflappable Sean's voice. 'Go, Sean.'

'*Mia, sheesh, what are you up to? Find some cover and wait for us, over.*'

Mia kept on her path, alternately following the tracks and checking her surroundings. She was scared, but she was also excited. As tempting as it was to wait for help, she knew that she needed to keep on the trail of these men. She would not be able to live with herself if something happened to Laura. The girl had been in her care.

'Sorry, Sean, you're coming through garbled,' she lied.

Mia turned the volume of her radio down and clipped it back on her belt. She paused briefly to touch some blood spatters on a leaf. When she lifted her finger, she felt its wetness. She was close. *What have those bastards done to her?* Mia asked herself.

Horrible thoughts flashed through her mind. Her discussions about umuthi with Bongani and with Jeff had conjured up some terrible scenarios in her head. Some izangoma, operating outside the law, had been known to use human body parts to prepare their potions. Corpses were stolen or bought from morgues, graves had been robbed and, in some awful cases, children or certain adults – people with albinism were particularly at risk in some parts of Africa – had been kidnapped and murdered.

Was Laura dead already?

Her fears multiplied inside her. She had not heard the faintest noise, let alone a scream, from Laura since she had been abducted. Had they killed her, silently, on the spot?

'*Mia, Mia ...*' She turned off the radio. If she was close to these men she did not want her position to be given away by noise.

Mia looked down and saw a long scuff mark, a flattened area of grass, and a wet patch of blood on the ground. At least one of the men had stumbled and fallen. Good, she thought to herself, every misstep by her quarry gave her precious seconds to catch up. Mia dropped some of her caution and broke into a run, her eyes methodically moving from ground to the front and flanks in a continual motion. She held the R1 at the high port across her chest, using it to brush aside twigs and branches.

Woo-oop.

Mia slowed to a walk and listened.

Woo-oop.

Ringing eerily through the bush came the unmistakable call of a spotted hyena. With their acute sense of smell and sharp hearing, the hyenas had possibly picked up the blood trail and heard her and the men she was pursuing crashing through the bush. While hyenas were excellent hunters in their own right they were also consummate scavengers, often following other predators with the intention of stealing their kills. The hyena clan could very well be on her trail right now, just as they might tail a pack of wild dogs or a lone leopard.

'Shit.' Animal interference was the last thing she needed right now. Mia picked up her pace.

Woo-oop. The hyena was louder, closer.

Mia heard another noise, this one man-made. She stopped.

A man was talking, low and rapid. There would have been no point in one stopping to lecture the other; this man had to be talking into a phone or radio, although his words were indistinct. Mia brought the butt of Phillip's rifle up into her shoulder and crept forward, all senses on high alert. She caught the coppery scent of blood and her stomach turned. Her hands tightened on the black plastic handgrip and stock of the military-spec rifle. Mia remembered Bongani's instructions, belatedly, and quietly spat out the muthi she had been chewing.

A grey go-away bird mocked her with its eponymous call. It was too late for that. The hyena whooped in anticipation of death to come.

The talking ahead of her stopped.

Mia looked around her, searching for landmarks. There was a granite koppie, a cluster of boulders piled into a hill, which she knew well and told her she was less than two hundred metres from the western boundary fence of the Sabi Sand Game Reserve. On the breeze she heard the faint hum of a motor vehicle engine.

Got you, you bastards.

Mia heard the voice again.

'*Hi ta vonana.*'

'I will see you,' the man had just said in Xitsonga, but then he ended his call.

Mia lowered herself into a crouch and watched each footfall, concentrating on not treading on a dry twig that might snap and give her away. She peered *through* the bush, just as she told her guests to on game drives, only this time the stakes were life and death.

She risked taking one hand off the stock of the R1 to take a fresh pinch of Bongani's muthi from the paper packet in her pants pocket, put some more of the concoction in her mouth and chewed on it, then spat out a little.

The ritual of chewing and spitting, and maintaining her noise discipline, focused her, calmed her a little.

The foresight and tip of the barrel of the AK-47 came into view.

Guests were sometimes amazed that either Bongani or Mia could spot a chameleon after dark, on their evening drives back to the lodge. The tiny reptiles had such a distinct silhouette that, with practice, they were easy to pick out in the beam of a spotlight, silhouetted on the branch of a tree. Mia's eyes were so attuned to the shapes, colours, surfaces and movements of the natural world that something so stark, angular and unnatural as a rifle leapt out at her.

Whoever was holding that gun had shot Phillip and Askari and tried to kill Bongani and her.

A girl, someone who had been in her charge, was missing, most likely bleeding.

The toll on rhinos and other animals was mounting.

Mia raised the R1 and peered down the sights. She knew that if she aimed about a metre to the right of where she could see the tip of the rifle barrel she would, most likely, hit the man holding it. There was a very good chance that the heavy 7.62-millimetre slug waiting in the breech of Phillip's weapon would kill.

She knew one thing for sure: *Whoever sees the other first has the strongest magic.*

She chewed the last of the potion and spat it out as she took up the pressure on the trigger.

A cool, calm energy flooded out from her heart and her soul to her fingertips. The power of life or death was in her right index finger. She had tracked this man and his companion, and now she had the power to kill him.

Mia knew she should call out to the man to drop his weapon. She knew she should wait for Sean.

The tip of the rifle started to move, swinging in a slow arc until it was nearly pointed at her.

Mia squeezed the trigger.

Chapter 13

Sannie heard the shot through the open window of her car and accelerated. She saw the camouflage-painted Sabi Sand anti-poaching vehicle parked up ahead and pulled over in front of it.

Julianne Clyde-Smith had been on the road behind her, in the open game viewer, with Sue, Elizabeth and Samantha on board. Sannie had told the women to go back to the lodge, where they would be safe, to await news, but Julianne and Sue would not listen and Sannie's friends, whether they liked it or not, were along for the ride. This was too many civilians in an area where gunshots were being fired, but in these crazy times there seemed to be nothing she could do to control them. As Sannie got out of the vehicle and drew her pistol she was annoyed but not surprised to see the game viewer also pulling to a halt. She could not waste time on them now.

She ran through the bush. Even with her very novice tracking skills she could not miss the path made by the poachers, Mia and Bongani, the dog team and Sean Bourke and the rest of his men. They had trampled a virtual freeway through the yellow grass and mostly denuded, khaki winter vegetation.

There was yelling up ahead.

Sannie ran as fast as she dared, her pistol pointed down at the ground.

Ahead of her was a pair of men, one sitting, one lying. The able-bodied of the two stood, raising his hands.

'Police,' she said.

'I am from Kaya Nghala,' the African man said.

'You're Bongani, the tracker?'

'Yes. This man is injured.'

The man on the ground looked up at her. His leg was bandaged. 'I'll live.'

Sannie gave a curt nod. 'There's an ambulance on the way. Stay here.'

'Affirmative.'

As she left the men, she radioed police emergency control and gave them instructions to pass on to the paramedics. She had called for an ambulance just in case, hoping they might find the girl.

A little further on she came to a green-clad ranger who half raised his rifle as she approached.

'Lower that weapon.'

The man did so, on seeing her uniform.

'Afternoon,' the ranger said. He looked downward. 'This man, he is dead.'

Sannie, panting a little from her run, stopped next to him and looked down. A barefoot man dressed otherwise in black lay sprawled on his back, an AK-47 in the dust by his right hand.

'Who shot him?' Sannie asked. There was no time for pleasantries.

'Mia, madam.'

'The guide?'

He nodded. '*Yebo.*'

'Where is she now?'

'She and Mr Bourke and the others are now following the other poacher together.'

'Just the two poachers?'

'Yes, madam.'

'There are four women in the game viewer back there. Don't let them see this body. All right?'

He nodded. Sannie ran off again, following the tracks, now minus one poacher.

There was more yelling, more gunfire ahead, and Sannie caught a glimpse of another man in green. He was bare-headed and she recognised the red-brown hair. 'Sean!'

He paused and turned, his face streaked with sweat and grime.

'Sannie. Howzit. Mia's gone ahead again. She thinks there's one more kidnapper on the run. I've sent two of my guys with her as backup.'

'And Laura?'

He shrugged. 'They say from the tracks the suspect's by himself. I've been looking for Laura in case ...'

Sannie swore to herself in Afrikaans.

They both stopped talking as they heard an eerie, almost other-worldly cackling noise.

'Hyena?' she said.

Sean nodded. 'Yes, but that's not good. That laughing sound is the call they make when they're in a frenzy.'

'Like, feeding?'

'Yes.'

Sannie's heart lurched as she followed Sean at a run, in the direction of the bizarre noise. Fortunately, Sean had an LM5 rifle.

Sean powered ahead of her, heedless of the whip of thorny acacia branches. Sannie stayed close to him.

'Sheesh,' he said, stopping. He raised his rifle and fired three shots in the air.

Sannie peered around Sean and drew a breath as she saw four hyenas, almost comically posed in the midst of their gory business. Two were frozen in a tug of war, a piece of skin stretched between their powerful jaws.

Sean fired again and the animals dropped their prize and loped off.

'It isn't ...' She was too scared to finish her sentence.

Sean moved forward, rifle still at the ready, and checked the blood-spattered grass and bushes. He shook his head. 'No, thank God. An impala.'

Sannie exhaled. 'And Mia?'

Sean reached for the radio at his belt and spoke to one of his men, Foster, asking for a sitrep, a situation report.

'She's at the spruit. Not far from here.'

As they set off again, Sean continued talking into his radio, the handset pressed to his ear.

'My guy, Foster, says they're looking for the other man. He went into the drainage line, but because of the recent rain there's water in it and they haven't been able to pick up his tracks. They're casting up and down the bank looking for him.'

'Is he armed?'

'We don't know, Captain.'

'No sign of the girl?'

'Negative,' Sean said. 'No tracks and no visuals.'

They ran on, but both slowed to look up when they heard the sound of a helicopter pass over their heads.

'Any lower and he'll be cutting the branches,' Sannie said.

'That's Julianne's pilot, Mike, from Lion Plains,' Sean said. 'At bloody last.'

The radio squawked. '*Sean, Sean, this is Mike, over?*'

'Go, Mike,' Sean said into his radio, while Sannie waited next to him.

'*Checking something on the ground. There's a clearing here.*'

'Roger.' Sean turned to Sannie. 'Let's go take a look.'

They ran, following the noise of the chopper, but just as they arrived at the clearing Mike had mentioned they saw his white Robinson R44 helicopter lifting off.

'*False alarm,*' Mike said into the radio. '*I saw a flash of colour, but it was just a plastic bag.*'

They crossed the clearing and saw the brightly coloured yellow bag. Sannie picked it up, inspected it and sniffed it. 'There was food in here, maybe some pap or something like that.' She balled it and stuffed it in a pocket. 'Maybe we can get some prints off it.'

Sean nodded. He received a message Sannie didn't catch, then spoke into his handheld again.

'My two guys, Oscar and Graham, are down by the spruit,' he reported back to her.

They cut through some thick bush lining the watercourse, between some wild date palms that were probably nurtured year-round by underground water. The two rangers were standing by a stretch of water that was flowing.

'Graham?' Sean said when he got to them.

The white man, young, fair-haired, muscled and sweating, shook his head. 'Lost him, boss.'

'Damn,' Sean said.

The other ranger, Oscar, pointed along the watercourse. 'He ran into the water here, to try to shake us off his trail.'

'And it worked?' Sean asked.

Oscar looked down at the ground. 'Yes.'

Sean turned to Sannie. 'It's a classic tactic. They go into some water and run either way along the spruit.'

'We've cast up and down the banks for a hundred metres in one direction and two hundred in the other,' Graham said. 'No sign of where he exited.'

'Why only a hundred metres that way?' Sannie asked, looking where the young ranger had just been pointing.

'The natural flow ends there this time of the year, and there's no sign of tracks beyond or around it.'

Sean glanced around. 'Well, keep searching. Don't come back until you find this *ou*. Understood?'

'*Yebo*,' Graham said. 'And Sean?'

'Yes?'

'It's Mia, she's ...' Graham nodded and Sannie and Sean both looked to see the woman sitting under a big jackalberry tree, her back to the trunk, her head between her drawn-up knees.

'We'll take care of her,' Sean said. 'You two, go!'

Oscar and Graham set off.

'Mia?' Sannie said softly as they came to her.

She looked up, her face streaked with tears.

'Mia, this is Captain Sannie van Rensburg,' Sean said.

'Hello, Mia,' Sannie said. She did not need to ask how the woman was.

Mia just looked up at her and blinked. She wiped her nose with the back of her hand.

Sannie dropped to one knee, beside her. 'Mia, I need to ask you a couple of questions.'

Mia nodded as Sannie took out her notebook.

'You shot the man, the one who is deceased?'

'Yes.' Her lower lip was trembling. 'I've lost them all, I've lost Laura.'

'There are others searching ... a helicopter,' Sannie said.

Mia shook her head. 'She was *my* responsibility. I'm supposed to be able to track ...'

'The man you shot,' Sannie said. 'Tell me about him.'

Mia brought her hand up to her mouth. 'I saw his gun. He shot Phillip, and the dog, Askari, and fired at Bongani and me.'

Sannie patted her arm. 'I'll need to interview you later, but in cases of self-defence we open an inquest docket into the shooting.'

Mia looked up at her and blinked. 'I took a man's life, Captain.'

'Yes, but he was trying to kill you.'

Mia shook her head. 'You don't understand. The reason doesn't matter; I *killed* a man. I've seen what that does to the person who pulls the trigger. My father ... he was in the war, in Angola. You don't know what it's like.'

Sannie held her tongue. She did not want to tell this girl about what had happened in her own life. 'I have used my pistol in the course of doing my duty. You should talk to someone, Mia. I'll speak to Julianne. She should arrange for you to see a counsellor. It's only natural, what you're feeling.'

'Natural? I'm not Graham, or Oscar, or you, Captain. It's not *natural* to kill someone. I'm not cut out for tracking people.'

'You did your best, Mia.'

She nodded. 'And a man is dead and a girl is missing.'

'The girl, Mia,' Sannie prompted gently. 'We need to find her.'

'I know!'

Sannie gave her some space. Right now this distressed young safari guide was probably their best chance of tracking down Laura. 'Mia, please.'

She sniffed and wiped her eyes again. 'Sorry. I *know* we have to find Laura, but I just don't know where she is.'

'The tracks from the scene?'

Mia closed her eyes, concentrating. 'There were signs of a scuffle, and her jacket was on the ground at the termite mound.'

'We found that.'

'I left it there. I thought that if the dog team arrived they could use it to pick up her scent.'

'Good thinking,' Sannie said, encouraged that Mia had calmed somewhat. She waited for her to carry on, eyes still closed.

'There was blood. I thought it was Laura's. Two sets of footprints leading away from the termite mound. Bongani had picked up tracks of men dragging an impala – they'd tried to make it look like a leopard with a kill.'

Excellent tracking, Sannie thought to herself. 'Poaching?'

She nodded. 'Yes, but what? They took an impala and went to a lot of trouble to cover up their tracks. It doesn't make sense, unless they took Laura because she was a witness to what they were doing, or they ... they know the value of a child. One could have had the impala over his shoulder and the other carried Laura the same way, but if they'd decided to take the girl, why bother with the impala? I don't know.'

Sannie tried to remain patient. She made a note in her book.

Mia looked up, her face pale with shock. 'I heard hyenas. They didn't ...'

'No,' Sannie said quickly. 'That was not Laura. The hyenas were feeding on an impala.'

Mia put a hand to her head. 'I need to think, to go take a look again.'

'OK, if you're up to it,' Sannie said.

Sannie helped Mia to her feet and the pair of them caught up with Sean who, like Graham and Oscar, had been casting along the watercourse, desperately looking for spoor.

'Nothing,' Sean said to them when they reached him. The helicopter buzzed over them, working a search grid between where they were and the fence line.

'Mia wants to see where the hyenas were,' Sannie said.

'Sure,' Sean said, without questioning why. Sannie could tell they were all desperate for a lead of some kind.

When they got to the scene there was little left of the impala. It seemed that after Sean's initial shots had scared the hyenas away they had returned to finish the job. Mia knelt and touched some blood on the grass, then stood and followed the trail back in the general direction from which they had all come, though not, Sannie noticed, along the tracks of the poacher they had been tracking.

Mia stopped and peered ahead through the bush.

'Do not shoot me,' a male voice called.

'Bongani, it's me,' Mia replied.

The two trackers met on the trail.

'The helicopter came,' Bongani said, 'for Phillip and the dog.'

'Yes,' Sean confirmed for Sannie's benefit. 'Mike picked them up and dropped them just outside the reserve, where they met up with an inbound ambulance. The paramedics said Phillip and Askari would be fine on the drive and Mike wanted to get back to the search here.'

'Makes sense,' Sannie said, thinking out loud, and remembering how the pilot had touched down, briefly.

Mia handed her R1 rifle to Sean. 'This is Phillip's.'

He took it. 'Don't you want to keep it for now?'

She shook her head and wiped her hand on her shirt front, as if the weapon had contaminated her.

'I have been following the hyenas' trail,' Bongani said.

'Me, as well,' Mia said, 'from the other end.'

'The hyenas caught the impala here?' Sean asked.

'No,' Bongani said. 'This impala was already dead when the hyenas found it. There is no sign of a chase or the violence of a kill. I think this was the impala the two poachers were carrying back at the termite mound.'

'Not Laura?' Mia asked.

Bongani shook his head. 'After you killed one man, the other carried the impala. But his tracks end where we all lost his trail.'

Sean pinched the bridge of his nose with his free hand, the LM5 rifle still in his right. 'So where is the girl?'

Bongani looked to Mia, and Sannie saw something in the older man's eyes.

'What do you think, Bongani?' Sannie asked.

He turned and stared at her for a few moments, not saying anything.

'Bongani?' Mia prompted.

'There was grass, tied like string across the trail, where the poachers were waiting for us by the termite mound,' Bongani said, looking at Mia again.

Mia, Sannie saw, swallowed, and gave a small nod.

'What is that?' Sannie asked them. Time was ticking away and they had wasted much of it, so it seemed, on a false trail.

'A trip-wire?' Sean ventured.

Sannie knew that Sean, who had worked for a while as an explosive detection dog handler in Afghanistan, was an expert in IEDs, improvised explosive devices, which had also been set by poachers to catch rangers in South Africa.

Mia shook her head. 'No, grass woven into string and placed like this signifies something else. Evil.'

'Umuthi?' Sannie asked.

Bongani looked at her. 'Those two men were never carrying Laura. They made her disappear.'

Chapter 14

Mia looked from Bongani to the police captain and she could see that the woman was struggling to control herself. Captain van Rensburg had closed her eyes for a moment, one hand balled into a fist as she holstered her pistol.

'Captain ...' Mia began.

Sannie opened her eyes and held up a hand. 'I respect your beliefs, Bongani, but a child is missing and I need more than evil spirits as a reason why we have not found her. Maybe the poachers disturbed Laura when she was behind the termite mound, and she ran off into the bush. Come, we must look again, start at the beginning.'

Sean got on his radio and called Mike in the chopper. Mia heard Mike report that he had found nothing. 'Mike,' Sean said, 'fly to my place. Get Benny. Tell Christine to give you my pack with Benny's tracking collar and other gear.'

'*Roger, Sean.*'

Mia could appreciate the seriousness of Sean's request. Benny was Sean's personal dog, retired from work after being shot by a poacher and attacked by a leopard that had climbed over the fence and into his kennel. Benny, a Belgian Malinois like Askari, was a legend in the reserve for his tracking ability, but Sean had sworn his best friend would never have to be put in danger again.

'Bongani,' Sannie said, 'tell me what you really think happened to the girl.'

Bongani handed Mia's rifle back to her, then started walking the way they had all come, and beckoned the rest of them to follow. Mia caught up with him and also checked the ground.

'Here is where they were shooting at us, and Phillip and Askari,' Bongani said, raising his hands to pantomime a rifle firing.

Mia saw the spent cartridges on the ground and pointed them out for Sean and Sannie.

'Did they have Laura here, at this point?' Sannie asked.

Mia cast about, then stopped and pointed at the ground. 'See this indentation here, this is where I thought they had laid Laura down.'

Bongani squatted and took a closer look. He ran his fingers through the grass and picked up some short strands of hair. He held them up. 'From the impala.'

Mia felt terrible, seeing the evidence of her mistake. A poor tracker, she reminded herself, set out with a suspicion and then looked for proof of what she thought.

'Where's my daughter?'

They all looked up to see Sue Barker storming ahead of Julianne.

'She's walking all over the tracks,' Mia said softly.

'Mrs Barker, Sue,' Sannie said. 'I asked you to stay with the vehicle.'

Elizabeth arrived at the clearing and Samantha, stumbling and almost falling over a tree root, came up behind her. 'We were too scared to stay in the vehicle by ourselves,' Samantha said.

Sannie bit her tongue.

'Sorry, Captain,' Julianne said, 'but I'm sure you understand Sue's concern.'

'Completely,' Sannie said, maintaining her composure, 'but, ladies, this whole area is a crime scene and the more people who walk over it, the more valuable evidence is destroyed.'

'Where's my daughter?' Sue said again, as if Sannie had said nothing.

'We're trying to find her tracks,' Mia said.

Sue fixed her with a stare. 'You. You shouldn't have let her go off by herself, behind that bloody termite mound.'

The words cut Mia to the core.

'And now I find out you knew there were armed poachers all around us and yet you took us out on a drive, put us in harm's way.' Sue turned to Julianne. 'I'd call my lawyer if I wasn't so worried about Laura.'

Mia looked to Julianne, who put a hand on Sue's arm.

'Sue,' Julianne said softly, 'we assessed the risk and decided it was safe to carry on. We had no idea there were more poachers close to us and Mia was actually taking us away from danger, or so she thought.'

Sue bellowed to the sky: 'Where is my daughter!'

Julianne tried to hug her, but the woman shook her off and came to Mia, who stood, hands on hips, ready to fend her off or to take what was coming.

Sue jabbed a finger at Mia's chest. 'You'll never work in this business again if you don't find her. It's all your fault.'

'We will find Laura,' Bongani said. His deep voice and deliberate delivery seemed to calm the situation.

Sue wiped fresh tears from her eyes. 'My daughter can't have just bloody vanished into thin air.'

'The magic these poachers are using is very strong,' he said.

Mia looked skywards.

'What did you just say?' Sue asked slowly.

'We need help, from a sangoma, but we will find your daughter,' Bongani said.

Sue looked from him to Mia, and then to Captain van Rensburg. 'What. The. Absolute. Fuck.' Her face became flushed with rage. 'Are you telling me that black magic is responsible for the disappearance of my daughter?'

'We do not call it that,' Bongani said. 'If you will allow me –'

'Get this madman away from me and do your bloody jobs!'

Mia felt for the woman. It was impossible for her to begin to understand what was going through Bongani's mind, and hers, if she admitted the truth to herself. There seemed something otherworldly about their run of bad luck at tracking lately. Who was she, Mia asked herself, to mock Bongani when she had been chewing on his magical potion as she stalked the poacher, looking for any advantage she could get over her prey?

Sannie intercepted Sue and Mia thought that was just in time, as she feared the woman was about to launch herself at Bongani. Mia went to her friend and took him gently by the arm. 'Come, let's go check the trail again.'

Bongani nodded and let her lead him away. 'I am sorry,' he said to Sue over his shoulder.

'You should both be ashamed of yourselves,' Sue said to their backs. 'You call yourselves trackers? You can't find your own two feet and now my baby is gone!'

Julianne again tried to fold Sue into a hug and this time the other woman did not resist; her body heaved with sobs. Mia and Bongani took their cue to move off.

'Jesus, Bongani ...'

'Do not blaspheme, please, Mia.'

'Sorry.' She had to remind herself that Bongani's deep traditional beliefs did not detract from his devout following of Christianity. 'But that woman can't understand the way you think.'

He looked up from the ground to her. 'The way *we* think. You feel it as well, don't deny it, Mia.'

'We're definitely dealing with something we don't understand, something illogical. That's for sure.'

They walked on, side by side, studying the tracks for something they had missed, although by now so many humans, and a dog, had covered the tracks of the two men that they were almost indistinguishable.

Almost. Here and there Bongani or she picked up a footprint or a partial track left by the two men. Mia stopped and examined an impression of half of a bare foot.

Bongani reached over to a thorny branch and took a pinch of impala hair from it. 'So where is the girl?'

'That is the question.' Mia stood and brushed dirt from her hands. She had the .375 rifle slung over her shoulder.

Bongani sighed. 'We all did the wrong thing – you, me, the police, Sean and his men. We *assumed* that the men we were tracking were carrying Laura but all the while they were running off with an impala.'

Mia caught up to him. 'Go on.'

'So, we were looking for proof that we would find the girl, but the old man fooled us, with his muthi, which caused us to become confused.'

Mia did not truly think she had been fooled by umuthi, but Bongani was right – they had all been labouring under the misapprehension that the two men who had been carrying the buck had also taken the girl.

'You said "the old man". How do you know he's behind this? Didn't you say it was his tracks that were leading away in the other direction from where we saw the leopard?'

'They were his tracks,' Bongani said. 'But he is also behind this.'

'How do you know?' Mia asked.

'His muthi is strong.'

'What makes you think that?'

Bongani stopped and straightened his back, looking to where they had just been. 'Ask yourself this. Why would those two men bother carrying an impala? It was not worth their lives and they knew we would be coming after them.'

Mia had been thinking the same thought. 'They were a decoy.'

'Yes. For the old man, so that he could get away, or go kill another rhino, or –'

'Take the girl.'

Bongani nodded. 'There have been two girls who have gone missing in the village.'

'You think Laura might have been taken for the same reason as the other two?'

Bongani shrugged. 'I cannot say, but it seems unlikely to be a coincidence. I think when we find Laura, we might find the other girls too.'

'We?'

'It is our duty,' he said. 'And Laura was our responsibility. The old man put umuthi on the trail.'

'The grass rope, strung across the game trail?'

He nodded again. 'I didn't tell you, but it was the same when we were chasing him, in the rain. He used the same magic. It is powerful. It confused me then, just as it did this afternoon. It is getting dark.'

Mia looked at the red sky. Soon the light would be gone. There was still no sign of the crime scene investigation team that Captain van Rensburg had summoned. Mia called Sean on her radio and asked for an update.

'*Negative, Mia,*' Sean said. '*Graham and Oscar have been sweeping up and down the spruit, and there are no more tracks on either side. Maybe you should come take another look. I've got no idea how this guy disappeared or where the girl is.*'

Mia looked to the sky. This confounded reason. 'Thanks, Sean. We're going back to the termite mound, to start over again.'

'*Roger.*'

Mia retraced her steps, trying to keep the images of the man she had shot from flashing back across the TV screen of her mind. It was difficult. The more she tried to forget him, the more he barged his way back in. She stopped in the clearing and screwed her eyes shut for a moment. When she opened them, Bongani was staring at her.

'You will need to do something about him, or he will haunt you forever,' Bongani said.

Mia nodded. 'Yes, but first we have to find this girl.'

They went to the termite mound and started casting about.

'There was a struggle, here, by the base of the mound, but it looks like they tried to cover up their tracks as well,' Mia said.

'Like they wanted to confuse us,' Bongani said.

'They've done a good job of that. We need to reconnect the dots, Bongani, to work out what happened here, and fast.'

The light was fading as they circled the mound again and tracked back to the dirt road. The tyre marks, footprints and other signs told the story of the group stopping for sundowners, of Mia scouting about for danger, and of Laura walking away from them and behind the mound.

Mia walked in ever wider circles, first concentrating on finding Laura's tracks which, when they could be seen, were distinct by the small size of her feet and the clear imprint of her hiking boots, which Mia guessed had been bought for her safari holiday and possibly never used elsewhere.

'You can see here, where Laura came in from the road.'

Bongani came to her and checked. 'Yes, I noticed that.'

'And I can't find any exit trail from her, so I don't think she ran off in panic, or was lured away.'

'Agreed,' Bongani said. 'And there's no sign she was taken by a leopard or any other animal predator.'

'But all the tracks around here have been brushed away, by a human.' Mia looked around and saw a broken branch lying on the ground a few metres away. She walked to it and picked it up. 'Here's the broom they used.'

Bongani took the branch from her and inspected it. 'Cut with a sharp panga.'

Mia grimaced and dropped to one knee. Carefully, she ran her hand through the top layer of dirt and sand. 'At least there's no blood mixed in with this. So, where did she go?'

'Laura disappeared into thin air.'

Mia sighed. 'That is not possible.'

'You cannot keep saying or thinking that, Mia. It has happened. Laura is gone, as are the tracks of the men we have been following and searching for. It is their magic.'

'Bongani ...'

'No, listen to me, Mia. You have to understand. Something is affecting us, or hampering us, and it is not our lack of skills, or bad luck, or anything like that. Think about it. We were both ill.'

'That's got nothing to do ...'

He held her gaze.

'Really?'

Bongani shrugged. 'Do you think it was just a coincidence?'

'I *did*, but do you think it's possible we were deliberately poisoned, by someone working for the poachers?'

He nodded emphatically. 'I am certain of it.'

'That doesn't explain this afternoon ... I was feeling fine after a bit of rest, weren't you?'

'No,' Bongani said, 'my heart was heavy.'

Mia tried to concentrate on the tracks again, on tangible evidence. How did a person, a girl, disappear into thin air?

Mia snapped her fingers. 'Air!'

'What about it?'

Mia pointed up to the sky. 'Thin air. Laura disappeared into thin air.'

He blinked at her. 'I don't understand.'

Mia unclipped the radio from her belt. 'Sean, Sean this is Mia, over.'

She waited a few moments then tried again.

'*Mia, this is Sean. Go.*'

Mia smiled at Bongani. 'Sean, we need to talk to Julianne's helicopter pilot.'

*

Sannie and Sean, along with his anti-poaching rangers, made it back to the spot where Laura had disappeared just as the sun set.

Sannie was relieved to see her crime scene investigation unit pull up, finally.

'Sorry, we got lost on the way,' the sergeant in charge said to her.

Sannie hid her annoyance. 'No problem. Just get to work, please.'

Another vehicle from Kaya Nghala Lodge had arrived to collect Julianne and Sue who, despite initially insisting that she stay on the scene, agreed to be taken to her accommodation after she began feeling faint and nearly collapsed. Sannie had taken statements from Elizabeth and Samantha, then allowed them to go home from the lodge.

'What's all this about the helicopter pilot?' Sannie asked as she, Sean, Mia and Bongani came together in the light cast by Mia's Land Rover's headlights.

'Mike,' Sean said. 'He's new, a temporary replacement, as it happens. He only started a month or so ago. Rick, the normal pilot, came down with bad food poisoning and ended up in hospital in Joburg. After he recovered, he couldn't cross the provincial border back into Mpumalanga to come back to work. Mike showed up out of the blue, looking for work.'

'I saw the chopper touch down, briefly, while we were chasing the poacher,' Mia said, 'after I had shot that guy.'

'Yes,' Sannie said. 'Sean and I also saw that. It wasn't far from us. He said he'd seen something, a flash of colour that caught his eye.'

'It was a plastic bag,' Sean said for Mia's benefit.

'And then?' Mia asked.

'Then he took Phillip and his dog, Askari, outside the reserve, where an ambulance collected them. After that he returned to his search,' Sean said.

Mia looked to both of them. 'The action all took place so close to the perimeter fence that it would only take him a minute or two to come and go from the reserve.'

'Plenty of time to fly a poacher out, as well,' Sannie said.

'He took his sweet time getting to us in the first place,' Sean said.

Mia nodded. 'Meaning that while we were tracking the two guys with the impala, the helicopter could have been picking up Laura and our disappearing old guy.'

Chapter 15

The police crime scene investigation unit set up under floodlights, with much tutting and muttering about the number of people who had trampled the area where Laura had last been seen. Sannie did not hold out much hope that they would discover anything useful.

She decided to drive to Kaya Nghala Lodge. Sean Bourke travelled with her and made a couple of calls to try to ascertain the whereabouts of Julianne Clyde-Smith's relief helicopter pilot. He ended a call.

'That was Alison Byrne,' he said to Sannie, 'Julianne's super-efficient lodge manager. She says Mike flew to Nelspruit this morning, to the local airfield there, where some avionics guy was going to fix his radio, which wasn't working properly. He returned this afternoon, as we saw, then picked up my dog, Benny, from my house and dropped him with my guys, out in the field. However, he's now on his way to Nelspruit to fix something else. She's given me his cell phone number.'

Sean put his phone on speaker and dialled the pilot. The number went through to a computer-generated voicemail, giving the number of Mike's phone.

'We need to talk to this guy, ASAP,' Sannie said.

'Seems like it,' Sean said.

'The poacher was heading west when we lost him,' Sannie said, thinking aloud. 'I'm going to find some more officers and go to Killarney. We'll see if anyone saw anything.'

'Let me know if I can help,' Sean said.

Sean and Sannie arrived at Kaya Nghala, and Sannie parked in a visitor's spot near the thatched portico. They got out of the car and nodded to Mia and Bongani, who were standing, waiting, by their Land Rover. In the reception area, they spotted Julianne leading Sue Barker, now wrapped in a blanket, into her office. A few moments later, Julianne emerged from the office alone. 'She's calling her husband. I think she's in shock.'

Sannie nodded. 'I need the full name of your helicopter pilot and his date of birth.'

Julianne ran a hand through her hair. 'I'll have Audrey print out his employment record. Do you think he's in on it?'

'Maybe,' Sannie said. Julianne spotted Mia outside and called her over to join them.

'Yes?' Mia said.

'The captain wants to talk to Mike, the new helicopter pilot. Was he involved in your contact with the poacher this morning?'

'It was Mia who came up with the theory that the pilot may be involved,' Sannie said.

Julianne nodded. 'Good work, Mia.'

'Mike was in Nelspruit this morning. He took off at dawn, as we were leaving to go on our game drive,' Mia said.

Sannie took out her notebook and started writing.

'Could Mike have touched down and picked up the poacher and taken him away this morning?'

'I think it's possible,' Mia said. 'The bush was quite thick where we lost him, and we got sidetracked, following a second man. Mike was supposed to be in Nelspruit by then, but who knows if he actually went?'

Sannie looked up. 'Could he have landed, though, if there was no open space?'

'He wouldn't have needed to,' Julianne said. 'I had the Robinson, the chopper, fitted with a winch and a jungle penetrator, at Sean's suggestion. The penetrator looks like a little bomb on the end of a cable, but it has four flaps that fold out so an anti-poaching ranger, and a dog if required, can be lowered or extracted through the treetop canopy.'

'I'm afraid that's true,' Sean said, 'it was my idea, but I didn't think it'd be used to help criminals get away.'

'So, the pilot could have extracted the poacher, and not even have left much evidence on the ground, like wind-blown debris or what-what-what?' Sannie said.

Julianne nodded. 'Exactly.'

'Alfred was following a poacher who also seemingly disappeared,' Mia said. 'When a rhino was killed, three or four weeks ago.'

'Alfred?' Sannie said.

'One of our other senior rangers,' Mia said. 'He claimed it was the poacher's muthi that turned him into water so that he could not be recognised. The chopper was up during that contact, helping us look for the guy. And Captain ...?'

Sannie looked up. 'Yes, Mia?'

'It could be a coincidence, but Bongani and I both came down with food poisoning earlier this afternoon. It was only a mild dose, but it might be worth us checking the source of the former pilot's poisoning.'

Julianne had her phone out. She dialled a number and waited. 'Audrey? I need our new helicopter pilot's full name, date of birth, contact details – everything you have on him.'

A camouflaged anti-poaching vehicle pulled up outside under the portico and Sean went out to meet it. On board were Oscar and Graham, and another man in the back of the vehicle, with a dog. As soon as the black and tan Malinois jumped out and ran to Sean Sannie recognised it as Benny, Sean's personal dog. Sean spoke to the men, took something from one of them, then came back inside, with Benny trotting happily alongside him.

'Anything new?' Julianne asked, a mix of hope and desperation plain in the question.

'Yes and no,' Sean said. 'Oscar and Graham said Mike was in a hurry to get away from the reserve after he dropped Benny off to them. Get the mother for me, please.'

'I'll go,' Mia said. She walked towards Julianne's office.

Sean held out a woollen beanie. 'Benny found this, near the waterhole where we lost the second guy, in that clearing where the chopper touched down.'

Hearing his name, the dog looked up at them.

'One of the other handlers took Benny to the termite mound, where Laura was last seen,' Sean said, 'and he went crazy, indicating all over the place. He had her jacket to work off.'

'And then?' Julianne pressed him.

'They followed the trail to where Mia killed the one guy, then further on, and Benny picked up the girl's scent again near where the chopper landed, and found the beanie.'

'So, if the poachers didn't have Laura they at least took her beanie?'

Sean shrugged. 'Looks like it.'

'To fool the dog, maybe, with a false trail?' Sannie realised they couldn't wait around until they got all the details on the helicopter pilot and started an official criminal record check. She moved a few paces away from the others, took out her phone and called Henk de Beer in Nelspruit.

'Henk, there's a chopper heading for the general aviation airfield at Nelspruit. I need you to send a car there and pick up the pilot for me. The helo belongs to Lion Plains Game Reserve.'

'Jissus, but we're busy, Sannie. Is it urgent?'

'This is important, Henk. We've got another missing kid, Laura Barker, a Brit.'

Sannie could hear a sigh down the phone line. 'All right, then, you've got it, Sannie.'

'Thanks, Henk. I owe you. Call me when you have the guy. I need to talk to him, as soon as possible.'

'Hundred per cent. Oh, and I meant to say this morning, I'm sorry about Tom. We're all praying for you.'

The good thing, Sannie thought, about being busy in this crazy time, was that for a few seconds every now and then, she did forget. Of course, that just made it harder when someone said something nice.

'Thanks, Henk. Let me know how you get on with the pilot.'

'Will do.'

Sannie ended the call and then dialled her son Christo's cell phone.

'Hi, Mom.'

She heard gunfire in the background, but assumed it was *Call of Duty*. 'How are you, my boy, and how's Tommy?' Sannie saw movement out of the corner of her eye; Mia escorted Sue Barker to Sean, who was showing her the beanie.

'*Ja*, I'm fine, Mom. Tommy went to bed early. He's not so good, you know. Crying again. I made him dinner.'

Sannie closed her eyes; Christo's words pierced her. 'Thank you, my angel, you're a good brother. I'm tied up on a case and I'm about to make my way to Killarney. I don't know when I'll get home.'

'No problem, Mom.'

'You sure you're OK?'

'We're *fine*, Mom. Bye.'

Sannie ended the call. Mia was leading Sue back into the lodge. Sean walked over to her.

'The beanie?' Sannie asked.

'Laura's,' Sean confirmed. 'Did you say you want to go to Killarney?'

She checked her watch. 'I do.'

'Then let me and Benny ride along,' Sean said.

Sannie pursed her lips. 'You don't have any authority outside the reserve, Sean.'

He let a small grin escape. 'Hasn't stopped me chasing poachers there before.'

'*Ja*, no, well, I'll pretend I didn't hear that. Fine. But I call the shots, OK?'

'OK. This poacher got away somehow – even if we don't know how. I'll have my guys and the other dog and handler, when they get here, keep checking this side of the perimeter fence, though it's dangerous for the dog at night with leopards and lions and such around.'

'Worse for Laura.'

'True. I'd love to know how these guys are getting in and out. If it's that chopper pilot I'll *moer* him myself.'

'Well, someone from the organised crime division in Nelspruit should be questioning him soon.'

They made for the entrance as Mia returned and intercepted them. 'Where are you going?'

'Killarney,' Sannie said.

'Bongani and I will come with.'

'No,' Sean and Sannie said in unison.

'We can't just sit around here twiddling our thumbs. Bongani's from Killarney; he's well respected there. People will be more likely to talk to him than you, Captain.'

Bongani joined them. 'Let us come with you, Captain.'

'No,' Sannie said again.

Bongani looked to Mia. 'We have information,' he said.

Mia looked up at the thatched roof and Sannie noticed her cheeks colour. 'What is it, Mia?'

Mia shot Bongani a disapproving glance, then turned back to Sannie. 'There's a young man.'

'What young man?' Sannie asked, impatient.

'When our volunteer, Sara, was wounded in the attack this morning, we tracked two poachers. They both got away, but I got a look at one of them.'

'He is just a boy,' Bongani said. 'We planned on going to visit him in Killarney, to get him to tell us about the poacher who has been eluding us. Then all this happened.'

'This boy might be able to give us some information,' said Sannie. 'What's his name?'

'I don't know,' Mia said, too quickly for Sannie's liking, and she noticed the funny look Bongani gave Mia.

Sannie had no time for games. She would get the name from her, but they needed to get moving. Mia was probably right, as well, Sannie thought, about the benefit of having Bongani with them to help put the community more at ease. 'Very well, follow us, Mia, but you are to point this young man out to us, or take us straight to him.'

'Yes, Captain.' Mia jogged off to her Land Rover before Sannie could admonish her further.

Sannie drove through the night with Sean and Benny the dog, who, with his head out the window and tongue lolling, barked at an elephant when Sannie stopped to let it cross the road. At least someone was having fun, she thought.

Sannie gripped the steering wheel hard. Driving after dark in the bush posed extra dangers, because animals could wander out onto the road without warning. The speed limit was there for a reason, but she again felt her patience wavering. When they exited the gate she pressed the accelerator pedal into the floor as she changed gears. Sean, she noticed, was holding on to the armrest.

Ten minutes later she slowed as they entered the village of Killarney. A dog barked at their approach, but other than that there was no sign of movement on the darkened street. Mia and Bongani had been hanging back in their open vehicle, to avoid Sannie's dust, and she waited for them to catch up.

'Do you know the boy's house?' Sannie asked as they pulled up alongside her.

'Third on the right,' Bongani said, 'the one with the blue door. He's a strange child; they call him "the snake boy".'

'Snake boy?' Sannie said. As she suspected, Bongani and Mia knew exactly who their prospective quarry was. Sannie recalled her interview with the girl, Sonto. 'Is his name Sipho?'

'Yes. You know of him?' Bongani asked. Sannie nodded. 'He collects reptiles. Most of us are terrified of snakes, but this boy likes them.'

'He's got a pangolin in there somewhere as well,' Mia said. 'He was carrying it this morning.'

'Great,' Sannie replied. 'We can probably take him in for questioning based on the pangolin alone.'

'Let's leave the vehicles here,' Sean suggested. 'Go in quietly.'

They got out and Sannie drew her Z88 pistol from its holster. Sean clipped a lead to Benny's tracking collar. Mia and Bongani followed them as they moved quietly down the street.

'Take Benny around the back, Sean,' Sannie whispered, 'in case anyone inside makes a run for it.'

A dog somewhere nearby started barking, perhaps catching Benny's scent. The noise set off a rooster from the yard of the house next to the one with the blue door.

Sannie went up to the tin door and banged on it. 'Police, open up!'

Sannie heard a noise inside, like scuffling feet, then the squeak of another door opening somewhere. She tried the handle in front of her; the door was locked so she rammed it with her shoulder. It was solid, so she stepped back half a pace and shot the lock, then kicked it open.

'Benny!' Sean called from the rear of the house. '*Rim hom!*'

It was the command, Sannie knew, for the dog to attack. As soon as she stepped into the small house, however, her pace was checked by the sight of a Mozambican spitting cobra rearing up at her from the floor, its hood flared.

Sannie had the presence of mind to turn her head to one side and bring up an arm as she took a step back and collided with Mia and Bongani. 'Snake!'

The cobra expectorated a stream of stinging venom at her, most of which went onto the sleeve of her shirt, though some splashed her cheek. Sannie knew that the stuff would blind a human or animal victim in minutes if it wasn't washed off.

Bongani took a pair of reading glasses from his pocket, put them on and looked around. He found a broom and pushed past Sannie, also averting his eyes as he chased the now angry snake.

Sannie and Mia backed out into the yard.

'Are you OK?' Mia asked.

'*Ja*, fine. Let's go around the back.'

They ran down the side of the modest house.

'*Auf,*' Sean said to Benny.

The Malinois had the boy on the ground, the dog's jaws clamped around his right shoulder. Benny let go and looked up at Sean, grinning.

'Good boy, Benny, good boy.' Sean pulled out a chew toy, a ball on the end of a short piece of rope, from the pocket of his cargo pants and tossed it a little way away. Benny raced for it.

Sannie took a pair of handcuffs from her belt pouch as she strode to the young man. 'Face down, hands behind your back!'

'That dog tried to kill me,' the boy protested.

Mia peered over Sannie's shoulder. 'There's not a mark on you.'

'Benny's trained to bite with the back of his mouth, so the teeth don't break the skin,' Sean said. He ruffled his dog's fur as Benny trotted back over to him. 'Good boy, Benny.'

'What do you want with me? I'm innocent,' the boy said.

With the cuffs locked on him, Sannie rolled him over and hauled him to his feet. 'What's your name?'

He looked at the ground, but Sannie put a finger under his chin and tilted his face up.

'I am Sipho Nyarhi.'

'Sipho – you're the friend of the girls who disappeared, Lilly and Thandi, yes?'

He looked at her, then away, and shrugged.

'Answer me.'

'I know them, yes, but I don't know what happened to them.'

He could not, she noticed, continue to meet her eyes. She was sure he knew more. 'This lady here,' she gestured to Mia, 'says she saw you in the Sabi Sand Game Reserve this morning, and that you had a pangolin. Where is it?'

Sipho kept his head lowered. 'I don't know anything about a pangolin and I was never in the reserve.'

Sannie grabbed Sipho's upper arm and marched him back inside the house, through the back door.

Bongani met them in the cluttered, cement-floored room that passed for a kitchen. 'I caught the snake, put it back in one of the glass cases.'

Sannie wrinkled her nose as she walked through to the lounge area. All around her, stacked against the walls was an assortment of old bird cages, fish tanks with partially shattered glass and anything else that could contain a live creature. There were several snakes as well as a tank with mice crawling over each other – presumably food for the reptiles – and an assortment of lizards of various sizes.

Sannie glimpsed movement on the floor from under a battered old sofa, stuffing spilling from wounds in the fabric. She side-stepped quickly, but was marginally relieved when she saw a fat monitor lizard, nearly a metre long, waddle into the centre of the room and make its way languidly towards a single-bar electric heater, which it lay down next to.

'Do you have permits for any of these?' Sannie let go of the boy – he was cuffed and surrounded by all of them now in any case. Benny the dog snarled up at the cobra that had spat at Sannie; the snake struck back, its fangs tapping on the glass of its enclosure. Benny retreated to Sean's side.

Mia walked along the rows of specimens. 'Puff adder, rinkhals, house snake, large plated lizard, boomslang ... sheesh,' Mia crouched by the largest of the old fish tanks, 'there's even a juvenile rock python here – endangered.'

'No paperwork?' Sannie pressed.

The boy nodded to the far wall. 'I am famous.'

Sannie walked over and studied a faded press clipping from *The Lowvelder* stuck to the wall with tape. '"*Snake man of Killarney charms savage serpents*". That's not a permit, Sipho.'

Bongani took a step closer to the shackled boy. 'I've seen cars from out of town parked outside this house. Expensive – Range Rovers, late model Beemers, Mercedes – I thought you might have been dealing drugs. But snakes? *Eish.*'

'Who are your customers, Sipho?' Sannie asked.

He looked up and stared at her, defiance plain in his eyes and the set of his mouth.

Bongani's hand shot out, faster than any striking cobra, and slapped the young man on the cheek. Sipho rocked on his feet.

'Answer the captain,' Bongani said.

Sannie did not condone brutality and certainly not torture, but three young girls were missing and she did not have the time or the resources to spend on this insolent young criminal, even though she probably had enough to open a docket and take him to Skukuza Police Station at Number 1 Leopard Street, at least overnight.

Sipho rubbed his jaw. 'You can't hit me.'

Bongani turned and walked across to the terrarium containing a puff adder. He took the glass lid off and carefully reached in, grabbing the snake behind the head. Sannie took an involuntarily step backwards.

'You know why this is the most dangerous snake in Africa, boy?' Bongani said as he came to Sipho.

The young man flinched. 'Because it bites the most people. It waits, in ambush, for someone to step on it. It doesn't try to escape, like other snakes would.'

Bongani nodded. 'You have no escape, boy.'

Sannie held her breath as Bongani brought the snake, now wriggling in annoyance, up to Sipho's face.

'Bongani ...' Mia said.

He glared at her. 'Not now. This boy has betrayed his people. You think you care for wildlife, by keeping these creatures here in unsanitary conditions, barely alive. You make me sick, boy. You know what this venom will do to you, when the snake bites you, how it will eat away the skin of that young face?'

Sipho gave a small nod. Bongani brought the puff adder closer. The fat reptile's tongue was flicking in and out, the forked tip almost brushing Bongani's cheek.

Sannie knew she could not let the boy be bitten.

'Wait,' Sipho said.

'What is it?' Sannie asked.

'Some men came to me, from Johannesburg.'

Bongani moved the snake so that it was in front of Sipho's eyes.

'All right, all right,' Sipho protested. 'These men, they offered me money to find more snakes for them.'

'So you *were* in the reserve this morning?' Sannie said.

'I knew it was him,' Mia said.

Bongani eased the snake back into the terrarium. 'You were with the poacher who shot the woman,' Bongani said.

Sipho shook his head. 'No. I heard the shots, but I was not with that man. I was not trying to kill a rhino.'

'Taking a pangolin is just as bad,' Mia said.

'I'm going to take Benny to search out the back,' Sean said.

'Fine,' Sannie said, then turned back to Sipho. 'Who were the men who wanted you to find a pangolin?'

Sipho shrugged his shoulders.

'Do you want me to ask Bongani to get the puff adder again?'

Sipho looked past her. Clearly he was afraid of Bongani, who glared at him. 'No. I don't know their names.'

'Had you ever seen them before?'

He pursed his lips.

'We can go to the police station, Sipho.'

'All right. Yes. They have been a few times in the past, to buy snakes from me. Is that against the law?'

'Probably, but I've got more important things on my mind right now. Why did they want snakes?'

'For umuthi.'

'Serious?'

He nodded. 'Yes. They said a sangoma in Johannesburg wanted deadly snakes, a mamba in particular.'

'What for? To kill someone?'

'No, the opposite, to protect people. Some izangoma, they use pieces of snake,' he held up his cuffed hands with one pinkie finger extended, 'maybe this long, to sell to protect people from bullets.'

'So, a few centimetres of dead snake will keep a hijacker safe from being shot?'

He nodded. 'Yes. They say it is very strong umuthi.'

'And you, the snake man of Killarney,' she glanced over at the press clipping on the wall, 'who supposedly "loves" snakes, will sell his friends the reptiles to be cut into little pieces to make umuthi.'

He sneered. 'There are plenty of snakes around here, Captain.'

'That's what the rhino poachers say about rhinos, but if you keep killing them, then there will be none left.'

'How else must I eat? There is no work here.'

Sannie did not have time to address the fundamental problems of the South African economy. 'The old man you were with, in the game reserve –'

'I was alone,' Sipho interrupted.

'The others say you were a decoy, that you were in the park, without a weapon, as bait. The plan was that you would run, the rangers would chase you, while the other poacher, an older man, would kill a rhino and escape with the horn. Who is he?'

'I don't know.'

Sannie held his eye. 'I don't believe you, Sipho. I can arrange a polygraph, a lie detector test. You will fail.'

He shrugged. 'You can do whatever you want to me, even bring back Bongani with my puff adder, and I will tell you that I was in the reserve alone. I was looking for snakes, but I found a pangolin instead.'

'Worth more.' Sannie tried to read him. She sensed that he was not going to say anything else, and that he was lying, because he was afraid. What or who he feared was more dangerous than any snake.

'I have been bitten by snakes before,' he said, as if to confirm what she was thinking. She doubted he had been bitten in the face, but Sannie was not about to allow Bongani to make good her terrible threat.

'Sipho, it's the girls I'm worried about. There are now three. Another has gone missing.'

There was a flinch, the ever-so-slight raising of his eyebrows.

'I know nothing about that,' he said quietly.

Sannie heard barking from outside.

'Good boy, Benny,' she heard Sean call from the rear of the house. 'Captain!'

Sannie turned Sipho around and grabbed the handcuffs and propelled him ahead of her, out the back door. 'What is it, Sean?'

'A dead body.'

'Keep an eye on Sipho,' Sannie said to Mia, and rushed out.

*

'Bongani,' Mia looked to her partner, 'please go outside and see if the captain needs help.'

Bongani hesitated for a second, then nodded and walked out.

'Sipho,' Mia said in Xitsonga, 'listen to me. The police captain wants the missing girls. If you cooperate I am sure we can find a way to keep you out of prison. You know me, don't you trust me?'

He eyed her warily. Bongani had scared him, but Mia now had to quickly win his trust. He said nothing.

'Sipho, you know me,' she repeated. 'Now, you must help them. The pangolin will die if they take you away.'

He looked into her eyes. 'Can you protect me?'

'I swear I will try.' She knew this village. It was more than likely that the local people would deliver Sipho a beating, but the boy seemed worried about something more sinister. 'Help us. Help the girls ...'

He hesitated, then said: 'I will tell you where it is, if you help me.'

'Where?' Mia asked. She sensed that if she could get him to show her the pangolin then she would have breached his defences and he might tell her more.

'In the cupboard, in my bedroom.'

She followed Sipho. Mia had to sidestep to avoid the monitor lizard, which scurried out of her way and under the sofa. God knew what else was crawling or slithering around this place. She went into Sipho's bedroom, which was furnished with a rusty old metal bedframe and a stained mattress partially visible under a yellowed sheet. In the corner, however, was a flat-screen TV with a DSTV satellite decoder; young Sipho was making reasonable money from his part in the muthi trade.

Mia went to the chipboard wardrobe in the corner and, tentatively, opened it, not knowing what might spring out at her. In the bottom was a hessian sack. She dragged it out and opened it.

The pangolin, a hefty sample, was rolled up to the size of a basketball. Mia gently caressed its armoured scales. The pangolin was engaging his primary means of defence, curling himself into a ball and doing nothing. It was what made the creatures so laughably easy for poachers to pick up and transport. The meat was prized in Asia as a delicacy and the scales were worth a fortune in Chinese traditional medicine – the pangolin was doubly doomed. The jury was out on whether the market in pangolins would die off because of their reported links to coronavirus, or if the temporary halt in trade would just increase their value once international borders were open again and bans on Chinese wet markets lifted.

'There isn't even any water in here for it.'

Mia had read that many trafficked pangolins died because the poachers who took them did not know what to feed them or how to care for them. She had at least expected slightly better from the 'snake boy' of Killarney.

'Sipho, the captain just wants to find the girls, and I think you want to help them as well. If you agree to talk to her, I will speak up for you.'

He licked his lips. His nervousness was palpable and Mia sensed he was not just scared about going to the Skukuza cells.

'I want to help, but I need the police to protect me.'

'Come,' Mia said, 'we will go see the captain.'

*

Sannie, Bongani, Sean and Benny were standing over the body of a man.

'Male, aged about forty, I'd say,' Sean said. 'Shot, though I didn't hear anything.'

'Forty-two, same age as me,' Bongani said.

'You know him?' Sannie asked.

Bongani nodded. 'Richard Baloyi. I went to school with him. I knew him, but he was not a friend. He was always in trouble.'

Sean clipped Benny's tracking lead on him and pulled him away. Sannie appreciated Sean's thinking – Benny was getting too close to the body and risked contaminating the crime scene.

'It's the second time his name has come up,' Sannie said. 'In trouble with the police?'

'With everyone,' Bongani said. 'Women, other men. He stole, and more than once the community took matters into their own hands.'

Sannie knelt by the body. 'I saw this man today. He ran from me, so that fits with what you say of his background, Bongani.'

'He had been working at the community project,' Bongani said, 'volunteering.'

Sannie thought Bongani said the last word with some disdain.

'Him and a man named Solly,' Sannie said. 'You don't think Richard was the type to volunteer?'

Bongani shrugged. 'I suppose anyone can find redemption, eventually, and there is not a lot else for people to do. He was a *skelm*, a criminal.'

Sannie called her crime scene investigation team in the Sabi Sand reserve and asked them to come to Killarney when they finished there. It was going to be a long night for the technicians.

Mia came out of the house, took one glance at the body then looked back at Sannie. In her arms she carried a pangolin. Sipho walked behind her.

Sannie couldn't resist having a look at the creature. 'You know,' she said, 'in all my life of living near the bush and going to the Kruger Park and working there, I've never seen one of these things.'

'That's part of the problem,' Mia said. 'They're not as well known as rhinos or elephants, so they don't get the same level of media coverage or public interest. I'll get it some water, at least, for the ride.'

'The ride?'

'Sipho's agreed to talk, Captain,' Mia said, 'but maybe it would be better at the station.'

Sannie looked to the boy, who nodded. She saw the fear in his eyes. 'All right. Let's get moving then.' Sannie led the way back through Sipho's house and out the front door.

As Sannie took out her car keys there was a series of bangs, something hitting the metal panels of Sannie's Fortuner, and a side window shattered.

Sannie grabbed Sipho's shoulder and shoved him forward so that he landed hard on the road. She knelt next to him, one hand holding him down, the other reaching for her pistol.

The others were all taking cover, though Sean, down on one knee behind Sannie's car, was looking for source of the gunfire.

Another round slammed into the vehicle and Sannie was able to get a rough fix on where the gunman was. 'Silenced rifle, fifty metres down the road, Sean, past the house with the green door.' It wasn't unusual for poachers to have suppressors fitted to their rifles when sneaking around the game reserves. Sannie fired two shots at a window next to the door.

'Seen!' Sean squeezed off four rounds. Benny lay obediently next to his master. With his high-powered rifle, Sean had a better chance of hitting the shooter, or at least keeping his head down. The other weapon opened up, two rounds in quick succession, forcing Sannie to duck behind the cover of her vehicle.

'Sipho!' Mia cried.

The boy had managed to roll away from Sannie and struggle his way up onto his knees, then feet. He sprinted down the street.

'Get down!' Sannie yelled at him.

Sipho kept running, away from them and the incoming fire, legs pounding. At one point his toe clipped a rock and he started to pitch forward. In the weak glow of a lonely streetlight it looked like he was going to get away.

The rifle opened up on them again, pinning them all down.

Sipho was just about out of sight when the bullet hit him.

He stumbled again, the momentum of his run propelling him mercilessly into the unforgiving surface of the gravel road.

'Sipho!' Sannie called.

There was no answer. The gunfire stopped.

Mia ran to Sipho and dropped to the ground next to him.

By the time Sannie reached them, it was clear Sipho was dead.

Chapter 16

Mia returned, dirty and bloodied, to her quarters. It was after ten pm and Captain van Rensburg had told her she was no longer needed in Killarney, which had become a crime scene thronged with police.

Julianne was with Sue Barker, and despite Mia's offer to stay with the traumatised woman, Julianne told Mia to get some rest. Her protest had been half-hearted – she was shattered, emotionally and physically, by the day's events. She and Bongani had been on the move for longer than any of the others now involved in the search and investigation, starting with chasing the poachers just after dawn. Graham and Oscar were helping the police with a door-to-door night-time search of homes in Killarney.

As she reached for the doorhandle a man appeared from the room next to hers, which had been vacant for some time.

'Hi.'

It was the Canadian, the researcher.

'Jeff,' he reminded her.

She tried a smile but had no idea if it showed on her face. 'Hello.'

'You look beat.'

She managed a small, unexpected laugh. 'You know how to flatter a girl.'

'Tough day?'

'And night.' All she had wanted was to crawl into bed and, like a child, pull the covers over her head to hide from the horrors she had witnessed. Now, however, she found herself on edge, almost scared to go inside, in case there was something, or someone, lurking there. *I killed a man.*

Jeff reached into the pocket of his khaki shorts and pulled out a joint. 'I hope you don't mind.'

She shrugged. Drugs were banned – Julianne sometimes employed one of Sean's dogs, cross-trained in narcotics detection, to sweep the staff and back-of-house areas of the lodge, although marijuana was technically legal for personal use in South Africa.

'No problem with me,' Mia said. 'Just don't let Julianne catch you.'

'She *was* kind enough to let me stay here a few days while I carry out my interviews.' He started to put the cigarette back in his shorts.

'Be a shame to waste it,' she said. 'I'm, like, so exhausted, but I don't think I could sleep.'

Jeff smiled. He was a good-looking guy. He took out a lighter and lit it, took a hit to get it going, then passed it to her. 'You don't mind breaking social distancing protocols?'

She inhaled deeply, held the smoke in and passed the *zol* back to him, then exhaled. Jeff pulled up two plastic chairs, one from outside each of their rooms. He took a drag and passed it back to her. A scops owl chirped nearby; normally the shrill call calmed her, but now it set her nerves further on edge.

Mia settled into the chair, hoping the drug would soon take effect. She passed it back to Jeff.

He took another toke. 'Pretty shitty day and night, from what I've heard around camp.'

She nodded.

'Want to talk about it?'

Mia closed her eyes.

'That bad?'

She nodded, exhaling a stream of smoke towards the starry sky. Mia rubbed her eyes.

'Want a beer?' Jeff asked.

Mia looked at her watch. 'Why not?'

He got up, returning a minute later with two green bottles of Windhoek Lager.

'At least you've learned about good beer since you've been here.'

'My first lesson.' He used one bottle, upturned, to lever the cap off the other. 'That was my second lesson.'

She took the proffered bottle. 'Third?'

He pulled his cigarette lighter out of his pants pocket again and used the end of it, hooked under the cap and over the crook of the finger around the neck of the bottle, to flick this one open. He clinked glass on glass. 'Third.'

Mia chuckled. 'You're almost African now.'

'I kind of am. My father's South African; he moved to Canada in the early 1990s and met my mom there. I was born there. Sure you don't want to talk?'

Mia closed her eyes again and drew a breath. Her head was fuzzy, not quite spinning, but the smoke and beer were calming her. 'I killed a man today.'

'My God. I'm sorry. I heard a poacher was shot and a girl went missing, but I didn't know …'

'It's all right.' She rubbed her temple, feeling a headache coming on. She should have remembered from her university days that dagga did not agree with her. 'In fact, it's not all right. Two men were killed in Killarney and two more girls have gone missing recently. It's a fucking nightmare.'

'That's crazy.' He sucked the last from the roach. 'I'm not the greatest at consoling people, but do you, like, need a hug or something?'

That sounded crazy, but she could not think why not. 'Sure.'

He scooted his chair closer to hers and put his arm around her. She rested her head on his shoulder. He smelled of marijuana smoke and Sunlight soap. Mia wondered what Graham would think if he showed up now. He would be jealous, but she wondered if he really cared for her, or just wanted sex. She sometimes wondered the same thing about her feelings for him.

'What's going on in this place?' Jeff said. 'I thought Julianne Clyde-Smith prided herself on running the safest reserve in Africa, for wildlife at least.'

'She did, does.' Mia eased out of his embrace. It had been nice, if weird, to feel the warmth of another, but she did not want to lead Jeff on. 'And it was the safest, for a time, though she's had troubles in the past. Everyone thought that was all over, but now she's lost several rhinos and, worse, the girl, just as tourism is starting to open up again. This could crush her.'

'How did – whoever – get away with the girl, do you think?'

Mia went over the facts as she knew them, as much for own benefit as his, trying once more to work out what had happened. 'And then I killed the poacher and everyone, Bongani and me included, lost the tracks of the remaining guy.'

'He vanished?' Jeff said.

'*They* vanished.'

'Wow. Like, totally disappeared?'

'Yes. I can't work it out.'

Jeff stubbed out the last, tiny remains of the joint. 'There must be a rational explanation.'

'Says the man studying umuthi for a living.'

'I didn't say I believed in it, well, not all of it.'

Mia rubbed her head again. 'What do you believe in?'

'The power of suggestion.'

'And?'

He shrugged. 'Love? God? I don't know. Ritual.'

'Let me ask you a direct question, no philosophical bullshit,' Mia said, fixing him with her gaze.

'Shoot.'

'Do you believe this poacher we're trying to track – and failing at it – is defeating us with umuthi?'

Jeff held her stare for a while, the corners of his mouth eventually turning up. 'You've just answered your own question.'

'How so?'

He held up a hand. 'First up, it helps that you're now stoned.'

'Yes, agreed, but it's a serious question, and I don't see how I answered it by asking.'

'You *did*,' Jeff said. 'The very fact that you are considering the intangible, the paranormal, that you are the tiniest bit willing to suspend belief and stop looking for a rational reason for how this guy is running rings around you is proof that his medicine is working.'

She shook her head. 'Bullshit.'

'Tell me,' he said, placing a hand on her forearm to make her look back at him. She did, but didn't move his hand, and nor did he. 'Did the poacher leave anything behind, any signs of his magic?'

'Yes. He placed some woven string across the trail he'd been using.'

'And what happened?'

'Bongani freaked out, is what happened,' Mia said. 'I've heard of that sort of distraction being used, but never seen it in action. I'm normally tracking animals, not people.'

'There you go.'

'*There you go*, what?'

'The fact that Bongani had a reaction meant that the poacher's muthi worked, that it did the trick. It forced him, for however long, to lose concentration and stop focusing on the job at hand.'

Mia slumped back in her chair again, the fatigue once more catching up with her. The marijuana might have given her mind a moment's reprieve, but the fatigue and beer were now winning the battle for her body again. 'Yes, but not for long.'

'That might have been enough.'

'I lost the tracks as well,' Mia said.

'I'm not surprised,' Jeff said.

'Ha! I'll have you know I'm a pretty good tracker.'

'Very good,' Jeff said, 'from what I hear, but unlike Graham you're a believer.'

'In umuthi?'

'In power,' he said, spreading his arms wide, 'the force, whatever you want to call it. Tell me, when you track an animal do you try to get into its mind?'

'Yes, we do.'

'That's not out of a textbook, that's power; shape-shifting, irrational anthropomorphic shit.'

'Yes and no. It's partly out of a book, like the field guides we read to learn about animals, birds and reptiles. We learn their behaviour and try to use that knowledge to predict what they're going to do at certain times of the day. Like, if it's hot, they'll go towards water for a drink, or seek shade from the sun.'

Jeff shook his head. 'You just admitted, you try to get into its *mind*. Don't tell me you never stop, close your eyes and try to think like whatever it is you're following.'

She only had to consider that for a moment. 'OK, so, maybe, yes.'

'That's what the San, the bushmen, used to do, same as native Americans and many other first nations people with a strong affinity to the land. You're just learning to use the magic that tens of thousands of years has bred out of white European people.'

'Sounds nice and romantic, but here's the deal, Jeff. There's a man out there who's better than us and he's getting away from us, even from the dogs, every time.'

'Because his magic's stronger than yours.'

'Now that's just the dagga talking, Jeff.'

She shivered, and knew it was because she was tired and had stopped moving. Her bed was calling, but now she felt guilty, knowing the police, Graham and probably Sean and the others were all still out on the job. Bongani had stayed in Killarney, to sleep the night at his sister's place. His family – his wife and three children – had been staying with her parents during the rolling lockdowns, further north, at Acornhoek, on the way to Hoedspruit.

'Anything that puts you at a disadvantage creates an advantage for your opponent.'

'Even a piece of string across the trail?'

He nodded. 'Even that. Just think about it. The string of umuthi distracted you. It might have been put at that precise place for a reason. It might have been there that the poacher started work on a false trail, or doubled back, or –'

'Or put some socks over his shoes.'

Jeff raised his eyebrows. 'Really?'

'Yes. They do that because it makes it harder for us to make out a tread pattern or footprint. I didn't think that the poacher might have combined two tricks with one.'

'Then his muthi worked. Want another beer?'

Mia shook her head. 'I need to at least try to sleep, Jeff.'

'OK. Put your head down, even if only for an hour or two. You'll be no good to anyone dead on your feet, Mia.'

'I guess.'

He yawned. 'And I've got some more interviews in the morning.'

'OK, 'night.' She got up and went to go into her room.

'Oh, Mia?'

'Yes?'

'Which umuthi did you take today?'

She felt her face flush a little, despite her tiredness. 'Who said I did?'

He looked in her eyes. 'You're a believer, or, at least, you hedge your bets. There's nothing wrong with that.'

'You think you know everything.'

He shook his head. 'No, not at all, but this is what I do, I study this shit. And it's nothing to be ashamed of or embarrassed about. Did you know that Russian cosmonauts piss on the wheels of the vehicle that takes them to the launch pad?'

Mia let out a little laugh. 'No, I did not.'

'These people are scientists, military people, no-nonsense types. Even when they've taken non-Russians up to the space station they make them piss on the wheels as well. It's a ritual.'

'Superstition, more like it.'

He shrugged. 'Same thing, except what those cosmonauts have in common with poachers, and you and Bongani, and probably most of the other rangers I've spoken to, is that you're involved in high-risk, high-reward activities.'

'Reward as in money?'

'Partly, but for you the reward would have been successfully tracking someone – the poacher you're after.'

She thought about it. 'Maybe.'

'Let me ask you again,' Jeff said. 'Which umuthi did you take?'

'OK, you got me. Bongani has this stuff he chews, powdery stuff made from some kind of ground-up bark. It's to keep him safe from danger, like wild animals.'

'Why did you take it?'

'Because I was going after a guy with a gun.'

'Yes, but why did you think it would help you any more than your own skills would?'

She paused to think again, then shrugged. 'I don't know, I guess I was, like you say, hedging my bets.'

'You were going into a high-risk, high-reward situation.'

She nodded. 'When I chewed the stuff, it helped me. I won't say it was physical, or physiological or whatever, but the act of taking something focused me, calmed me, maybe. Perhaps there was actually something in the powder?'

'Or maybe,' Jeff said, 'the act just gave you that little bit of confidence. And in this case, you could say it worked – you weren't shot, and you got one of them.'

'I ...' Mia choked on her words and her eyes started to burn as the image of the man she'd killed flashed up in her mind. She blinked to try to hold back the tears, but they squeezed through her tight-pressed lids. 'I ...'

Jeff wrapped his arms around her again and she did not resist. Mia sobbed into his shirt, her body heaving with release as she did so.

'Come on,' he said gently, 'let's get you inside.'

Mia let Jeff lead her into her room. He kicked the door closed behind him with his foot, but she felt nothing but solace in his embrace as he steered her towards her bed.

He eased her down on the bed and she kicked off her boots. She sat there on the edge, almost as if she had forgotten how to get into bed. He lifted her legs and swung her onto the mattress.

'God, I'm exhausted,' she muttered.

He pulled back the cover on the other side of the double bed. 'Roll over.'

She did as he commanded and, awkwardly, she wriggled under the covers that he held up for her.

''Night, Mia.'

She blinked up at him. 'That guy I killed – I can't stop thinking about him.'

He looked down at her and nodded. 'I figured it was something like that.'

She started to cry again. 'Will you stay with me, Jeff, just a little while, please?'

'If you're sure?'

'I'm sure.'

'Then OK.' Fully clothed, and smelling of weed and beer, he lay down on his back next to her, though on top of the blankets, folded his hands across his chest and closed his eyes.

Mia felt his warmth, and it was enough just to know there was another human being in the room with her, to allow her to close her own eyes and let the tiredness wash over her and take her away.

Sleep came quickly, but so, too, did the nightmare. She heard the man talking again, in Xitsonga, telling his comrade he would see him again.

'*Where?*' Mia asked the dead man as he stood there, in front of her, bleeding from the gunshot wound she had inflicted on him, but showing no other ill effect.

'*In your life,*' he said to her, in English.

'*What do you mean?*'

'*You have killed me, so now I will be with you, forever.*'

He was going to haunt her, and he had said it so matter-of-factly, so calmly, that it made the curse all the more terrifying. In her dream Mia ran through the bush, past an elephant, who turned his big head to watch her as he fanned himself with his ears.

Breathless, Mia leaned against a leadwood tree, but when she peered around it the bleeding man was there, watching her. He had materialised, like the ghost he was, out of nowhere. She carried on, trying to escape him, but he was always there, appearing from behind the next tree, or waiting for her, here, when she returned to her room.

Jeff was there, as well, and he was naked, above her now, making love to her, and she felt bad, because she was supposed to be in love with Graham, but he was not there.

Is this a dream? she asked herself. She could feel Jeff's hands, soft, unlike Graham's. Mia smelled the marijuana and knew she was still stoned.

Real or dream?

Her arousal felt real, the warmth spreading from her lower belly out to her fingertips, her heart fluttering as Jeff kissed the inside of her thighs. She tried to call Graham's name, or was it Jeff's? She was confused and couldn't tell if a sound escaped her mouth.

Jeff didn't care. He began kissing her, down there, softly at first, gently brushing the insides of her thighs as his lips fluttered over her. He was mapping her, drawing each part of her into his mouth and sucking, tasting, until his tongue parted her and found the spot that was so hard, so swollen for him. She felt his hair, long, soft, between her fingers. Graham had a crew cut; Jeff's hair was almost like a girl's.

She wanted him now, but not soft and gentle, not his caresses. Mia was opening herself to Jeff, whispering to him, dirty words, hidden secrets, urging him on, and she could feel the change start to come over him.

Good, she smiled to herself.

This *is* a dream, she told herself, but then the guilt surfaced again. This could *not* be happening. Jeff was touching her now, in the dark under the covers, his finger finding her, rubbing her, becoming more slippery with each movement. She was arching her body, tilting her pelvis to reach for him, pushing herself onto him.

Was she? Really?

She was beyond caring as she felt her arousal mounting, like riding the crest of a perfect wave one time at Ballito, on one of the rare holidays her father had taken her on. He had gone to the coast for an army reunion, got drunk, abusive, and Mia had cried, but for the one moment when she had been on one of his friends' kids' boogie boards, she had felt the weightless rush of freedom and ridden that wave right in to shore, grinning all the way.

Jeff was taking her back there, giving her that feeling of pure bliss, of freedom, and she knew it was what she needed right now, to escape this terrible nightmare that her waking life had become. All she needed to do was surrender to his touch, whether that was happening in a dream or otherwise. For now, she enjoyed the sensation of his fingers on her.

'Yes,' she heard herself say.

Mia felt his stubble on her chin, scratchy, raw, possessive, not caring that he might mark her as he kissed her, passionately. She opened her mouth to him as she moved her legs to help him. She wanted him. It felt bad, wrong, but good and unstoppable, as though she had no hand in this, no say in the morality of it. She existed, in that moment, for him and his touch.

Mia's eyes felt like they were glued shut, so that even if she wanted to open them, to double-check whether or not this was a dream, she was incapable. Part of her wanted to tell him to get his hands off her, but the other wanted him to get her off. She *needed* this, to clear her mind, she told herself.

'Hey.'

Hey what? she asked herself in reply.

'Hey, what the fuck?'

Jeff was on top of her now, between her legs, rubbing himself against her. Her sense of pleasure, of anticipation, was heightened to the point where she wanted to scream at him to stop.

The problem was, someone was speaking – no, yelling.

'Get the fuck out of here, man!'

Mia thrashed in the bed, arms reaching up, to push Jeff off her, but she could feel nothing. Her hands flailed in thin air. She flung an arm out to the side in her bed and it connected with something.

'Ow!'

Her brain was foggy with fatigue, unable to comprehend what was happening here, whether she was moving from sleep to wakefulness, or if she had been conscious the whole time. If she was in the here and now, then why wasn't Jeff still touching her?

'What the hell are you doing?'

Mia saw the man she had shot, standing in her doorway, bellowing at Jeff, who was on his feet, still fully clothed.

Her heart pounded with fear and at last she was able to open her eyes properly. It was not, she saw with a relief that was immediately overtaken by dread, the dead poacher, but rather Graham, and he was punching Jeff.

Chapter 17

'Graham, no!'

Mia scrambled out of bed just as Jeff hit the screed concrete floor next to her.

Graham growled like a bear and stood over Jeff, reaching down for him and picking him up with one big hand wrapped in his shirt-front. The Canadian looked groggy, blood already flowing from his nose.

Mia had time to register that Jeff was fully clothed, and from the indentation on her mattress and drawn blankets on his side it looked as though he had remained on top of the bed and had not, in fact, been trying to make love to her. It had been a dream. That was a relief, but now Graham looked ready to kill Jeff.

Graham drew back his free right hand and prepared to knock Jeff unconscious.

Mia stepped between them and Graham's blow bounced off her forearm.

'Ow!' she protested.

'Sheesh, sorry. I mean, what were you up to?'

Jeff seemed barely conscious as he hung in Graham's grasp.

'Why was he in bed with you?'

'He was *on* my bed, you bloody brute.'

Graham let go of Jeff, who stumbled backwards a step, trying and failing to regain his balance. He fell to the floor and tenderly touched his nose, then shook his head.

'What was he doing *on* your bed in our room?'

'It's not "our" room, Graham,' she said, hands on hips. 'And you can't just storm in here and beat people up. Jeff was kind to me. I thought I couldn't sleep after yesterday and he helped me get to bed.'

Graham sneered. 'Then crawled into bed with you. Hell, Mia, what are you doing to me? I came here to see how you were getting on. I didn't know you'd be ... entertaining another man.'

'What is this, the nineteenth century? I wasn't entertaining any-one.' She looked at her watch. It was one in the morning. What the hell had Graham come here for anyway, a middle-of-the-night booty call? 'For goodness sake, get a Coke or a beer or something out of the fridge and apologise to Jeff. He didn't do anything.'

'Yeah, man,' Jeff said, at last able to speak, 'nothing happened.'

Mia turned to Jeff. 'Thank you for looking after me, but ...'

He touched his nose and winced. 'Yeah, maybe I should go. I don't want a broken arm.'

Graham glared at Jeff.

'Say sorry to him,' Mia said.

Graham said nothing.

'Sheesh, men.' She turned to Jeff. 'I'm sorry for what happened.'

'OK. Just do me a favour and think about what I said to you, about medicine – umuthi.'

'Ah, *kak*,' Graham said. 'Has this *oke* now been filling your head with more of that ... more of that shit?'

'Graham, please –'

He waved a hand in the air. 'These bastards are running rings around us and we're all contemplating our flippin' navels and talk-ing about black magic. It's crazy, Mia.'

Jeff ignored him. 'You've been through a trauma, Mia. You should think about doing something to help yourself. Maybe talk to a sangoma.'

'*Jislaaik*, I'm going to shoot someone just now,' Graham said.

Jeff held up a hand and backed out of the doorway.

'I'm sorry,' Mia said again.

Jeff shook his head. 'You don't need to apologise, Mia, and be-sides, I can understand how Graham might have felt.'

'Graham is in the *fokken* room, man,' Graham said.

Jeff nodded to her and closed the door.

Mia turned to Graham. 'There was no need for you to act like a bloody Neanderthal.'

'I'm no caveman.' He stabbed a finger at her. 'And you shouldn't let strange men into your room when you're alone.'

Mia seethed. 'Get out.'

'What?'

'Out!'

'Babe ...'

'Don't *Babe* me. Get out.'

'Mia, listen to me.'

She put her hands on her hips. 'No. You listen to me. Nothing happened with Jeff. He was kind and he helped me and I was so tired. I don't belong to you, Graham.'

He looked her up and down, as if appraising some farm animal. 'No, you're right. You don't.'

He turned and walked out. Mia slumped, her anger gone as fast as it had risen. She wondered if she had reacted so strongly because she did feel a tiny bit guilty over what had turned out to be her dream. It had seemed so real, though, Jeff gently though expertly and effectively coaxing her arousal. Graham was not like that when he made love. He was not ungenerous, but he was always in a hurry. That was not all bad, and she liked sex with him.

Liked.

Too tired to stay awake worrying about men, Mia lay down and drifted back to sleep, still in the grip of the joint and the beer.

Another nightmare, in which the man she had killed had Laura in his grasp, woke her again. It was still dark outside her window. Mia checked her watch and saw she had only slept another three hours or so. She sighed. She was still tired, but there was still so much to be done. She found her phone and texted Julianne Clyde-Smith, asking if there was any news of Laura. Her phone rang a few seconds later.

'Hello, Julianne, how are you?' she began.

'Still no sign of Laura.'

Julianne was English, so she spoke directly, straight to the point. African people, black and white, placed a high stock in manners and always asked after one another before getting down to business. Mia couldn't blame her employer this time, she supposed.

'Sue is under sedation,' Julianne continued. 'Did you sleep?'

'A few hours. Not well.' She left out the business of the boys fighting.

'I told Graham and Sean and the others to get some rest,' Julianne said. 'However, Sean's still out searching with his dog teams.'

'What do you want me to do?' Mia asked.

'There's nothing you can do.'

Mia was fairly sure the comment was not meant as a direct criticism, but nonetheless it stung.

'Bongani and I can help man the Vulture system again,' Mia said. 'We might pick up something.'

'Yes, sure, fine. Anything else?'

'No,' Mia said. Now sure that she was being chastised, she ended the call.

For God's sake, Mia thought to herself, I *killed* a man trying to catch these people. She closed her eyes and saw the dead body again.

A hot shower helped revive her, marginally. Afterwards she dressed in fresh clothes and WhatsApped Bongani. He was awake and agreed to meet her at the Vulture monitoring room.

Mia stopped by the kitchen for a cup of coffee, which she took in a takeaway cup, along with a muffin.

Pretty, the cook, looked distraught as she served her. 'Ah, Mia, I am so very, very sorry.'

'What for?' Mia sipped her coffee.

'The food poisoning yesterday. I have no idea how it happened.'

'Oh.' With the shootings and the kidnapping, her temporary bout of an upset stomach had faded away as the least of her problems. 'No problem, Pretty, these things happen in any kitchen.'

Pretty pursed her lips, looking more defiant than contrite now. 'Not in *my* kitchen.'

'I didn't mean any offence.' *Sheesh*, Mia thought, *I was the one who ended up throwing up.*

'I mean, I am still sorry, but I can't imagine how it happened. I taste all my food myself, hygienically of course, while I'm cooking.'

'I'm sure you do.' Pretty's waistline and boobs did not for a moment suggest that the chef was lying.

'And there was nothing wrong with me.'

'Might have just been one bad batch of fish, I guess,' Mia said.

Pretty shook her head. 'My supplier has never let me down, and nor has my refrigerator. Miss Clyde-Smith has asked me to investigate.'

'Well, I'm sure you'll get to the bottom of it.' Mia had bigger problems right now than a bug in Pretty's kitchen. She took her coffee and muffin, assuming it would not make her sick, and walked out to the Land Rover. Bongani was waiting for her. Dawn was coming earlier every day and the sky was turning pink. 'Did you sleep?'

He smiled. 'Like a baby, for a few hours. I snuck out of my sister's place an hour ago. I wanted to be here early.'

'How do you do it?'

He shrugged. 'We – you and I – must be rested and strong in order to catch this man whom we seek. We will find him.'

She shook her head slowly. 'Your confidence never ceases to amaze me,' she said, climbing into the Land Rover and starting the engine.

Bongani got in next to her, in the passenger seat rather than on his tracker's perch. 'Your problem is that you are a woman.'

She laughed, despite her fatigue and fear and frustration. 'Do you know that in most of the rest of the world you could be busted for sexual harassment for a comment like that?'

'Yes. But it is true.'

'Hey –'

He held up a hand. 'You are the best tracker I have ever met, apart from myself.'

'Gee, thanks.'

'You know what I mean.'

Mia shrugged.

The morning air was chilly as they drove the short distance to the anti-poaching rangers' camp, where the Vulture system was located. Bongani was looking over the edge of the Land Rover's door as they went. 'Stop, there are tracks.'

They had work to do, but she pulled over.

'Switch off the engine, get out.'

Mia frowned. 'I told Julianne we'd go man the Vulture system.'

'I know, but this is important.'

She pulled over and turned the key. A nearby spurfowl was squawking its morning call like a bush rooster. Mia listened for other sounds. Off to their left, she heard the faint *ka-ka, ka-ka* of monkeys who had clearly been woken by something scary.

'They're alarm-calling.' She got out and walked around the front of the vehicle to where Bongani was standing, looking down.

'Lioness,' she said.

Bongani nodded. 'And?'

Mia looked up and down the dusty road and took a few steps. She circled the area. 'It's One-eye from the Little Serengeti pride.'

He smiled broadly. 'How do you know?'

Mia started to look at her watch, but checked her impatience. 'She's huge and heavily pregnant, as you very well know. A lioness only moves off by herself if she's about to give birth to her cubs. So, those tracks are hers, for sure.'

'Of course.'

'So, I've told you what I know. What does that mean?'

'That means that you are as good as any tracker here, and that you know this land intimately. Yet, because you are a woman you feel as though you need to be better than the men, just to be grudgingly seen as their equal.'

She supposed he was right. 'So?'

'So, you need to let go of that, Mia, of trying to be the best. You need to just *be* who you are, which is the best tracker on this property, probably in the whole of the Sabi Sand Game Reserve.'

'I thought you were the best tracker?'

He smiled. 'No, I am just a man. And, because I am a proud man, I sometimes cannot say out loud what I know to be true.'

It was his way of complimenting her, or stating the fact that he – perhaps *grudgingly* – acknowledged that she was not just as good as him, but possibly better.

'So why can't we find this poacher?'

'Because you are letting your self-doubt get in your way, just as I am allowing my pride to cloud my judgement.'

'What do we do about that?' she asked.

He looked down at the tracks. 'We go find this lioness, quickly.'

Mia rolled her eyes. 'Bongani, there's a girl missing, and a poacher busy killing our rhinos. How can tracking a cranky old lioness help us? You know One-eye; she's not keen on people. You've seen her charge our vehicle enough times. And now, if she's had her cubs, she'll be extra protective. It's crazy.'

He folded his arms, immovable, implacable, and he seemed to tower above her. 'If you do your job, she will not know that we have even found her.'

Mia drew herself up to her full height. She would not let him intimidate her. 'No.'

He turned and walked off, into the bush.

'Bongani!'

Mia balled her fists. She reached into the Land Rover, pulled out her gun case and unzipped it. She took the rifle and set off into the bush after him. He had gone mad, clearly, and she felt that if she ended up having to shoot the lioness because Bongani spooked her and the cat charged, then she would save the next round for him.

'Bongani,' she hissed.

She came to him, and he had his hand raised. Mia crept up behind him. 'What is it?'

'I have lost the spoor.'

Her eyes felt like they might spin out of her head at this rate. 'Sheesh, man, let's go to the Vulture.'

He turned and stared at her. 'What's wrong with you?'

Now she was becoming angry. 'There's *nothing* wrong with *me*.'

'I thought you had it, but it seems you've lost it.'

'What?' Now he was talking in riddles.

He stopped and looked her in the eyes. 'The hunger. You know, we have talked about this before. What makes a good tracker?'

'Yes.'

'Then tell me,' he said.

She sighed again. 'Technical competency, an understanding of animal behaviour ...'

'And?'

'And a devotion to tracking bordering on the fanatical.'

He nodded slowly.

He was right. She did not feel it. Normally as soon as either of them picked up a track it was like a compulsion, an inability not to follow it, as long as it was something they wanted to find. They had both, for different reasons, lost it when searching for the poacher.

'We gave up,' she said softly.

'Yes, Mia. We did. I was blinded, scared even, by umuthi. You let the pressure get to you.'

She wanted to scream, *But he disappeared!*

And she had killed a man.

Did that not count for anything? Police, even soldiers these days, received counselling from professionals. Was she just expected to suck it up and head back out into the bush and find their man? Maybe, Mia thought, Captain van Rensburg was right, and that she should ask Julianne to organise some counselling for her.

Their soul searching was interrupted by the sound of a vehicle. They backtracked to the road to find Sean's Land Rover parked next to theirs.

'Phew,' Sean said as they emerged. His eyes were red-rimmed and his chin stubbled. 'I was wondering where you two had got to.' Benny barked in the back of the vehicle, excited to see them.

From the front passenger seat, on the other side of the vehicle, a blonde woman emerged.

'Sara!' Mia said, surprised.

Chapter 18

'**I**'m back.' Sara grinned and held up a bandaged arm. 'I made them let me out of hospital last night and stayed with a safari guide I know in Nelspruit. He was taking an early game drive into Kruger so he dropped me at the gate, where Sean spotted me. With the whole coronavirus thing I think the hospital was happy to have the bed back, and I was happy to get out.'

Sean leaned an arm out of the driver's side window. 'So here we are. Sara insisted on being taken to the Vulture system so she could help.'

'You sure you're OK?' Mia said.

Sara waved off her concern, though Mia noticed a small wince. 'I heard what happened,' Sara said. 'What are you guys looking for now? The poacher?'

'No, a lioness,' Bongani said.

'Serious?' Sean shook his head. 'I've got work to do. Sara?'

She looked at her watch. 'My shift on the Vulture starts in an hour – I called ahead.' She looked at Mia. 'Can you guys take me?'

'Sure,' Mia said. 'We were heading there, eventually.'

Sean directed his question to Mia: 'Is this important, tracking a lion now?'

She gave a nod. 'You know, I think it is.' She needed to recalibrate herself, to find again her hunger for tracking. 'Call us if you need us sooner, Sean.'

'Roger that; there's nothing you can do right now anyway.' Sean started the engine again, to the delight of his dog, and drove off.

'This is so cool,' Sara said.

'What is?' Mia asked.

'I'm back in the bush five minutes and I'm off on foot with you guys, the best trackers in the country, looking for a lion.'

Bongani set off, but not before Mia noticed the smile curling at the sides of his mouth.

Mia closed her eyes and tilted her head upward. She tried to centre herself, her being. Sara's enthusiasm was infectious, and she could almost feel it penetrating her veins. All that was stopping her was her own doubt, and the spectre of the man she had killed, who lurked at the corners of her consciousness, quietly mocking her weakness.

I should have killed you, the dead man whispered to her. *I wanted to. I will.*

'Are you OK?'

Mia opened her eyes at the touch of Sara's hand on her forearm. 'Yes. No. I mean, I think so. I think I understand now.'

Sara looked puzzled. 'What?'

'Something Bongani just said to me, about what I'm lacking.'

'You are not lacking anything,' Sara said. 'You are a natural.'

'It's not skill I'm talking about.'

'What then?'

'It's dedication, devotion, whatever, the fanatical desire to track, to seek, to find.'

'Yes, well, I have enough of that for both of us,' Sara said.

Mia gave a little laugh. 'Yes, you do.'

'Then let's find this lion!'

They caught up with Bongani and he stopped walking, motioning for Mia to take the lead. 'Give me the rifle. You track.'

Mia heard the monkeys calling again and looked up, scanning the trees ahead. The morning sun was burnishing the trunks a lustrous red-gold, the air crisp and clear thanks to the early rains the day before. Mia centred herself. 'The monkeys can see her.'

'Yes,' said Bongani. 'And now we must go find her.'

Mia moved off, scanning the ground, but also listening, for the squeak of tiny cubs calling for their mother. She stopped every now and then to sniff the air for the damp fur smell that might give the lioness away.

The monkeys chattered away. That was good and bad, Mia told herself. The lioness would know that she had been spotted, so she would not be stalking, but it also told Mia that the cat was close, and every step they took brought them all closer to danger. She felt it again, the flutter in her chest, the tingle jolting down to her fingertips.

Ahead of her, on a hippo trail they had picked up, was the crisply indented, almost perfect track of the lioness. The pathway was like a mini dual carriageway through the bush, where the hippo's big four-toed feet had pounded furrows either side of a middle-*mannetjie*, the hump running down the centre of the trail. The lioness was moving with a long, sleek, energetic stride.

The vervet monkeys ceased their chattering and Mia also stopped, the others closing up behind her. Bongani waited patiently, saying nothing.

Mia listened. The silence meant the lioness had gone to ground, or left the monkeys' line of sight. She thought about where they were. 'There's a waterhole ahead, to the left. That's where she's going.'

Bongani's silence now meant that he either agreed with her, or that he wanted her to learn from her mistake. Mia felt a moment's hesitation. There were no more tracks visible on the hippo trail and she could not, immediately, pick up the lioness's spoor. The female might just have meandered off the path and Mia might find another perfect print ten metres further down the trail, or it was possible her instinct, that the cat had gone to drink at the closest water, as she might normally do at this time of day, was correct.

The lioness either had a belly full of babies, or she had given birth, stashed them somewhere and, most likely, had been out hunting all night to rebuild her strength and help her produce milk. Either way, she needed water, and at this time of the dry winter there were no other alternatives within easy reach.

Mia left the pathway.

She could sense Bongani move to the next stage of alert behind her and imagined him gripping the rifle stock just that little bit tighter. They were moving into thicker bush now, their own visibility becoming more limited.

Mia looked down.

She felt the tiny, rewarding pulse of adrenaline as she saw something, only a partial print, but without a doubt it was fresh and that of the lioness. She had been right. Mia did not allow herself to breathe easier, because the danger was still there – enhanced if anything – but she felt a sense of calm descend over her. It had been a comfort to her, the security of knowledge and experience, and it had been terrifying how quickly it had left her.

The world had gone through something similar these past months. All that was ordered, everything that had seemed so natural, so effortless, for so long had been turned on its head. People had lost their jobs, their livelihoods, and their lives to this unseen enemy.

So it had been for her. It was not even the visible threats – the man who had been shooting at her, the one she had killed – that had shaken her most, but rather the vanishing act of the poacher who seemed to mock the combined years of skills and experience that Bongani and she had amassed.

Mia knew that there was something she and Bongani were missing, and it was not the correct kind of umuthi or magic. There was a clue, somewhere, a track or other piece of physical evidence, like what she was searching for now on the ground or in the bushes, or it was something they had missed about the poacher's behaviour. Maybe it was something as simple as a criminal helicopter pilot, as she had suggested. There was something that man had done – or not done – that would eventually give him away.

She brought her mind back to the task at hand, doing her best to push the phantom poacher and the dead man out of her consciousness and to focus on the lioness. No, to *become* the lioness, to get into the animal's head and use her own knowledge and empathy and experience and devotion to decipher where the big cat was going and what it was doing.

Drinking.

Mia raised her nose and caught a faint, slightly rank smell.

Sara, full of excitement at being back in the bush and unable to contain herself, came up beside her, putting her mouth almost uncomfortably close to Mia's ear.

'What is it you smell?'

'Water. At this time of year the waterhole is stagnant. I can smell it.'

'OK. But I thought the waterhole was fed by a borehole, with a pump? Doesn't that keep it fresh?'

Sara's curiosity about everything that happened in the reserve was mostly endearing, but sometimes, like now, when there was work to be done, it bordered on annoying. 'The reserve only pumps when we absolutely have to, like in the drought a couple of years ago.'

'Yes.' Sara nodded. 'I read that man-made waterholes are going out of fashion in the Kruger Park and reserves that are environmentally conscious, yes?'

'That's right,' Mia said. 'They attract game, but then it affects the vegetation. Too many animals mean the land around an artificial water point becomes unnaturally overgrazed. It means that during a drought there might be water, but not enough food for the animals. It's hard to get the balance right. The property next to us has put in a big concrete waterhole and hide, just across the border, and Julianne was furious, not only because it will draw game away from Lion Plains, but because it's environmentally unsound.'

Bongani put his finger to his lips and nodded for them to continue walking. They did so, but there was no sign of the lioness.

Tempted to blame Sara for distracting her, Mia kept her excuses to herself and cast about in a circle, looking for signs. She was beginning to doubt herself again. Panic began to bubble inside her.

She started when she felt a hand on her shoulder and looked around to see Bongani, that self-satisfied half-smile on his face.

'Breathe,' he reminded her.

She closed her eyes and did as he said.

'Do not doubt yourself.'

Mia nodded and resumed walking in the direction of the waterhole. She still could see no sign of a pug mark – there was too much dry leaf litter about here, and there were no hairs or scat or anything else to guide her. She was relying purely on her experience.

Mia scanned the ground. There it was: a patch of dirt amid the leaves.

'What is it?' Sara said, unable to contain herself.

'The lioness has lain down here,' Mia whispered. A sound above them made her heart leap and she looked up.

Sara followed her gaze and they both saw a blur of pale grey and a shaking branch. 'Monkeys. This is where they were watching her, just now.'

It was now Mia's turn to shush Sara with a finger to her lips. Sara was right, though, they were only minutes behind their quarry. Her heart beat faster.

Ahead she heard the boisterous honking of a pair of Egyptian geese. As she knew, the waterhole was now very close. Here and there was a clear print, then the lioness's tracks veered sharply off to the right.

Mia felt a faint breeze on her face and knew that they were where they needed to be, downwind of the cat, so she would not smell their approach. If she had moved off and begun doubling around behind them, they would be in trouble. Mia called a halt and they doubled back about fifty metres, to where the lioness had been lying. Now, Mia set off to the right as well, trying to outflank her. She moved with patience. She did not want to bump into the animal she was tracking.

Mia heard something. She stopped and cocked her head, holding up a hand to make sure the other two stayed silent. She picked it up again: a faint squeak.

Slowly, Mia turned to lock eyes with Bongani, who was nodding and grinning.

Mia carried on and as she walked, watching each footfall to make sure she did not snap a dried stick, the noise became louder and clearer.

Ow. Ow. Ow.

Mia took them to a large jackalberry tree and they stopped there as she craned around the stout black trunk. There she saw a twitch of movement, the dark tuft on the tip of One-eye's tail, bobbing above a patch of long, dry, golden grass, the perfect place to hide a litter of cubs.

Slowly, Mia dropped to one knee and the others imitated her, not daring to make a sound. Mia pointed and Sara stared hard then put her hand over her mouth, just managing to stifle a gasp.

The lioness emerged into full view and Mia tensed, fearing that at any moment that single golden eye would turn on her, signalling that the animal had heard them. Instead, the big cat walked across their front and in her mouth, held delicately between jaws that could dissect a buffalo carcass, was a tiny cub.

Other cubs squeaked as their mother took the first from one position of safety to another thicket of undergrowth. The lioness returned and collected two more little bundles, their fur carrying the spots that would disappear as they aged.

When the lioness returned for a fourth time there was more squeaking, and when the new mother stood up, she winced, and not without reason. This cub was not in her mouth but hanging from one of her teats. The cub suckled as long as it could, swinging from its tortured parent, then dropped into the grass. One-eye circled and picked it up in her mouth, then set off to deposit the little one with its siblings.

Sara shifted next to Mia and her knee must have pressed down on a dry twig because there was an audible *snap*.

Mia froze as the lioness set down the cub, then pivoted to face the noise.

The three of them held their breath and Bongani, slowly, raised the rifle to his shoulder as the lioness took a few steps towards them.

The cat raised her big head and sniffed the air. Luckily, they were still downwind, so the lioness could not smell them, but she had heard the noise and was curious, alert.

Sara grabbed hold of Mia's shirt and Mia could sense she was about to lever herself up. Mia reached around and held Sara down, on her knee. The lioness must have seen the movement, because she lowered her body into a stalking crouch and started moving towards them again.

The single golden eye, now visible through a narrowed lid, fixed on Mia. The lioness lowered her ears, tail straight out like a tawny lance about to be launched. Mia could sense that Bongani was taking aim. She reached out a hand, slowly, and pushed the barrel down. Bongani challenged her with angry eyes, but she shook her head.

Bongani started to raise the rifle again as the lioness continued to close the distance between them.

Sara gave a tiny whimper, but stayed where she was.

Mia, like all of them, knew that if one of them got up and ran, he or she would be the first to die.

'Whatever you do, don't run,' Mia had drilled into Sara the first time they had been out in the bush together. 'Though that advice is not going to make any sense to you when you're staring down a lion.'

Even Mia felt it now, the primal urge to do the wrong thing, ingrained in humanity's DNA since prehistoric times. Lions, like house cats, hunted by sight and sound. If Sara got up now she would be like the mouse or lizard being toyed with by a moggy – if the prey lay still, the cat lost interest, but as soon as it moved, it was history. This lioness would be counting on one of them making a run for it and giving her the target she craved.

She came closer and closer, growing in bulk, the piercing stare of her one good eye becoming more focused with every step. The cat blinked.

Mia was rock-solid still. The predator paused, sank lower on her haunches and twitched her tail. She was getting ready to pounce.

Mia took a deep breath, closed her eyes for a moment to summon what inner strength she had, then slowly stood up.

She was aware of Bongani exhaling, of Sara clutching her ankle, but other than that every sense was focused on the lioness in front of her.

The cat seemed unsure what to do next, and that was a worry in itself. Mia knew that all animals had what was known as the 'flight or fight' zone. This invisible force field varied from creature to creature and depended on a number of factors but, basically, there was a point at which any animal, humans included, made a decision in their best interests, either to run away, or to stand and fight. To be more precise, this apex predator, ten metres to her front, was deciding whether or not to leap at her.

The lioness, Mia knew, would go for her head, crushing her skull in its jaws as if her skin and bone were made of papier-mâché.

One-eye growled.

Mia held her ground, stood straight, and raised her hands over her head, trying to make herself look bigger. '*Voetsek!*' she yelled, telling the lion to go away in Afrikaans.

The lioness wriggled her bottom, and ground back on her haunches a little more, as if preparing to gain the maximum amount of propulsion when she released her muscles and sprang onto Mia. She growled again.

Mia growled back at her. She could sense Bongani, to one side and just behind her, trying to surreptitiously get the cat in the sights of his rifle, but Mia had deliberately stood to block her partner. He would be cursing her now, and that was too bad, because she saw suddenly that they had been wrong to come after this animal.

Mia knew in her heart that no matter the merits of what Bongani had been trying to achieve in attempting to re-establish her confidence in her ability to track, they had done the wrong thing by deliberately trying to get close to a mother with newly born cubs.

The irony, Mia registered briefly, was that she had succeeded, and only Sara's snapping of the twig had given the game away. That couldn't be helped.

At that moment the lioness sprang forward.

Mia steeled herself. Now every single nerve or brain cell or instinct that had told her not to run was screaming at her body and mind to turn and flee. Instead, she stayed rooted to the soil.

As the lioness closed on her a calmness washed over her, like an antidote to the adrenaline that had been coursing through her body.

With each bound the distance between them rapidly reduced to nothing, but Mia sensed that she was protected.

Bongani had his muthi, which she had tried, and she had the benefit of years of experience and training that told her that if she found herself in this position, she must stand still and do nothing.

Mia could smell the lioness, see the bared fangs, and that one eye was fixed on her and nothing else. She was vaguely aware of movement beside and behind her, of Bongani perhaps using his body to shield Sara. If the lioness did pounce on her and kill her, then at least the other two would get away. That gave Mia an added sense of calm.

It had all taken less than two seconds and Mia felt a mini sandstorm blast the skin on her legs, bare beneath her shorts. Almost absent-mindedly she looked down and marvelled at the sight and sensation of individual granules of dirt, tiny stones, and leaf litter pattering against her shins and upper thighs.

The lioness had skidded to a halt, not more than two metres from her, her front paws digging into the ground to slow her and thereby sending up the dust storm.

She growled at Mia again and this time, Mia felt and smelled the cat's foul breath wash over her.

Sara whimpered.

Bongani had his face turned, unable to watch what must surely transpire next.

'Go!' Mia yelled at the lioness.

The lioness drew herself up to her full height, shook her head, gave Mia one last glare, then turned and walked away.

Mia exhaled. She kept her eyes on the cat as Bongani helped Sara to her feet. The lioness stopped, and Bongani started to raise his rifle again, but there was no need.

The big cat started scratching the ground, a precursor to urinating, which she did a few seconds later, just as Mia knew she would.

Yes, Mia thought.

Chapter 19

Sannie, hands on hips, surveyed the task force she had put to-gether to search the entire village of Killarney by the light of the new day.

There were four uniformed officers, two men and two women, and a pair of guys from the Kruger Park Stock Theft and Endan-gered Species unit there on the promise that their search might turn up a weapon used in the reserve or some rhino horn. There was also Sipho's illegal reptile collection to deal with.

'Be careful,' Sannie said to them. 'We've had people shot in cold blood here and let me remind you that this sort of thing usually does not happen here. This is not Joburg. This is Mpumalanga.'

'What do we do about the snakes?' one of the male officers asked.

'You can work on loading them – *safely* – as long as someone else is with you. I don't want anyone getting bitten in there and then passing out.'

'And us, Captain?' one of the two policewomen asked.

'We continue going door to door, talking to people, trying to find out what is going on in this place. We've got two murders in as many days and three missing girls. Lockdown or no lockdown, virus or no virus, this sort of *kak* ends now. Got it?'

There were nods and murmurs of assent.

Sannie, along with the private security guards Graham and Oscar and their superior Sean Bourke, had made a start on questioning the local people the night before, but it had been difficult going, rousing angry people from their sleep. On top of that Sannie had needed to coordinate the crime scene technicians who complained about working overtime, having been called from the first scene, where Laura had disappeared and the body of the slain poacher had to be examined, to Killarney where Sipho and Richard had been gunned down. It was a long and trying night for all of them. Sannie had snatched an hour of sleep in her car and was running on adrenaline.

'I'm going to talk to the village's best-known sangoma, who lived where the two local girls were last seen,' Sannie said.

'You think umuthi is a factor in the killings?' a male officer asked.

She shrugged. 'Maybe. I'm not ruling it out. Some strange stuff has been happening around here lately and Sipho, the snake boy, was selling reptiles to some guys from Joburg for umuthi.'

The female officer squared up to her. 'I hope you are not insulting my traditional beliefs, *Captain*.'

'No,' Sannie said, 'I am keeping an open mind because I have several parallel investigations going on here, and not enough resources to do my job. If anyone here does not want to be here and give one hundred per cent effort, then I need to know that now, and I will send them off to issue lockdown infringements.' She looked to all of them, her eyes coming back to rest on the female officer. 'Understood?'

The woman looked down and mumbled: 'Understood.'

'Right,' Sannie said. 'Door to door, everyone. Something's going on in this *dorpie* and it stinks. I know people here won't want to talk to the police, but we're talking about kids going missing, and locals being killed. Someone here will have had enough.'

The officers split into their teams. Sannie walked through the settlement, ignoring the sullen looks of residents who, she knew, were feeling more like inmates than citizens these days. Her phone rang.

'Van Rensburg.'

'Henk here. Howzit, Sannie?'

'Good, and you?'

'Sannie, I've finally found that chopper pilot, Mike de Vries.'

'Good work.'

Henk had driven to the general aviation airfield at Nelspruit the previous evening, at Sannie's request, expecting to find at least Julianne's helicopter. Calling the after-hours number for the avionics company that was supposedly working on the chopper, Henk had learned that de Vries had never shown up.

'The guy from North East Avionics called me an hour ago. He got a call from de Vries, who said he'd had to make a forced landing on some farm near Hazyview, but it was a false alarm or some such rubbish. And he was flying to Nelspruit now-now.'

'Where is he now, Henk?' Sannie's patience was wearing thin, due to sleep deprivation, and Henk, she knew, liked to draw a story out as long as possible.

'In handcuffs in my car.'

'Really?' She also knew Henk de Beer was a tough guy, but she had just expected him to question the pilot, not lock him up. 'What did he do?'

'We were waiting for him at the airport, keeping out of sight, but when he touched down one of the uniform guys took it upon himself to walk out to the flight line and put his hand up, telling the *oke* to get out.'

Sannie shook her head. 'What did the pilot do?'

'De Vries started to take off, but we showed ourselves and our guns and put a couple of rounds over his head,' Henk chuckled, 'then I think he *kak*ked himself and landed.'

'What was he panicking about?'

'Wouldn't say,' Henk said, 'but when I told him we suspected him of ferrying poachers in and out of the game reserve he hit the roof, claiming he'd never do such a thing because he loved rhinos and what-what-what.'

'OK, Henk. Do you feel like a ride in the chopper?'

'I was hoping you would say that. I've got him here at the airfield now. I was looking for an excuse to get out of Nelspruit.'

Sannie checked her watch. 'I can be at Kaya Nghala in an hour. I'll see you and the pilot there. I need to talk to him in person and I don't want him flying off and getting lost on purpose on the way.'

'Affirmative,' Henk said. 'I'll be the bad cop and you can be the good one.'

'In the mood I'm in, that might not be possible.' Sannie said goodbye to Henk and ended the call.

Although she was in the middle of an increasingly complex investigation, Sannie still had a family to worry about. She called Tommy on his phone.

'Hi, Mom. How are you?'

'Fine. Is everything all right with you, my boy?'

'Ja, hundreds, Mom. Christo made breakfast, but then he went to Gita's place.'

'Did he now,' she said, unable to keep the smile from her face. Gita was the daughter of Kubashnee Venkatraman, one of the Kruger Park's vets. Christo and the pretty Indian girl had grown up together, going to the same schools, though Gita, like her mother before her, had been studying at Onderstepoort, the country's premier veterinary college. Sannie knew that Gita had come home for lockdown and both she and Kubashnee had noticed the two childhood friends spending more and more time together. She was pleased she had something to cheer her, a little.

'Kubashnee's home,' Tommy said, as if to ensure everything was above board, or maybe to reinforce his older brother's story. Sannie didn't have time to worry either way; she trusted Christo and both she and Tom had brought the boys up to respect women and girls in every way.

She sighed. The thought of Tom momentarily stopped her train of thought.

'It's fine. Do your schoolwork and I'll see you later today, hopefully. I'm going to get *Tannie* Samantha to come look in on you. Eat something healthy for lunch, please.'

'Yes, Mom. Love you.'

'Love you,' the words caught for an instant in her throat, 'bye.'

Sannie called Samantha Karandis and told her she was still away from home, working.

'Sure, Sannie, no problem. I'll fix him some lunch, and just call if you need me to take the boys some dinner as well.'

'Thanks a million, Sam.'

'Happy to help. How's the investigation going? They're saying on the radio this morning that two guys were shot dead in Killarney.'

'*Ja*, but sorry, I can't go into details.'

'I understand. Take care and don't worry about Tommy.'

'Oh, Sam.' Sannie remembered part of their drunken conversation at Samantha's house. 'You said something about Liz having a helicopter pilot boyfriend?'

'Sannie, I talk too much after a few wines. It was indiscreet of me.'

'Who does he fly for?'

There was a pause on the other end of the line. 'Um, one of the larney lodges in the Sabi Sand.'

'Kaya Nghala Lodge? That place is very fancy, as you know.'

'Sannie, please. Liz asked me not to say anything.'

'That's not a "no", Sam. This could be important. Is the pilot she's seeing Mike de Vries, from Lion Plains? Yes or no?'

There was another pause. 'Liz hasn't done anything wrong, Sannie.'

'I'm not saying she has, but please, this is official. Yes or no.'

'Um, yes.'

'Tell me about the pilot. What do you know about him?'

'Sannie, we're all friends. You really need to ask Liz about this, not me.'

Sannie knew Sam was right and that it was unfair of her to press her friend in this way. She and Henk already knew de Vries was guilty of something – evading arrest, for a start. She would make an official call to Liz later if de Vries was not forthcoming when they spoke to him. 'I will. Thanks, Sam. And thank you for looking after Tommy, I value our friendship. Bye for now.'

She put her phone away and continued walking. The area she was in was a buffer zone between the settlement of Killarney itself and the Sabi Sand reserve. The community project had encroached into this area, which before that had mainly been used by the locals to graze livestock. She heard the clanking of a goat bell somewhere nearby.

Sannie was sure that this was also a prime spot for poachers to come and go from the reserve, although these days the perimeter fence was quite an obstacle. It was electrified, reinforced with coils of razor wire along its lowest levels, and covered at regular intervals with security cameras. Added to that, the Vulture system was pointed to cover this sensitive sector of the reserve.

Sannie thought about how she would question the helicopter pilot. She wondered if he was maybe moving contraband, such as alcohol and cigarettes.

Sannie heard a noise and stopped. A cape turtle dove called nearby, but that was not what she had heard. This was more like a cracking noise – not a gunshot but more like something big, breaking. She left the well-trodden path she was walking on and headed through the scrubby bushveld in the direction of the Sabi Sand Game Reserve's fence. She heard the noise again, coming from the direction in which she was walking, and smiled as she quickened her pace.

Soon she came to the rough dirt perimeter road that ran alongside the fence. Beyond the barrier of wire and electronics there was another road, this one smoothly graded and well used by security patrol vehicles inside the reserve. Past a firebreak of slashed dry grass there were tall, mature trees, and the bush was thicker than on this side. It took her a moment to notice the swaying, slender trunk of a young tree. She smiled to herself as she saw the first of the elephants.

A cow, distinctive by the angular shape of her forehead – males' heads were more rounded – was bending the sapling in order to strip the nutrient-rich bark from it. From between her legs came a tiny baby.

Sannie's heart lurched again, though this time it was from pure, ingrained maternal love rather than pain. She relished the feeling and felt the sting of tears welling in her eyes as the little one took a few brave steps ahead of its mother into the cleared zone.

'Hello,' Sannie said quietly.

The baby's trunk flipped and flopped about as it walked. Sannie knew that it would take time for the little one to work out how to use his unusual appendage. The mother paused in her foraging and raised her own trunk in the air.

Sannie realised, only now, that the wind was at her back and the mother had probably caught her scent. The cow made a grumbling noise from deep in her belly and the little calf turned and trotted back to her. Silently, almost magically, the huge animal and her tiny newborn disappeared into the dun-coloured vegetation, leaving Sannie to wipe her eyes and turn back to the path she had been on.

She felt alone, adrift, and sad that she had, if only briefly, contemplated ending her own life the previous morning. Only now could she fully imagine what Tommy might have thought of her. At the time, as she had looked at the Z88 pistol in her hands, her own grief had been all-encompassing. Seeing the mother elephant and how its tiny calf depended totally on her had reminded her that she was not alone in the world even though Tom was gone.

Tom.

She did not have to let him go back to Iraq, but at the same time she knew there was nothing she could have said or done that would have stopped him. The creeping, gnawing feeling that she had not *minded* him leaving was still there. She did her best to brush it aside, but the guilt threatened to consume her.

For now, though, she had work to do.

Chapter 20

Mia, Bongani and Sara drove to the Vulture system headquarters.

They were quiet on the drive, all of them reflecting on what had gone on with the lioness and her cubs. When they arrived, they got out and went through the process of a handover with the two volunteers from a neighbouring lodge who were sharing the manning of the array of high-tech monitoring systems.

The departing men had seen nothing of interest. Bongani volunteered to make tea and coffee while Mia and Sara each sat in front of a double-screen work station.

Mia scrolled through the log of confirmed intercepts. She noted elephant, buffalo, giraffe, an array of buck and, of more interest, several rhino sightings. She pointed the listing out to Sara. 'Three white rhinos travelling together.'

'Is that unusual?'

'Yes and no. They're not herd animals,' Mia said, 'though sometimes they clump together.'

Mia clicked on the entry and pulled up video one of the other operators had recorded from the camera. It was black and white and grainy, shot at night. Mia paused it and tapped the screen. 'Yes, as I thought, see.'

Sara craned her head over. 'Is that a young one in the lead?'

Mia nodded. 'Yes, white rhino calves walk in front of their mothers. The idea is that the mom can keep an eye on the little one. It's

different for black rhinos – their calves walk behind the mother because they mostly live in thick bush and she needs to clear a path for
the baby. White rhinos live in country like this, more open and grassy.'

'And the big one at the back?'

'That's a male, for sure,' Mia said, 'following the cow, hoping
she's nearly ready to mate again.'

Sara swivelled in her chair. 'A tempting target for poachers.'

'For sure. If poachers pick up the tracks of those three, it will
be a bloodbath.' Mia wondered, in an afterthought, if someone had
tipped them off.

'What do you know about Julianne's helicopter pilot?' Sara
asked.

'You're reading my mind,' Mia said. 'Let's first see if we can find
these rhinos again.'

Mia's screen was covered with blinking dots, moving targets that
had been picked up by radar.

In the area where the rhinos had been reported she picked up
slow and steady movement by a couple of groups of animals. One
was a herd of elephants, which, when she clicked on a video from
an earlier intercept, showed that the family was eating on the move.
Based on the estimated speed and trajectory of the three rhinos she
watched a corner of her screen intently, hoping the radar would
pick them up again.

'Got you,' she said when a moving dot appeared. She clicked on
it, and a camera focused on where the animals were. She zoomed
in. It was the rhinos.

'Cool,' Sara said, looking across from her screen.

Mia double-clicked and entered the details of the three rhinos.
She would keep an eye on their progress from now on.

'I've got something interesting,' Sara said.

Mia slid over on the rolling office chair. 'Show me, please.'

Sara used her mouse and cursor to trace a line of intercept dots.
It was dead straight and moving fast – too quick for Sara to lock on
to it and focus with a camera.

'Human.' Mia felt a jolt of adrenaline. 'Has to be. Keep trying.'
She got her phone out.

'Bourke,' a groggy voice said.

'Howzit, it's Mia. Did I wake you?'

There was a cough at the other end and Mia heard a female voice in the background.

'He just fell asleep after being on the go for twenty-four hours,' Sean's wife, Christine, called.

'Sorry,' Mia said.

'No problem.' Sean sounded awake and alert now. 'What have you got?'

'Human traffic.'

'Where?'

'Coming in from the direction of Killarney, about five hundred metres this side of the fence.'

'And you only just picked them up now?'

Sean was probably tired, but Mia felt there was no need for the reproachful note in his voice. 'Hey, we just came on shift, blame the guys before us.'

'Sorry. I'll talk to them. For now, keep a watch on him, or them. Any idea how many?'

Mia checked the screen again. Sara was furiously clicking, trying to pick up the target. 'Not yet, sorry. They're moving fast and clever.'

'No problem. WhatsApp me the coordinates and direction of movement. Shame we don't have a bloody helicopter or pilot.'

'Shame or convenient?' Mia said.

He paused. 'Hmm, good point. Sannie is following up on that lead, Mia. For now, I'll get a dog team out there and some guys. What's their target? Any idea?'

'Three white rhinos, on our concession, and probably leaving a trail a tourist could follow.'

'Shit,' Sean said. 'Right, thanks Mia. Good work. Stay on them and keep me updated.'

'Roger.'

Mia ended the call then had a thought. She redialled Sean's number, but he was busy, no doubt mobilising his forces. It wasn't really her job, but she took Captain van Rensburg's business card out of her top pocket and dialled the policewoman's number.

*

'Van Rensburg,' Sannie said.

'Howzit, Captain, it's Mia Greenaway.'

'Yes, Mia. How are you?' After the brief pleasantries, Mia told Sannie that she had intercepted a suspected poacher on the game reserve and where she thought the man had come from.

'I'm actually at Killarney now,' Sannie said. 'Just by the fence line.'

'I'm enlarging the map on the screen now, Captain, and shifting the view to an aerial photograph image ...'

Sannie paused, not wanting to lose phone signal, as it could be patchy in rural areas like this one.

'Captain, you know where they're doing the building work for the new lodge and school?'

'*Ja.*'

'I think they probably entered the reserve somewhere near there, not long ago.'

'I'm close by.' Sannie felt her heart rate pick up. 'I'll go and check now. Have you alerted your own people?'

'Yes, Sean's sending a team and a dog to check.'

'When do you think they entered?'

'They're now about seven hundred metres inside the reserve and look to be moving at a good pace, on a mission, so maybe fifteen or twenty minutes?'

'Good work. Call me if you see anything else. Leave a voice message if you can't get through.'

'Affirmative,' Mia said.

When Sannie got to the fence, she scanned the ground in front of her. Legally, there was nothing to stop people on the Killarney side of the fence from walking on the pathway, and here and there she picked up footprints, though they seemed to be old.

Sannie looked for any sign of the wires on the fence having been cut. A skilled poacher might take the time to bend any severed strands back into place, so that a breach might not be visible to a casual observer, or a patrol driving past.

As well as checking for poachers, she told herself that she *must* find and interview the sangoma, a task which had already slipped down her list of priorities.

Sannie carried on for about three hundred metres, checking the fence and pathways either side of the barrier, but saw nothing out of the ordinary. At one point she came to a culvert, a likely place for someone to try to crawl under. She also got down on one knee to inspect the lowest part of the fence, where it crossed the dry watercourse. This was the sort of spot where even a warthog or other animal might try to burrow through the soft sand. A pile of bricks had been laid in the stream bed to block the gap beneath the razor wire fence. Sannie checked it and looked for tracks – there was no sign of disturbance.

She stood, wiped her hands on her blue uniform trousers and turned and retraced her steps. Sannie carried on another three hundred metres along the fence in the opposite direction, but, again, found no sign of disturbance. She took out her phone and called Mia.

'Yes, Captain?'

'Nothing this side of the fence,' Sannie said. 'What's your system showing?'

'We've lost him again.'

'Him?' Sannie said. 'Just one man?'

'Yes,' Mia replied. 'We got a few seconds of video of him and he appears to be alone, masked and armed with a hunting rifle and silencer. He's using dead ground – riverbeds and dongas – to keep out of sight of our cameras and sensors.'

'Can you pick up his trail?'

'Yes, Captain, Bongani and I are certainly going to try. We're going to leave Sara here to watch the system while we try to pick up his spoor.'

'Good,' Sannie said. 'And good luck. Give Sara my number and if you catch sight of him turning and making a run for the fence let me know and I'll try to intercept him on this side. He's got to have crossed over or under it somewhere.'

Sannie turned back towards the settlement of Killarney, once more cutting through the sparse trees of the buffer zone. A cow mooed nearby. She found the track she had been on and followed it to the right, in the direction she had originally been heading.

The sangoma's house was an older-style rondavel, a roundhouse built in the traditional style of mudbrick and a grass thatch roof.

The satellite dish and solar panels on the roof were a concession to the twenty-first century.

'Can I help you?'

Sannie turned to see a plump, elderly woman in a neatly pressed floral dress and blue canvas tekkies, simple sneakers. The woman had a basket made of woven reeds over her left arm.

'I'm looking for the sangoma,' Sannie said. 'Do you know if he's in?'

The woman shook her head. 'Tsk, tsk, tsk.'

'Do you know where he is?' she asked again.

'He was never here.'

Sannie was tired. She had not been sleeping well, generally, and she'd had precious little rest the night before. She was not in the mood for riddles or jokes.

'The truth is, he never existed,' the woman said before Sannie could rephrase her question.

Sannie looked at the woman and opened her mouth to speak. Again, she was beaten to the punch.

'You are troubled.'

Sannie sighed. She didn't have the energy to pretend. 'More than you can imagine, but can you –'

'Come inside. I will make you a cup of tea, Captain van Rensburg.'

'You know my name?'

'My old eyes are not so bad that I cannot read a name tag, and I'm not so senile that I can't recognise police ranks. *Police* is one thing I know about.'

The woman went to the door of the hut and opened it. Sannie followed her inside.

'You're the sangoma?'

The woman looked back at her as Sannie crossed the threshold. She raised her eyebrows. 'You're surprised? And you a female senior officer?'

Sannie shrugged. 'Not really, I know that many izangoma are women.' Sannie did recall, however, Sonto saying the local children had been warned to stay away from this particular sangoma. Right or wrong, that had made her assume the healer would be a man.

The woman gave a little chuckle and set down her basket on a carved wooden table. She had a kitchen, of sorts, and some old laminate-topped cupboards that looked like they had come from another house, propped against the wall. The woman placed a black kettle on a gas cylinder and lit the burner.

Sannie looked around. The walls of the hut were decorated with brightly printed fabric wraps, many with motifs of animals – there were several lions, but also a rhino with his horned head held high, and a sneaky leopard. Another wall hanging was of the sun, with a face in the middle.

The hut smelled musty, and faintly of decaying meat or skin. Old death. Home-built shelves of rough timber followed the curve of the wall wherever there was space. Hundreds of boxes and old Cremora and coffee jars contained a variety of ingredients and medicines, made, Sannie guessed, of both plants and animals. The windows were also blocked with wraps.

The woman further busied herself, though taking her time, lighting a paraffin lamp. The smell of sulphur in the air came from the Lion match the woman had just struck, but all the same, Sannie couldn't help but recall some scary Sunday School stories of hell from her youth.

'I save my solar electricity for the television. *Rhythm City*, my favourite soap and my one vice each night.' She gave a small laugh.

Sannie smiled politely, but she was impatient. 'I need to ask you some questions.'

The woman blew out the match and put it back in the box.

'I can see you are troubled,' the woman said again.

'I'm sorry, I don't know your name.'

'I am Virtuous Mathebula.'

'Captain Susan van Rensburg, from the Stock Theft and Endangered Species unit, based at Skukuza.'

'You must be proud to have attained such a senior rank, though I know it has come at a cost to you.'

Sannie frowned. She was used to suspects trying to put her off a line of questioning, even immune to it, but she felt this woman was doing her best to annoy her. 'If I may –'

'Is it a loss?'

'Is what a loss?' Sannie asked.

'Is that what you are suffering from, the death of a loved one, perhaps?'

Sannie closed her eyes for a moment, to compose herself. 'Ms Mathebula ...'

'Mrs. My husband is no longer with us, but I retain the title.'

'*Mrs* Mathebula, I need to ask *you* some questions, not the other way around.'

Virtuous waved her hand in the air. 'Suit yourself, but if you don't mind me saying so I think you'd be better able to do your job with a clear mind and a clear conscience.'

Sannie felt a flash of anger. 'Clear conscience?'

Virtuous opened one of the old kitchen cupboards, its chipboard door swollen with damp, and took out two chipped mugs. She had her back to Sannie as she unscrewed the lid of an old jam jar. 'You look tired, my dear. I have something that will help you.'

Sannie started to stand up, worried the woman was going to slip her some strange concoction.

Virtuous turned to her, smiling, holding up two tea bags. 'Rooibos?'

Sannie sat again. 'Fine, thank you.'

Virtuous laughed. 'Did you think I was going to drug you with one of my potions?'

'No, no, of course not,' Sannie said quickly.

Virtuous chuckled. The kettle whistled to a boil and she turned off the gas and poured for them both. Sannie took out her notebook and pen. 'You're aware of the missing girls?'

Virtuous handed her a cup. 'Be careful, it's hot. Yes, I am aware of the missing girls. Ah, but this is a terrible business.'

'What do you think happened to them?' She *was* tired after being up most of the night; she'd snatched an hour of sleep in her car. The tea was a godsend.

Virtuous picked up her own cup and sat down on an old tubular-framed kitchen chair. She blew on her tea. 'This country happened to them, Captain.'

'What do you mean by that?'

'You are a policewoman. You must know the evils of mankind.'

Sannie sipped her tea. She certainly did. 'Specifically?'

The woman shook her head. 'You of all people must know of the problems of violence against women and children. Lord knows it is in the news media enough, but our menfolk are not getting the message. I fear for those children.'

Sannie made a note and looked up. 'Did you know the girls?'

Virtuous nodded. 'Yes, but not well. The second girl to go missing, Lilly, was not the type to be easily led astray, even by her friends. She was smart, with an enquiring mind. I had spoken to her – she was interested in studying medicine one day.'

'A competitor?'

Virtuous smiled. 'Not at all. I don't seek to persuade people to ignore science or the benefits of modern medicine. People come to me for a different kind of healing.'

'Poachers?'

She arched her eyebrows. 'If a poacher came to me with an ailment, or a problem, should I turn him away?'

Sannie shrugged. 'I don't know. It probably depends on what he wants from you. What if, for example, a man came to you asking for umuthi that would protect him from bullets, or make him invisible?'

Virtuous regarded her for a few long seconds. 'I hope you're not mocking me or my beliefs, Captain?'

'Not at all. I am sure the poachers who come to you believe in whatever it is that you're selling them.'

Virtuous set her cup down on the table. 'I am not in the business of sending young men to their deaths with false notions of their own immortality, Captain. I am one of a number of traditional healers who signed a memorandum of understanding with South African National Parks a couple of years ago agreeing not to aid or abet poachers. I can show you the article from *The Lowvelder*, if you wish?'

'Thanks, but I'm sure I can find it online.'

Virtuous took up her cup again and sipped her tea. 'I can tell you that this poaching business worries me, Captain. Too many of the young men from our community have been corrupted by greed and have found themselves either in prison or an early grave. I want nothing to do with something that kills my people. I do, where I can, try to counsel the people who come to me to not break the law and to respect the environment and the wildlife that lives on our doorstep.'

Sannie glanced around at the jars and containers on the shelves. 'Yet many of the ingredients in your medicines come from wildlife, don't they?'

Virtuous shrugged. 'Some yes, some no. You've heard of umuthi markets?'

Sannie nodded. 'I have.'

'There is a big one in Faraday, in Johannesburg. I go there two or three times a year to buy what I need. I am assured that any animal products I buy have been sustainably sourced.'

Sannie kept her face passive, but she was sure Virtuous had bought illegally poached products among her 'sustainably sourced' ingredients. Now was not the time to threaten her, though, in case she stopped talking. 'That's good to hear.'

'I can see you don't believe me, but I rest easy at night, knowing I am not contributing to this problem of poaching.'

'Of course,' Sannie said, though she held on to her doubts. 'The boy who was killed –'

'Sipho.'

'Yes,' Sannie said. 'He was selling snakes to a sangoma in Johannesburg, or to a middleman.'

Virtuous shook her head. '*Ai, ai, ai*, that boy. I told him he would get into trouble, and look what happened to him.'

'More than just "trouble", don't you think?'

'He was dancing with the devil, that one.'

Sannie made a note. 'You don't sound very remorseful.'

Virtuous shrugged. 'You ask me if I buy animal parts, if I help poachers – that boy Sipho was keeping snakes illegally and dealing with criminals. He is fuelling the myths about my calling, that we are in bed with poachers and thieves. I warned him about those snakes and I warned him not to deal with those men from Johannesburg. They are bad news.'

'You know them?'

'They came to me looking for umuthi to protect their gunmen. They sell it to the hijackers who steal cars and hold up the cash in transit vans. It's them you should be chasing, not me or the likes of Sipho.'

'Tell me about these men from Joburg,' Sannie said.

'Gangsters, every one of them. I'm afraid to say that pieces of a reptile, a young girl, even a young boy, are all just commodities like any other to the sorts of men we are talking about here as we sip our tea, you and me, Captain.'

The thought chilled Sannie to her bones. She thought of her own children.

'You are troubled,' Virtuous said again.

'So you said.'

'You know, that is something a sangoma can help you with.'

'Loss?'

'Loss ... guilt?'

'I'm not guilty,' Sannie said, too quickly. How did this woman know so much about her? It was unsettling, and not a good position to be in when conducting a police interview.

'Not of a crime.'

'There's nothing you can help me with, apart from my investigation.'

Virtuous set her teacup down. 'May I make a suggestion, Captain?'

Sannie shrugged her shoulders.

'You might see more clearly, in your investigation, if you were not carrying around so much sadness. It is, I feel, clouding your view, and perhaps your judgement.'

Sannie took a deep breath. This woman was trying her patience and Sannie was smart enough to know that one of the reasons she felt her own annoyance – anger, perhaps – rising, was that there was an element of truth in what Virtuous was saying.

'You read people.' Virtuous said it as a statement, not a question.

'It's my job.'

'Mine too. I know you are good at yours. If you weren't you would not, as a woman, and a white woman at that, have risen to the rank you have attained. Yours is not a political appointment; you must have worked hard.'

'I have. Thank you, now if we can get back to the girls –'

Virtuous held up a hand. 'Let me help you.'

'I am fine.'

'You are not.'

Sannie gritted her teeth. If she did need help she would not get it in this place, from this peddler of –

'Half-truths.'

Sannie blinked. 'What?'

'You think that I am not someone who can help you, that I am a purveyor of half-truths, of *black magic*.'

'I would not say something like that.'

'No, you're politically correct. You have to be, in order to hold a senior police rank these days, especially as your people no longer run the country. You pay lip service to traditional beliefs, perhaps you even have something of an understanding of their importance to people, yet you still think of all this as a sham, as a collection of half-truths designed to rob the gullible.'

Sannie felt that if she had been her normal self, the woman she was before Tom's death, that she would have been in command of this interview, that she would not have let this woman get to her. Now, however, she felt an almost physical weakness. Her vision seemed to blur at the edges. She took another deep breath. For a moment she wondered if she *had* been drugged.

She shook her head. No. She was very tired but she was in possession of all her faculties. The woman's words and her obfuscations had unnerved her.

'It was someone close to you. A family member.'

Sannie blinked. 'Yes.'

'Who, dear?'

'My husband,' she said softly.

Virtuous leaned forward and put a hand on her arm.

Sannie felt the emotion well up inside her, like a flooded river pressing against a weakened dam. She had to hold on or her defences would burst, and now was *not* the time, and this was *not* the place.

'You are safe here,' Virtuous said.

'I have … I have to find these children, and I need you to tell me who the poacher is who is killing the rhinos in the Sabi Sand.'

'My dear,' Virtuous reached out again, but Sannie snatched her arm out of her reach, 'I don't know any poachers.'

Sannie wiped her eyes, and even though the woman's face was soft with sympathy, all Sannie felt was her weakness exposed. 'The men from Johannesburg. Tell me about them.'

Virtuous frowned. 'You should let me help you.'

Sannie sat up straighter, squaring her shoulders. 'You can come with me to Skukuza Police Station. We can talk there.'

The other woman held up a hand. 'All right. I'll tell you what I know. I owe those men nothing and they are a disgrace to my calling. They are the ones who got poor Sipho killed, I am sure of it.'

'Why would they kill him?'

'Because he knew too much and they knew that if you took him into custody he would talk.'

'About snakes and umuthi?' Sannie asked.

Virtuous shook her head. 'No. Sipho was working with the rhino poachers as well; I am sure it goes deeper than him just selling imithi.'

Sannie regarded Virtuous. 'I have eyewitnesses who say the poacher was an older man, and that Sipho ran off with a pangolin. The anti-poaching rangers were chasing two different men.'

'And they did not catch them, yes?'

Sannie said nothing, but wondered why Virtuous had so quickly broken the unspoken code of silence that so often pervaded communities such as this. Was it because Sipho was dead that Virtuous did not mind airing her thoughts that he had been into more than trading in snakes, or … ?

Virtuous folded her hands in her lap and said nothing more.

Perhaps, Sannie thought, this wise, smiling sangoma also had something to hide, and Sipho was a convenient decoy for her to use, just as the poachers had.

Chapter 21

'Where the bloody hell has this man gone?' Mia said to Bongani. Both of them stared at the Vulture system monitors, with Sara keeping watch over their shoulders. 'We should be out there tracking as well.'

'You heard what Sean said,' Bongani said.

While Mia had told Captain van Rensburg that she and Bongani were going out to track the poacher they had detected with the Vulture system, Sean had emphatically countermanded her, saying it was up to him and his men to follow an armed suspect. He did not want a repeat of the previous day's events.

The radio hissed to life. *'Benny's lost the scent again.'* All of them in the air-conditioned cabin could hear the frustration in Sean's voice over the radio speaker. They were all feeling the stress. *'Have you picked up any more intercepts, Mia, over?'*

Part of Mia wanted to tell Sean that she would have called him if she had, but there was no sense in her losing her temper any more than she already had. 'Negative, Sean.'

Mia's phone rang. 'Hello?'

'Mia, hi, it's Jeff Beaton.'

'Jeff, I'm kind of busy right now.'

'Sure. I just wanted to say sorry, for what happened last night.'

Mia rolled back on her chair, stood and went to the door of the cabin. Sara seized the opportunity and scooted in so she could take over Mia's screen. Mia went outside for some privacy. 'You don't need to apologise,' she said quickly, 'it was Graham who acted like a fool.'

'Yeah, well, I can see how he might have got the wrong idea.'

'Yes, I suppose so,' she said, 'but he has no right to tell me what to do or how I should act.'

'Oh.' He paused. 'So you're not, like, boyfriend and girlfriend?'

It was her turn to collect her thoughts. 'We're friends, Jeff. Good friends, maybe more. But he doesn't own me.'

'Right. So, well, this is a little awkward, but if you and Graham are only friends ... I really like you and I'd like to see you again.'

That took her aback. She had found Jeff attractive, and thought he was a nice, sensitive guy, but she was romantically involved with Graham, no matter how she'd just fudged it. Not to mention that they were all neck-deep in a crisis. 'Um, we can't exactly go on a date anywhere right now, Jeff.'

'I know that, and it's difficult. I also wanted to talk to you more for my research, kind of off-the-record stuff. I'm really interested in your upbringing and your closeness to the Shangaan people – how you bridge the gap, if you know what I mean.'

It was flattering, his shy-boy approach, but she had a job to do. 'Like I said, now is not a great time. We've got a poacher – at least one – somewhere on the reserve right now.'

'Wow. Are you at the Vulture command centre? I'll be right over. My other interviews were cancelled due to all the drama.'

Jeff hung up before she could tell him, again, that now was not a good time.

'Mia?' Bongani called.

She went back inside. 'Find something?'

'No,' Bongani said, 'but Sean just called again. He's been on the phone to Captain van Rensburg. Another policeman, de Beer, has found our missing helicopter pilot. The cop's on his way to Kaya Nghala with Mike in the chopper. He asked if you can go meet them. Mike is under some sort of arrest.'

Mia frowned. Part of her wanted to stay and search for the poacher, but she also had questions for Mike. She was proud that she had planted the idea in the minds of Sean and the police that Mike might have something to do with poachers – and perhaps girls – disappearing into thin air. The helipad was close by so she would hear the Robinson coming in to land and be able to get there in time to meet the men.

'Tell him I will,' she said, staring at the screen over Sara's shoulder. 'Where has this guy *gone?*'

Sara traced a line on her screen. 'I think he's picked up the tracks of those rhinos.'

Mia bit her lip. 'What's his speed?'

Bongani called up the last intercept of the poacher and used his cursor to draw a line that ended where the poacher was last seen. 'Roughly six kilometres per hour, straight line.'

Mia nodded. 'Fast for that terrain, as if he's on a mission. I don't think he's tracking. Sara?'

Sara looked over her shoulder. 'Maybe he was moving fast until he picked up a track. His path does point to him intercepting those rhinos.'

Bongani clicked on the rhino intercept again and then pointed to a spot on the screen in the direction in which the animals were heading. 'They are making for this waterhole.'

'Yes,' Mia said. 'And so is our poacher.'

'How come?' Sara asked. 'Does he know rhinos will be there at this time of day?'

'Not instinctively,' Mia said.

'Then how?' Sara asked.

They heard a helicopter fly low over them, on approach to the Kaya Nghala airstrip.

They all exchanged glances and Mia walked out to the Land Rover. Jeff was walking briskly up the path towards her.

'Hi,' he said.

'I've got to go to the helipad, Jeff.'

He looked disappointed.

'Get in,' she said, pointing to the Land Rover.

*

Sannie's phone rang and she saw that it was Henk de Beer.

'Excuse me,' Sannie said to Virtuous, and went out of her hut to take the call. It was good to get some fresh air. She had nearly been overcome by her emotions and the strange smells of the woman's workplace.

'Howzit, Henk?'

He spoke loudly over the noise of an engine. 'I'm just coming in to land at Kaya Nghala, with the pilot.'

'OK,' she said. 'Did you know there's been another poaching incursion?'

'*Ja*, we heard over the radio. We've been flying around looking for him, but now we must land to refuel. And I guess you want to talk to the pilot?'

'I do,' Sannie said. Henk's arrival would give her the excuse she found she had been craving to terminate her interview with Virtuous.

She would not have said she had failed with the sangoma, but the woman was adept – at least as skilled as Sannie was – at turning the conversation to her own agenda. Admittedly, it seemed the woman just wanted to help her, but Sannie was not ready for some kind of traditional healing for her grief.

'I'm coming now,' Sannie said. 'Sean Bourke has arranged for the head ranger from Kaya Nghala, Mia Greenaway, to meet you with a vehicle at the landing pad.' Sannie's phone beeped and she glanced at the screen. 'Got to go, Henk, I've got another call coming in. I'll drive to you now and meet you and the pilot at the lodge.' She ended the call and accepted the incoming one. 'Van Rensburg, hello?'

'Captain, it's Mia again.'

'Yes, Mia? Any sign of the poacher?'

'No, sorry. But I just heard Julianne's helicopter fly over.'

'Yes, I just spoke to Detective de Beer and told him you'll meet him.'

'Sure, yes, on my way, but I need to talk to you. This poacher is on a mission to get to a waterhole, Captain, and we think he's going to try to intercept some rhinos there.'

'Is he tracking them?'

'No,' Mia said. 'I think he's being fed information by someone.'

'The pilot?'

'Yes. Or someone else inside the reserve. I don't know.'

Sannie thought about what Henk had just told her. 'The pilot's just been flying over your concession, supposedly responding to the report of the poacher being seen.'

There was a pause, then Mia said what Sannie had been thinking. 'That pilot's not looking for the poacher, he's somehow working with him. I'm sure of it.'

'OK. But leave the interviews to me. I'll see you at the lodge, Mia.' Sannie ended the call.

*

Henk de Beer had enjoyed the low-level flight over the Sabi Sand Game Reserve. It took him back to his time as a conscript in the old South African Defence Force.

He remembered the fear mixed with excitement and adrenaline as he sat in an Alouette helicopter, the wheels almost brushing the thorny uppermost branches of acacias as they raced across the dry bushveld of South West Africa, now known as Namibia.

Mike de Vries, the wayward pilot, was not a bad *oke*, Henk had already decided, and he had accompanied him in the helicopter to Kaya Nghala not so much to keep him under some loose form of arrest and assist with the interrogation as to get a joy flight out of Nelspruit.

'Shame we couldn't find the poacher,' Mike said to Henk as he settled the helicopter onto the landing pad.

'*Ja*,' Henk replied. 'Maybe if we can clear all this stuff up you can refuel and get back out there.'

The pilot smiled. 'That's what I like doing best. Hey, I need to let the engine cool down.'

'All right,' Henk said.

'You can get out, I'll see you once I've shut down. I'll be there now-now.'

Henk hesitated. He supposed he really should stay with the young man, but a quick glance over at the fuel gauge confirmed what the pilot had said, that the needle was in the red. His tank was almost empty.

*

Mia and Jeff pulled up in her Land Rover just as the chopper settled onto the ground. A burly man with a grey crew cut got out, bent at the waist and jogged over to them.

'I'm Henk,' the man began, then turned as the engine note behind him changed to a high-pitched whine.

'He's leaving!' Mia yelled.

Henk turned and started running back towards the helicopter, drawing the pistol from the holster on his belt.

The helicopter lifted off and the pilot banked away steeply as soon as he could. Henk fired twice, but both his shots flew wide. He swore, then pulled out his phone.

Mia got on the radio. She knew the frequency and the call sign Julianne's normal pilot used.

'Eagle, Eagle, this is Mia, go.' She released the press-to-talk switch. There was no reply, but that did not mean the pilot could not hear her. 'What are you playing at, Mike? Come back here and tell us what's happening, over.'

Henk was talking into his phone now, to Captain van Rensburg by the sound of it.

'What direction is that, where's he headed?' Henk called to Mia.

'West. Straight towards Killarney.'

'He's heading your way, Sannie,' Henk said. 'No, not into the reserve. Stay where you are for now.'

Henk ended the call and came to her. 'Let's go.'

'Where?' Mia asked.

'To the gate, then Killarney.'

'We won't catch a helicopter,' Mia said.

'I know, but he's almost out of fuel. He has to put down somewhere.'

'Wait,' Mia said. She called Bongani. 'Howzit. Can you expand your view on the Vulture radar to cover more of Killarney?'

'Sure,' Bongani said. 'Why?'

'I need you to look for Julianne's helicopter; Mike just flew off, last seen heading west.'

'Roger,' Bongani said.

Mia got into the Land Rover and Henk climbed in the back, introducing himself to Jeff.

'This is exciting,' Jeff said.

'Just another day in Africa,' Henk said.

Mia drove off, racing up through the gears and going as fast as she dared through the bush towards the entry to the Sabi Sand reserve. Bongani came back on the radio.

'Go, Bongani,' she said, hanging on hard to the steering wheel as the Land Rover lurched into and out of a dip in the road.

'*I've picked up the chopper. You were right, headed to Killarney.*'

'Good work.'

'*Wait, I'm losing him … he must be landing already.*'

'Where?'

There was a pause, probably while Bongani zoomed in on his map.

'*Got it. By the new schoolhouse, most likely using the football field as a landing zone.*'

'Roger. Keep an eye on the area. I'm heading there now.'

Mia sped on, hoping she could maintain her resolve. She needed answers to what had been going on. She respected people's traditional beliefs, but she did not believe anyone's muthi, not Bongani's nor the poacher's, could make a person disappear into thin air.

But a helicopter could.

Mia arrived at the gate. Rather than trying to convince the security guards on duty that she was in too much of a rush for them to do their routine search of her vehicle, she used the break in driving to radio Bongani again.

'Any news?' she asked him, without preamble.

'*He left the chopper and went into one of the schoolrooms – a new building that's still under construction,*' Bongani said. '*I haven't seen him come out. There are no kids there because of the lockdown, but it seems like he's hiding there.*'

'OK, call me if he leaves.'

'Affirmative,' Bongani said.

Mia called Captain van Rensburg and updated her on Mike's location.

Clear of the gate, Mia pressed the accelerator pedal to the floor, and her two passengers gripped anything they could to stop the coil spring suspension from catapulting them from the vehicle as she raced along the dirt road leading to the community of Killarney.

*

Sannie got out of her car well short of the new Killarney school construction site near the new hotel on the outskirts of the community and approached on foot, her Z88 up and at the ready.

She mentally debated the merits of waiting for Henk, who could provide backup. The pilot, she assumed, was unarmed – Henk would have made sure of that.

Looking over her shoulder she could see the cluster of granite boulders where the local teenagers had been hanging out, and where the missing girls had last been seen.

There was no one around the empty school, not even kids flouting the lockdown regulations. The wire mesh fence around the construction site for the new classrooms was festooned with plastic shopping bags. A dog barked nearby.

As Sannie walked closer to the school she could see Julianne Clyde-Smith's helicopter sitting in the middle of the empty rectangle of rocky earth that served as a soccer field, just beyond the new building, which was substantially complete and roofed.

She advanced, her pistol held in a two-handed grip.

Sannie stopped still and took out her phone. It was too quiet for Africa. She felt, in her bones and in the downy hairs standing up on the back of her neck, that it was time to call for backup.

'De Beer,' Henk said. 'We're almost there, Sannie.'

'*Lekker*. I think I'll wait for you. I'm by the school and –'

*

'Gunfire,' Henk said to Mia, but she had also heard the shots over his phone's speaker.

Mia red-lined the four-wheel drive's engine as she pushed it up into sixth gear.

De Beer had drawn his pistol. He was on his phone, calling for backup as Mia swung into the village.

Faces watched them from windows and a mother dragged a curious child from the *stoep* back indoors.

'Someone's shooting,' Jeff said from the back of the Land Rover. 'Give me the rifle.'

Mia wanted to argue, but was too busy concentrating on the road ahead.

'No ways,' Henk said for her. Ignoring Jeff, he spoke into his phone again. 'Sannie, talk to me, if you can.'

Mia looked to him.

Two shots rang out.

'Sannie, we're coming in. Talk to us.' Henk held up the phone for Mia to hear as they pulled up two hundred metres short of the school buildings and all got out of the Land Rover. Mia unzipped her gun case and took out her .375 rifle.

'One guy, AK-47,' van Rensburg replied, at last, 'in the school building. I'm hit.'

'Sheesh, Sannie. How bad?'

'Leg. It's not bad, but I won't be dancing tonight.'

'Got you. Are you in cover?'

'More or less. I'm behind the water bowser trailer, to the left of the construction site.'

'Got it.' Mia pointed out Sannie's location for Henk and Jeff, who crouched beside her.

'I'm going to outflank the guy in the schoolhouse,' Henk said.

Mia gave a sharp nod. 'I'll be right behind you.'

A burst of fire rang out, echoing up the empty road. Mia felt a mix of fear and excitement and flashed back to the man she had killed. Would she, could she, do it again? She was happier she was with, and behind, the detective this time.

There were more gunshots. It sounded to Mia like a pistol, Captain van Rensburg's. At least she was still alive.

Henk stopped to assess the situation. 'There's a drainage ditch on the right. Looks like they've been digging it for a water pipe. We go through that way, catch him on his blind side.'

Mia nodded. It wasn't much of a plan, but it was all they had. Henk had kept the line open to Sannie so he told the policewoman what they were going to do.

'I've got one spare mag of ammo, Henk,' she replied. 'When you give me the word, I'll pump it all into the building, try to keep his attention off you.'

'OK. Be careful, Sannie.'

'You as well.'

Mia turned to Jeff. 'You stay here with the Land Rover.'

Jeff looked like he was about to argue, but Mia didn't have time. Henk got up, darted to the ditch and slid down into it, barely keeping his balance. He was a big guy and was huffing and puffing already. Mia guessed he didn't chase too many suspects on foot. She swallowed her fear and jumped down after him.

They were like a couple of World War I soldiers, she thought, heading along a trench to certain doom on the front line. She wanted to be out of this nightmare and, at the same time, perversely, she felt the adrenaline supercharging her body with excitement and anticipation. It was a rush – she was sure her father had once described going into combat as a young man in the same way.

As they got closer to the half-finished schoolhouse they passed cement mixers, a bulldozer lying idle, and an earthmoving machine. The sound of more gunfire, louder now, focused her.

Henk was walking bent at the waist, keeping his head below the lip of the deep trench. He turned to look at her. 'All right?'

She shrugged. 'We're going into a gunfight.'

He gave a small nod of understanding. 'You stay here. Call for an ambulance. We're going to need one for Sannie – at least.'

Mia thought about Jeff and when she turned to look for him, she found him right behind her.

Jeff grinned. 'Sorry.'

Mia shook her head, then said to Henk: 'I'm staying with you.'

'You sure?'

'Yes.' She was anything but. She gripped her rifle tighter and turned to Jeff. 'Go back to the Land Rover and wait for us there.'

'No,' Jeff said. 'You can't order me around like that. Besides, you might need me.'

They heard Sannie fire two shots from her pistol, which were answered by a long burst from the gunman in the schoolhouse.

'I've been counting his shots. He's changing magazines after thirty rounds,' Henk said. He held the phone close to his mouth and said 'now' to Sannie. He glanced back at Mia. 'Run, if you're coming!'

The big detective lumbered along the trench line and, when it came close to the half-finished building he started scrambling up and out of the excavation. Mia was on his tail and was out of the cover before Henk. Jeff, now beside her, reached down and gave the detective his hand, hauling him the rest of the way out. It was a less than auspicious start, Mia registered, to their valiant assault.

Henk raised his pistol and ran forward. A silhouette darted across an open window space and Henk fired two shots.

Mia held her breath, even as she ran, and it was only when she began feeling dizzy that she remembered to breathe again.

'Ow!'

Mia spun around and saw Jeff had tripped and fallen headlong into a shallow trench that looked like it had been dug for electrical cables or some other services.

'I'm OK,' Jeff called.

A person emerged from the front door of the building site. Henk swung to fire, but checked his aim at the very last second. It was a girl. She was African, young and lithe, and she ran like an impala fleeing a pack of wild dogs.

A man followed her out and Mia, like Henk, had her gun up ready to fire.

'Don't shoot!' He held his arms high as he ran and Mia recognised that it was Mike de Vries, Julianne's missing chopper pilot.

The shock of seeing the girl and the pilot, unarmed, fleeing, caused them all to pause. Mia and Henk took cover behind a large cement mixer.

There was the distinctive *pop-pop-pop-pop* of an AK-47 firing on full automatic again and the pilot pitched face forward into the dirt. More bullets chased the girl, but she continued to run, headlong, arms windmilling in panic.

Henk started moving. The dark-clad figure appeared at the window again.

Mia could see that the man was raising his rifle, but Henk already had his gun up and was firing. The man ducked below the windowsill.

The ground Henk was running over was furrowed and churned, the money for landscaping having probably run out when the pandemic hit. He stumbled and sprawled forward, landing on his belly.

Jeff had dusted himself off and caught up with her again. He was almost pressed up against Mia. He stuck his head around the cement mixer. 'I can see him, Mia.'

'Keep your bloody head down!' Mia yanked on Jeff's shirt to pull him back behind the cement mixer, where he crouched down.

Mia didn't know whether to follow Henk or to turn and flee. Henk was exposed, working the slide of his pistol, either to clear a misfeed or reload. The man in the building raised his head and the barrel of his rifle, taking aim at Henk and making the decision for her. Mia fired, then worked the bolt, chambering another round in one fluid movement. Her drills were quick; she had trained on the rifle range to take down a charging lion or buffalo. A chip of brick-work flew off the building's wall next to the gunman's face.

The man switched his aim to her and fired; Mia felt the billow-ing fabric of her untucked khaki safari shirt snatched away from her body. She hunkered back behind the mixer with Jeff, trying to escape the next round. Henk was shooting again. Mia aimed and fired again. Her target disappeared. The gunfire stopped.

*

Sannie gave it five minutes then got to her feet and moved towards the school building, advancing from cover to cover. She was being cautious and her leg was now throbbing in pain. Fortunately, the bullet had only grazed her, but her blue uniform pants were turning purple with blood. The wound needed to be dressed, but as Tom had told her more than once, the best treatment for a gunshot wound was to first kill the person who had inflicted it.

Tom. She pushed him from her mind and tried to calm her breath-ing as she advanced, both hands up.

'Sannie!'

She looked over to see Henk, now back on his feet, brushing dirt from his clothes as he and Mia and a young man also closed on the school building.

'Are you all right?' she called.

'*Ja*, fine,' Henk replied. 'I think Mia got him.'

Sannie touched her first two fingers to her eyes then pointed them to the building, reminding them all that they needed to keep watch for more danger. Sannie had told the wide-eyed, running girl – she didn't yet know if it was Thandi or Lilly – to go straight to Mama Nomvula's house in the village and to stay there until she could get to her.

'There could be two more girls somewhere in that building,' Sannie called to the others.

She paused beside the helicopter pilot and quickly, painfully, dropped to one knee. A quick touch of her fingers to his neck confirmed what she could tell from looking at him and seeing him fall. Dead.

Sannie got to her feet again, took a couple of steps, then stopped. She held up a hand until the others all noticed, and also paused.

There was something not right about this.

Then the schoolhouse exploded.

Chapter 22

Jeff was kneeling by Mia's side as she opened her eyes.

'*Eish*,' she said, blinking up at him. 'What happened?'

'Shush.' Jeff wiped her head with something. 'You were hit in the head by some debris. Thank God you're alive. You were blacked out for a couple of minutes.'

Her head hurt, now that he mentioned it. She remembered an explosion. 'The school?'

He shook his head. 'Gone. That place was rigged to go off.'

Mia was aware of someone in her peripheral vision. She craned her neck, the simple movement causing her to wince with pain. 'Captain ...'

'Mia,' Sannie said, limping a few steps so Mia could better see her, 'good to see you're all right. I have to go. I've just met your friend Jeff and he's called an ambulance.'

Mia sat up and felt dizzy.

'Stay still,' Jeff said. 'Lie down.'

'No. Where are you going, Captain?'

'The girl.'

'I remember now – she ran from the building, with the pilot. Is he ...?'

'Dead,' Sannie said. 'I've got no idea what's going on here. I've asked for a forensic team to go through what's left of the building.'

'Let me come with you.'

'Mia ...' Jeff began.

'I know these people,' Mia said. 'I speak their language. Let me come with you. It's just a bump on the head.'

Jeff looked up at Captain van Rensburg.

Sannie shrugged. 'All right. Might be better if we're all together. We still don't know who else might be around here.' Sannie looked over at the remains of the school. Henk de Beer, covered in dust from the explosion, was gingerly picking his way around the wreckage, pistol still in hand. 'Henk?'

He waved back at her. 'You go on. I'll stay here until the forensics guys arrive. I'll see what I can find. You don't want to see what I'm looking at right now.'

Mia drew a breath. 'The other girls?'

Henk shook his head. 'No, no sign of anyone else. Just what's left of the *oke* who was shooting at us.'

'Call Sean Bourke.' Mia grabbed hold of Jeff's forearm, using him for support as she hauled herself to her feet. 'His old dog, Benny, was trained to detect explosives, and last I heard they were having no luck tracking the poacher inside the reserve.'

'Yes, good idea,' Sannie said. 'It'll be hours before I can get a police canine team here.'

Sannie headed back to the cars, making the call to Sean on the way, with Jeff supporting Mia. They were the walking wounded, Mia thought, as they followed.

'I'll drive,' Jeff said.

'Let me come with you,' Sannie said, 'my leg is not so *lekker*.'

They climbed in and Sannie directed them to Mama Nomvula's house.

When they arrived Mia saw Virtuous, the village sangoma, standing at the gateway.

'*Ai*, what has happened?' Virtuous asked.

Mia was not a close friend of the sangoma, but they knew each other by sight and greeted each other. Mia filled her in.

'Captain, you are also injured. Let me take a look at that wound.'

'We're here to visit Nomvula and to see the girl.'

'The girl?'

'A girl escaped from the new school building, just before the explosion. I very much hope it is one of the girls who are missing.'

Virtuous looked heavenward and clasped her hands. 'Praise be. I received a call from Nomvula to come, now-now. She said it was an emergency. Is it Thandi or Lilly?'

'I don't know yet,' Sannie said. 'We've called for an ambulance.'

'Yes,' Virtuous said calmly, 'but the paramedics are not here yet. I am.'

'Wait here, please. Mia, come with me.'

Mia glanced at Virtuous, giving her an apologetic look, and the sangoma replied with a polite nod.

They went into the house to find Nomvula with her arms around a thin young girl who was shivering, even though the day was warm, and she was swaddled in a thick grey woollen blanket.

'Are you hurt?' Sannie said to the girl.

The child looked up at her, eyes wide and brimming with tears.

'It's all right,' Sannie prompted, 'you're safe now.'

'This is Thandi,' Nomvula said, and Mia saw the sadness in the older woman's eyes. 'She thinks my Lilly is alive.'

'Did they hurt you?' Sannie asked again.

'A man ... he hit me sometimes. I couldn't sleep, I was so afraid,' Thandi said.

'Did he ...' Sannie began.

The girl shook her head and lowered her eyes. 'No, but he threatened me with that.'

Mia seethed quietly. Her head was throbbing and she felt nauseous. She needed fresh air. She got up and went outside.

Virtuous was still outside, sitting on the *stoep*, with Jeff standing nearby.

'I'm sorry the captain was so rude,' Mia said to her.

Virtuous smiled. 'She is hurt, under pressure, and it is not just her leg that is wounded. She has suffered a terrible loss.'

'She has?'

Virtuous nodded. 'Someone close to her has died. Her husband.'

'Shame,' Mia said, meaning it. 'I need to make an appointment to see you.'

'I know.'

'How?'

'You killed a man.'

'Word travels fast,' Mia said.

'This is a small community. Nothing happens without me knowing about it, Mia.'

Mia narrowed her eyes. 'Then what happened to those missing girls, the one inside?'

'That did not happen in this community. The police captain will not find anyone from Killarney guilty.'

'Outsiders?' Jeff weighed in.

Virtuous gave a small shrug. 'Maybe. Or it could be that the men who hunt the rhinos are getting desperate; rhinos are not as easy to come by any more as ...'

'Children?'

Virtuous looked away. Mia felt a chill.

*

Sannie waited while Nomvula made Thandi a cup of tea, with condensed milk and three heaped spoons of sugar. The girl took it between her grubby fingers, blew on it and sipped.

'Did you see the other girls?'

Thandi blinked at Sannie, seated opposite. 'I heard things, but never saw anyone else. I was kept alone.'

Sannie took out her notebook. 'Where did they keep you?'

'In a room.'

'Can you describe it?'

'The walls were made of cement, no windows, just the one doorway. They put a bag over my head, when they took me.' The girl wiped away some more tears. 'But the sack was not tied tight so I was able to get glimpses of them, and where I was.'

'You heard the other girls?' Sannie asked her. 'This is important. We need to find them, to know if they are still alive.'

'One time, I heard Lilly; I know her voice. She was crying for her grandmother.'

Nomvula put a knuckle to her mouth.

'Go on, you're doing very well,' Sannie said. 'When did you hear her?'

The girl looked puzzled. 'It was hard to keep track of days. I think it might have been two days ago, three, maybe?'

A groan escaped from Nomvula, who got up from her chair, turned and tried to busy herself boiling more water.

'Any more?'

'Another time I heard a girl screaming, calling for help, but her voice was different, she sounded white, like, maybe British.'

Sannie exhaled. 'And when did you hear her?'

'It must have been yesterday. She was crying for her mother. She said that if anyone heard, they should call her mother, Sue someone.'

Sannie made a note. She didn't know whether to feel hope, or to expect the worst. 'You are doing a terrific job. This is very, very important for us. We need to find those other girls.'

'I understand. I am trying.' Thandi started sobbing, deeper, louder, her skinny shoulders shaking. Nomvula adjusted the blanket and wrapped her big arms around the child.

'I know this is difficult, but their lives depend on anything we can learn now,' Sannie said.

Thandi sniffled and composed herself. 'It is all right, I will help you.'

'Who took you, and where?'

'It was not far from here, near the sangoma's place. We – my friends and I – would go there to talk.'

Nomvula interrupted: 'And smoke and drink and meet with boys, like that poor stupid Sipho.'

'Poor?' The girl looked to each of them.

'Nothing,' Sannie said, not wanting to upset her with news of the snake boy's death. 'Unless Sipho hurt you, or was part of this?'

'No, he had nothing to do with it. He wasn't even there when I was taken.'

'What else can you remember? Did you get a look at the men who took you?'

She shook her head. 'No, not really. I was surprised by them. They grabbed me from behind.'

'How many of them?'

'Two. I fought them, but they were strong. And it wasn't two men; there was one man, one woman – I smelled her perfume. They wore gloves and before the one put the bag over my head I could see he was dressed in black.'

Sannie raised her eyebrows and made a note. 'From their voices, could you tell where they were from? Were they local?'

'They did not say very much. But, yes, the man was. He had a deep voice, like a Shangaan man.'

'The woman?'

Thandi shrugged. 'I just knew she was a woman – she did not talk.'

'How did they treat you?'

'My food – it was mealie pap and some sauce – was handed to me through a slit in the door. No one ever spoke. I had to … had to use a bucket. It was only emptied every few days. A man would look through the slit and tell me to put the hood, the bag, over my head and to sit on the bed, quietly, while he took my empty food bowls and the bucket away. The last day, up until now, I was tied to my bed. I was starving. I had no water or food for maybe one or two days. I lost track of time.'

Interesting, Sannie thought. Perhaps the couple wanted her weaker, more compliant, for something. Maybe they were planning on moving her, or something worse.

'How did you get free?'

The girl closed her eyes as if concentrating on recalling the details. 'There was a noise, like an engine, but louder. I would hear men working, often, but no one could hear me from the room or through the door.'

'A truck? A helicopter?' Nomvula prompted.

Sannie frowned at her, indicating that she was the one asking the questions.

'Yes, I think so,' the girl said. 'It must have landed close by. There was the sound of two men arguing outside the door and then a white man came in. He was saying something to someone else about how he had orders from "the boss" to move me, urgently, to take me away.'

'In his helicopter?' Sannie asked.

'I don't know. There was a fight, and the white man cut my ties. He was taking me away, I was so full of hope, and then the man with the gun came and stopped him. He hit the white man with his gun and knocked him out. I saw one of the other man's hands during the fight – he was African.'

'Did the pilot, or the other man, say anything about the other girls?'

Thandi closed her eyes again. 'I heard him say something like, "where are they", and the man with the gun swore at him. I didn't think to ask, I am sorry.'

Sannie reached out and put her hand over Thandi's. 'Don't be. It's just good that you made it out.' She thought it might be positive, maybe, that the pilot was asking about the others – at least that meant he didn't think they were dead, or gone somewhere. Perhaps there was another hiding place.

'Were you taken anywhere else?' Sannie asked.

'No.'

'How did you manage to escape?'

'After about ten minutes the pilot woke up, and he used the frame of my bed to break the door open. By that time the gunfire had started and the sound of it covered the noise of the pilot breaking down the door.' She sniffed and started to cry again. 'It was so scary.'

Sannie patted her hand again. 'It's OK.' She could picture the rest. The pilot, whatever his involvement in all of this, had perhaps at least tried to redeem himself by freeing Thandi, or maybe he was just trying to get away himself. 'The pilot ...'

Thandi blinked up at her. 'He saved me. The man with the gun tried to stop us and the pilot charged right at him. The pilot could have run out – he was already in front of me – but he chose to stay inside and he got between me and the man with the gun. He hit him, and then ran himself – I think the gun was out of bullets – but when we got outside he just yelled to me, "run, run, run", and I did. And then I think the man with the gun reloaded and ...'

Thandi was sobbing again, unable to carry on. It did, indeed, seem like the pilot had given his life to protect hers.

Which did not explain the explosion.

'Did you see any explosives?' Sannie asked.

Through her tears, Thandi shook her head.

'Ah, they were blowing up lots of things,' Nomvula said. Sannie looked to her. 'Sorry for talking.'

'No, no,' Sannie said to the older woman. 'It's fine. Tell me. There have been other explosions?'

'In between the lockdowns, sometimes there were men working on a new road, as well as the school, the hotel and the pool. Nothing lately.'

'But there are explosives onsite?'

Nomvula nodded. 'Yes. In a building with a red skull and crossbones.'

Could the explosion have been an accident? Sannie wondered. Perhaps a stray round had detonated some explosives. It sounded far-fetched, though. More likely, Sannie thought, the blast was designed to conceal something. Perhaps it was a booby trap.

A siren outside drew their attention. Sannie went to the door and saw two paramedics in green jumpsuits getting out of an emergency ambulance. Sannie directed them inside the home. A police *bakkie* pulled up behind the ambulance. Sannie was glad to have some backup, even if it was late. This village was turning into a war zone.

Mia, Jeff and Virtuous had been waiting in the shade of a tree beside Nomvula's house. They came to her.

'I've finished inside for now,' Sannie said to Virtuous. 'If Nomvula wants to see you, then it's fine.'

'Thank you,' Virtuous said, and went to Nomvula.

One of the paramedics came back out of the house.

'The captain here needs someone to take a look at her leg,' Mia said to the man.

'I'll be fine,' Sannie said.

Mia shook her head. 'Not if you pass out on us from blood loss.'

'They're all under control inside,' the paramedic said, as he bent to take a closer look at Sannie's wound. 'Unlike you. Please take a seat.'

Sannie sat in an old kitchen chair on the *stoep* as the paramedic shrugged off his bag and got to work.

The two police officers, the man and the woman who had been canvassing the village, reported to Sannie as the paramedic cut away part of her trouser leg and took out antiseptic and bandages from his bag.

'You called for backup, Captain?' the female officer said.

'Yes. There's been an explosion and multiple homicides in and around the new school buildings just up the road. Two dead males, though you'll have trouble finding anything of the one in the destroyed building. Secure the area, please, and beware of other suspects.'

'Yes, Captain,' the sergeant said.

The paramedic finished bandaging Sannie's leg. 'I'll help you to the ambulance now.'

'No way,' Sannie said. 'I've got work to do.'

'But, Captain, you'll need a couple of stitches.'

'That can wait. I'll go to the doctor later. Mia, can you drive me back to the school and my car, please?'

'Of course,' Mia said.

'Thank you,' Sannie said to the paramedic, who was shaking his head as he zipped up his bag.

Mia drove them out of town to the new school. Just as they arrived, Sean Bourke pulled up in his camouflaged Land Rover, with his dog in the back.

'Sean,' she said.

'Sannie, howzit?'

Mia and Jeff waited in the Land Rover as Sannie climbed down. Sannie briefed Sean on what had happened and her theory about a stray bullet setting off some explosives.

He shook his head. 'Highly unlikely. Modern explosives are pretty stable. You could fire a machine gun into common explosives like C4 or nitropril, and nothing would happen. If it was the Middle East I'd say a suicide bomber, or a command detonation, but as no one in this part of the world likes deliberately heading for heaven, I'd say the latter.'

'Remote controlled?'

'Yes.' Sean, hands on hips, looked around them. 'Someone might have been watching, waiting for the right moment to press a button on a wireless device, like maybe a garage door remote, or even sending a message on a cell phone, to detonate the explosives at the right time.'

'There was a guy inside, shooting at us when the bomb went off. Why would whoever this was kill one of their own men?'

'Were you closing in on them?'

Sannie nodded. '*Ja.*'

'I said people here don't like killing *themselves*, but I know plenty who wouldn't think twice about throwing someone else under the bus. Maybe someone's trying to hide something?'

'Like missing teenage girls?'

Sean shook his head in disgust and went to the back of his truck and opened the tailgate. Somewhat awkwardly, Benny jumped down, but when Sean reached into the cab and fetched the dog's tracking collar the canine barked and ran in a small circle, clearly eager to get to work.

'Hello, Benny.' Sannie winced as she transferred her weight from one leg to the other.

'I'll take Benny and we'll cast about a bit, see if we can find any bomb residue or components.'

'Be careful, Sean.'

He reached into the cab of his vehicle and took out his LM5 assault rifle. When Sean cocked his rifle Benny's whole demeanour changed. He stood alert, ears up, tail out.

'When he hears that sound, he knows we're working,' Sean said to Sannie, then looked down at his dog, 'Yes, you do, don't you, boy?'

Both of them, Sannie thought, looked in their element.

'*Soek*, Benny!' Sean pointed towards the ruins of the school building and Benny set off on his own.

'Will he be all right?' Sannie asked.

'I'm working him off lead because there aren't any predators around, no lions or leopards. Also, if he finds something ...'

Sannie didn't need or want Sean to finish the sentence as it was too terrible to consider. If Benny found and accidentally tripped a booby trap bomb then there was less risk of a human being injured if the dog was ranging ahead by himself.

'Don't worry,' Sean said, 'what I meant to say is that if he finds something, he'll know exactly what to do. This isn't Benny's first rodeo. He was the best explosive detection dog in Afghanistan, and although he's getting old, I'd stack his nose up against any other tracker dog.'

Talk of Benny's olfactory powers triggered something in Sannie's memory. 'One more thing. Come with me, please Sean.'

'Sure.'

Sean followed Sannie as she limped to her car. She popped the boot and took out a plastic evidence bag. She opened it and gave Laura's beanie to Sean. 'See if Benny can pick up her scent again.'

'Hundred per cent. You think Laura and the other girl might be in the school buildings somewhere?'

'Maybe, but after you've checked that, I'd like you to also take a look up there.'

Sean's eyes followed to where she was pointing, to the sangoma's hut.

Chapter 23

Bongani picked up the radio handset in the Vulture control room. 'Mia, go for Bongani, over.'

There was no answer. He tried again, three times more, and wondered if she was out of range or just away from the Land Rover.

Bongani kept his eyes on the computer screen in front of him, not allowing himself to lose sight of the poacher who was walking resolutely through an open, grassy clearing, an AK-47 balanced with arrogant casualness on his shoulder. It was as if, Bongani thought, he did not care if anyone saw him. Sara sat next to Bongani, similarly transfixed.

'Bongani this is Jeff, over. I'm the guy who's been doing the research into umuthi.'

'Copy, Jeff, I've heard of you. Where's Mia, please?'

'She's with the cops. Can I pass on a message?'

'Just tell her the poacher is crossing Little Serengeti now-now. She'll know what that means.'

'Roger, Bongani.'

'Oh, and one more thing, Jeff.'

'Yes?'

'Tell her I'm going to get him.'

'Roger, will do.'

Bongani stood and Sara looked up at him. He knew she would want to come with him. 'Sara, you must stay here and watch the screens.'

'But –'

'No buts,' he said. 'We cannot lose this man again. I will find him, but if his magic is strong once again and I lose him, then you will be able to guide me. If he heads too far east, out of the Vulture's area of coverage, you can re-task the system.' He showed Sara the commands to redirect one of the long-range cameras. 'You can follow him like that.'

'We shouldn't have let Sean and Benny go to Killarney.'

'There is no use in regretting decisions once they are made,' Bongani said. 'There was a bomb in Killarney and that dog, Benny, is an expert at detecting explosives. I am an expert in tracking people.'

'Be careful, Bongani.'

'I will. And I will be safe with you as my guardian angel, watching my back with your fancy cameras and radars.'

She smiled and turned back to the screens. It was time for him to end this nonsense once and for all. From the Vulture system cabin he went to the main lodge. In the back-of-house area was a walk-in safe, which housed the reserve's armoury. Bongani opened it, using the combination entrusted to very few. From the rack on the wall he selected an R1 rifle they sometimes took on walks. He took two magazines of 7.62-millimetre ammunition and put them in each of the side pockets of his cargo pants. He took the keys to one of the Land Rover game viewers from a hook in the safe, went out to the car park and started the vehicle.

He drove fast, eyes darting left and right looking for animals. In less than ten minutes he was racing along the road next to the open area known as Little Serengeti. He picked the spot where he had last seen the poacher, drove on another half a kilometre and parked.

On foot, he left the road and had little difficulty picking up the poacher's path. The grass was long – the passage of animals was evident through flattened pathways – but the individual stems had begun to bounce back on these meandering tracks.

One pathway was still flattened, still dead straight. That of a man.

Bongani broke into a jog, the sure-footed, soundless pursuit of a wild dog on the hunt. He kept an eye on the spoor in front of him, but especially on the way ahead, as he knew he was not far behind the wily poacher who had led them on a merry dance across the reserve where Mia and he had once reigned supreme. He was sure it was the old man, experienced and arrogant enough to hunt alone. Nothing, not the canny leopard nor even the shy nocturnal aardvark had eluded them when they picked up its tracks or heard of its presence.

Except this quarry.

Bongani felt the challenge laid down, of a gauntlet dropped by one knight to another, something Bongani had seen in an old movie once. His honour was at stake, as were the lives of rhinos and who knew what else this man was after – be they children or pangolins. Bongani would find him and stop him.

He caught a glimpse of movement between some trees about a hundred metres to his front. The Little Serengeti had given way to bushveld. He paused by a tree and scanned ahead.

Bongani's hands tightened on the pistol grip and the stock of the military-style rifle. This was not a gun for hunting or protection, this was a weapon for mass killing, multiple shots, one after another. He did not have it in mind to kill the elusive old man, but the poacher was carrying an AK this time and Bongani did not doubt that the man would use it without hesitation.

He paused.

Why was the man carrying the Russian assault rifle and not a heavy weapon? he wondered. What was the poacher after this time?

Bongani studied the ground. Now that there was shelter from trees there was not as much grass and undergrowth, and Bongani was able to discern the man's boot prints on bare ground here and there.

The stride was long, which meant he was still moving quickly. There was the slightest sign of an uneven gait, a short scuffing of the right foot that told Bongani he was tracking an older man. Of course, there was no way to be certain it was the same man, but Bongani *felt* it.

As clever as this poacher was, he wouldn't be a threat much longer, Bongani thought. This time he would not escape.

Bongani resisted the urge to run. Had the man become so cocky that he thought he could take down a rhino just with his AK-47, on his own? It was possible – Bongani had seen rhinos killed by a long burst of fire. While the rounds from an AK were smaller than those of a big-bore hunting rifle, a poacher could kill a rhino with one by firing a number of bullets into the animal's body and disrupting its vital organs.

A wary old criminal like this one, Bongani knew, could probably even bring down a rhino silently, with a tomahawk. Perhaps that was his plan, to sneak up on a half-blind, dozy white rhino and hack into the tendons of one of its rear legs. He would then chase the wounded creature and kill it with his hand-axe. It was dangerous work, and skill was needed to get close enough to the rhino to deliver the first, crippling cut, but Bongani had no doubt this man was up to it. If that was the case then the AK was probably just for the man's personal protection. Yes, Bongani said to himself, that all made sense.

He did not judge the poacher, nor think him evil, as some would. They were warriors on different sides of a war, that was all. Bongani's father and grandfather before him had been hunters and they had roamed these lands taking what game they needed, to eat or to trade. Bongani was a convert to the idea that big game, such as rhinos and elephants, needed to be protected to provide jobs and income through tourism, but he did not judge a hunter harshly.

That said, Bongani knew the man would have no qualms about shooting him if he discovered Bongani was on his tail. He wondered if he knew the man. Whoever he was, he was an experienced hunter and, therefore, dangerous.

Bongani moved with cautious haste, walking, watching, checking spoor and always looking ahead, left to right, for dangerous game and a deadly man. They carried on, crossing the Manzini Spruit, heading further east with every step.

'This time you will be mine,' he whispered.

He reached into his pocket, took a pinch of the sangoma's herbs from the little packet and put the mix into his mouth and started chewing. He needed all the help he could get. If this guy could make himself invisible or impervious to bullets then so, too, could Bongani.

Bongani carried on for another fifty metres then paused and listened. A spurfowl began its crowing call. The birds normally made a noise at dawn and dusk, or when they sensed danger. It might be his prey. He carried on, slowly now, rifle at the ready.

The sun was climbing high and Bongani felt the sweat drizzle from his armpits. He stopped to wipe his brow.

A blur of movement made him bring the R1 up into his shoulder and he tracked the flash of brown with the tip of the barrel. It was a bushbuck. Bongani cursed – he should have seen the antelope before it saw him. What was wrong with him? He was supposed to be focusing all his attention on the way ahead.

His mouth felt dry. Perhaps it was the heat, but he had not moved too far. He should not feel exhausted, but his feet felt as though they were weighted down, with lead in his boots. His head felt woolly.

What is wrong with me?

He blinked away sweat that stung his eyes. Why was he perspiring so much? His hands felt slick on the rifle's pistol grip.

From his front he heard a high-pitched squeal followed by the drumbeat tattoo of heavy feet pounding the dry ground. Another person might have wondered what kind of animal could squeak like that here in the bush, but Bongani knew, instantly, that it was a rhino, making one of its rarely heard calls. He feared he was right about how the poacher might take his next victim.

Bongani looked down, forcing himself to concentrate. There were the man's boot prints, but there was also a new set of tracks, several of them, and very fresh. It was the crash of three rhinos they had seen on the screen. The poacher had intercepted them and he had turned right, his footprints now overlapping the big, three-toed spoor of the giant animals. The man was making no effort to conceal himself, though he was also now moving more slowly.

Bongani tried again to focus his thoughts. He looked at the ground, knowing that he, too, must now veer to the right and follow the tracks of the man and the rhinos he was pursuing.

He wiped his face with his left hand, holding the rifle in his right, took two steps then stumbled. Bongani hauled himself to his feet and carried on, but the same pattern kept repeating itself. He would push himself onwards, fall, or stagger, then carry on, like a drunken man.

What is wrong with me? he asked himself again.

The radio clipped to Bongani's belt hissed to life. He had the volume set to low, but he could hear Mia's voice, broken by static. He fumbled for it, barely able to stay standing. His knees felt weak.

'*Bongani ... this ... Mia,*' she said.

He held the handset to his mouth and moved his lips, but he was unsure if he was making any noise as he mouthed the words: 'Bongani ... over ... poacher ...'

The words would not come.

Bongani drew a deep breath and staggered on. It was an effort to lift each leg, to put one foot in front of the other. His vision swam and he had trouble concentrating, but he knew he must go on.

Ahead of him, Bongani saw fresh blood on the ground. One of the rhinos had begun running – he had heard them all take off – and the man was giving chase. He had to run, as well, but did not know if he could.

He forced himself onwards, feet clumsily landing on earth and grass as he fought to stop himself from pitching over headfirst. What spell had this man cast on him? he wondered, because this was like nothing he had encountered. Except, perhaps, his recent bout of food poisoning.

What if ...

Bongani heard the squeals ahead.

Then his radio hissed again and this time Mia was either closer or there was a clearer line of sight between them for the radio waves to navigate, because the message came through undistorted.

'*Bongani, Bongani, this is Mia. Send your location please. I'm coming back to Lion Plains and I've got Captain van Rensburg with me, over.*'

Her voice was loud enough for the poacher to stop his grisly business.

Bongani needed to silence Mia, and he fumbled with the volume control on the radio on his belt. He had to look down to locate the knob. His body seemed incapable of doing what his fuzzy brain told it to do.

'*Bongani, Bongani ...!*'

His mind swam. Should he mute her, or should he call her? He felt himself losing control, not only of his motor skills, but of his brain. Bongani pressed the transmit switch and held it in.

He sensed movement in his peripheral vision and looked to a large termite mound ahead and to his left. It looked familiar. The silhouette of a man appeared. He carried an AK-47, distinctive with its banana-shaped magazine.

Bongani raised his R1, one-handed, and pulled the trigger, twice. Even in his diminished capacity he knew he had no chance of hitting the man, but the shots might scare him off, or bring Mia to him.

He dropped to one knee and released the transmit button.

'*Bongani, Bongani, I hear gunfire, two shots. Is that you, over?*' Mia asked.

He had the presence of mind, through the fog that was enveloping him, to press and release the transmit button once, the signal for 'yes'.

Bongani tried to raise his rifle again, to draw a bead on the poacher, but the weapon seemed impossibly heavy, his arms next to useless. The man stared at him, no more than thirty metres away now, an easy shot, normally.

The man brought his AK-47 up into the firing position and aimed at Bongani. Before the man could pull the trigger, Bongani felt his legs give out and he fell, tumbling backwards and knocking the back of his head on a tree root.

His chin was close to his chest and if he rolled his eyes downward, which took all his powers of concentration, he could look down the length of his body in the direction where he had last seen the poacher.

Bongani saw, through vision that was becoming increasingly watery, the shape of the man walking back towards him. He now carried a long rhinoceros horn in one hand, a small axe in the other. He had slung his rifle over his shoulder.

He stood there, by the big termite mound, staring at Bongani for long seconds. Bongani kept his eyes half closed, feigning death, which was not hard as he felt as though he was probably paralysed.

The man slid the tomahawk into his belt, handle first, and set the rhino horn down on the ground. He unslung his rifle and once more brought it up into his shoulder, left leg forward, bracing himself, in a soldier's stance. He took aim at Bongani, who prepared himself for death, even though he already knew he was dying.

The man seemed to peer over the barrel, perhaps convincing himself that Bongani was already dead. He thought better of delivering the coup de grace and, instead, slung his rifle again and picked up the horn. Then the man reached up and pulled off the balaclava he was wearing, probably believing Bongani was dead.

Bongani had to bite the inside of his lower lip to stop from crying out as the poacher glanced back at him. Through his slitted eyes Bongani could see, without a doubt, that the man they had been chasing all this time, the one who had eluded him, was, in fact, a very good tracker in his own right. He was, as Bongani had guessed, one of them.

It was his cousin, Alfred.

'*Famba kahle*,' Alfred said in Xitsonga, wishing Bongani safe travels. Alfred turned and walked to the big termite mound.

Bongani's vision swam and he could not lift his head to get a better look, or open his eyes wider – not because he feared he would alert Alfred, but rather because his body was refusing to obey the commands his mind was issuing. Alfred disappeared from view.

Bongani tried to reach the radio to tell Mia what he had just seen, how the poacher, Alfred, had vanished, just as surely as he had every other time they had tried to catch him. But his hands and fingers would not move.

Then Bongani died.

Chapter 24

Sean and Benny searched the second, still-standing empty school building and found no traces of explosives.

Captain Henk de Beer, who had been picking over the ruins of the other building, along with a police crime scene investigation team of two, came to Sean.

'Captain van Rensburg wants us to check out the hut where the sangoma lives, but I'm not sure about search warrants,' Sean said.

'Let me worry about that,' Henk said. 'Come. Her instincts are usually right. She didn't get to be a captain by being just a *mooi vrou*.'

They walked past the ruined building and headed up the rise towards the rondavel.

Sean held Laura's beanie under Benny's nose then let his dog off his leash. Benny bounded away.

'You think the captain believes there's a connection between the missing girls and the muthi trade?' Sean said.

'Wouldn't be the first time.' Henk made hard work of the gentle uphill climb, huffing as he walked. 'I've seen some things, I'm telling you.'

Benny was scratching at the front door of the circular hut when they caught up with him.

Henk put his hands on his hips and drew a deep breath. 'You trust that dog of yours?'

'With my life,' Sean said.

Henk tried the doorhandle and found the door locked. 'Police, anybody home?'

There was no answer.

Henk grinned at Sean, drew his pistol, lifted a leg and kicked the door open.

Benny darted inside and the two men followed him in. Sean took in the garish animal prints on the wall and the musty smell, and saw Benny scratching under a bed in the second of the hut's two rooms. Benny lay down on a zebra skin on the floor, tail out and ears back, indicating.

Henk stood over Sean, pistol at the ready as Sean got down on his knees and reached under the bed. He pulled out a black top with an 'Under Armour' logo. He held it up.

'Women's, small size.'

'Jissus,' Henk said. 'I'll get Sannie to call the lodge, where the mother is. Something tells me she's going to say her daughter was wearing this. Let's take more of a look around.'

'Good boy,' Sean said, ruffling Benny's neck. 'Fetch your toy, boy, fetch!'

Benny turned tail and ran out the door.

'Toy?' Henk said as he opened a chest of drawers. 'It's work time, not play time.'

'Benny needs to be rewarded every time he makes a successful indication,' Sean said. 'He's got a conk, a ball on a rope, that he loves to play with. He'll be back at work just now.'

Sean opened some old kitchen cupboards fixed to a wall above a table with a kettle and gas cooker plate. A minute later Benny trotted back in with Sean's daypack clamped in his jaws. He dropped the bag at Sean's feet and Sean unzipped it and took out the toy. Benny bit the conk and Sean tugged on it, patting and congratulating him at the same time.

Henk opened a chest deep freezer, set up against one wall of the hut, and suddenly reared back and swore.

Sean left Benny to chew on his toy and went to the detective. Looking over his shoulder he saw what the detective had discovered under some frozen chops and a bag of chicken feet.

A severed human arm, wrapped in cling film.

*

'Bongani, Bongani,' Mia kept saying into the radio as she and Jeff drove through the reserve. Tears of frustration ran down her cheeks. Captain van Rensburg was in the back of the vehicle, fatigue plain on her face.

'Mia, this is Sara, I'm mobile now, and I'm close to Bongani.'

'Where, over?' Mia asked.

'By the big termite mound. I'm pulling up now.'

'He's been shot, I know it,' Mia said.

They came to another Land Rover, a short wheelbase model with a video camera mounted on the back, another of the webcast filming vehicles. Mia stopped, leapt out and sprinted into the bush.

Not far from the mound, Sara was on her knees, bent over Bongani, her mouth over his as she blew air into his lungs, causing his chest to rise.

'How ... how is he?'

'Mia,' Sara drew a breath, 'get us a chopper. Now!'

Sannie and Jeff arrived at the clearing. Sannie took out her phone. 'I'll organise the chopper. What's his condition?'

Mia dropped to her knees and started compressions, pushing the heel of her right hand down on Bongani's lower chest with her left hand.

'No gunshot or other visible wounds,' Sara said. 'No pulse when I arrived. I saw him fall down on the Vulture monitor – he showed me how to move one of the cameras in order to follow him – and I got straight in a vehicle. I was here within five minutes, but I don't know when he stopped breathing or why.' Sara lowered her mouth to Bongani's and blew in another breath as Mia removed her hands.

Sannie started dialling. 'Best guess?' Mia asked, as Sara broke contact.

Sara shrugged. 'I think it's a cardiac arrest, brought on by something. Poisoning? Snake bite? I haven't been able to check all over his body. Mia, I know it's hard to believe, but I saw the poacher on the camera. The resolution was too grainy for me to identify him, but I watched him disappear, for real.'

'I'm calling the MAJOC.' Captain van Rensburg got through to the Mission Area Joint Operations Centre, the headquarters for the fight against poaching in the Kruger Park, located near Skukuza Airport. She asked for the air operations officer.

Between them, Mia and Sara kept up the routine of breaths and compressions. Mia didn't have time to dwell on what Sara had just said about the disappearing poacher.

'OK, one of the national parks' helicopters is on the way, but the doctor's busy elsewhere delivering a baby,' Sannie said.

Mia looked to Jeff, who glanced away from them, staring at something in the bush, then bent and grabbed Mia's rifle.

'Hey, what are you doing?' she said.

He put a finger to his lips with one hand. 'I thought I just saw someone.'

'Shit, Jeff ...' Mia said as she went back to administering compressions.

'I'll be fine,' Jeff whispered. He crept away, towards the nearby termite mound.

Captain van Rensburg was back on the phone, giving more directions to be relayed to the pilot.

Jeff crept off into the bush, but right now he was the least of Mia's worries. She looked down at Bongani, who was still not breathing. 'Please, Bongani, please.'

Bongani opened his eyes wide.

'*Ka faen!*' Sara sat back on her haunches, exhausted.

'What?' Mia said.

'That's Norwegian for "WTF",' Sara said. 'He's breathing!'

Mia took Bongani's hands in hers. 'Can you hear me?'

Bongani seemed dazed, and any sound he could have made was temporarily drowned out by the noise of the national parks' green and yellow helicopter flying low overhead.

Sannie dashed to the gravel road nearby to guide the pilot in and, moments later, returned with a crewman.

'How is he?' the man asked.

'He's breathing, but only just, and we don't know how long he was without oxygen,' Sara said. 'He needs to get to a hospital, as fast as possible.'

Jeff had returned from his foray into the bush, giving Mia a shrug that she assumed meant 'false alarm'. The four of them each took an arm or a leg and lifted Bongani. Mia felt every wince and cry that he made as they did their best to quickly but gently get him to the waiting chopper.

'Lie him on the back seat,' the crewman yelled over the noise of the engine. 'There's only room for one more.'

Mia was torn between wanting to be with Bongani and finding the man he'd been following, especially if the fugitive had poisoned Bongani in some way. Gone was her remorse and conflict over shooting the first poacher. Now she wanted nothing but justice – revenge.

'You brought him back to life,' Sannie said to Sara.

'I learned advanced combat first aid, from my time in Afghanistan,' Sara said.

'Good, then you go with Bongani,' Sannie said.

Sara looked crestfallen, as if she wanted to take back her words. 'But I am also a soldier. I want to get that bastard poacher. He's responsible for this, somehow.'

'You're still recovering,' Sannie said, pointing to the dressing on Sara's shoulder, 'and Bongani could die if you don't go with him. Get on the bloody helicopter.'

As Sara reluctantly obeyed, Mia leaned into the helicopter and kissed Bongani on the cheek.

'*Famba kahle, madala*,' she said to him. She squeezed his hand and his lips began moving, as if he was trying to form a word. 'It's all right,' Mia said, smoothing his brow with her hand.

In the silence left by the departing helicopter Sannie looked around her. 'So where did this poacher go?'

Jeff shrugged. 'I'm no tracker, but I thought I caught a glimpse of someone moving through the bush, over past the big termite mound. I went to have a look, but I couldn't see anything. Maybe Mia can.'

'I know this place,' Sannie said, looking around in a circle.

'Yes,' Mia said, going to Jeff and taking her rifle out of his hand, 'it's the spot where Laura disappeared.'

'Ah, yes,' Sannie said.

'Coincidence?' Jeff asked.

'As a detective I don't believe in coincidences. What do you think, Mia?'

Mia pointed to the west: 'That way's the shortest route to the fence and Killarney. He must have been heading from there, when Bongani picked him up.'

'It's odd for him to be travelling in broad daylight,' Sannie said. 'Poachers are most often active at night, during full moon. Do you have a map of the reserve, Mia?'

'Yes.' Mia went to the Land Rover and took a plastic laminated map from the cubby hole between the two front seats. She handed it to Sannie. 'Maybe this guy heard or knew about what was happening in Killarney and thought all the authorities would be tied up there. This might have just been an opportunistic mission for him.'

They started to walk towards the mound and Mia checked the ground. There were some tracks, but they were Jeff's. Out of habit she had mentally registered the tread pattern of his boots.

Something caught her eye.

'What is it?' Sannie asked, following her.

Mia walked close to the earthen mound and bent at the waist. 'There are too many tracks here.'

'What about those over there?' Sannie pointed to another set.

'Yes, that's the poacher.' Mia left the area immediately around the termite mound and picked up the other tracks. She followed them into the bush. 'Blood here. And it looks like he *was* following a crash of rhinos.'

'More than one?'

Mia nodded. 'Three. A cow and her calf and a bull – we saw them on the Vulture system earlier. That was his target.'

'And he was tipped off?'

'We guess so, yes, maybe by Julianne's pilot.'

'Why the blood, here, when there's no carcass? Is that from the poacher?'

Mia shook her head. 'No, the rhino. Here, see, the poacher hamstrung it, cut its rear leg. We'll find it just now.'

They walked on.

Sannie looked over her shoulder. 'Where's your friend, Jeff?'

Mia glanced behind her and rolled her eyes. 'Off playing Rambo again, maybe. Men.'

She heard a low mooing noise and stopped.

'What is it?' Sannie asked.

Mia held up a hand. 'Buffalo. Now we're in *kak*, if we bump into some dagga boys. They're ...'

'I know about buffalo,' Sannie said, 'you don't need to tell me the old males are the most dangerous.'

There was a whooshing sound from the tree canopy above them and Mia saw a white-backed vulture gliding past. It was a bad sign, she thought. The vulture was descending, coming in to land to their front. Mia carried on, rifle at the ready. As soon as the birds became aware of her approach they took off, or aborted their landings.

Mia saw the rhino. She knew instantly when she saw the size of the body that it was the big old bull, the one that had been following the calf and its mother. There was some tiny consolation that at least the other two had escaped. Moving closer, she saw the grisly truth, that this majestic animal had been hacked to death.

Sannie joined her, hands on hips, surveying the horrible scene. She had, Mia guessed, given up asking why. Sannie took out her phone and held it up, looking at the screen. 'I need to call this in, but there's no service here.'

Mia nodded, not even bothering to check her phone. 'Yes, it comes and goes here, but we don't do anything to improve it, to avoid aiding poachers.'

'Understood,' Sannie said, taking a picture of the crime scene instead, then putting her phone away. 'I need to get somewhere to make a call.'

'OK.'

'Hey!'

Both of them turned, each raising their weapon then lowering it when they saw Jeff walking back, through the bush.

'You could have got yourself killed,' Mia called out to him. 'Did you find anything?'

'Some tracks, I think.'

Sannie was checking her phone again. 'I really need signal, Mia.'

'Jeff, we can check the tracks just now. The captain needs to get back to the Land Rover first. We need to get to Little Serengeti so she can use her phone. We found the dead rhino.'

Giving up, for the moment, on trying to make a call, Sannie took another look at the map Mia had given her. 'Mia?'

She went to the captain, who shared the map with her. 'Show me where Killarney is, approximately where the new school is located.'

Mia checked the map and placed her finger in the white border outside the coloured area, which as well as showing roads, water-holes and prominent features, was adorned with sketches of the big five.

'Now show me where you've lost the tracks of poachers in the past, including this area, please.'

Mia ran her right index finger along the laminated surface. 'Here, by the Manzini Spruit, where there's a small waterhole in the dry stream bed, and here, where we are now. And this is roughly where the termite mound is, where we lost Laura.' She thought about what Bongani had said to her about his cousin, Alfred. 'And here is a spot where another anti-poaching patrol claimed a poacher disappeared.'

Mia looked up from the map and into Captain van Rensburg's blue eyes.

'You see what that was, on the map, all these spots?' Sannie said, retracing the route Mia's finger had just taken.

The realisation hit Mia. 'A straight line. That doesn't happen in nature.'

'Nor crime. Criminals are rarely as organised as films and TV make them out to be, but –'

'My goodness.' Mia put a hand over her mouth. 'That's how –'

'Guys,' Jeff called to them from where he had stopped. 'I really think you're going to want to take a look at this. Hurry.'

Mia looked to Sannie, who rolled her eyes in reply.

They were retracing their steps, but Jeff had moved off the game trail they had been following, about twenty metres deeper into the bush. Out of habit, Mia checked the ground to see what might have led him there, and then she saw it. 'Tracks.'

'Yep. *I* found them, like I said,' Jeff said proudly. 'There's some muthi lying about as well. You're just about to cross it.'

Mia looked down, and sure enough she saw the plaited grass twine, the same sign that had freaked Bongani out just before their contact with the poachers in which she had killed the man. She shuddered again at the memory. It seemed so long ago.

Jeff had carried on. He looked over his shoulder. 'There's more, Mia.'

'More tracks?'

'Magic.'

'Stop talking in riddles. We have serious business to attend to,' Sannie said.

'No jokes, no riddles, no games,' Jeff said. 'I'm talking about real life, honest to goodness magic. Watch.'

Mia paused, catching her breath. She was finding the constant surges of adrenaline through her body very draining, and she was operating on too little sleep. 'Jeff ...'

He smiled at her, bent, grabbed a handful of dirt, brought it up to his mouth and blew on it. The cloud of dust billowed out towards Mia and Sannie, and Jeff disappeared.

Chapter 25

Sannie and Mia stood at the spot where Jeff had just disappeared and looked into the hole in the ground. Jeff grinned up at them.

'A tunnel.' Mia shook her head in wonderment, although, having seen the straight line that Sannie had just pointed out on the map, she had herself just come to the conclusion that the only way the poachers could have kept entering and leaving the reserve undetected was underground.

'Exactly.' Sannie looked around them and down at the ground around the entrance that Jeff had discovered. She knelt beside a circular steel cover, its concave surface filled with a mix of sand, leaves and twigs. It was like an expertly camouflaged manhole cover, lying in the grass by the hole in which Jeff stood, looking up.

'The ground was disturbed, and the cover wasn't fully concealed,' Jeff said. 'I guess the guy jumped in here in a hurry after I saw him and didn't have time to replace it completely.'

'How could he hide all signs of it, though,' Mia asked, 'if he was already in there, pulling the cover back in place?'

'Sipho,' Sannie said.

'Who?' Jeff asked.

'He was the young guy who Mia and Bongani chased through the bush yesterday.'

'Of course,' Mia said. 'Yes, there's a pattern here. Now I can see it. Whenever a rhino was killed there was always a decoy poacher for us to chase.'

'Or something to throw us off the trail, like Laura's jacket being left by the termite mound,' Sannie said, 'and her beanie being found later. That meant the dog handlers rewarded their animals for finding something, meaning they wouldn't keep looking and maybe find a tunnel entrance.'

'Yes,' Mia said, 'and like Sipho, the two guys with the impala were also decoys. Laura must have seen them or the tunnel opening and then they or another guy forced her underground, covered up the entrance and lured us away. The decoys' job must have also been to make sure the tunnel entrances were covered up properly. Sipho was, like, cannon fodder, to protect the old guy. But why would he have risked it?'

Sannie had the answer. 'When we caught Sipho he had a pangolin, and he was known for going into the park to catch snakes. He – and the syndicate he was part of – would have known that he would get off with only a slap on the wrist, a fine or a month or two in prison. They would have promised to pay him.'

'Then who killed him and why?' Mia asked.

Sannie shrugged. 'Good question. Maybe they thought they could no longer trust him to stand up to interrogation, or maybe taking the teenage girls wasn't part of the deal he had with them. We know at least one of the girls was close to him – maybe Sipho was worried for the girl and the bad guys found out he was sweet on her. When they saw we were about to take him into custody ...'

'Makes sense,' Mia said. 'Poor kid. He knew he was at risk.'

'This is a hell of a logistical effort to go to,' Jeff said, looking up at them.

'Yes,' Sannie said, 'but the stakes are high. How many rhinos have you lost in this area lately, Mia? Fourteen?'

'Fifteen, all big ones. It's been our worst few months in years.'

'How big was each horn?'

'Hard to say, exactly,' Mia said, 'but maybe two kilograms on average.'

Sannie did the mental arithmetic. 'On the street, in Vietnam, that's getting close to two million US dollars. That's a hell of a big incentive to dig a tunnel, particularly if you've got machinery and workers sitting idle.'

'Like during a government-imposed lockdown,' Jeff said.

'Exactly,' Mia said, 'but if this thing goes all the way to the fence line, to Killarney, then it's crime on an industrial scale.'

Sannie nodded. 'It's a hell of an investment and it would have needed some serious muscle or machinery to excavate. The school and tourism project ...'

'Is right by the fence,' Mia said, continuing her thought.

'They had labourers coming in from outside and the local community was warned to keep well away from it. I've got to call this in.'

Jeff disappeared into the tunnel.

'Where are you going?' Mia asked.

'Not far,' came his muffled reply. 'Just having a look.'

'OK,' Mia said to Sannie. 'We can guard this end. If anyone comes out, we'll take care of them.'

Sannie stood and started to turn when Jeff called out from underground. 'Come quick, I can hear something. Maybe voices!'

*

Laura Barker sat on the bare wooden slats of her bed, knees drawn up against her chest. She knew, now, that she was underground, having been led from the cement-walled cell where she had been kept so far to a pit and forced to scramble down a ladder.

With the hood over her head she had been unable to see where she was putting her feet and she had fallen the last two metres, banging her knee on the floor. She had been led to a crude room, carved from the earth and lined with rough wooden boards. It smelled of fresh earth and human waste, perhaps from whomever had dug it.

Above her she had heard gunfire and, soon after, the ground had shaken from the effects of an explosion. Clods of dirt had rained down on her and for a moment she had thought she would be buried alive.

Left alone, Laura had screamed for help until she was hoarse, thinking the shooting was the prelude to a rescue mission, like in the movies when someone was kidnapped.

The steel door clanged as someone fiddled with a latch or lock on the other side.

'In here! Help me!'

When the door opened, however, a voice said: 'Come with me.'

The person who entered did not bring news that they were here to help. The hand that grabbed her was that of the woman. Her heart sank.

'Where are you taking me?' Laura blurted out.

'Do you want to live, girl?'

Tears rolled down her cheeks under the hood, but she gave a small nod.

The woman dug her fingers into Laura's forearm and dragged her off the bed and out of the makeshift cell and into a tunnel.

*

Mia and Sannie climbed down the shaft into the tunnel below. Jeff had jumped, when he did his disappearing act, but it was about three metres down, so they used steel rungs set into the wall, which had been roughly plastered with cement.

At the bottom, Sannie saw that the tunnel extended in two directions. Jeff had headed off to the west, towards Killarney. 'Jeff, come back here, now.'

'But …' He came back towards them.

'If you did hear voices, Jeff, we need to be extra careful. We move together as a group. First we need to find out where this thing goes, and we need to organise backup. There has been one explosion already today so we have to assume that whoever dug or developed this thing knows explosives – they may have wired all the entrances to blow if they're discovered.'

'The nearest phone signal is this way,' Mia said, pointing east. 'The border of the next property, Leopard Springs, is only about a hundred metres away, across the road, and the signal starts deeper into their reserve.'

'We need to establish where the other entrances or exits are,' Sannie said, 'so we're not ambushed. Let's head east.'

'OK,' Jeff said.

Sannie led the way and used a torch app on her phone to see in the dark. She ran her hands along the walls of the tunnel as she went. The structure was perfectly cylindrical and as her fingers trailed over a seam – a machined tight fit – she realised that the interior of the tunnel was made of pre-cast concrete sections of pipe. She reckoned the tube they were walking along was two metres in diameter.

'How did they do this?' Mia asked aloud.

'A machine,' Sannie said. 'A tunnel-boring machine. Tommy, my youngest, he's always watching that Discovery Channel. He watched this one show about how they dig those massive railway tunnels under cities. The machine is circular, with cutting heads, and it first drills underground, and then sections of pre-formed tunnel are dropped down a hole and pushed along by big jacks, one piece at a time, to fill the void behind the machine, like a concrete sleeve.'

'Amazing,' Jeff said.

Sannie had only walked for a few minutes, pistol out and at the ready, when she came to a dead end. The others came up behind her as she ran her hand over a smooth concrete wall in front of them.

'What the hell is that all about?' Jeff asked.

Mia snapped her fingers. 'I know where we are. We're under the next property and they've been building a new hide and a waterhole. Julianne was furious about the whole project – it's more like a dam.'

'So, is that a dam wall we're looking at?' Jeff asked.

Mia shook her head. 'No. The worst-kept secret in the Sabi Sand is that our neighbours at Leopard Springs have been building a big underground hide. They're becoming more popular – guests sit below ground level so they can view animals coming to drink at water level; it's better for photography.'

Sannie looked around them. 'Makes sense for the entry/exit point to be at the big termite mound, where we entered. If there was an entrance here then there would be too much risk of people visiting the hide seeing poachers coming or going.'

'Then why bother digging the tunnel all the way to this hide or dam or whatever's on the other side of that wall?'

273

Sannie already had the answer, thanks to her son's enquiring mind. 'Because that's where the tunnel-boring machine was extracted from underground.'

'Really?' Jeff said.

'I think so,' Sannie said. 'A shaft has to be dug and reinforced with concrete, and the tunnel-boring machine is then lowered into it. At the other end another shaft has to be constructed so that they can lift the boring machine out.'

'That's it,' Mia said. 'They must have removed the machine when they built the underground hide and upgraded the waterhole at Leopard Springs. With the COVID lockdown no one would have noticed.'

'So, where's the machine now?' Jeff asked. 'And who owns a thing like that?'

Sannie had an immediate thought about the second question the young Canadian had asked. Her friend Elizabeth Oosthuizen's husband, Piet, had the contract for construction of the school, lodge and 'infrastructure' to benefit the people of Killarney.

'The best place to hide a tunnelling machine is back underground,' Mia said.

Jeff nodded. 'You could be right.'

'There's a new big empty concrete swimming pool by the new hotel,' Mia said.

Sannie had just been thinking exactly the same thing. The abandoned hotel development would have been the perfect location to start drilling a new tunnel. It also made some sense that the tunnel operators would blow up the school to block and hide the entrance to one tunnel if they knew they had another one to fall back on. Elizabeth's husband had supposedly run off with his secretary – but what if he'd been working underground all this time? And if so, was Elizabeth involved?

'We need to check in the other direction,' Sannie said, 'now that we know no one will be coming from this end. Mia, how far do you think it is to Killarney from here?'

'Maybe a kilometre, as the crow flies.'

'Or as the mole burrows,' Jeff said.

They retraced their steps and passed under the open manhole cover near the termite mound, heading west, towards the perimeter of the reserve and Killarney. About fifty metres along, Jeff stopped.

'A locker,' he said.

Sannie closed up to him and saw that recessed into a cut-out section of the concrete pipe was a double-door metal storage locker. Jeff opened it and Sannie winced, half-fearing a booby trap might go off.

'First-aid kit, flashlight, water. These guys are organised,' Jeff said.

Sannie had to agree. Jeff unclipped the battery-powered torch, switched it on and moved off again, leading the way.

'Let me go ahead,' Sannie said, pushing past Mia.

Jeff shook his head. 'I'm not going to put a woman at risk while I hang back.'

'This is no time for misplaced gallantry, or chauvinism,' Sannie said.

Mia put a hand on the captain's shoulder. Sannie looked back at her and their eyes met. 'We need you alive.'

'Better to save the battery on your phone, Captain.' Jeff carried on, the light of his torch bouncing off the smooth, curved walls. Sannie saw that an electrical cable ran the length of the tunnel above their heads and at intervals there were lights encased in protective metal cages. Jeff was right, the builders and operators of this criminal enterprise were well organised.

Jeff stopped and held up a hand.

Sannie closed up to him. 'What is it?'

He put a finger to his lips and waited a few seconds. 'I heard a voice, I'm sure of it. A woman's, or a girl's.'

'That could be one of the missing children,' Sannie said. 'Everybody stay cool, keep the noise down. We may be outnumbered, certainly outgunned.'

'Shine the light on the floor here, please, Jeff,' Mia said softly. He moved the beam. 'There's blood here, fresh.'

Sannie took a closer look. 'That rhino was scalped to the bone. Perhaps the horn and skin brushed the wall here.'

Mia looked down again. 'Blood on his shoes as well. So, he's ahead of us.' She carried on then stopped at a plastic box, like an electrical wiring junction on the wall, with an offshoot of cable running from the central line above. She stepped closer to take a look.

'Careful,' Sannie said.

The box had a sliding cover. Mia opened, it, gingerly, and saw a tiny green light on a smaller black box. 'What is this? It looks almost like an internet thing?'

Sannie took out her phone.

'It is. There's bloody wi-fi down here,' she confirmed. 'The network is called "Tom".' The detective bit her lower lip. Everything was reminding her of Tom, today, it seemed. Then something occurred to her, and she held up a hand. 'Wait. My husband's favourite movie was *The Great Escape*, an old war film, about all these guys who escape from a Nazi prisoner of war camp.'

'I'm not sure I know it,' Mia said.

'Before your time. But it was based on a true story – the POWs who escaped dug three different tunnels from the camp. They named the tunnels Tom, Dick and Harry.'

'You think it's the same here?' Mia asked.

Sannie shrugged. 'Could be. It also means whoever is in charge here saw the film, and is arrogant enough to call his tunnels whatever he likes in the knowledge no one will ever find out what he's up to. It supports the theory that there's another tunnel – maybe even two more.'

'Great white male,' Mia said, softly.

'What?'

'Private joke,' Mia said. 'The wi-fi extender makes sense. There's no signal in the reserve, but if they've placed these gadgets all through the tunnel – or tunnels – the poachers can communicate with each other about rhinos, anti-poaching patrols and all that sort of thing underground. Password-protected, I'm guessing?'

Sannie checked her phone and tapped on the network, showing Mia the screen. 'Afraid so.'

'OK,' Mia said, 'do we push on or go back topside and call for the cavalry?'

Sannie put her phone back in her pocket. 'We don't know what's ahead. There could be booby traps, armed poachers. Also, we have to assume that the end of the tunnel under the schoolhouse was blocked by the explosion. As we haven't seen anyone coming this way it's logical to assume that if there is a second – or even third – tunnel coming from Killarney, then there might also be tunnels linking each of the main lines. It's too risky for us all to blunder about underground. We need help.'

'We're with you, Captain, whatever you want us to do,' Mia said. Jeff nodded in agreement.

Sannie took a deep breath. Any decision she made now could cost the lives of innocents – or her own – but she had a duty to do, especially if one or both of the remaining missing girls was alive down here somewhere.

'Jeff, if it was one of the girls you heard ahead, then that's my responsibility,' Sannie said. 'You two, backtrack and get out of the tunnel. Drive as fast as you can to somewhere with a reliable signal or use the Land Rover's radio to call Sean and get him to relay as much information as he can to the police. I'm going to carry on.'

'You sure, Captain?' Jeff said.

'I'm not sure about anything, but I can't put you two at risk. The best thing you can do for me is to get me some backup. Now.'

'OK. You should take this,' said Jeff, handing Sannie the torch.

'Good luck,' Mia said.

Chapter 26

S annie moved as fast as she dared, pistol up and torch held out to one side. Her arm soon began aching from holding the torch at an unnatural angle, but she had been trained to adopt this position when entering darkened buildings – the theory was that an armed assailant would aim for the light, and therefore not her body. Moving alone in an underground tunnel, she figured she needed every advantage she could muster.

The uniform smoothness of the concrete tube that encased her was broken after four hundred paces. Playing the light of the torch upward, she saw that a hole had been cut in the roof of the tunnel. Cautiously she moved below the opening and took a quick glance. It was a shaft, leading above ground, with ladder rungs in the wall of the vertical escape chute. She was about to holster her pistol and start climbing, hoping that if she broke through the entrance above she might find a phone signal, when she heard voices.

Sannie switched off the torch. Jeff had been right. She heard the sound again, echoing along the tunnel from the direction in which she had been heading, so it was not Mia or Jeff. The words were indistinct, but she felt she had to carry on. At least, she thought, now that she had found the exit shaft she had an additional escape route.

*

'You know, in a way, it's almost disappointing,' Jeff said, as he and Mia walked through the tunnel.

'What?'

'That the tunnel was discovered,' he said. 'It was almost beginning to seem as though the poachers' muthi really was working.'

'Jeff, you don't really –' Mia began.

'No, no. I never thought people could really make themselves invisible, but the power of suggestion is a strong thing. It was almost as if you and Bongani and the other trackers, even the dogs, had lost the ability to track poachers because something was messing with your minds.'

She thought about that proposition and realised that there was probably a grain of truth in it. For now, though, she had a concrete explanation about how a man, perhaps several men, acting in cooperation with each other and some decoys, had been able to miraculously vanish from the Vulture system radars and leave no trace for the trackers or dogs to follow up. She wondered if coopting Julianne's pilot had also been part of the elaborate decoy strategy, to give the rangers someone to blame if the people behind this needed to protect their secret tunnel.

'This whole set-up is unbelievable, even for Africa,' Jeff continued.

'Yes and no,' Mia said. 'Aren't there tunnels under the border between Mexico and the US, for people-smuggling and drugs? Even here in South Africa we have illegal miners working underground in goldmines, like, every day, blasting away and digging.'

Jeff shrugged. 'I guess you're right.'

'I'm worried,' Mia said. 'I'm starting to feel like we've been lured into a trap, Jeff, like we were drawn in here. The guy you saw has disappeared and you kept hearing voices. I wonder if there's some hidden way out of here that we've missed, in the dark. It would make sense for them to have escape routes at various points, so they can get out if there's a cave-in, or to evade us.'

'Hmm. Yes.'

'Jeff, let me take the lead, please.'

He quickened his pace. 'No way, Mia.' Jeff took out his phone, which also had a torch app, and turned it on.

He could be impetuous and pig-headed, Mia decided. But he was brave.

'At least when we get above ground we'll have the radio to call in some help,' Jeff said.

'Thank goodness.' Mia hadn't realised until just now how important it was and how much she took for granted the ability to communicate with others. 'This has to be linked to the disappearance of the girls.'

'You think so?' he asked from the gloom ahead.

'For sure. Where they went missing was just near where all the work was going on and that must have been the camouflage for the entry to the tunnel and whatever machines they were using.'

Jeff's phone torch seemed to be getting weaker, or he was moving faster than he should. Mia had to quicken her pace to catch up with him.

'Jeff, slow down.'

'Hang on, I think I see ...'

The beam of light was getting further and further away. Mia felt the darkness pursue her, then envelop her, like a predator chasing her down, consuming her. She didn't dare scream, in case Jeff had seen someone.

She ran.

Mia carried the heavy rifle across her front, at the ready, but as she could not see where she was going, every now and then the tip of the barrel or the rubber cushion on the end of the butt grazed the smooth wall of the tunnel.

'Jeff,' she hissed.

Then the weak glow she was following disappeared.

Mia's heart began to race and she felt the familiar rush of adrenaline powering her on, elevating her fear and anxiety levels. The walls felt closer with every step. She ran on, but she was becoming more and more disorientated. First her rifle and then her elbow collided, painfully, with the side wall. She tried to turn on the move, but tripped over her own feet and went down. Her knees, bare beneath her shorts, were skinned on the unforgiving floor and the rifle clattered away from her in the darkness as she reached out to stop her face from hitting the cement.

Mia took a breath. Her right palm and the knuckles of her left hand were now sticky and bloody as she crawled, pain shooting through her knees, and groped for the rifle in the dark.

Mia reasoned that she had made so much noise with her fall there was no point in staying quiet any longer. 'Jeff, come back!'

Her hand came into contact with her rifle, and as she dragged it to her it clanged against the metal locker they had stopped at earlier. Mia hauled herself to her knees and felt up the door for the handle. She found it and opened it and fumbled inside, feeling for another torch.

She located the first-aid kit, lifted it, and underneath, her fingers went into a recess. She could make out another doorhandle, by touch. She turned it, and the whole wooden backboard of the locker swung out. A door.

'Hey, Jeff?'

Mia felt in her pocket. She didn't smoke, but she carried a cigarette lighter with her as part of her essential kit, in case she needed to make a fire. She lit it.

Beyond the hidden door, partially illuminated in the flame of the cigarette lighter, was another tunnel.

This one was narrower than the concrete tube she was in, and instead of being lined with concrete pipes it was braced with timber boards. The floor was bare earth.

'Jeff!'

'Stay back, Mia!' he yelled, 'there's someone here!'

*

The shockwave from the explosion, which raced down the tunnel, sent Sannie sprawling onto her hands and knees first, and then flat on her face as a wall of dust and grit washed over her.

She coughed, dusted herself off, then stood. Sannie ran back up the tunnel in the direction from which she had come, towards Mia and Jeff. Had they set off a booby trap? she wondered. Were they still alive? Vaguely she recalled that she had heard and felt the twin thumps of two blasts going off, a split second apart.

Choking on dust, she made it to where she had discovered the exit shaft, only to find her way blocked by a landslide of shattered concrete and dirt. Someone had blown the shaft. There was only one way to go now and she had to hope she would find an alternative exit.

Sannie headed back through the tunnel towards Killarney, gun and torch at the ready. Counting off another four hundred paces she worked out she had probably passed under the perimeter fence. She decided to switch off her torch. She ran a hand along the smooth concrete wall to keep herself orientated.

Her right hand clanged against something metal. It was another cabinet, recessed into the curved wall, like the one near the termite mound opening where Jeff had found the torch.

Sannie moved on, and after another hundred and fifty paces she came to another wall of rubble. This, she realised, was the end of the line, where the school building had been blown up and had fallen down into the cavity below, blocking this end of the tunnel.

But she had heard voices.

Sannie turned and ran back to the cabinet. She switched on the torch and opened the double metal doors. Like the first cupboard that Jeff had discovered, this one had a first-aid kit and a torch clipped to a wooden backing board. There was also a five-litre plastic container. Looking at it, Sannie realised just how thirsty and hungry she was. She unscrewed the cap on the small jerry can and sniffed it, confirming it was water. She gulped down several mouthfuls.

She went to remove the first-aid kit, hoping to find some sustenance in it, but when she grabbed it, she found it was fixed to the board at the top. Lifting it up, she found a hollow behind it, inside of which was another doorhandle. Sannie grabbed and turned the handle and opened the concealed door. Beyond, bathed in red light, was another tunnel, this one lined with timber.

Sannie felt a mix of relief – to have found a way out of this tunnel and that her theory about cross-tunnels was right – and fear about what she might find next. She wondered if the first locker, which Jeff had discovered, was also a hidden entrance to a cross tunnel. Someone, somewhere, in this network had the power to set off explosives at will. She was no expert on bomb-making, but she now wondered if instead of someone having a wireless remote-control device, like the one Sean had mentioned, the whole network might be hard wired, with detonators at various locations. Had all the entrances now been blown? she wondered. She ducked her head and stepped through.

If the main, concrete-lined thoroughfare had been running roughly east–west, then this excavation was heading north.

She put her torch in her pocket and carried on, pistol at the ready again.

Sannie came to another door, made of steel, on the left. It was half open. She kicked it all the way open, ducked back behind the doorframe and peered in. There was a single wooden bed with no mattress, just an old blanket. Sannie thought of the missing girls.

She went back into the hall and looked at the ground. In the weak red light she saw tracks – a bare foot and a boot sole.

She checked the screen of her phone, hoping that she might pick up a signal from above. There was nothing, though when she looked at the wi-fi networks again she saw that another connection had appeared. This one was also named after a man, 'Dick', and was stronger than 'Tom'. Her theory about the naming of the tunnels had been right, though it gave her no sense of satisfaction. It simply meant there were more places for kidnappers and poachers to hide, or lie waiting in ambush.

Sannie carried on down the tunnel, faster now, hoping that one of the missing girls might be just minutes ahead of her.

The passageway curved to the right, and as she rounded a bend she saw them, a figure dressed in black pants and top and a ski mask, ushering on a white teenaged girl. Laura.

'Police, stop!'

The kidnapper spun around and Sannie recognised the swell of hips and breasts. A woman. She raised a handgun and fired two shots at Sannie.

Laura screamed in fear and desperation. The bullets went wide as Sannie dropped to her knees and took aim. In the low light and with the woman pushing Laura into a run Sannie couldn't risk pulling the trigger.

Sannie took a deep breath, got up, and set off after the woman.

'Help me!'

The call was muffled, and had not come from Laura. It made Sannie slow down. She came to another door recessed into the wall, and heard the muted sound of hands banging on steel from the other side.

'Help me, they've been keeping me locked in here!' It was a girl's voice.

'Stand back, away from the door.' There was a padlock securing the door. Sannie fired at it, twice – shooting a lock off was not as easy as it appeared in the movies – then kicked the door open.

The girl retreated to the corner of her cell.

'It's OK, I'm here to rescue you,' Sannie said. 'What's your name?'

'Lilly.'

The girl came to her and threw her arms around her neck. Sannie hugged the girl tight, briefly, allowing herself just a moment's temporary relief that at least both of the girls who were still missing were alive, for now. She gently prised the girl off her. 'Who kidnapped you?'

'A woman ... two men. They kept me locked in a room somewhere else. There was an explosion, then they brought me down here. There are other girls – my friend Thandi, and another girl, a white girl, foreign. I heard her talking and screaming.'

'Thandi is safe,' Sannie said. 'The woman has the British girl, Laura. I just saw them.'

Lilly nodded. 'Yes. I think she was coming for me, as well. I heard the key in the lock, then she ran off, with the other girl screaming again.'

'I have to go and help Laura too, so you need to hide,' Sannie said. 'Head down the tunnel that way,' she pointed back the way she had come, 'then turn to your right, into the concrete pipe. At the end the entry is blocked, but I'm sure someone will realise what's happening and start digging just now. You need to wait there for me. If people come, tell them what you know and that Captain van Rensburg is trying to find Laura.'

Lilly grabbed Sannie's uniform shirt. 'Don't leave me, please.'

Sannie took Lilly's skinny shoulders in her hands and locked eyes with her. 'Listen to me, Lilly. You must go. Hide, where I told you. I will come back for you, I promise.'

After a moment Lilly nodded then turned and set off down the tunnel, with a nervous backward glance. Sannie broke into a jog, in pursuit of the kidnapper and Laura. Around another gentle bend – this hand-dug tunnel was not nearly as straight and precise as the other – she saw a dead end and the open wooden door in the rear of a second locker, just like the one that had hidden the entrance to this tunnel. Sannie approached the door, ready to shoot.

The red lights went out.

'Put down your gun,' a trembling girlish voice said from the darkness.

'Laura?' Sannie called.

'The woman is telling me what to say. She says to tell you she has her pistol pointed at the side of my head. If you come for me she will kill me.'

The woman was not calling out herself. Why? Sannie wondered. The only obvious answer seemed to be that if the kidnapper spoke, Sannie would recognise her voice. She took a guess.

'Tell the woman that if she puts down the gun, we can talk nicely and I will recommend the court treats her fairly.'

There was a pause, then Laura called back: 'She says to tell you that if you insult her intelligence again she will kill me.'

'What do you want?' Sannie yelled. She leaned against the frame of the hidden door. Peering through, she saw a tunnel like the first one she had entered, made of cast concrete pipes, and once more heading east–west. From the distance she had travelled in the hand-dug tunnel Sannie reckoned that this one must have its entrance somewhere near the new, but empty, hotel development.

'She says to put your hand through the doorway and to show you are holding your pistol by the barrel.' The red lighting came on again.

Sannie knew there was no way she could close the gap between her and the woman and kill or disarm the kidnapper without being shot herself, or Laura being killed. She needed to buy time.

'She says you have five seconds. Five, four, three –'

'All right,' Sannie called. She held her arm out into the main tunnel, her pistol held as directed, the barrel facing down.

'She says for you now to walk towards us, hands up.'

Sannie stepped through the doorway and, hands in the air, started walking slowly down the tunnel.

'That's it, she says to keep walking,' Laura said. Sannie could see that the kidnapper had her mouth close to Laura's ear and was whispering into it as they carried on deeper into the tunnel for perhaps another hundred metres onwards. 'Now stop. Put the pistol on the ground.'

Sannie did as she commanded.

'Now take three steps backwards and get down on your knees,' Laura said, her voice starting to quake.

Sannie lowered herself down, already planning her next move. The woman would not be able to pick up Sannie's Z88 without letting go of Laura, and Sannie intended to give the girl a clear chance to escape. Sannie focused, through the red gloom, on the body of the kidnapper – what she could see of it.

The woman whispered something to Laura, who then moved away from her, towards Sannie. When Laura was halfway between the two women she lay down, face first on the concave floor of the concrete tunnel.

Sannie cursed to herself. The woman was cleverer than she had imagined.

The woman pointed her pistol at Sannie, but then reached into a pocket and took out a mobile phone and glanced quickly at the screen.

Laura had her neck craned, looking at Sannie. She saw tears running down the terrified girl's face.

'Don't worry, Laura,' Sannie said softly, 'others – many more – are coming. They are already underground.'

The woman walked down the tunnel towards Sannie, pistol in one hand, the phone in the other. She paused by Laura and pushed the barrel of her weapon into the back of the child's head, forcing her to face downward.

Sannie looked hard at the woman. 'I know who you are.' The build was right, and it all made sense now, who would go to such lengths and why. Sannie was seething with anger, but had to force herself to stay calm.

'I know who she is as well,' Laura blurted out, 'she's –'

'Shut up.' The woman dug her pistol harder into Laura's head, silencing her. 'In any case, it doesn't matter. You had to find out eventually.'

She crouched by Laura, put the phone on the floor of the tunnel and pushed it so that it slid along the smooth floor. When it came to rest in front of Sannie, what she saw made her draw a sharp breath.

On the screen was a photo of her youngest child, Tommy.

Sannie glared at the masked woman again. Cooly, calmly, she whispered to herself: 'I am going to kill you.'

Chapter 27

'Jeff?' Mia coughed and spat dirt. The blast had knocked her backwards and her ears were ringing. Her voice sounded muffled to her own ears.

She crawled out of the side tunnel into the main thoroughfare and went left, but the air was still thick with dust and the light from the exit Jeff had been headed for was gone.

'Jeff,' she coughed again.

Using her lighter she went back and had another look at the false door and this time was able to locate another torch clipped to the reverse side of the hidden door, which explained why Jeff didn't find it earlier. She switched it on and particles danced in the beam.

There was no answer.

Mia stumbled along, the beam from her torch barely able to penetrate the cloud she found herself in. Very soon she met a wall of broken concrete, earth and rock. She dropped to her knees and started digging with her hands.

'Jeff!' She could hear herself better now, but there was still a ringing in her ears.

The last thing he had said to her was that he had seen someone. She wondered if he had somehow managed to get outside before the blast was triggered.

She thought about that. Sean had said the bomb at the tunnel entrance, the one that had killed the man who had shot the helicopter pilot, was command-detonated. That meant someone had to be nearby. It also meant someone was above ground. Jeff had said he had seen someone when he first discovered the tunnel. Perhaps, she thought as she continued shovelling dirt with her hands, the man had led Jeff towards the tunnel mouth, but then slipped off into the bush instead of heading underground. That way, all of them had gone underground, leaving the way clear for the poacher to press the switch, detonating the explosives and entombing them.

But maybe Jeff had got clear.

'Jeff! Can you hear me?'

She stopped digging to listen. There was nothing.

She felt her fingernails, which she kept practically short most of the time, start to give way, but she carried on scraping out handfuls of dirt and rock.

Mia felt something soft under her fingers. It was fabric. She cleared away more soil and freed the garment. By torchlight she could tell that the piece of material she was holding was the torn remains of Jeff's shirt. Most likely, she thought, it had been blown off his body by the force of the blast.

Mia started to cry.

'Jeff!' There was no reply to her repeated calls. Mia took a deep breath and coughed up more dust particles. She tried to work out what to do next. Shining the torch around her she tried to find her rifle, but realised she had, stupidly, probably buried it by mistake while scraping out handfuls of dirt in the half light.

Sobbing, she turned and ran westward along the main tunnel, towards Killarney. With luck she would catch up to Captain van Rensburg or maybe find another way out. Poachers had disappeared from view and the Vulture monitoring system at more than one location on Lion Plains, so Mia thought there might be more entry and exit points.

However, the further she went the more she became engulfed in new, lingering clouds of dust. She slowed as she was confronted with what she predicted and feared – there must have been another exit here, but it had also been blown and had caved in.

Pure panic surged through her body. It was, she told herself, adrenaline. She needed to calm down and to get herself out of this tunnel. As with the charge that had gone off when Jeff had tried to exit, the explosives at the central exit had brought down large chunks of concrete from the pipe and the shaft above. There was no way she could clear that by hand. She turned and forced herself to walk, conserving oxygen and energy, back to the side tunnel she had discovered through the false locker.

Stepping in, she followed it for some sixty or seventy paces, to where it ended. On the ground was a pick and a shovel and an up-turned wheelbarrow left by whomever had been working there last.

Mia played the light of the torch behind her. By holding the torch at a ninety-degree angle and narrowing the beam, she could see that this tunnel had branched off from the main pipeline tunnel at an upward angle. The diggers were angling towards the surface. From what she could tell, the end of the tunnel might be only one and a half metres below the surface – less than half the distance of the shaft that she, Jeff and Captain van Rensburg had descended, near the termite mound.

Mia grabbed the shovel and attacked the roof of dirt above her head.

*

Sean and Benny searched in and around the sangoma's home, but turned up nothing more than the grisly remains and item of cloth-ing that had already been discovered.

The overworked male and female duo from the police crime scene investigation team had arrived, after Henk de Beer summoned them from the ruins of the school building.

Henk was briefing them at the door to the rondavel as Sean came up to them. If the crime scene officers were shocked by the prospect of seeing a human body part in a freezer, they gave no in-dication. Sean guessed they had seen some terrible things.

'Any news from the school?' Henk asked.

The female officer nodded. 'Something odd, there. We'll need more labour and maybe an excavator.'

'Why? We're stretched thin for manpower as it is,' Henk said.

'That blast,' the woman said, 'as well as destroying the building and the guy inside, it imploded.'

'Imploded?' Henk said.

'*Ja*,' the male officer weighed in, 'the floor of the building collapsed, and much of the rubble fell downward. There's like a cellar or something under the building. There would be a crater, but the building has mostly collapsed into it, filling it.'

'Could the bomb have been detonated below ground?' Sean asked.

'Very possible,' the female said. 'No sign of blast residue or other markers on the walls still standing. Good theory.'

'OK, we'll leave you to the contents of the freezer and whatever else you can find in here,' Henk said to the forensics team. 'Sean, we need to try to find the sangoma.'

'I just need to let Benny pick up her scent.'

Henk nodded, went inside, and came out with a floral dress, while the male crime scene investigator protested from inside about Henk disturbing his workplace. 'I found this in with some dirty clothes. It could be evidence, but we can't waste time.'

Sean held the dress under Benny's nose. '*Soek*, Benny.'

Unencumbered by his lead, Benny trotted away immediately, with Sean and Henk half jogging to keep up. Benny picked up a trail that led them down the path from the rondavel and onto the gravel road that led to the new developments. Benny went past the ruined school building and carried on directly towards the empty, though substantially completed, hotel.

Benny trotted over rough ground, mounds of dirt that clearly needed to be levelled and landscaped if the hotel was ever going to open to tourists. It still largely resembled a construction site and two shipping containers sat next to what would one day be a substantial concrete in-ground swimming pool.

Thick power cables joined the two containers via holes in the walls. A flexible tube, about thirty centimetres in diameter, extruded from the side of one of the containers down to the ground. On the other side, a section of tubing ran from the steel box into a squat concrete cube of a building abutting the pool, a structure that was half buried in the ground so as not to interrupt the view of tourists sunbathing on a future deck. Benny sat down in front of a black-painted steel door in one side of the cube.

'He's indicating,' Sean said as they caught up with him.

'Inside that thing?' Henk said.

'Looks like it.' Sean shrugged off his daypack, took out Benny's chew toy and gave it to him to play with. 'Good boy, Benny.'

Henk banged on the door with a closed fist. 'What is this?'

'Pump house?' Sean guessed.

'More like a bunker or a prison cell.' There was a sliding bolt on the outside of the door, but it was open. Henk drew his pistol and motioned for Sean to take Benny to one side. The detective kicked the door open, bringing his pistol up at the same time.

Sean joined Henk and when they moved in, they saw that the ground dropped away before them into a shaft, with steel ladder rungs embedded into a concrete wall. The flexible tubing and electrical cables they had seen above ground ran down into the pit.

Benny, finished with his solo game, walked into the room, carrying his chew toy in his mouth.

'*Eish*, I've got to call this in,' Henk said. He looked at the screen of his phone. 'No signal. I'll have to go back out near the sangoma's house. I had three bars of signal there.'

As Henk turned to leave, the steel door they had entered through slammed closed and they both heard the bolt slide home on the outside.

After banging on the door, they took stock of their surrounds and discovered that the building was little more than camouflage for the opening of a shaft, which they climbed down.

'A bloody tunnel into the reserve,' Sean said, 'dug by some machine.' Red lighting allowed them to see. At the bottom of the shaft they found signs of human habitation – a stretcher and sleeping bag, camp chairs, a table, and several containers and boxes of various sizes.

'Someone's been living here for a while,' Henk said, opening a plastic storage box. 'Food, toiletries, there's even a camping fridge here.' Henk opened the lid and Sean saw beer, juices, meat and vegetables.

A bank of a dozen large twelve-volt batteries ran along one wall and was connected to an inverter that hummed away noisily, as did the fridge. They had worked out that the cable coming from above must be from a generator, most likely housed in one of the two shipping containers they had seen by the empty swimming pool.

The same type of flexible tubing they had seen passing through each side of the other container stretched away from them, along the tunnel, as did the thick black snake of bundled electrical cables and what looked like a high-pressure water pipe.

'The power to run a drilling or boring machine is coming from that shipping container above,' Sean said, training the cables and piping. 'This pipe must supply water to lubricate the machine's cutter head and then slurry must be pumped back out via the bigger pipe.'

'And all the waste gets hidden on the construction site. Clever,' Henk said.

Sean found some military ammunition boxes and a toolbox with explosives, electrical components, a soldering iron and other specialist tools. 'Explosives,' Sean said. 'This is like a Taliban bomb-maker's workshop.'

Sean sat on a folding chair at the desk, working away after sorting through another two boxes filled with detonators, timing devices, garage door remotes, batteries, detonating cord and plastic explosives. He took out his Leatherman pocketknife and pliers combination tool.

'What are you doing?' Henk asked.

'Working on a plan to get us out of here.'

Henk kept searching around them. 'Gas cooker, magazines, torch. One set of men's overalls, but nothing to ID the guy.'

Sean worked away for a few more minutes, then leaned back and surveyed his handiwork. 'That should do it.'

Henk looked over his shoulder. 'That will get us out of here?'

Sean nodded and held up the sixty centimetres of detonating cord, fuse and a striker, for use as a detonator. 'Standard breaching charge; that should blow open that steel door upstairs and we can then find out who locked us in.'

'The sangoma?' Henk theorised.

Sean shrugged. 'Could be, though Benny thinks there's still something interesting down here.'

Benny had, indeed, been sniffing around impatiently while Sean worked.

'Maybe she did come down here,' Henk said, 'then doubled back out before we arrived. She could have been hiding somewhere close by, then sprung the trap on us by locking us in.'

Sean wondered if the criminal gang were busy blowing all the entrances to the tunnels to seal them in.

'I'm going to set the charge, blow the door open, and then we can go get some help,' Sean said to Henk. 'Stay here, and get ready to take cover when I come back down the ladder.'

'OK.'

Sean put the breaching charge, a roll of duct tape and his Leatherman in his daypack, shrugged it on, and started climbing the metal rungs in the wall of the tunnel shaft. Near the top, however, the red lights under which he had been working abruptly went out.

Next, from far away along the tunnel came a rumbling noise, like an engine starting up, followed by a hum which carried down the length of the concrete piping sections.

'Shit, what was that, man?' Henk said from the pitch darkness below.

Benny growled.

'Easy boy,' Henk said.

'Quiet, Henk,' Sean called from above, having to raise his voice over the noise rolling down the tunnel. 'Benny's not scared of the dark, he's picked up on something.'

'*Ja*, I'm going to take a look. Do you think someone's started up that tunnel-boring machine?'

Sean looked down the shaft and saw a beam of light stab the dark.

He silently cursed. It was the detective's business if he wanted to head off into the dark like Rambo, but Sean could not blow the door unless he knew Henk was taking cover somewhere. Also, the policeman should have called him and Benny to provide backup. Better yet, Sean could have sent Benny into the tunnel first to sniff out any threat and, if necessary, attack.

Sean was almost at the bottom of the rungs when he heard a loud clanging noise followed by a dull thud from down the tunnel where Henk had been heading.

Benny looked alert, ears up, ready for action.

'*Soek*, Benny.'

His dog set off down the tunnel, searching and sniffing.

Sean set foot on the tunnel floor and unslung his rifle. Cautiously, he headed towards the still-on torch, which was lying on the ground thirty or so metres down the concrete pipeline.

As he got closer, he could see Henk, lying motionless. His out-stretched gun hand was empty. Benny had given Henk a cursory sniff, but had moved on into the darkness.

Sean knelt and put a hand to Henk's neck. His pulse was strong and the detective was breathing. Sean used the torch to do a quick check and saw a nasty lump and abrasion on Henk's temple – he'd been hit with something and was out cold.

Sean started to get up, then felt the cold steel of a gun barrel digging into the back of his skull.

'Drop your rifle and get out your handcuffs, and the cop's,' said the man standing behind him in the dark.

*

'Sean, this is Graham. I say again, do you copy, over?'

Graham was doing his best to stay cool, just like Sean, the combat veteran, would have. Oscar, kneeling next to him, eyed him anxiously, sweat beading on his upper lip, his hands gripping his rifle tightly.

They had heard two explosions, almost simultaneous, nearby, and from their vantage point on top of a small koppie they had seen a man with a rifle moving through the bush. They had begun following him and were still on his tracks. There was no one monitoring the Vulture system to track the poacher via camera or radar, just the two of them.

'Where is Sean?' Oscar whispered.

Graham shrugged. *How the fuck do I know?* he wanted to yell at his friend and partner. Perhaps it was the unexplained disappearances of the mythical poacher, or the bomb blasts, but Graham was feeling truly rattled. 'We can't lose this *oke*, bru.'

Oscar nodded and licked his lips. 'I know. I wish I had some muthi.'

Graham swallowed. 'Me, as well.'

Oscar stared at him, and then his face broke into a broad grin. 'Did you just hear yourself, bru?'

Graham shook his head. They were all going crazy. He was worried about Mia – her safety and the fact that she had been spending too much time with that drug-smoking hippy, Jeff.

'Come,' Oscar said. 'We need to finish this guy, one time.'

'Affirmative, bru,' Graham said, doing his best to sound confident.

They stood and started forward, covering each other as they moved in tactical bounds – one would advance while the other watched over him.

As they ran through the bush the poacher's tracks took them towards a dry riverbed. A purple-crested turaco gave its distinctive clucking call from one of the big leadwoods or jackalberrys that lined the bank. It was Graham's turn to overtake Oscar.

When Graham came to the edge of the sandy watercourse he realised he would need to quickly cross the open space, just like Sean had taught them. He looked back and checked that Oscar had a good position, behind a tree, from which to cover him. By Graham's reckoning, the poacher was still maybe a hundred metres ahead of them, if he had kept to the same steady pace with which he had been patrolling.

Graham had broken cover and started to jog through the sand when a figure dressed in black stepped from behind a bush on the other side of the spruit.

'Graham!'

Graham stopped dead in his tracks and raised his rifle, shocked and confused to hear his name.

The man held an AK-47 in one hand, but raised his other and waved. The man's face opened into a broad smile.

'Alfred!'

Graham looked over his shoulder and saw Oscar walking down the riverbank.

Graham lowered his rifle. 'What the hell are you doing here, man?'

'Alfred, you had us worried,' Oscar called, also holding his rifle loose by his side now.

Alfred gave his deep signature laugh. 'My brothers, I was driving my car and I saw this *tsotsi* running through the bush, so I carried on like I hadn't seen him, then parked up and got out. I'm off duty, so I don't have my radio, but I thought I could get him myself. I am following his tracks.'

Graham exhaled loudly, some of the stress involuntarily escaping his body.

'What's in the bag?' Oscar asked Alfred.

Graham noticed for the first time the old canvas satchel slung around Alfred's neck, a dark stain purpling the faded khaki where something inside the bag was sticking out. 'And why the AK-47?'

Alfred grinned. 'It's the one we use for training. You know it. Sean's always telling us how we need to know how to use enemy weapons as well as our own. I was taking it to the rifle range to do some shooting practice.'

Oscar looked to Graham. Their eyes met.

Graham saw the tomahawk stuffed into Alfred's belt.

Oscar started to raise his rifle, and while he was quicker than Graham, Alfred was faster than both of them and he flicked his Russian military assault rifle to full automatic and pulled the trigger.

Oscar fell and Graham dived for the sand. Graham was aware of a bullet striking his upper body, but registered no pain. His chin dug into the coarse river sand, but he was able to slide his LM5 rifle into his shoulder as Alfred turned and ran. Graham stilled his breathing and took aim at the centre mass of Alfred's back and squeezed the trigger twice, just as he had done in training so many times.

Alfred pitched forward into the bush on the other side of the riverbank.

Graham was on his feet in an instant, charging forward, rifle up. He ran up the loose soil of the stream bank and stopped, chest heaving, blood pounding in his ears as he stood over Alfred. He kicked the AK-47 away and used his foot to roll Alfred over. His comrade, a man he had considered a brother in arms, stared up at the sky through dead man's eyes.

With the threat neutralised, Graham ran back to his friend. Oscar was lying in the sand, clutching his stomach. Blood welled through his fingers.

Graham got down on his knees and shrugged off his backpack. He reached for his radio, which was clipped to his chest pouches, and only then saw where he had been hit. One of Alfred's bullets had smashed the radio and torn a furrow on the canvas of one of Graham's pouches. He guessed he had been turning side on, diving for the sand as the bullet sliced its way across his equipment. He had, he realised, been a split second and a centimetre away from a bullet in the chest.

Graham took out a wound dressing and eased Oscar's hands away from his stomach. Oscar screamed.

'Oscar, listen to me, bru. My radio's finished and there's no phone signal here. I'm going to have to carry you out.' He unwrapped the bandage, placed it on Oscar's wound and eased him over so he could tie it.

'Leave me here, brother. You can move faster without me.'

'True, that. But, hey, if I leave you here the hyenas and vultures will finish you off.' He was only speaking half in jest. Also, Graham could not be sure Alfred had been alone in the bush.

Graham picked up Oscar's rifle and slung it around his neck, then sat Oscar up, took his arm and torso over his shoulder and lifted him up into a fireman's carry. Holding his own rifle by the pistol grip in his right hand and steadying Oscar with his left, he set off, trudging through the sand, up the stream bank and into the bush, heading east towards Leopard Springs Lodge. The neighbouring property was much closer by foot than Kaya Nghala.

'Hold on, bru, you'll be fine.' Graham felt a lump in his throat. He wished he could believe his own words.

Chapter 28

'Samantha.' Sannie shook her head, trying once more to contain her rage, although she had already guessed it was her friend dressed in black, even before she removed the ski mask.

Laura, once again on her feet, was back in Samantha's grip. She swivelled her head to look into her captor's face. 'You were on the drive with us. I recognised your voice, anyway.'

'Clever girl,' Samantha said. 'I thought as much, and as there was no other way for me to talk to Sannie than through you. I had to assume that it was time for the games to end.'

Sannie breathed through her nose, teeth clenched as she looked at the phone again. There were two pictures on the screen, the first of Tommy, smiling and looking at the camera; the second, when Sannie swiped, showed Elizabeth next to Tommy, also grinning, and holding up his creative writing assignment with today's date on it.

'Elizabeth ...?' Sannie sneered.

'In on it as well, I'm afraid,' Samantha said. 'Shame, so was Julianne's handsome young helicopter pilot, who Liz was bonking. He was smuggling booze out of Kaya Nghala during lockdown, so we had enough on him to blackmail him into helping us. He was also our fall guy if the police started to get some idea about a tunnel, or how poachers were miraculously getting in and out of the reserve.'

Sannie nodded slowly. 'Yes, you had us fooled, for about five minutes.'

Samantha sighed. 'He didn't have the stomach for kidnapping.'

'So, what do you do now, kill me?' Sannie asked. 'Kill Laura now that she knows your identity?'

Samantha shook her head. 'I don't want to do that, Sannie. You know me. I'm a hotelier, not a serial killer. The truth is, the last thing I want is for half a dozen people including two senior cops and the head of anti-poaching in the Sabi Sand Game Reserve to go missing, or show up half-eaten by hyenas. I don't need a task force swarming all over Killarney and the reserve until they find our tunnels.'

'Why did you do it, Sam?'

'Why?' Samantha's cheeks turned red. 'Why? The fucking virus, that's why. The fucking government turned its back on the tourism industry. John and I put our life into that bloody hotel and the government pulled the pin on all the funding they promised. On top of that our business partner from the local community buggered off with his half of the grant money before we even had a chance to pay our suppliers. We were left with two kilometres of concrete piping to bring clean drinking water and a modern sewage system to the good people of Killarney and we got royally screwed. Don't ask me why!'

'I went to your fundraisers, Sam, to help support the honorary rangers and anti-poaching dog units. You seemed so passionate about saving rhinos. And now you turn out to be just another common poacher, a criminal.'

Samantha sneered. 'Don't you lecture me, with your job and your government salary. My husband *killed* himself over this bloody pandemic. It took him from me, so I took a few rhinos – big deal – to keep the hotel we dreamed of afloat, to hold out the promise of hope for a hundred unemployed people in Killarney who'll get a job there once the tourists start coming back. I'll stop the poaching then. We're already planning to open the tunnels one day as a tourism attraction, so people can walk into the hides in the reserve, all the way from our hotel, and schoolkids can visit from the basement of their own classroom.'

'And you don't think anyone will be suspicious of how you dug these tunnels without any planning permission?'

'Hah,' Samantha said. 'This is Africa. I can buy any approval I need, once I'm solvent again, and with my good friend the head of the Skukuza endangered species unit, Captain Sannie van Rensburg, telling anyone who'll listen what a good idea it is.'

'Me?' It dawned on Sannie what Samantha really wanted. 'You want my soul.'

'Spare me the moral indignation, Sannie. You won't be the only corrupt cop in South Africa.'

'And if I don't? What, you'll kill my son?'

'No. I'll have to kill you. Liz and I will make sure Tommy's looked after.'

Sannie balled her fists by her sides.

'Better yet,' Samantha continued, 'you'll go topside and quietly explain to Laura's mom, Sue Barker, that if she agrees to invest in my hotel, as a twenty-five per cent partner, she'll get Laura back, un-harmed, and they, like you, will be sworn to secrecy. With the sort of money Sue has I won't need to kill another rhino and we'll be sitting on a goldmine. I'll cut you in on a share of the hotel as well, some-where for you and the kids to spend your holidays, in luxury.'

'I don't want your blood money,' Sannie said.

'Too late.' Samantha smiled. 'There will be two hundred thou-sand rand in your bank account in the morning and a rhino horn in your car boot later today. If I kill you, Sannie, your disappear-ance will be less likely to cause outrage when the police get a tip-off about you being involved in the murky world of poaching. Shame, the kids will probably be affected, knowing their mom was actually a criminal, but such is life.'

Samantha had given plenty of thought to this. Sannie had to play along, reluctantly, to buy herself and Laura some time. She had to hope that Mia and Jeff had survived the blasts and called for help.

'All right. But I want Tommy released, now.'

Samantha shook her head. 'Not going to happen. Liz is going to take Tommy into the Kruger Park for a few days – you're going to record a nice, neutral, loving, cheery WhatsApp message for Tommy – and then, as I mentioned, you're going to make contact with Laura's mom as though you're now part of the kidnapping syndicate. Which, in effect, you are.'

'Whatever you say,' Sannie said as she thought about how she would disarm Samantha and, if necessary, kill her as soon as she could. She was thinking cooler now, more rational, though she knew she would not hesitate to kill her former friend if she had to.

'There's one more thing.'

'What's that?' Sannie asked Samantha.

'We need to go find that other brat, Lilly.'

'What's going to happen to her?' Sannie asked.

'Shame, you shouldn't ask questions like that. She was snooping around, probably looking for her friend, Thandi, who also found our little underground venture. Clearly, I should have spent more on security, but you really can't trust anyone in this country any more, hey?'

Sannie heard footsteps behind her and turned. Samantha, too, was looking past her, pointing her pistol down the tunnel.

'It's all right,' came a voice from the gloom. 'I have her, Samantha.'

Virtuous Mathebula, the main sangoma of Killarney, stepped into the light, with a gun in one hand and a frightened Lilly Ndlovu in the other.

*

Clods of earth rained down on Mia, making her cough and splutter. Dirt filled her eyes and she had to stop after every few strikes with the shovel to clear her vision. Digging upward, she was discovering, was easier than digging a hole, but a hell of a lot messier.

She looked down at the tunnel floor and blindly thrust the blade of the shovel into the earth above her. At any moment, she thought, she could be buried, but she needed to get out of here. Mia had no idea if this was going to work, or how long it would take her to break free to the surface if it did. Something told her, though, that there was no point going back.

At least, she thought as the dirt cascaded through her hair and down the back of her shirt, she would have the upper hand on the poachers once she was above ground again, on her own turf. She was confident that wherever she emerged she would be able to find her way to the nearest road, and from there, back to her Land Rover.

Now that she'd found out their secret, these bastards would not get the better of her again.

She thought about Jeff for a moment, then forced him from her mind. Someone would pay for all this bloodshed and the rhinos that had been killed on her watch.

Mia thought of all the times, recently, when the poachers had eluded them, either by making their tracks disappear, or hiding themselves from the long-range eyes of the Vulture system. She visualised all the spots where they had lost the trail of intruders.

Before she could continue her analysis, an avalanche of soil and rock knocked her to the floor of the tunnel and half buried her. She wriggled backwards, shaking the spoil from her back and her hair. When she was able to stand she moved cautiously forward. When she looked up, to her great relief she saw blue sky.

Her next challenge was to get out. The opening, she calculated, was about two metres above her. She picked up the shovel, also nearly buried, and started digging foot holes in one side of the new shaft she had created.

Mia reached up with the tool and cautiously widened the hole she had made. When it was just big enough for her to wiggle through, she put a foot in one of the holes and boosted herself up. Using the shovel for support, she slid her back upward along the bare earthen wall. Mia gritted her teeth against the abrading pain and managed to get her foot into the next hole she had dug. By bracing herself there, she was able to dig her next foothold and re-peat the process.

As she neared the top she reached up and laid the shovel across the entrance, then grabbed the stout wooden handle and used it to help lift herself the rest of the way. By the time she had her head and shoulders out she was sweating and gasping for breath from the effort of the short but painful climb. With a hand either side of her she managed to boost herself up and out. The boring hours in the Kaya Nghala gym had, at least, paid off.

Mia took a moment to catch her breath, then brushed herself down and took a look around her. She had made a mental note to go back down into the tunnel and try to exhume her rifle once she escaped, but now she was in the fresh air she thought her best course of action would be to get moving and find help; she could always go back for the weapon. There were no obvious landmarks in sight, so she looked for the sun and headed east, sure she would soon hit the border road between Lion Plains and Leopard Springs.

Out of habit she checked the ground ahead of her for tracks. For now, she was more worried about whatever two-legged predator had blown the opening to the tunnel and killed Jeff.

He had come into her life so swiftly, and made such an impact in a short time that she could not fully process her feelings for him. Right now, though, her first priority was to get to safety and alert the police and other authorities to what was happening underground. Given the number of explosions that had happened, it was quite possible the police captain was still trapped underground – if she wasn't dead already.

Branches whipped at her arms and face as she jogged, certain she must hit the road at any minute. Once she got there she would turn right, retracing the path she had taken down the hand-dug side tunnel, and that would bring her back to the big termite mound, the exit Jeff had been heading for.

Mia heard an engine and stopped and listened.

'Hey! Hey!' She ran through the bush, as fast as she could. She *had* to catch that vehicle.

Mia burst out onto the road and saw a Land Rover – her vehicle – coming towards her. She waved her hands in the air and the driver looked left and right, then broke into a grin she could see from a hundred metres.

It was Jeff.

He stopped the car and jumped down and they ran, crashing into each other's arms, and hugged. Jeff kissed her and through her tears she felt it the most natural thing in the world.

Mia held him at arm's length. He was filthy, his bare torso covered in dirt.

'Oh Mia. I'm so sorry. Someone set off some kind of booby trap. I got buried in dirt at the entrance; it caved in, but I managed to somehow get my hand out and that gave me some air. I tried digging down for you, but there was too much damn concrete, and ...'

'I know,' she said, wiping her eyes, 'I tried the same thing. I found a side tunnel, which I think was heading for the surface, and I was able to break through.'

'Really? Is that what you were trying to tell me –'

'When you called out to me, yes. What were you trying to tell me?'

'I saw a guy, the poacher, I guess, as I got under the entrance. I think he must have had a remote or something to blow it up.'

'We've got to let everyone know; we have to find Captain van Rensburg. There were two explosions, Jeff. I'm worried about her.' They got into the Land Rover and Jeff got behind the wheel. Mia was too relieved and exhausted to argue about who was going to drive.

'It's OK, I've radioed it in, to Kaya Nghala. I found the security channel as well on the radio. I've told them everything, about the tunnel, the explosion, the captain. Help's on its way, Mia, but I just heard some gunfire.'

Mia thought about where everybody was. Sean Bourke and the other police detective, de Beer, were in Killarney, and Captain van Rensburg was possibly trapped underground.

'I'll try to raise Graham and Oscar, they should be on standby or on patrol.' Mia took the radio from the dashboard. 'Graham, Graham, this is Mia, over.'

She waited, but there was no reply, so she tried again, only to be met by more silence.

'I'm worried, Jeff.'

'The gunfire was over there,' he pointed to their left front, 'so I was heading that way.'

Mia opened the passenger door, got out and climbed up onto Bongani's tracker seat on the front left fender. 'Let's go.'

As Jeff drove, Mia thought about where Bongani had fallen ill, and remembered the direction of the poacher's tracks. If there was, in fact, another main tunnel, then the one she had found could have been an unfinished linkage route, heading towards it. She cast her mind over other spots where poachers had supposedly disappeared and realised they were heading for one of them, not far from another dry stream bed.

Mia was about to tell Jeff to turn left, into the bush, so she could navigate by dead reckoning towards the spot on the spruit where she thought the poacher might have been heading, when she saw tracks on the road. 'Stop!'

Jeff put on the brakes and Mia jumped down and checked the dirt road. She looked back at Jeff. 'There's a man carrying a heavy load, staggering, and someone's bleeding. They're heading towards Leopard Springs.'

'Why?'

'It's the closest lodge, the nearest place where someone would find help, or phone signal. Kaya Nghala's a lot further by foot from here. Let's go.'

'Yes, ma'am.'

Mia got back on the tracker seat as Jeff turned right, leaving the road and crossing into the Leopard Springs property. Now was not the time to be worried about border protocols and traversing rights.

Jeff drove slowly, allowing Mia to follow the man's tracks through the grass. The blood was fresh and, alarmingly, there was plenty of it.

Peering ahead, looking through the bush, not at it, as she always told her guests to do, Mia saw movement.

'Hurry, Jeff!'

Chapter 29

Sannie looked back at Virtuous, who, like Samantha, had a gun to her captive's head.

'What do you want?' Samantha called down the tunnel to Virtuous. 'Are you here to save the day?'

Virtuous gave a little laugh. 'No, I'm here to join you. Your tunnels have been very good for my business. Every would-be poacher and criminal in the lowveld has been hearing about the disappearing poachers of Lion Plains and they all think I'm the one supplying this super-strong muthi that truly does make people disappear. You thought you could lead the police to me, to cover up your little underground operation, did you?'

Samantha shrugged.

'We can work together, you and I, but from what I just heard, in the dark, you want our police lady friend in on this as well.'

'You seem to know it all,' Samantha said.

'I do, now, and I know this woman.' Virtuous pointed at Sannie, who glared at her. 'I have spoken to her and looked into her soul. Whatever she has told you, she will not agree to work with you. She is too honest, this one.'

'So what do I do with her?' Samantha asked.

'Kill her.'

Baie dankie, Sannie thought to herself.

'She's my friend,' Samantha said.

'Yes.' Virtuous nodded. 'I gathered that from what I heard earlier. And because she is your friend you should know that what I am telling you is the truth. As soon as she gets the chance she will betray you and these tunnels, and she will prevail. I'll make it easier for you. I will kill her for you.'

'No!' Lilly screamed and broke from the sangoma's grip. She ran to Sannie and threw her arms around her. 'She saved my life!'

Sannie rolled on top of Lilly, smothering her with her body, expecting to feel someone's bullet – either from the sangoma or Samantha – at any second.

Lilly was fumbling under Sannie. 'Be still, girl,' Sannie said.

Samantha dragged Laura a few steps closer to Sannie and Lilly, maintaining her stand-off with Virtuous. 'Quiet, everyone!'

'Please, Captain, take this,' Lilly whispered into her ear, 'it's from the sangoma.'

Sannie felt the girl press something angular towards her, made of steel warmed from concealment. It was another pistol, small, perhaps a .32 calibre. Big enough.

The sangoma drew a deep breath, closed her eyes and took a step towards Samantha before opening them again.

'Stay where you are.' Samantha looked rattled. 'I'll shoot you.'

'You need me,' Virtuous said.

'Throw down your gun.'

'I want the girls,' Virtuous said.

'What?'

The sangoma's mouth curled into a grin. 'Do you have any idea how much they are worth in my business? Dead or alive?'

'Seriously?' Samantha said. 'You're sick.'

'Really? What were *you* going to do with them?'

'Ransom them.'

'Lilly's grandmother has no money. I brought her to you as an offering just now, but I will gladly take her and get out of your life. Your secret will be safe with me, as long as you keep mine. I will pay you for the other one.'

Laura whined. 'I want my mother. I'll say whatever you want.'

Virtuous shifted her aim, slightly, to Laura, mocking her fear.

Sannie could see that all of Samantha's attention was on the san-goma, who she clearly thought was even crazier than she. Sannie slowly, centimetre by centimetre, moved her hand. Using her thumb, she could feel that the hammer was back, meaning the pistol was already cocked and loaded.

Samantha instinctively moved Laura to one side, half turning her body to shield the child from Virtuous. Virtuous and Lilly had clev-erly engineered the moment for Sannie, but Laura was still too close to Samantha for her to risk taking a shot.

A growl emanated from the Killarney end of the tunnel and a black bundle of fur raced into the middle of the stand-off and started barking at Virtuous.

'What the hell …' Samantha said.

'Benny,' Sannie called.

The dog looked to her.

'*Rim hom!*'

It was the word of command that Sean used to make his dogs attack. Benny seemed to pick up that Sannie was looking at Saman-tha, though he hesitated.

Samantha, seeing the dog take a step towards her, fired her pis-tol, but missed the dog. Laura cowered at the noise and managed to duck out of Samantha's grasp.

Sannie rolled, raised both hands, left wrapped around right, took aim and fired.

The bullet hit Samantha and she spun side-on, but pulled the trigger again on her own pistol, sending another bullet ricocheting off the curved tunnel wall. Virtuous and Benny charged forward, and Laura grabbed Samantha's free arm and bit it, hard.

Samantha screamed and fell in a heap as Sannie launched herself onto the other woman, grabbing her gun hand and slamming it against the concrete. The girls joined her and they disarmed and held Samantha as Sannie took out her handcuffs and put them on her one-time friend.

'*Auf*, Benny,' Sannie called, telling the dog to back down from the melee.

'Girls, girls, forgive me,' Virtuous said, opening her arms wide. First Lilly, then Laura came to her, and lost themselves in her embrace, their tears soaking into her ample bosom and sundress. 'I would never hurt you, or any child.'

'Sheesh, you shot me,' Samantha said to Sannie.

'Shut up. Samantha Karandis, I'm arresting you on suspicion of kidnapping and rhino poaching. You have the right to remain silent and the right to legal representation. Anything you say can be used against you.'

'I'm bleeding!'

Sannie had hit Samantha in the right upper arm – Samantha had been lucky as Sannie, by virtue of her training, had been aiming for the centre mass of her body. Although the shot was at close range, the relatively puny bullet had lodged in the flesh of Samantha's muscle. Sannie picked up the other woman's discarded ski mask, stretched it until it ripped, then tied it tightly around the wound.

'I'm feeling faint,' Samantha said. She rested her back against the tunnel wall and then slid down until she was sitting.

Sannie saw that Samantha's face was pale. She was probably suffering shock, but would not die from the wound. Sannie let her rest for a moment, but kept her eyes and gun on her as she went over to Virtuous.

Virtuous let the girls go and they, too, sat down, talking quietly to each other, sharing their experiences.

'Where did you get those guns?' Sannie asked the sangoma.

'I'm very sorry, Captain. I have to confess that I injured one of your colleagues.'

'Tell me what happened, quickly,' Sannie said.

Virtuous nodded. 'When I left Nomvula's house I walked back to my home, but I saw police there, and the anti-poaching man with the dog. I went around the back, through the bush and from their conversation I could hear that they had found something terrible in my freezer.' Putting a hand to the side of her face, so that Laura and Lilly could not see or hear what she was saying, she mouthed the words: 'Body parts.'

'Go on,' Sannie said.

'Well, you know how we izangoma are often accused of trading in such things – I would never – I panicked. I thought the police would arrest me, so I tried to pinpoint where the body parts could've come from. There is a shipping container near the new hotel, by the pool, and it hums, like from an engine, and I had wondered for some time whether the workers there had a cold room, like a big refrigerator. I thought to myself, perhaps there are dead bodies in there? Then I wondered if the girls might ...'

Sannie nodded.

'So I went to investigate and found that the container door was locked, but there was a nearby entrance to a concrete building that was unlocked. Inside I found the shaft leading down to this concrete tunnel. I climbed down, and found a place where someone had been living. I picked up a frying pan, the closest thing I could find to a weapon, for my protection. I walked a little way along the tunnel then found another tunnel to the right, this one dug in the earth, with wooden boards on the walls and roof. It led to another tunnel, which was blocked at the Killarney end ...'

'Where you found Lilly?'

'Yes,' Virtuous said. 'I waited with her and she told me that you had found her and not long left her. We planned on staying put, but then the lights went out and I heard other men moving about, talking, but too far away to understand what they were saying. I thought these people were bad men, so I snuck back along the off-shoot tunnel, into this one, crept up behind the one man, and hit him over the head with the frying pan. I'm afraid it was a detective, named de Beer. The poor man is unconscious.'

'I'm sure Henk – Detective de Beer – will forgive you, if you haven't given him brain damage. Two pistols?'

'He was carrying one and had the small one, which I gave to Lilly to give to you, in a holster strapped to his ankle, like in the TV crime shows.'

Sannie nodded. Typical Henk to be carrying a backup weapon. 'You did well.' Sannie looked to Lilly. 'Both of you. You were very brave.'

'Where do we go now, Captain?' Virtuous asked.

It was a good question. Sean could be coming their way now; hopefully with a conscious Henk. Her main priority, however, was to get out of this network of tunnels. Now that it was quiet, Sannie could hear a deep, rumbling, grinding noise somewhere in the distance. With a sinking heart, she realised it must be the boring machine churning on somewhere down the pipeway under Lion Plains. Someone, Sannie reasoned, must have turned it on somewhere. That felt ominous.

'Who else is underground?' Sannie said to Samantha.

'No one right now, but as you said, I have the right to remain silent.'

Sannie went to Samantha, grabbed her by the shoulders and pulled her to her feet. She leaned in closer so that their faces were just centimetres apart. Samantha flinched. 'If I were you, Samantha, I would start cooperating if you want to minimise your prison time. What's the quickest way out of here?'

Samantha flicked her head behind her, in the direction of the boring machine. 'There's an exit, about two hundred metres that way. You'll come up inside the reserve.'

Sannie decided she needed to get everyone out as soon as possible. If Sean and Henk were behind them, then hopefully they would come running, having heard the gunfire. The other possibility was that Sean had taken the injured Henk back out the entrance by the hotel swimming pool. 'All right,' she said, pointing her own pistol, which she had retrieved, at Samantha, 'lead on.'

Samantha, complaining that she was in pain, shuffled along, with Sannie prodding her in the back every now and then. Virtuous offered to bring up the rear of their little column, with the girls safely in the middle. Benny was enjoying the attention of the two teenage girls as he walked protectively alongside them.

They came to a shaft identical to the one Sannie had passed under in the other tunnel. She was taking no chances, in case of booby traps. 'You first, Samantha.'

Wincing, and making slow work of the climb because of her wounded arm, Samantha made her way slowly upward, with Sannie just below her. At the top, Samantha grunted and heaved until she was able to shift the manhole cover and light flooded down below.

'Don't try to make a run for it,' Sannie cautioned her.

'In my condition? I need to sit down.'

Sannie climbed out of the tunnel, gulping down the fresh air. Samantha sat dejectedly by the tunnel entrance.

The girls, who were both young and fit, were able to share the load of carrying Benny up the ladder, holding him by a carry handle stitched onto the back of his tracking harness. Finally, Virtuous, struggling on the ladder rungs, made it to the top, with Lilly and Laura helping her out into the open air.

Sannie patted Samantha down and found her phone. They had lost the wi-fi signal and had no reception here. Just then they all turned at the sound of an engine.

'The cavalry?' Virtuous said, fanning her face. She sat on the ground in the grass, Henk's pistol by her side.

Sannie had her Z88 out and ready, but lowered it when the familiar sight of Sean Bourke's distinctive long-wheelbase camouflaged Land Rover Defender emerged through the trees.

Benny's ears pricked up and he trotted to the rear of the vehicle as it pulled up. He must have recognised either the truck or his master's scent on board. Or perhaps, Sannie mused, he just wanted his chew toy.

Sannie started moving towards the Land Rover, peering at the tinted windows. *How did he know where to find us?*

Three men burst from the canvas-covered load area on the back of the vehicle, all dressed in blue workers' overalls but carrying AK-47s. They fanned out and took up positions of cover facing her.

Sannie raised her pistol and took aim at one of the men as the driver's-side electric window came down. A man, vaguely familiar, stared at her. 'Put down your gun, Captain. Predictably, there's another man in the back with a weapon pointed at Sean Bourke's head. I've seen you together in Killarney, so I know you know each other.'

The armed men moved forward and Sannie lowered her pistol.

Samantha stood and told the gunmen about Sannie's spare pistol and the one that Virtuous was carrying. The men came to them and disarmed them.

'How are you, my *liefie*?' the driver said to Samantha.

'I'll live, but I need to get to a doctor soon.'

'With a fine tale for the *Hazyview Herald* of how you fought off some poachers.' The man got out. He was fair-haired, in his late fifties, wearing cargo pants and a khaki bush shirt. His skin was pale – probably, Sannie thought, from being underground. She recognised him – the last time she'd seen him was pre-COVID, when he'd played a round of golf with her late husband.

'Piet Oosthuizen,' Sannie said. 'Elizabeth said you ran off with another woman.'

He gave a tight smile. 'Now all your comrades here know my name as well. That might not bode well for them, Sannie.'

Sannie glared at him.

Piet shrugged and drew a pistol from the waistband of his pants. 'I see Samantha's little plan to convert you didn't work.'

'Give up now and things might not go too badly for you in court,' Sannie said.

'With the penalties they're handing out for rhino poaching these days? I don't think so. Get in the Landy, all of you.'

Sannie saw Benny scratching up at the tailgate of the four-by-four. 'Benny –'

'Stop!' Piet pointed his gun at Benny, who looked to Sannie. 'I really don't want to kill the dog, but if you say one more word to it, I'll shoot it before it lifts a paw.'

Sannie did not doubt him. She felt for the dog.

Laura started crying and Lilly put an arm around her as the gunmen ushered them all to the rear of the Land Rover.

'Keep the policewoman in the back seat, away from the others, so she doesn't rouse the rabble,' Piet said to his men.

Sannie was escorted past the open flap of the canvas-covered load area and when she looked in, she saw Sean lying on the floor, hands cuffed and feet hobbled. Piet had been bluffing about the extra gunman in the back, covering Sean, but it made no difference as Sannie knew she had been outgunned. Sean had a gag in his mouth but he made eye contact with her.

Henk? she mouthed.

Sean could only shrug his shoulders. Sannie noticed that Benny was waiting by a tree, a few metres away from his master. As a consolation, he had managed to pull Sean's daypack out of the back of the Land Rover, no doubt hoping someone would let him play with his chew toy.

Her guard shoved her between her shoulder blades and took her around to the back seat of the double cab. He pushed her inside and took the seat beside her, the barrel of his AK-47 pressed into her ribs.

Sannie closed her eyes and said a quiet prayer for the safety of her children, especially Tommy.

Once they were all on board, with Samantha sitting in the front passenger seat and the other gunmen and captives in the load area, Piet drove off.

'Are you going to kill us all now?'

Samantha looked over her shoulder. 'I gave you a chance, Sannie.'

Piet nodded. 'Sean's too gung-ho for his own good – said he'd rather die than take money from rhino poachers. Such a shame his little daughter will grow up without a father.'

'What about the girls?' Sannie asked.

'I never wanted to take any of them,' Samantha said. 'The first two were just too damn inquisitive for their own good, and silly Laura went behind the termite mound for a pee just as two of our men, who had snared an impala for rations, were about to go down the tunnel. She saw them and fortunately I happened to be in the bush as well so that when we threw her down there I had just enough time to close the hatch and cover it up. Piet caught her. We'll still ransom her and give her back to Sue once she's handed over the money and we're sure she's all right with our … arrangement.'

'I'll do it,' Sannie said.

Samantha looked back again. 'What?'

'I'll join you, work with you.'

Samantha smiled. 'We'll see.'

Piet had joined one of the main arterials through the Sabi Sand that served as the boundary between Lion Plains and Leopard Springs. He took a left onto one of the Leopard Springs roads. No passing vehicle would think twice about the presence of the big camouflaged anti-poaching truck whose driver had carte blanche to be anywhere on the reserve.

Piet sped past a herd of buffalo, scattering a few who were trying to cross the road, and a lone elephant bull who trumpeted in anger at the dust cloud the vehicle raised.

The presence of more game – a herd of impala and a trio of giraffes – told Sannie they were nearing water, and sure enough, Piet turned onto an access road with a sign that said Leopard's Rest Dam.

He pulled up in a circular clearing overlooking a large expanse of water. Piet got out and he, as well as the gunman covering Sannie, and Samantha, looking pale and slightly unsteady as a result of her bullet wound, took Sannie to the edge of an open pit.

The hole was about two metres wide by six long, and six metres deep. The walls were sheer and stabilised with concrete that looked like it had been sprayed on three sides, but the fourth side, she could see, was smooth and actually part of what appeared to be a dam wall, sunk into the ground. Amazingly, three metres from the bottom of the pit was a green-tinged window that was a metre in height and ran almost the full length of the wall. It looked to be made of thick, armoured glass.

'Brilliant, isn't it?' Piet said.

Sannie looked along the waterhole. A pair of warthogs that had been drinking at the far end, maybe a hundred metres away, stared at the noisy humans. A herd of waterbuck was filing in for a drink and a fish eagle gave its distinctive, mournful call from the branch of a dead tree that had been flooded by the manmade water point. Wallowing in the muddy shallows was a large white rhinoceros, a bull by the look of his bulk and the size of his horn.

'This is where the tunnel-boring machine will be extracted,' Piet said, 'and when it's removed, we'll enlarge the hole, put in steps and a roof, and guests will come here and be able to view game drinking at water level. They'll also be able to see the crocodiles, hippos and fish through the underwater viewing window.'

As if on cue, a hippo honked from somewhere. Sannie felt a shiver down her spine at the thought of the reptiles that were no doubt lurking somewhere in the dam.

The other two gunmen had unloaded Lilly, Laura, Virtuous and Sean, who hobbled over to them. They were all ushered to the edge, and the gunmen took several paces back to cover them.

Piet checked his watch and looked to Samantha. 'We don't have much time. Let's get on with it.'

Samantha turned to Sannie. 'Did you mean what you said, just now, in the truck?'

'I did.'

'Fine. Push Lilly in.'

'Why? What's the point of putting her in there?'

Piet lowered his voice. 'The machine will break through in a few minutes. It will be over quickly. Her remains will be, well, turned to slurry, and sent back down the tunnel through the pipe. There will be no trace of her, and what there is will become part of the land-scaping around the new hotel.'

Sean launched himself at Piet, even though his hands were cuffed and ankles tethered. Sannie went for Samantha, who squealed and ran, as Piet dodged to one side, put out a foot and tripped Sean. Lilly and Laura both screamed as Sean toppled over the edge and into the pit, head first. Not even able to use his hands to break his fall, he landed with a sickening thud. Sannie, realising the moment was gone, glanced down. Sean was not moving.

'You heartless bastard,' Sannie said to Piet.

'Heartless? No more than the government that was prepared to see Samantha and her husband go bankrupt and become homeless, or my business destroyed and all my workers out of a job. People are murdered every day in this bloody country, because those in charge won't give police like you the resources and manpower you need. This is just us trying to survive.'

Sannie looked to the men with guns, probably ordinary con-struction workers who had been wooed by the same fatal, sick logic that their employer was now using to try to justify killing animals and humans alike.

Virtuous had brought the girls to her again, one under each arm. She had her eyes closed and her face tilted to the sky.

'The girl,' Piet said.

Just then, they all heard a voice come over the radio through the open door of the Land Rover.

'*Mia, Mia, this is Sara, over.*'

'*Sara, this is Mia, copy. What are you doing back here, over?*'

'Mia, Bongani's in hospital, they think he'll be fine. I got a lift back with the national parks helicopter to Kaya Nghala and took a Land Rover. I'm looking for you. Are you OK?'

'I'm fine and Jeff's with me. Oscar's been shot, but he and Graham killed the poacher. It was Alfred, from security! We're taking Oscar to Leopard Springs Lodge. We're in a rush, let me call you back soon.'

'Roger, standing by.'

Samantha looked to Piet and nodded.

'Right, let's get on with it,' Piet said. 'If you're with us, Sannie, now's the time to prove it.'

'No!' Laura yelled.

Virtuous opened her eyes and shepherded Lilly behind her. 'You will have to kill me first.'

Piet walked to Virtuous and pointed the pistol at the middle of her forehead.

'You may take me,' Virtuous said. 'But please do so in exchange for the girl. She is young and fit. Perhaps she can work for you underground, but let her live.'

Virtuous ignored the pistol, walked around Piet to the pit and stepped off the edge. She landed hard, but managed to ease herself to her knees and slowly stand. Once more she closed her eyes and looked to heaven.

'Sannie?' Piet said.

She looked at Lilly. 'I can't. Think about what Virtuous said.'

'What about me?' Laura cried.

Sannie went to the edge of the pit and looked back at Laura. 'Do whatever you have to in order to survive.'

Then Sannie jumped, and focused on landing with her feet together and knees bent. She landed harder than she'd anticipated, but went into a controlled roll. She checked herself and found she was uninjured. Sean, however, was unconscious, and Virtuous had dropped to one knee and was holding her right ankle tightly.

Sannie looked up at the top of the pit. Piet had Lilly by one upper arm. Laura was screaming, somewhere out of sight. Piet shoved Lilly, and the gangly teenager windmilled her arms as she fell. Sannie did her best to break the girl's fall, though both of them ended up winded on the floor of the pit.

Gasping for air, Sannie saw Piet take one look down at them, then turn his back and walk away. Moments later she heard the Land Rover start up. The noise of its engine, and Laura's wails, disappeared into the bush.

Sannie managed to stand and went over to Lilly to make sure she had survived the fall. As she helped the girl to sit up, they both sensed movement in their peripheral vision and turned to look through the thick glass window. A crocodile, perhaps three metres long, glided lazily through the water, watching them through one beady eye.

Chapter 30

Mia and Jeff had found Graham, staggering in the unforgiving afternoon heat under Oscar's weight, and loaded them into the Land Rover game viewer.

As Mia had told Sara, they were following Graham's original plan, to head to Leopard Springs as the nearest lodge. Jeff had already radioed for a helicopter evacuation from the lodge's helipad.

Mia was in the first tier of seats, behind Jeff, who was still driving. Oscar was lying along the centre row of seats. Mia held one of his hands and Graham, seated with his comrade, held the other. There was not much more they could do for him right now. Oscar, while in terrible pain, was still conscious and trying to be stoic.

'Not long now, bru.' Graham used his free hand to wipe tears from his eyes every now and then.

Mia was touched by Graham's show of emotion. 'You really do care for him, don't you, Graham?'

'The big bastard's like my brother. I don't want to lose him.' Graham swallowed a sob. 'Or you.'

With Mia giving general directions based on the position of the sun and her knowledge that they would hit a game-viewing road soon enough, Jeff bashed through the bush, weaving in and out of larger trees.

They came to a dirt road and Mia told Jeff to turn right, mentally picturing the layout of Leopard Springs as best she could. She did not know the reserve well, but arrogant Jake, the guide who had hit on her at the airport, had invited Mia and Bongani and a few of the other staff from Lion Plains over for a weekend a few months earlier when all of them were suffering the lockdown blues. They had been on a few game drives. Jake had hinted that there was big work being done on the Leopard's Rest waterhole, but had made a point of telling them all that they were forbidden to visit the dam as there was some sort of revolutionary new attraction being built there. Whether or not anyone at Leopard Springs was aware of what was really going on underground would probably be the subject of a future police investigation, Mia thought.

'Jeff.'

He looked back at her. 'Up ahead somewhere you'll see a turnoff to a place called Leopard's Rest. Take it, even if it says no entry. It should be a quicker route to the lodge.'

'Yes ma'am.'

Graham reached for her hand and she took it and squeezed it.

What on earth was she going to do about these two – Jeff and Graham? That was also going to be the subject of future questioning and investigation, she decided. Almost to her shame, she had felt something intense with Jeff, though now was not the time to be reliving crazy dreams.

*

Sannie stood at the bottom of the pit, feet apart, legs bent in a squat position, hands braced against the rough concrete wall. Her shoulders took terrible strain as Lilly helped Virtuous up onto them.

Her thighs and calves burned and Sannie emitted an involuntary yell as she pushed herself until her legs were straight. Although the bullet wound she was carrying was not much more than a graze it was hurting like hell now. The sangoma, no lightweight, wobbled precariously as lithe young Lilly used hands and bare feet to climb Sannie and then the older woman like a human ladder. Even though Lilly probably weighed no more than fifty kilograms, the extra weight felt like it was going to crush Sannie's body.

'I can't stay here for much longer,' Virtuous protested.

'I'm almost there,' Lilly said.

Sannie was staring at the wall, perspiring with the effort of holding the weight of the other two. 'What can you see, Lilly?'

'I ... I ... can't reach the top.'

Sannie felt a tremor through the sangoma's legs and Lilly squealed as their shaky human pyramid collapsed in a tangle of arms, legs and screams.

When they had caught their breath Sannie asked if they should try again.

Lilly wiped her eyes. 'It was no good. I still couldn't reach the top and there was nowhere for me to put my hands or feet to grab hold. I'm sorry, Captain.'

'Don't cry, Lilly,' Sannie said, giving her a hug. 'You did your best.'

She left the other two and went to the wall closest to Killarney. She put her hands against it. The last time she had checked she'd thought she detected vibrations, but had convinced herself she was just imagining it. Not so now. The other two came closer and they could all see particles of cement dust cascading down the face of the roughly rendered wall.

Virtuous had painfully lowered herself to her knees and invited Lilly to join her.

'What are you doing?' Sannie asked.

'Praying.'

Sannie felt a helpless rage within, trying to overtake her. She knew it would do her no good. Perhaps the sangoma was right. She eased herself to her knees and joined hands with Virtuous and Lilly while the woman led them in prayer.

Sean groaned. Sannie opened her eyes and looked over at him. She excused herself from the others and went to him. He was coming to. She had removed his gag and other restraints as soon as she jumped into the pit. 'What's your name?'

'Sean.'

'Sean what?'

'Sean.'

He was not looking good.

'Benny ...' Sean said.

Sannie cradled Sean's head, which was badly cut and bruised from his fall. 'Benny's fine, Sean. He's OK.'

The cement on the wall was shedding more powder now and Sannie could feel the vibration in the ground. If the machine was about the same size in diameter as the tunnels, then she realised there would not be enough room for any of them, not even thin little Lilly, to escape to one side of it as it smashed through the wall and continued its unstoppable journey into the recovery pit.

Virtuous and Lilly kept on praying.

Sannie started at the sound of an engine, thinking the machine was about to break through, then she heard a different noise and looked up. Standing at the rim of the pit was Benny, and he was barking. The motor noise behind him was switched off. She realised Benny must have followed Sean's Land Rover all the way to Leopard's Rest Dam, but who, she wondered, had just pulled up in a vehicle? Was it Piet, come back to check on his grisly work?

'Good boy, Benny,' said a female voice, and then Mia's face appeared over the edge of the precipice. 'So *that's* where you all are!'

Sannie's heart leapt. 'No time for jokes, Mia,' she called up. 'The tunnel-boring machine's about to break through and mince us.'

'Shit. I've got a long towing strap,' said Mia, as she turned and sprinted away from the edge.

'Hallelujah,' Sannie said.

Virtuous and Lilly hugged.

*

Mia opened the tailgate of her Land Rover and pulled out the canvas bag containing her recovery gear. She knew exactly what was in it. Graham knelt down and looked into the pit.

'I'm Graham Foster,' he told the occupants. 'Mia's rigging a tow strap to the back of the Land Rover and we're going to pull you up one at a time. Do you need help down there? How's Sean?'

'Yes please, Graham,' Sannie said. 'I don't think we can get Sean onto the rope by ourselves. He hit his head when he fell. Hurry, this wall is starting to crack.'

'Roger that,' Graham said.

Mia finished doing up the bolt on the shackle at the end of the tow strap, fastening it to one of the Land Rover's two rear spring hanger brackets. She tossed the other end to Graham.

'Reverse, Jeff,' she called.

The vehicle backed up and Graham took a firm grip of the end of the strap and lowered himself over the edge. As the Land Rover reversed, Graham was lowered down into the hole.

Mia watched on from above as Sannie directed Graham to help her fasten the strap around Sean.

'No!' Sean, perhaps concussed, was trying to push them away. 'The kid first, then the woman.'

'No, Sean, you're injured,' Sannie said.

Above them, Mia shook her head. Bloody men.

Jeff had hopped out of the car and was standing beside her. 'You don't have another strap, do you?'

'Yes, I do, a recovery strap. Good idea.' Mia went to her bag again, found the second strap and shackle and fixed it to the Land Rover's other spring hanger.

Sannie and Graham were making slow work of getting the tow strap around Sean and Mia realised that the sangoma and Lilly would both probably need assistance. With the Land Rover now parked at the edge of the drop-off she grabbed the recovery strap, climbed over the precipice and lowered herself down using muscle power. She grinned up at Jeff. 'Get ready to haul ass, literally.'

He gave her a thumbs up. 'Good to go.'

Mia eased herself down.

'Mia?' Jeff called down to her.

She looked up, impatient to get on with it. 'Yes?'

'I'm sorry, if I came between you and Graham. I didn't mean to.'

Graham also looked up at the mention of his name. He grinned up at Jeff. 'All good, bru. Just get behind the wheel.'

Jeff ducked out of sight, but Benny returned to the pit to watch all the activity below. He barked, presumably to get Sean's attention. Mia touched the ground at the bottom of the pit and ushered Virtuous over. She also protested, saying Lilly should go first.

'No, Mama,' Lilly said firmly. Lilly helped Mia get the strap around Virtuous and secure it under her arms with a shackle.

'You'll need to hold on, as well,' Mia said, 'so the strap doesn't tighten too much around you and squeeze you.'

The sangoma nodded. 'I understand.'

'The wall,' Sannie said. 'Hurry.'

Mia looked over and saw fine, but long, vertical cracks beginning to appear in the cement. Sannie and Graham had managed to get Sean on his feet and ready to go, with a strap around him. Jeff would have his work cut out for him, helping these two over the lip, Mia thought.

'OK, Jeff!' Mia called. 'Go for it.'

They all looked up as Jeff started the Land Rover. He revved the engine and they heard him start to drive away. But when both Sean and Virtuous tugged on their straps, ready to be lifted, the heavy metal shackles on the ends that had been attached to the vehicle slid through the grass and over the lip of the pit, and they all ducked to avoid being hit by them as they crashed down.

Benny was barking furiously.

'Something's wrong,' Sannie said. 'He's leaving us!'

For a moment they all looked at each other, aghast.

Jeff had disconnected the straps. Lilly started to cry. The sound of the Land Rover disappeared on the warm afternoon breeze as the wall started to open up behind them.

Chapter 31

Sara had taken one of the filming vehicles, a short-wheelbase, older-model Land Rover with just enough room for the driver in front and a camera operator in the back. She was parked on a rise which, although low, had a marvellous view over the open plain of the Little Serengeti.

She checked her watch. It was coming up to two in the afternoon, the time when the second Stayhome Safari of the day was normally broadcast.

In this sector of Julianne's reserve they had phone signal, which was why most of their webcast game drives were held around here, where they could guarantee transmission. She took out her phone and called the producer, Janine.

'Hi, Janine, it's Sara, the camera operator at Lion Plains.'

'Sara!' Janine said. 'What's with you guys, you've been offline since all that drama with Mia and the poacher. Is everything all right? We've been flooded with comments from people on Facebook and Twitter wanting to know what's happening there.'

'Long, long story. There was a gunfight – it's probably all subject to a police investigation now, so I'd better leave that to Mia. I'm by myself, but I can look around and maybe go on camera myself.'

'Sure, we're desperate for content from Lion Plains after yesterday. This is your big break.'

'Thanks!' Sara ended the call then climbed into the back and switched on the camera. It would be difficult, as without an operator she would have to point the Land Rover at whatever she was trying to film, although there was a remote she could use to stop and start and zoom and she could see a feed of what she was filming via an app on her phone.

Sara took out her binoculars and scanned the view in front of her. 'Yes!' she said to herself when she spotted a pair of rhinos, a mother and a tiny calf. She started her engine. Off to her right she saw a dust plume. She took out her binoculars and picked up two vehicles. One was Sean Bourke's camouflaged double-cab anti-poaching vehicle, and the other was a game viewer, with one person on board.

Sara focused the binoculars and realised it was Jeff, the cute Canadian researcher guy, driving. He was shirtless, probably working on his tan. That must be Mia's vehicle, she thought. She wondered if Mia and Graham had hitched a lift on the chopper with Oscar. It had been like a regular shuttle service between Lion Plains and the hospital in Nelspruit. She wondered how much of the story she could or should tell online when she went live.

*

Jeff caught up to the anti-poaching Land Rover and flashed his lights. Piet Oosthuizen, driving the other vehicle, pulled over.

Jeff stopped and got out and went to the other vehicle. Piet opened his door, went to Jeff and the pair embraced.

'My boy,' Piet said.

Jeff swallowed hard, fighting back tears. 'Dad.'

'The girl? The anti-poaching rangers?' Piet asked.

Jeff took a breath to steady himself. 'Mia and Graham went ... went into the pit. I didn't even have to force them. It was their idea. They climbed down to help the others. The wounded ranger's still in my vehicle.'

Piet smiled. 'If anyone ever finds any evidence – which they won't once that machine has done its work – people will most likely think it was a terrible accident. Think of it that way, my boy. Someone fell in and your friends went in to save them. It will be over quickly. Trust me, I've seen people die worse deaths. What's the condition of the wounded guy ...?'

Jeff looked over at the man still lying in the Land Rover. 'Oscar. He'll die if he doesn't get urgent attention. He's barely conscious – I doubt he knows what's going on. We could drop him at a clinic and –'

'Now's not the time to go soft, Jeff. Look, you probably should have left him in the pit as well. But what we can do is slot a rhino and leave this guy at the scene, let him die there. We'll tell the authorities we came across him doing some freelance poaching. We can say that some accomplice got away with the horn.'

Soft was one thing his father could never be accused of, Jeff thought. He had killed Sipho and one of his workers with a hunting rifle from long range in Killarney, concerned that they would not stand up to police interrogation and would reveal the existence of the tunnels. Piet had also exhumed and dismembered a worker who had died in a cave-in while digging one of the cross tunnels, and planted his arm in the sangoma's freezer. Jeff feared his father just as much as he craved his approval. He felt he needed to explain what had happened.

'I had to get Mia and the police officer into the tunnel, Dad, to trap them and stop them calling it in. They had just worked out how we were doing it. I had to blow the shafts on the Tom tunnel, and –'

Piet held up a hand. 'Enough, now. You have done what had to be done, as has Samantha. We can all put this behind us now.'

Jeff looked around his father and into the cab of the Land Rover. An armed man kept his gun trained on Laura, the British girl, who slumped in the back seat, her eyes red from crying. His father's new girlfriend, Samantha, was in the front passenger seat, her face pale and sweaty. She raised a hand weakly. 'Good work, Jeff.'

Piet clapped him on the arm. 'I would have been proud to have you by my side in Angola.'

Jeff's father had served in the border war between South Africa and the communist-backed forces in Angola during the apartheid era. While he would talk about his time in the army often, usually funny stories, Jeff had often wondered what it was his father had seen or done that caused him to wake, shouting, in the middle of the night. In civilian life Piet had worked as a mining engineer after the war. He blamed the loss of his job at a goldmine in the late 1990s on the company's push to employ more black African engineers, but Jeff suspected his father's love of drinking and gambling had more to do with his career limitations than political correctness.

Piet and his first wife, Maria, had moved from South Africa to Canada when Jeff was still very young. Jeff had only known a life of privilege, as an only child growing up Canadian. When asked by friends in Canada about how the immigrant family had done so well for themselves, Piet would talk of an inheritance or an investment windfall that had helped set him up in his adopted country. It was only when his mother Maria was dying of breast cancer that Jeff had learned the truth: that his father had been part of a gang that had tunnelled underground from a vacant shop in Krugersdorp, on Johannesburg's West Rand, to the nearby Standard Bank and broken through to the vault. Their haul was worth a fortune at the time and no arrests were ever made.

Just before he learned the news about his father's criminal past, Jeff had also been in trouble with the law, suspended from university for dealing drugs. He'd started using grass in his midteens and had moved on to ecstasy, MDMA and a little coke – dealing to his fellow students had been a good source of income while studying. His father had hit him when he found out. Jeff had tried to stop his own use, but had re-offended, and ended up doing six months in prison. Funnily enough, in prison he'd been able to restart his university studies and continue them when he got out, majoring in anthropology. With his family ties to Africa he'd been truly fascinated with the world of traditional beliefs and medicine.

After Maria had died, Piet had been drawn back to Africa, expanding his Canadian construction and engineering business abroad. On a business trip he had met Elizabeth, several years his junior, and eventually married her. While he put up a smooth and professional business front, Jeff's father, ever the gambler, had, in fact, been overextending himself. He'd gone into partnership with Elizabeth's friend, Samantha, her husband John and their local African partner to build the hotel and install a new water and sewage plant and drainage system, as well as the new school, and it had all fallen over as soon as COVID hit.

Jeff had been in South Africa researching his thesis for his masters. That part of his cover story was true, though he'd adopted a fake surname, Beaton, when his father coopted him into his plan, in case Julianne Clyde-Smith or any of her people connected him with the guy doing all the construction work in Killarney, and on the neighbouring Leopard Springs property. As Piet's undercover man inside the Sabi Sand Game Reserve, Jeff, the earnest young Canadian researcher, had ample opportunity to pick up on intelligence about rhino sightings and to help seed the fear that poachers were using umuthi that actually worked. In fact, he'd proven very useful in this capacity, partly by using his own knowledge of illicit pharmaceuticals to slip first tranquillisers and later, poison, into the muthi packs carried by Bongani and some of the other African staff – and into Pretty's smoked salmon bagels, for good measure.

'Elizabeth didn't see you?' Piet asked.

Jeff shook his head. 'Samantha made sure to let me know their movements, so I could stay out of their way.'

Piet smiled at Samantha. 'Good work, both of you.'

Jeff exhaled. This ride was the most intense high he'd ever been on. He'd sought his father's approval all his life and now, he realised, he'd finally earned it by becoming complicit in murder. Jeff could see how war had made his father who he was. He felt he had crossed a line, in his father's eyes and in his own. He thought about Mia, for a moment. It was a shame she had to die – he'd wanted to get her in the sack. He smiled to himself; maybe he was more like his dad than he'd ever dared to dream.

Piet seemed to have spotted something in the distance. He reached into the cab of the anti-poaching Land Rover and took a pair of binoculars from the dashboard. 'Bingo. Rhinos. Two of them. Easy money.'

'Dad ...'

'No one's manning the Vulture system – you said so yourself. Samantha called Julianne to *check* on Sue Barker and found out that Audrey and Alison are there busy looking after the distraught mom. There's another hundred thousand US dollars sitting over there in the open, waiting to be plucked. Charles, Shadrack?'

'*Yebo*,' the two men with AK-47s in the back of the vehicle answered. They and their companion had been workers in Piet's construction business and they had turned to poaching in order to keep their jobs. They climbed out.

Piet pointed to the rhino. 'Go. Take that one. I'll bring the Landy around the other side of it. Let the calf live.'

'All right,' Charles said.

'Julius,' Piet said to the third worker in the truck, 'you stay in the truck, watch the girl.'

'Dad, don't you think we should make a clean break?' Jeff said. 'You told me you'd made enough to keep the bank off your back. We should get Samantha to a doctor, lie low for a while. The country's about to reopen for tourism, so we can get the hotel up and running soon. We've been lucky so far.'

Piet shook his head. 'We make our own luck in this life, Jeff.'

*

Lumps of cement render and clods of earth were raining down from the face of the wall and the faint outline of the two-metre circular cutting face of the tunnel-boring machine was starting to show.

The machine did not move fast, but Sannie knew it would be un-stoppable. Beside her, Sean looked up suddenly from where he was lying on the ground, still dazed from his fall.

'My backpack, Benny's chew toy ...' he said.

At first Sannie thought he was rambling, but then she thought about how much Benny liked the chew toy he received as a reward. 'Is there something in the bag we can use, Sean?'

He nodded, his lips trying to form words.

Sannie could tell it was important. 'Graham, put Mia on your shoulders. Lilly, climb up on them and call to Benny.' Sannie knew that her own leg, once more aching and bleeding from where the bullet had grazed her, would not take another two people's weight.

'We tried that and I couldn't get out,' Lilly sniffed.

'I know. I just need to you to try to reach Benny. We need him to fetch Sean's bag.'

Graham braced himself against the wall as Sannie had and Mia, then Lilly, quickly scrambled up. Lilly's outstretched fingers were still about a metre short of the top of the pit.

'Benny!' Sannie called. The dog came to the edge, looking down inquisitively. Seeing Sean lying motionless he barked again. 'Benny, get your toy, boy.'

Benny tilted his head.

'Play time, Benny,' Lilly said. 'Fetch your toy, boy.'

The dog darted away and they all looked to the wall and the now nonstop rain of rubble and dirt. Virtuous dropped to her knees to continue her prayers.

Benny returned with Sean's green nylon daypack in his mouth. As Sannie had hoped, Benny had carried his beloved toy through the bush with him. When Lilly got on her toes on Mia's shaking shoulders to try to reach Benny, the dog backed up, as if this was a game.

'Benny! Drop it!' Lilly's voice was stern. Benny came to the edge and opened his mouth. Lilly tried to catch the falling pack, but missed it and it fell, bouncing off Mia's back. Sannie caught it. The others climbed down.

Sannie opened the pack. There was a Leatherman pocket tool – useless against several tons of rotating cutting heads – as well as Benny's toy, a roll of duct tape and a long flexible tube.

Graham and Mia stood over her. 'Yes!' Graham punched the air. 'That's det cord – explosives.'

'Thank you, Lord.' Sannie reached out and squeezed Sean's shoulder. 'Good thinking, Sean. You've given us a chance.' Sannie could see the det cord was already rigged with a detonator and initiator. 'This is a breaching charge, like our tactical squad uses to blow open doors,' she said for the benefit of the others.

'Can we stop the machine with that?' Mia asked. 'Blow it up?'

The ground was shaking. They all looked over at the sound of a high-pitched whine and screeching sound. The spinning blades of the cutting head were now starting to show through. Instinctively, they all retreated to the furthermost wall of the pit.

Sannie picked up the breaching charge, weighing it in her hands. 'No. This has been rigged to blow a door off its hinges or destroy a lock. We'd need a two-hundred-kilo bomb to stop that machine.' She looked at the thick glass window, fish swimming on the other side.

'Flood the pit,' Mia said, reading Sannie's mind.

Virtuous had stood, and she moved with them to the window. 'There are crocodiles in there.'

Sannie looked to the disintegrating wall and had to raise her voice. 'We'll have to risk it. We've got no chance against that thing.'

'Let me help you,' Graham said.

They lifted the breaching charge to the viewing window. Sannie held it against the glass while Graham taped it in place.

'Hurry!' Lilly screamed.

The massive rotating face of the machine broke through and dirt, rocks and cement fragments cascaded down and outward. Free of resistance, the juggernaut trundled towards them, unstoppable until it reached its programmed destination.

'Everyone in the corner,' Sannie shouted. 'Lie flat. Glass will come exploding outwards. Help each other.'

'I cannot swim,' Virtuous said.

'I'll help you,' Mia said.

'I've got Sean,' Graham said, dragging his boss into the corner of the pit.

Mia placed Lilly in the farthest reach of the pit next to Sean and lay down over her. Virtuous then pressed her body against them.

'I can set off the charge, Captain. I know how it's done,' Graham said.

Sannie hesitated.

'Lie down, Captain. You've got children, right?'

'Yes.' She thought of Tommy, Ilana and Christo, and her poor dear Tom. She lay down against the sangoma and put her arms around her.

Graham played out the fuse line and got on the ground next to them.

The cutting heads on the round face of the boring machine spun like the weird rotating teeth of some alien behemoth, the deadly grinding blades now no more than a metre from Graham's back. The air was filled with dust, flying rocks and a roaring noise as the bulk of the boring machine rumbled ever closer.

Graham shielded the rest of them as best as he could with his body builder's bulk, lying on his side. He gripped the igniter in his hand; it was a tube with a pin that slid into the open end. He smacked the palm of his other hand onto the flat head of the pin, which produced a spark that ignited the fuse. A split second later the detonating cord went off.

Every one of them was either praying or screaming as the explosion added to the cacophony echoing off the walls of what was probably going to be their mass grave.

The blast was deafening.

Sannie, covered in dust and grit, managed to raise and crane her neck. Smoke temporarily obscured her vision, and when it cleared she felt like wailing, because it seemed the armoured glass, while cracked, was still holding.

'Lord, take care of my children,' she said aloud.

'I love you, babe,' Graham yelled to Mia.

'Me, as well,' Mia said.

'Tom ...' Sannie whispered.

But then the crack in the viewing window started to expand, growing tendril after tendril, like a star appearing in the green glass. The machine obscured half the window's length now and they felt the mechanical heat of it as it bore down on them, shaking the earth beneath them and the air around them.

The vibrations also shook the glass as, with the cutting heads almost on the prone humans, a fountain of water spurted out over them, sizzling and steaming on the hot metal of the boring machine. The spout turned to a gush and then a wave as all of the glass came away and the water cascaded out and into the pit.

Sannie felt herself at first pummelled and pushed against the others by the force of the brownish water from the dam, and then she was being lifted. She stood, checking the others around them as the pit began to flood. Graham had his left arm around Sean's chest, keeping his head above water, and Mia was desperately trying to calm Virtuous, who flailed at the rising tide. Lilly took hold of the sangoma's hand.

'It's all right, Mama,' Lilly said, 'let the water lift us.'

The water did nothing to impede the onward march of the machine and its cutter head, which still bore down on them even as Sannie felt her feet leave the floor of the pit. She kicked hard and used her arms to stay afloat. Above them, Benny, as scared as the rest of them, kept up a barrage of barking.

Sannie kept an eye on the water around them, fearing she might see, or worse, feel, a crocodile below her at any second. A hippopotamus honked in panic somewhere. Something broke the surface with a splash next to Sannie and she couldn't help but scream.

'Just a fish!' she said to the others.

Steam rose around them from the heat of the machine below and Sannie and the others all raised their feet as they felt its hot metal surface brushing the soles of their shoes under the water.

They were near the top of the pit now, and while they had all so far escaped being crushed and churned to mincemeat, their rate of ascent was slowing. Dog paddling, Sannie turned to look around her. She could see what was happening; as the machine exited the tunnel and moved further into the open pit, water was starting to escape around the borer's edges, seeping back down the tunnel towards Killarney. 'Everyone, get out! Grab the edge!'

They were still a metre from the top.

'Climb out, Lilly,' Mia said. Fighting to keep Virtuous afloat, Mia's head went under water. She resurfaced and spat out the foul-smelling liquid. She coughed. 'You can help us from there.'

Lilly reached up, hooked her hands over the edge of the excavation, and boosted herself upward. Benny's excited licking did not help, but she managed to get her torso onto the ground and wriggle out. Once there, she turned around and reached for the sangoma.

Sannie, also unencumbered, was next out. She reached back in to grasp Sean under the armpits. She strained to lift him out.

'Graham,' she panted, 'I'm not strong enough. I'll hold him steady while you climb out.'

Graham boosted himself out and Sannie jumped back into the churning water to push Sean from below. With considerable effort from them both, Graham was able to haul Sean up, and Benny barked with delight and licked his master's face. Graham then went to grab hold of the sangoma's arms and help Lilly lift her over the edge. With Virtuous out, Mia was also able to scramble clear of the water. She turned and looked down at Sannie.

Physically and emotionally spent, sleep deprived and injured, Sannie felt her strength disappearing. She reached up a hand for help.

Below her, though, the tail end of the tunnel-boring machine trundled through the hole it had just made, which had the effect of a plug being pulled from a bathtub. With nothing else blocking the tunnel behind it, the water from the pit surged away into the tunnel, sucking Sannie down with it.

Sannie managed to get her fingers on the ragged edge of the tunnel entrance and hold on for a second as the escaping waters rushed around her.

'You must look after the others, Graham,' Mia said, then jumped back into the pit as Sannie lost her handhold and was swept away into the darkness.

Chapter 32

Sara was giving a running commentary for the benefit of Stay-home Safari's live worldwide audience as she drove towards the anti-poaching Land Rover and the Lion Plains game viewer.

'You remember we saw the mother rhino and her calf a short while ago, well, now we can see what looks like a couple of anti-poaching rangers leaving their Land Rover and going off on patrol in the bush. They may have spotted something.'

In her earpiece, Janine, the producer, was giving her feedback. 'We're getting comments streaming in, Sara. Keep it up. This is the most interesting thing we've seen this afternoon. Give us a rundown on anti-poaching in the Sabi Sand.'

'Unfortunately, the problem of rhino poaching has not gone away during the lockdown,' Sara said. She did not want to get into trouble from Julianne by saying how bad it had been on Lion Plains. 'It's an issue that affects any game reserve in Africa that still has rhinos. Now we can see these rangers better ... for some reason they're wearing blue uniforms today, not their usual camo.'

Sara pulled over. If it was a patrol, or the rangers were tracking someone, she did not want to get in the way. She quickly took out her binoculars. Oddly, she could see Jeff Beaton standing on the roadside talking animatedly to a man who was not Sean Bourke, even though Sara was pretty sure that this was Sean's Land Rover.

She switched her gaze to the two men moving across the short grass plain of the Little Serengeti. Not only were they not wearing the correct uniforms, she also now saw they were carrying weapons she was very familiar with from her time in Afghanistan – Russian-made AK-47s.

Sara ignored Janine's request in her earpiece for more commentary. She picked up the radio and called Sabi Sand security. 'This is Lion Plains one,' she said. 'Confirm if you have an anti-poaching patrol on Little Serengeti, dressed in blue and armed with AK-47s, over.'

'*Negative,*' the officer on duty replied.

'Can you give me a location update for Sean Bourke, Mia Greenaway, and rangers Graham and Oscar, over?'

'*Negative again, Lion Plains one. We've had no word at all from Graham or Oscar – we've been trying to raise them, and Sean has gone missing in Killarney somewhere as well. If you have information, please relay, over.*'

'I was told by Mia a while ago that Jeff Beaton, a civilian based at Lion Plains, was taking her, Graham and Oscar to an evac chopper at Leopard Springs, over.'

'*Negative. I say again, negative, Lion Plains one. We've had no report of that. What's going on?*'

'You tell me,' Sara said. 'Get some air support and a ready reaction force to Little Serengeti ...' She heard gunfire. 'And turn on Stayhome Safari on your laptop, now! Out.'

Sara saw the two men in blue running now. One of them must have spooked the rhino, because she had set off with her calf, leaving a dust trail behind them. The man Jeff had been speaking to had got back in Sean's Land Rover and was driving fast, cross-country.

Sara put her vehicle in gear and accelerated. She switched on her camera again via the remote and glanced over her shoulder to look into the lens. 'Seems we have a situation, folks, and those guys might actually be poachers. Stay tuned.'

Jeff was back in the game viewer, Sara saw, and he also drove out onto the plain, but not towards the two gunmen. Instead, he was heading off to the left, to the tree line. When he got there, he stopped his Land Rover, got out and ran into the trees. Sara could see that he was also carrying a rifle.

Sara turned off the road and bounced across the savannah. She gripped the steering wheel hard for support as she accelerated.

'Lion Plains one, this is Sabi Sand security, over.'

Sara risked letting go of the wheel with one hand to pick up the radio. 'Go, Sabi Sand.'

'There's a national parks helicopter over the Kruger. They were on their way back to Skukuza Airport with an anti-poaching patrol on board, but they're diverting to your location now. They'll be there any minute, over.'

A herd of zebras was galloping away in the distance, no doubt frightened by the gunfire. Sara closed on the men in blue uniforms. Briefly, she wondered if she could get away with running them down while broadcasting to several thousand people around the world.

One of the men settled her internal debate for her. He turned, dropped to one knee and opened fire. A burst of three rounds bracketed her, sailing past the Land Rover. She swerved hard.

Janine chattered in her ear. 'Sara, be careful! Oh my God. We're going viral!'

A shadow passed over Sara and she pointed frantically at the two men in the open ground. The national parks helicopter came around in a sweeping turn and Sara saw the ranger sitting in the door, aiming his rifle at the targets below.

One of the poachers ran; the other, the one who had shot at Sara, made the mistake of standing and pointing his rifle at the sky. Sara had the presence of mind to grab the remote and stop filming as the ranger in the air opened fire and gunned the man down.

With the poachers distracted, Sara stopped, turned off the engine and climbed behind the camera. She tilted, panned and started filming again, making sure she framed Sean's double-cab Land Rover, which moved in and out of shot through the relatively open, scrubby bushveld.

The head and shoulders of another man emerged from the rear passenger seat of the Land Rover. He, too, had an AK-47, and he pointed it skywards and opened fire. The driver put on the brakes as he came to a donga, a deep dry watercourse bisecting the plain.

He had to turn right to find a shallow spot to cross and as he did so the rear passenger door opposite the gunman was flung open and a teenage girl came tumbling out. She fell, but managed to stand and run.

The helicopter made a low-level pass and this time two rangers returned fire, raking the vehicle from stem to stern as the girl ran clear.

Sara left the camera running, but climbed back into the driver's seat. The driver of the double cab, the man Sara had seen talking to Jeff, had either been hit or badly hurt because at that moment the big Land Rover lurched from one side to the other and then rolled.

The helicopter swooped in low and settled on the ground, and Sara whooped with the joy of victory as the four rangers on board jumped out and ran to the Land Rover. Sara drove as fast as she could to the girl, who headed her way.

*

Sannie fought to stay on her back and keep her head above water as the rushing tide carried her down the tunnel towards Killarney.

She hadn't been able to remove her boots and she felt them dragging her down. Henk de Beer, according to Virtuous, was somewhere down here, probably. She pictured the layout of the underground network in her mind – this tunnel led to the entry by the swimming pool at the new hotel, but just before then was the off-shoot tunnel that led to the first passageway they had discovered, the one that ran from the schoolhouse to the termite mound exit on Lion Plains. That tunnel was blocked, though, halfway, because of the explosions.

Looking up at the curved ceiling, just a metre above her, she saw a break in the pipe coming up – another vertical entry/exit shaft. She briefly thought about trying to get out there and then make her way back to Killarney. If she did, though, Henk might drown before anyone could get to him. It was a moot argument, however, because she passed under the shaft at such speed that she doubted she would have been able to catch a handhold and pull herself out.

She said another prayer and braced herself for the rest of the ride, wherever it took her, then heard a weak cry for help ahead of her.

'Anybody!'

'Hello!' she called.

'Sannie?'

'Henk.'

'Can't ... can't swim. Hands ...'

Sannie barrelled along down the tunnel. She caught a brief glimpse of the entry to the offshoot tunnel but realised something was wrong. The wave of water she was riding was not continuing down the side tunnel. Rather, it had stopped and was washing back. She realised that the hand-dug tunnel, far less structurally sound than the concrete pipeway she was in, might have collapsed, or else some other equipment might have blocked it, damming the water.

She ended her wild ride in a fast-filling chamber at the end.

'Help!'

The water was rising and in the dark Sannie could feel she was bumping into floating items – a camping chair, a camping stretcher. This must be the office-cum-campsite Virtuous had mentioned, she deduced.

'Henk? Talk to me.'

Sannie felt something move below her and grab her leg. She screamed.

Sannie kicked and reached down, ready to strike at whatever was about to kill her, when she felt fingers brush hers then grasp her again. Henk lost his handhold. Sannie took a deep breath and duck-dived. Unable to see anything, she blindly groped around underwater.

Her fingertips brushed something and whatever it was bucked away at her touch. She flailed about some more and felt the collar of a shirt, a neck, short-cropped hair. She hauled Henk upright and kicked for the surface.

She lifted him, hands around him now as she went. Henk's face broke the surface of the water, but he seemed unresponsive.

Mercifully, the water began to recede. Perhaps whatever blockage had been caused in the side tunnel had now cleared itself, as the level dropped with a gushing rush. Sannie locked Henk in a Heimlich manoeuvre hold and lifted and squeezed, realising now that his hands had been cuffed behind him, preventing him from swimming. To her relief, he vomited water and began coughing.

'*Eish*,' Henk said. 'Jissus, I thought I was *fokked*.'

Sannie slumped against him and laughed weakly.

'Look out!' Mia arrived, half running, half floating as the waters carried her towards them.

The lighting above them came on, glowing red. None of them spoke. It could, Sannie thought, have been some electrical malfunction righting itself now that the water had passed – or someone who knew how to operate the lights was in the tunnel.

Now and then a fish flipped and splashed at their feet, but other than that, silence was returning. The tunnel-boring machine had stopped, having reached its terminal destination.

The three of them, Sannie, Henk and Mia, stood together, wet and, now that the rush of adrenaline had passed, shivering. They heard a splashing noise and all of them spun around.

Jeff walked down the tunnel towards them, an LM5 rifle held up and ready to fire.

'It's over, Jeff,' Mia said. 'Graham escaped – we all did. We all know where the tunnels start and finish.'

'The best chance you have now is to come to the surface with us,' Sannie said. 'Put down your gun. Come on, Mia's right. This is the end.'

'The end?' He looked to Mia. 'How long do you think I'd survive in a South African prison?'

'To tell you the truth, Jeff,' Mia said, 'I don't care.'

'I climbed down the central entry shaft,' Jeff said. 'And pulled the manhole behind me. No one knows where I am. I came down here to get away. Throw me the keys to your car, Captain.'

Sannie reached into her pocket, took her remote out, shrugged and tossed it, so that it splashed in the water in front of Jeff.

He crouched, keeping the rifle held in his right hand, finger on the trigger, as he felt for the keys.

In her peripheral vision, Sannie saw Mia raise her hand to her mouth. Henk was wide-eyed, unable to hide the fact that he was looking around Jeff at something in the tunnel beyond. Sannie didn't dare breathe.

Jeff noticed the looks on their faces, and broke into a grin. 'What? The old "behind you" trick? You think I'd fall for that?'

Epilogue

One month later, Lion Plains Game Reserve

Tommy Furey sat in the grass next to Bongani Ngobeni, the tracker who had spotted a leopard for them all on the drive into the game reserve. Tommy's big brother, Christo, sat on his other side, messaging their sister, Ilana, on WhatsApp.

It was late afternoon and the bark on the big maroela tree was turning a red-gold colour.

Tommy's mother and Mia, the ranger who had driven them all into the reserve, were led out of the bush by Virtuous, the sangoma, who carried a metal bowl which she set down on the ground. Both women wore simple, cheap cotton nightdresses that they had bought especially for the occasion. Their feet were bare and their hair was wet, slicked back, as though they had both just had a shower. His mother caught his eye and winked at him.

Bongani pointed to the cleared patch of bare earth on the ground in the shade of the maroela. He spoke softly: 'This place, under the tree, has been cleared and swept clean by the sangoma so that it is purified, so that there are no bad spirits here, Tommy.'

He nodded. His mother had told him not to be scared of anything that he might see today, or anything that he might see her go through or hear about.

His mother had been so sad ever since his father had been killed overseas. Tommy had been sad as well, and cried at night sometimes. His mother had also had some nightmares lately. She had told him and Christo that the sangoma, with whom she had become friends, had suggested that the cleansing ritual they were going to witness today might help her.

'Really?' Christo had asked. Tommy didn't think Christo believed it would help. 'You're a practising Christian, Mom. How's this stuff going to make any difference?'

'Trust me, *boetie*,' she said, using her nickname for Christo, 'it can't make me feel any worse.'

Tommy had met the sangoma once, when she came to tea at their house last week, but then she had worn western clothes. Now she was wearing a more traditional outfit, swathed in red, black and white patterned wraps and also barefoot. Her wrists and ankles were decorated with thin, knotted strips of animal skin, still with the hair on, and several bracelets made up of red, black and white beads.

'Where were Mom and Mia just now?' Tommy asked Bongani.

'In the bush,' Bongani whispered, 'away from the purified area. The two women were washed, using water that contains various herbs, to cleanse the outside of their bodies. Then, the sangoma gave them a special drink, to cleanse their insides.'

That took a moment to sink in. 'You mean, like they made themselves sick?'

Bongani smiled and nodded.

'Really?'

'Don't look so horrified, Tommy. What your mother and Mia went through, the things they have seen recently, have polluted their spirits. They needed to get rid of this evil from their bodies, from their souls.'

Tommy nodded. The newspaper had reported that one of the criminals who had been responsible for the poaching and the tunnels, a man from Canada, had been killed by a crocodile underground, when the dam burst. Tommy had asked his mother if she had been there when that had happened, and she had nodded, but said nothing more about it. Her ex-friend, Mrs Karandis, was in jail, and *Tannie* Elizabeth's husband, Piet, had been killed. 'My mom's been having some nightmares lately.'

Bongani nodded again. 'So has Mia. She has been deeply troubled. You know she killed a poacher?'

'Yes,' Tommy said. 'I read that. She's famous, online. She's now the number one guide on Stayhome Safari.'

'Be that as it may,' Bongani said, 'she will be haunted by the spirit of the man she killed until she is able to cleanse herself of his memory, of his death. This happens sometimes, to soldiers and rangers, when they see terrible things or kill someone, even in the line of duty. The spirits, the evil, stays with them, and they have terrible dreams. Sometimes these dreams are so bad they may even take their own lives.'

'I think I understand. I've heard about people – police officers and soldiers – having those troubles.'

Tommy hushed himself as Virtuous began speaking. Her voice, however, was different from normal, deeper, almost like a man's.

'She is speaking a different language, not Xitsonga,' Bongani whispered to him. 'It is as if she is talking to the spirits.'

Tommy felt a chill, despite the sun's warmth, but watched on in fascination as Virtuous bent and reached into the bowl and took out an animal's organ. 'What's that?'

'The gall bladder, from one of the goats that I killed.'

He said it matter-of-factly. On the drive here, Mia had explained that elsewhere in the bush, while she and Tommy's mother prepared for their cleansing ceremony, Bongani would have the honour of killing two goats, using a spear driven into each animal's heart, to prevent it suffering. The goats were sacrifices, to appease their ancestors, one for Mia and one for Sannie, Mia had explained, and while Tommy wasn't sure how that worked, he was told they would all be having goat on the *braai* afterwards, so the killing was not done in vain or taken lightly.

Virtuous went to Mia and, squeezing the gall bladder that had come from 'her' goat, anointed her forehead, the back of her neck and her back with the liquid bile that came out.

Tommy watched on, fascinated, and Christo had stopped sending messages. Tommy glanced at the others sitting in the grass. There was Oscar, one of the rangers, who had been shot, but was now out of hospital. His friend, Graham, had his arm around

Oscar's shoulders as he also watched the ceremony in fascinated silence. Miss Clyde-Smith, the owner of the reserve, and a woman called Sue, and her daughter, Laura, who had been kidnapped, were also there, as was Lilly, a girl who had just won a scholarship to Tommy's school, and her friend, Thandi. Lilly saw him looking and smiled at him. Tommy smiled back.

Tannie Elizabeth – he was allowed to address her as 'aunty' again now – sat in the grass dabbing a handkerchief to her eyes. On the afternoon his mother had come back from those terrible two days in Killarney and the game reserve, she had done so with a police tactical unit, and they had pointed guns at Mrs Oosthuizen and her mother had accused her of kidnapping Tommy. It turned out that *Tannie* Elizabeth was innocent, but Mrs Karandis, who really was a *skelm*, had pretended Mrs Oosthuizen was in on the act. Tommy remembered *Tannie* Elizabeth's surprise when she was told that her husband was not off in Dubai with his girlfriend. She had been angry, and cried, because she also found out her stepson, from Canada, was in on the plan to kill rhinos. They were friends again, his mother and Elizabeth, but his mother never left him with anyone other than Christo these days.

'Why is the sangoma doing that, with that stuff?' Tommy asked, as Virtuous repeated her ministrations, this time for Sannie, using the second gall bladder.

'The ancestors live in our minds, and in our bodies, and the bile is a means of sending something to them, a message, asking them for help with our troubles.'

Tommy thought of his father and looked up at the blue sky. He hoped his dad would always be in his head and his heart, just as he lived on in his body and blood.

When the sangoma had finished speaking, the ceremony was over and she gave Tommy a strip of skin from the hind leg of the goat killed in his mother's name, and tied it around his right wrist.

'This bracelet is what we call *isiphandla*, Tommy,' the sangoma said. 'It is a connection between you and your ancestors – your dear departed father and all who went before him. As the son of the captain you must wear this until it falls off. By that time your mother will have moved on another step in the process of healing her heart. This symbol shows her, and the community, that you are here for her, Tommy, that you are supporting her in these troubled times and that you remember and respect your ancestors. Do you understand?'

'I do.'

His mother came to him and she smelled fresh and clean, except for the stuff on her head. She kissed him. Mia was being hugged too, first by Graham and then by Bongani.

Somewhere in the distance a lion called. His mother held him tight and drew Christo into their embrace.

'Your father loved that sound,' she said, 'and so do I.'

Acknowledgements

Warning: if you are, like my wife, the sort of weird person who reads the end of books before the beginning, there are some spoilers ahead.

The idea for this book came from a conversation I had with an academic over a cup of coffee in the town of Hoedspruit some time ago. That person told me of work being done to study the use of umuthi by both poachers and national parks rangers in South Africa.

I'm incredibly grateful to that first contact, who wishes to remain anonymous. That discussion led me to Dr Tony Cunningham, an expert in this field who patiently answered my many questions about umuthi and belief systems, and read the relevant sections of the manuscript. Tony was keen to stress how African traditional beliefs aligned with similar views, practices and religions around the world. I'd like to thank him for his help and stress that any mistakes in my representation of these often-complex ideas are mine alone.

I envisaged a story about poachers disappearing into thin air, but how was I going to pull this off? I didn't know, when I started writing. I did think about poachers being flown out of a reserve in a helicopter, climbing trees and even pole-vaulting fences and spruits, but it was a real-life story which gave me the idea for how my criminals could come and go undetected.

I wrote this story during a COVID-19 lockdown, at my home in Australia, and was surprised to wake to the news online one morning that thieves in South Africa had circumvented that country's lockdown restrictions on alcohol sales by tunnelling into a liquor store in Johannesburg from a neighbouring building.

I mentioned this story to my friend Dr Chris Wessels, a neighbour of mine in the real version of 'Hippo Rock Private Nature Reserve' (it's based on the place where I live in South Africa) and he then emailed me a link to another real-life story about one of South Africa's great unsolved crimes – a bank robbery in Krugersdorp, in 1977, in which thieves also dug a tunnel to gain access to the bank's vault. I used this as part of the back story for the fictitious Piet Oosthuizen, though fudged the date of the real theft.

My biggest challenge, how to write a novel set in Africa from the spare room of a two-bedroom apartment in Sydney, Australia, was solved the same way that many of us overcame the challenges of COVID-19. I reached out to people and talked to them.

My sincere thanks go to my friend and renowned artist Abbey Ndlovu, in South Africa, who talked to me at length via Facebook Messenger while I was doing my research. Abbey told me of his traditional beliefs and his experiences of visiting a sangoma.

Thanks also to Beryl Wilson, head of Zoology at the McGregor Museum in Kimberley, South Africa, for her information on the reptile trade and other conservation matters.

Like many die-hard safari fans, I got my 'fix' of the African bush remotely during 2020, watching live webcasts of game drives from South Africa. Tayla McCurdy, field guide, presenter and one of the former stars of the real-life inspiration for 'Stayhome Safari', WildEarth safari-iLIVE, also answered my questions during lockdown about tracking, and life as a woman in a traditionally male-dominated industry. Tayla also kindly read a draft of the manuscript and provided valuable feedback and career-saving corrections. Thank you!

Likewise, my anonymous friend and source read the book and made several (many, in fact) sensible and sensitive corrections, not only about umuthi, but also about my depiction of life in rural South Africa. Thank you.

Annelien Oberholzer, my go-to person for all things African and Afrikaans, provided corrections and feedback and once more proved she can pick up typos that the best editors (and average authors) miss. Baie dankie, mate. Thank you, as well, to my long-time reader and supporter Sara Skjold for her advice on Norwegian swear words. Thanks also to my friend, psychotherapist Charlotte Stapf, who answered my questions on Mia and Sannie's expressions of grief.

While writing this book I was honoured to be asked to read and endorse an excellent non-fiction book, *Changing a Leopard's Spots*, by master trackers Alex van den Heever and Renias Mhlongo. Their real-life story helped a great deal with my creation of Mia, Bongani and the fictitious places where they live and work, and their approach to tracking.

Thanks once again to my Miss Fix-it in South Africa, Michele Ferguson, who seems to know just about everybody employed in just about every facet of wildlife and nature conservation. Michele put me in touch with Charmaine Swart from South African National Parks' Environmental and Corporate Investigations unit and I am extremely grateful to Charmaine for providing corrections and advice about Sannie van Rensburg's role in *Blood Trail*.

Noel Kerr and Alison Windle from Bothar Boring came to my rescue on the technical side of things, providing explanations and videos of tunnel boring machines in action. I'm sure they thought I was crazy, or a criminal, or both, when I contacted them asking how someone might tunnel into a national park. Any mistakes or exaggerations in my depiction of this amazing technology, or indeed, about anything else I've covered in this novel, are mine and mine alone.

As with most of my novels I outsourced the naming of characters in this one to several worthy charities. The following people paid good money to good causes to have their names or those of loved ones, friends or relatives assigned to characters. I hope they like their fictional identities, even if they're baddies (you are all goodies in my eyes). Thanks to: Mia Greenaway, Sara Skjold and Jeff Beaton (Painted Dog Conservation Inc); Sue Barker (Belmont Rotary in support of the young people's mental health charity, Headspace); David Byrne on behalf of Bongani Ngobeni and the late Alison Byrne (Nourish Non-Profit Organisation, a community sustainability project in South Africa); Elizabeth Oosthuizen and Samantha Karandis (South African National Parks Honorary Rangers, K9 fund); and the

Foster family, on behalf of Graham Foster (Conservation and Wildlife Fund, Zimbabwe).

As always, my heartfelt thanks go to my team of unpaid editors – my wife, Nicola; mother, Kathy; and mother-in-law, Sheila. Thanks very much to the team at Pan Macmillan Australia and Pan Macmillan South Africa for all their hard work on the first edition of 'Blood Trail', and to Joel Naoum from Critical Mass Consulting for getting this edition into your hands.

And last, but by no means least, if you've made it this far, thank you. You're the most important person in this whole business.

www.tonypark.net

If you enjoyed 'Blood Trail', you can read about Sannie van Rensburg's earlier cases in **'Silent Predator', 'The Hunter'**, and **'The Cull'**.